PRAISE FOR T

The Heart Resort Series

"Marcelo loads their darling romance with touching drama and sweet moments while seamlessly weaving in Filipino culture, language, and food, adding depth and authenticity to the plot. The endearing protagonists, dramatic sibling rivalry, and idyllic coastal setting make for a feel-good romance that readers won't want to miss."

—*Publishers Weekly*

"Readers will yearn for more stories about these compelling characters."

—*Booklist*

"Compelling family tensions, a captivating second-chance romance, and an evocative beachside setting come together beautifully in Tif Marcelo's gem of a book. I fell in love with Heart Resort and the Pusos, and I can't wait to return to this world in the next installment!"

—Mia Sosa, *USA Today* bestselling author of *The Worst Best Man*

In a Book Club Far Away

"Marcelo captivates in this endearing story about the bonds of friendship . . . Making good use of army life as the backdrop, Marcelo skillfully layers the narrative with the three women's points of view, capturing both their singular and collective worlds. Themes of friendship, forgiveness, and women's independence make this propulsive, feel-good story a gem."

—*Publishers Weekly*

"Fans of book clubs will enjoy the discussions of the popular reading that Adelaide's book club favors . . . Told in a straightforward style, this story of women's friendship and commitment to the army lifestyle will appeal to fans of Kristin Hannah, Debbie Macomber, or Sarah Pekkanen."

—*Library Journal*

"With a wonderfully diverse cast, tantalizing descriptions of Filipino food, a realistic portrayal of the challenges of being a military spouse, and a hint of romance, Marcelo's latest will charm readers and could lead to a fruitful book discussion."

—*Booklist*

The Key to Happily Ever After

"Marcelo movingly portrays sisters who love each other to death but also drive each other crazy. Give this to readers who like Susan Mallery's portrayal of complicated sisters, or Jasmine Guillory's sweet, food-focused city settings."

—*Booklist*

"This sweet family story / romance will appeal to fans of Susan Mallery and RaeAnne Thayne. Especially suitable for public libraries looking for more #ownvoices authors."

—*Library Journal*

"Marcelo charms in this feel-good story . . . The layered plot, which includes a dark period in Mari's past that places a roadblock to finding love in the present, and the cast of colorful supporting characters, particularly sassy shop seamstress Amelia, are a treat. Fans of Jill Shalvis and Jane Green will particularly enjoy this."

—*Publishers Weekly*

WHEN JASMINE BLOOMS

OTHER TITLES BY TIF MARCELO

Heart Resort

Lucky Streak
It Takes Heart
Know You by Heart

Contemporary Fiction

In a Book Club Far Away
Once Upon a Sunset
The Key to Happily Ever After

Journey to the Heart Series

North to You
East in Paradise
West Coast Love

Anthology

Something Blue
Christmas Actually

Young Adult

The Holiday Switch

WHEN JASMINE BLOOMS

A Novel

TIF MARCELO

Published by Lake Union Publishing, Seattle

www.apub.com

Amazon, the Amazon logo, and Lake Union Publishing are trademarks of Amazon.com, Inc., or its affiliates.

ISBN-13: 9781542038782 (paperback)
ISBN-13: 9781542038799 (digital)

Cover design by Caroline Teagle Johnson
Cover image: © PhotographerOlympus / Getty; © enviromantic / Getty; © Oleksandr Kalinskyy / Getty; © Silmairel / Shutterstock

Printed in the United States of America

For April, Annie, Rachel, and Jeanette, and all we've shared in both our author and motherhood journeys.

AUTHOR'S NOTE

Dear reader,

When Jasmine Blooms is Celine Lakad-Frasier's story, but is an ode to Marmee, who I consider an aspirational literary mother. Drawn from Abigail Alcott, Louisa Alcott's mother, Marmee holds a special place in my heart.

Like Celine, in my earlier readings of *Little Women*, I barely noticed Marmee's character. I was enamored with Meg, Jo, Beth, and Amy. It was not until I became a mother to teens and young adults that Marmee stepped to the forefront as my protagonist. And it was then I began to wonder how Marmee and Abigail coped after their daughters passed away. Because being a mother isn't for the faint of heart. It isn't without its ups and downs, without loss, nor is it without joy and love and thrill.

When Jasmine Blooms isn't a retelling. It is Celine's own path through grief and hope, and that sneaky question of *what if?*

My friends, content guidance includes: death of a child (not on page), panic attacks, therapy.

Finally, these are books I read (and reread) while writing this novel.

Little Women, by Louisa May Alcott

Meg, Jo, Beth, Amy, by Anne Boyd Rioux

Marmee & Louisa, by Eve LaPlante

My Heart Is Boundless, edited by Eve LaPlante

Marmee, by Sandford Salyer

It's OK That You're Not OK, by Megan Devine
Beyond Tears, by Ellen Mitchell and others

Thank you for taking this first step into *When Jasmine Blooms*. I hope you enjoy it.

xo

tif

Chapter One

Standing in the dim study, lit only by an hourglass lamp on a scratched oak desk and the blazing flames of the fireplace, I ran a thumb against the dark-brown leather of the book in my hand. Though a storm raged outside, with raindrops drumming above and splattering against the old windows, my senses were focused on the craterlike divots of the embossed leaves on its cover and the crevices of the book's title. *Little Women.*

A classic that had guided me throughout my life, read silently and aloud to myself and then to my children—its characters were known to me as if they themselves were alive. Meg, Jo, Beth, and Amy March—I had been each of them at different phases of my life. Then, one day, Marmee had taken center stage. Marmee, the strong and brave mother, loving and intuitive.

For decades, I'd found confidence and comfort in Marmee's stoic and loving nature. And the similarities between her and me! Marmee had been a military wife, and she'd made a life helping others, just like me. She'd had a husband who loved people, as my Quinn did. She'd had four children.

She'd had *four children.*

A tear slid from my cheek and dropped onto the leather. It streaked down the cover and pooled in one of the leaves. Shutting my eyes to hold back the rest of my tears, I steeled myself against the stark upswing of breathlessness.

I had read this story so much that the pages were yellowed and wrinkled and annotated. Its contents were all but memorized and imprinted in my brain. And yet, despite years of study, I had missed something entirely. The true tragedy of Beth's death.

Marmee had lost Beth, but my eyes had glazed over the words; I'd turned the pages without pausing to consider what that had really meant to the family, to Marmee.

And now I knew why.

Her death had been suffered in silence. Life had moved on. Marmee had had no closure.

For the first time, *Little Women* had no answer and gave no consolation.

With a final look at the book, I tossed it into the fire. Heat blazed in the study. The pages and leather singed and curled into the flames, emitting the bitter smell of a day-old campfire.

And much like my heart, the book turned to ashes.

~

Cold fingertips against my wrist snapped me out of my haze, and I blinked to see a woman speaking in front of me. As my vision sharpened, her garbled speech turned into actual words.

". . . was the best baker in the neighborhood. I'm sorry for your loss . . . ," she was saying.

We had been introduced years ago by Libby herself, though at the moment, this woman's name had escaped my memory. Despite my overconsumption of coffee, my body was still going at half speed, my brain trailing behind it.

Still, I pressed my lips into what I hoped was a smile. "Thank you for coming."

"Of course. I just can't believe this. I remember when Libby . . . ," the woman continued, and at the sound of my third daughter's name on her lips, my body tensed, eyes shutting ever so briefly so my lungs remembered to expand and contract. In and out, fill and empty. Carbon dioxide for oxygen.

There had been so many stories today, tales from people who I didn't recognize that were meant to be reminiscent and lovely. Stories meant to console, to comfort, to add humor to the whisperings of a quiet room. But all of it had had the opposite effect on me.

My gaze traveled to the indoor jasmine plants growing next to the windows, the macramé wall hangings. Old family photos on the wall, intermixed with local artists' work, hung by Libby after Quinn and I had moved out of the house years ago.

How this home had changed since we'd moved to Maryland—it still took me by surprise. These walls had been witnesses to the fights, the laughter, the wishes, the conversations of our family of six. I'd named it Sampaguita for the national flower of the Philippines. While *Jasminum sambac* was not native to the US, a wild jasmine bordered the property, filling the air with an intoxicating scent—when the girls used to come in from playing outside, their clothing and skin had smelled of it.

The blossoms of the sampaguita reminded me of my little girls, each one unique and delicate and hardy all at once, each with a smattering of qualities from my Filipino and Quinn's Scottish roots.

My eyes landed on Quinn, standing in a group of men, sipping on a whiskey, a hand in the pocket of his slacks. The guy next to him half-heartedly mimicked shooting a basketball—they were talking shop, with Quinn's boys' recent loss in the Sweet Sixteen. My husband was nodding, though his expression was blank. Then, as if sensing me, he turned his eyes up to my stare. Despite his sad smile, his face was gaunt, with bluish half moons under his eyes.

He hadn't slept; then again, I hadn't either. While Quinn had paced the house most of the night, my sleep, or lack of it, was riddled with dreams of Libby playing her piano. Running in the backyard, chasing the neighborhood stray cat. Sprinkling flour over a mass of dough.

My husband's attention slipped away, to someone else speaking to him, and my next natural step was to seek out my girls. It was an unbreakable but necessary habit, to count my people like we were in a crowded amusement park. We were an unwieldy bunch, an over-full suitcase of personalities and priorities and demands. If we hadn't watched it, a moment's inattention would have led to someone getting lost or in trouble.

Their names appeared in my head next to blank checkboxes.

Mae, beside the buffet with an empty dessert plate in her hand, next to her husband, John—heads bent down as they negotiated dessert with their three girls, my darling granddaughters. Check.

MJ, sitting in an armchair, legs out and crossed, gaze down at the hands clasped on her lap. Across from her was Quinn's aunt Anne Frasier, sipping daintily from a teacup. Check.

Amelia, an arm interlaced in her fiancé Theo's as they meandered in from the kitchen, where Sonya, my best friend and executive assistant, managed the influx of covered casseroles. Check.

Libby . . .

My gaze darted in between and among faces for my third-born, for my tallest child with Quinn's chiseled jaw and high cheekbones and introversion that one could feel in her vibe.

At her absence, my heart rate spiked, followed a beat later by a brick-heavy realization that descended over my already weary body.

Libby was gone.

My breath hitched, and my eyes filled with tears, though their outpouring was interrupted by a nudge against my hand.

"If you could sign." Something cool was placed upon my open palm, and it startled me back to the present. I blinked my way to the woman's face, to her eyes, which widened with excitement.

Focus, Celine. This time, I forced myself to pay attention to the woman and exactly what she was saying, though the only things that stood out were her sky-blue eyes, framed by dark lashes. After inhaling a gulp of stagnant air, I asked, "I'm sorry?"

"Can you . . . sign it?" She gestured down to the thing in my hand—a book. My book, my debut, *It Will All Be Okay*, published a decade ago, was a mothering book, a self-help title, with the purpose of helping others harness their passions even in the thick of motherhood.

The sob that had ebbed earlier threatened to bubble up and out. *What the hell?*

Louisburg was loyal to a fault. A half hour west of Boston, this town was tight knit and proud. They'd rallied behind me eleven years ago, when I had started Celine Lakad Coaching, and become my first followers.

But even this was too much. On all levels.

In my silence, the woman's smile faltered. "I'm such a fan. I listen to your podcast and follow you everywhere on socials. Knowing how much you accomplished being a mom and an entrepreneur, you inspired me to create a business plan. I wanted to come to one of your conferences, but it was just too much with the three kids. You know how it is. I can't get away."

Her words passed like the horizon outside one's windows when going down the highway: swiftly and lacking purchase.

The last thing on my mind was work, especially when work had caused me to fail the most important test in my life.

And yet . . . this woman was Libby's friend. This woman was also a mother who'd had a need. It was an easy enough favor, so I accepted the pen that she was holding out to me. "Okay, sure. Who should I make it out to?"

The woman opened the book to the title page. "Nora. N . . . o . . . r . . . a."

I scrawled her name at the top of the title page. Then, after repositioning the pen above my printed name, I swiped the beginning of my signature.

But a disordered piano chord charged through my nervous system, sweeping the pen's trajectory to the bottom of the page. With it, a switch flipped inside me, where what had been muted was crystal clear and stark. I spun to the instrument, a gift from Theo's grandfather, our next-door neighbor, tucked in one of the corners of the family room.

A woman my age with dark skin and wearing a low bun was sitting on the piano bench—another neighbor named Lena, I remembered belatedly. Behind her was her partner, Deb, who was short haired and pale, with a hand on her shoulder. Both I'd met for the first time today, but with how Lena pressed on another chord while Deb hummed, they had clearly been friends with Libby too, with how comfortable they were positioned behind Libby's piano.

And when the notes came together into one of Libby's most favorite first pieces to play, Beethoven's "Ode to Joy," a shiver ran through me from the toes on up.

This is wrong. Absolutely wrong.

The thought catapulted me away from Nora, with her book still in my hand. Crossing the room took too long, and as I did, the vision of my little girl tapping "Chopsticks" on an electric keyboard rushed to the forefront in my memory.

How joyful Libby had been with her hands buried in the keys, writing notes in the margins of her sheet music, or dreaming up melodies. The piano had dashed her insecurities, and on it she'd learned to succeed and fail, to love and let go, to negotiate and win.

And this piano was sacred.

Lena's face lifted upon my arrival, expression falling. "Oh, I'm sorry . . . Libby and I, she gave me some lessons . . ."

"No one plays this piano." Voice cracking, I set a hand against the fallboard, a threat. To Lena's fingers, to another story about Libby, to everything that was unknown to me about Libby and her life in Louisburg. To these last ten days and the four years prior to them.

Lena scrambled off the bench in continued apology, and she and Deb scuttled away. I rounded the piano, eyes scanning the keys for signs of damage or evidence of Libby. Surely her fingerprints still remained, especially on the black keys. The flats and sharps had been her favorite; doing the different and taking the opposite had been exactly her style.

A shadow descended from above. Quinn. Just over six feet tall, he blocked out the light from the low ceiling, though it cast a halo around his reddish-brown hair. "Celine?" Worry laced his tone.

The explanation was at the tip of my tongue, ready to leap, but in my periphery, Mae, MJ, and Amelia watched me intently.

There could be no tears here, no outbursts. I couldn't slam the fallboard shut, nor could I scream from the top of my lungs. Not in front of these people, and especially not in front of my children . . . what was left of them.

With a final look at the keys, I lowered the fallboard. "I . . . I'm fine. I'm sorry . . . it's just . . . this was her most favorite thing."

A mumble of an apology came from Lena, and Quinn eased the moment by leaving my side and guiding her and Deb to the buffet table, plying them with plates of pastry and small talk. The uptick in his voice broke the ice that had built up in the silence, and the room seemed to reawaken.

I ran a hand down the smooth wood of the fallboard, thumb catching on a ribbon. It was attached to a key sticking out from an hourglass keyhole. The brass was cool, its presence an invitation, and I twisted the key to the right.

At the melancholy click of the lock, the tension in my chest eased.

I hadn't been able to protect Libby, but this . . . *this* I could do.

Chapter Two

The hotel room's automatic doors widened with a whoosh, and the cool air was a relief from my two-mile walk. After crossing into the foyer, I stood briefly to bask after what had felt like a thirty-minute hot flash, arms sticking out wide for maximum exposure in my shorts and T-shirt. Clearly, Boston wasn't pulling any punches, intent on welcoming me back to my home turf with record-high heat and humidity.

Thank goodness for AC.

A shriek snapped me out of my temporary reverie, toward the dining room area on the right, where the buffet breakfast was being served. It was packed with bodies, with the line snaking to the back wall. A low murmur sounded through the dining room as hotel workers wove among the tables and chairs, taking away trash and wiping down empty tables, which were quickly inhabited by other groups of people.

But what stood out from this group was that a majority were women, and most wore purple graphic T-shirts with the cover of my newest book, *Just One Step*, and lanyards around their necks. Some were taking selfies, flashing peace signs, and others flexed the bling pinned on their lanyards, a sign that this wasn't their first Celine Lakad Coaching rodeo.

I tugged the bill of my running cap lower, over my eyes, dipping my chin to my chest. With the elevator alcove as my target, I scurried past the dining room, avoiding eye contact with anyone coming my direction.

It had been a given for me to stay in the same hotel as my book-tour attendees. It had worked for my previous book tours, coaching workshops, and motherhood-to-career events because my being in the same building guaranteed that the event would start on time, with me being the last person to arrive. Also, oftentimes, attendees had extra questions about vision planning and goal setting, and I hadn't minded taking them after the lights had dimmed onstage, such as at mealtimes or during the hotel's happy hour. Connections were best made when everyone was at eye level, without a lavalier microphone attached to my lapel.

But this book tour had differed from the jump. It had started with *Just One Step*, my fifth self-help book, which had been published two weeks ago, becoming an instant bestseller after the viral explosion of my branded social media. What had followed was the coveted self-sustaining cycle of buzz, book sales, and publisher support.

For the first time in thirteen years, and to the surprise of me and my team, every seat in the tour was sold out. Which meant that for the last four stops, I had been swimming in a fishbowl of purple-clad inhabitants, adding to the pervasive, low-level exhaustion that hummed through me.

Not that I was complaining! But the expectation to be "on" was overwhelming, and did people really want to see me in my workout gear, without makeup, and looking like the fifty-three-year-old woman I really was? Yes, fifty-three was the new forty-three, which was basically thirty-three but with a lifetime more experience, but my retinol wasn't a magic potion.

These attendees held a specific image of Celine Lakad-Frasier in their heads. She was an edited, put-together individual, poised, and wise. The Celine they knew through her socials, her book, and her workshops gave them the tools, confidence, and permission to be better versions of themselves. She told them that they could accomplish their dreams with simple, measurable steps. Her actual image didn't need to be the focus of attention.

And I would do my best to keep it that way.

The elevator was empty, a respite, and I stepped in and pressed the button for the twelfth floor. In the general quiet, except for the elevator music piping through the speakers, the day's to-do list came to mind. My energy was waning—not a good sign—hence the walk this morning to wake my tired brain. It would be a full-pot-of-coffee kind of day. My primary care physician, Dr. Simpson, wouldn't be happy about it. *Coffee doesn't count as hydration, Celine,* she'd said time and again. *Hydration. Sleep. You need to lower your stress level.*

That coming from an MD who had a patient waiting list longer than that buffet line on the first floor, as if stress wasn't part and parcel of life.

And coffee—I would do what I had to do. In three hours, the hotel's main conference room would be filled, and the spotlight would be on me.

Heat clambered up my chest, and I pulled the neckline of my shirt. After tonight, our next stop was Milwaukee in two days, then New York City. Among and in between would be podcast and virtual interviews. All in addition to my usual blog posts and social media captions—though they were now managed by my team, I still provided the vision.

"You're living the dream," I said aloud and rolled out my shoulders, assuaging the rise in my heart rate. This moment, the way my book had been received? This book tour was the culmination of thirteen years of hustle, from my humble beginnings as a mommy blogger. And yet the joy . . . the joy I'd expected to feel reaching this point was absent. It was both anticlimactic and suffocating.

I'm just a little tired. A good nap and a full night's sleep will do the trick.

The elevator doors jostled and began to shut, but when the gap was only a foot, an arm wormed its way through. Three women in purple shirts and a couple of teenagers in their pajamas stepped in, and four other buttons were pressed.

Dammit. I inched my way to the corner and dipped my head, bringing my phone up to chest level and pretending to scroll. This was going to be a long ride up.

I loved my Steppers—this was the evolved name of my followers. They were supportive and loyal. They'd been by my side from the beginning of this journey with my first attempt at blogging my struggles as a stay-at-home mom and military spouse. *Attempt,* meaning that the result had been an unpolished mess, but it had been something, a vehicle for my on-the-spot lessons of finding one's passion even while in the thick of motherhood. They'd followed me to social media as I had built my brand as a life coach, though the term never had sat right with me—I'd considered myself an encourager, a sharer, and a connector.

It was my Steppers who'd paid the big bucks for my daylong workshops after I had become a coach, traveling miles to attend to see me and other life coaches and speakers. Steppers had filled bookstores as I'd churned out one book after another. They had been my audience for my blog, and then on my socials. In seeing them, I was inspired. In helping them, I was filled with purpose. I was more than *Mom*. Being among them came with this validation that motherhood wasn't supposed to be perfect. That nuance existed in this role. That as mothers, we could still want more, want different.

That was, it all *used to* feel that way.

I bit my cheek to readjust my attitude.

A nap. And maybe a retweaking of the schedule. Those were my next two steps after the tour.

The volume level in the elevator rose with the women's laughter, drowning out the elevator music.

"I cannot wait. T-minus one hundred and ten minutes. What should we do until then?" one of the women asked. She was White and appeared to be in her midforties, her hair in a perfect blonde bob. (How, in this humidity? Who knew.) Up her lanyard were enamel pins from previous events—she was truly a Stepper.

"How about mimosas? I'm all stocked in my room," a second woman with a soprano tone said. She was Black with a slight build.

"Morning happy hour before a cry fest," the third, a muscular Asian woman with a husky voice, commented back. She twirled her ponytail with a grin. "But the big question is, did we all wear our waterproof mascara? I'm sure to cry."

"I know. Especially when I think of what she went through. I don't know how she was able to move on," someone whispered.

My senses tingled with foreboding, and my eyes shut in earnest.

They couldn't see me here. This wasn't for my ears.

Another clucked. "I mean, technically, we *know* how she did it because we're seeing it now. She's completely changed."

"What do you mean, she's changed? If anything, she's totally more relatable. She wrote a book about taking the next step, and isn't that what she's doing too? She's literally showing us how she's trying to move on with life."

"But are you guys getting a different feeling about her content? It's so curated these days," another said in a whisper. "Like she's holding back."

The elevator doors opened, and the teenagers stepped out, silencing the chatter. Once the doors slid shut, the three women huddled even closer.

The woman kept going, and her words were like little pinches against my skin. "She hasn't come right out and talked about the thing . . . except for that official message. And I wish she would. She has to know how we're curious, that we want to support her. She even doubled down—the book, events, everything. She's put out so much content, though nothing about . . . you know."

Another voice chimed in, dipping in volume. "I don't know how she could have scheduled a tour this early after it all happened."

The tones were getting so mixed up that I couldn't discern who was saying what. One person added, "Five hundred people, multicity tour. The books, the merch. I guess it would be hard to walk away from that."

"Well, all her success doesn't replace what she lost. Though I do agree at how much she's changed in two years. You could even clock it to the day when her daughter died. She went from authentic and natural photos to filtered."

My eyes flew open, my breath lodging itself in my throat. *Breathe, Celine.* With pursed lips, I sipped in air.

"Gotta go. This is me." The doors opened, and one stepped out. "Text me!"

Two were left, and if possible, the temperature in the elevator rose, and what had been shock to have witnessed this conversation turned to annoyance. Holding back? Filters?

These people had not walked in my shoes. Nor did they understand my life, and how I valued this work. How much I put myself into this work. And what was wrong with filters? Filters were all but expected for a cohesive presence. The team had switched to filters and curated content to get with the times.

Thank goodness my floor was next.

"Everyone does filters. *You* do filters," someone said.

That's right . . . you tell them, I thought.

"True. But it's different," the other answered. "Maybe it's just me, but it all feels, I dunno, like she's in denial. Like her daughter hadn't died at all."

"If you feel this way, then why are you even here?"

"I mean, I still love her. Her content is still important, and I do believe she's a good person. It was because of her second book that I finally went into freelancing, and look where it got me."

Her friend hummed. "I know, Ms. I Formed My Own LLC."

"Right. But I can have my opinions. And I can be curious. Like, how does she really feel these days? But I'm invested. If she can get through something so horrible, then it makes me think I can deal with my own problems."

The elevator simmered into a silence, though the pounding in my chest migrated to my ears. My clothes felt too tight. The warm air had become suffocating, and I wanted out of there.

Had I been watched like a zoo animal? Did people discuss my life like these women had, curious at my natural habitat and all the while treating my history like a plot twist? They were supposed to be here for my work, for my contributions, not for my personal life.

Yes, I understood the consequences of this business, of being accessible, of being online. I also knew that a good image was paramount. It was why the team had veered to a more curated feed, to motivational quotes and edited snippets of what was going on behind the scenes of Celine Lakad Coaching. We were leveling up to a professional brand. We owed it to all the speakers I worked with, to the publishers I wrote for, and to my readers and followers, who were there for a boost in their motivation.

Not once had I thought the things I wasn't saying, my personal life, would become fodder.

Finally, *finally*, the elevator doors opened to the twelfth floor, and my body lurched forward as I mumbled, "Excuse me." Then, with long strides, my legs took me down the hallway. After turning left, now away from the view of the elevator, I halted, swallowing the ball of tension in my throat.

My mind ran through my tool belt of affirmations. Having a list in one's memory was part of online survival. I'd yet to encounter a comment section on one of my posts that hadn't had something negative, sexist, or racist.

My life is my own.

Others' opinions aren't my facts.

I choose gratitude.

And though my chest tightened with the start of dread, I pushed myself forward on my feet once more.

This was not the time to mull over the past, to go down memory lane, or to become defensive over what strangers had said. My sold-out events were evidence enough that my purpose had value.

Plus, today's event would begin in a couple of hours, and my presentation had to be perfect. I had to get with it.

But as I neared my hotel room, a woman was milling in front of Sonya's door, which was across from mine. She was my height, wearing cuffed boyfriend jeans and white Keds, with curly brown hair loosely tied in the back. A hard-shell carry-on stood beside her.

"Mae?" I sped up. "What are you doing here?"

Mae and John lived in Maryland too. After Quinn and I had downsized and relocated to Annapolis six years ago to be closer to Quinn's college-basketball coaching job, Mae and her family had soon followed so I wouldn't be too far away from my apos. Seeing my granddaughters grow was important to me and to Mae.

But she was a busy mother of three and a kindergarten teacher. While it thrilled me for my girls to attend my events, there was no expectation on my end. So, when Mae had told me a while ago that she couldn't meet me at this tour stop with the rest of the family due to her work schedule, I'd understood.

She turned to me with rounded eyes. They held a deer-in-the-head-lights kind of expression. "Oh, hey, Mom. I thought you were out walking." Belatedly, she hugged me stiffly and kissed me on the cheek.

Something was amiss. Mae and John were attached at the hip. I fished my key card out of my pocket. "Honey? What's wrong? Where's John and the girls?"

A stray hair was splayed against her cheek, and she tucked it behind her ear. Her light-brown eyes were glassy, the sclera pink.

"Yes . . . um. I'm here alone."

Chapter Three

The room card slipped from my fingers. "Alone?"

Mae bent to retrieve the card and swiped us in while I picked my jaw up off the floor.

"You didn't say you were coming. Did something happen?" I prodded.

Mae kicked off her shoes at the threshold, slogged to the bed, and perched on it. Then, she threw her body back onto the mattress, slinging her arms across her eyes. "Oh God, oh God."

My worry ratcheted up, though I tamped it down. My daughter had a flair for the dramatics, and a minor in theater to boot. There was a logical explanation to all of this.

"Mae?" I perched on the bed beside her.

Then she shot up, panic in her expression. "Where's Sonya? MJ? Amelia? Dad?"

Mae could never keep up a lie, and these whiplash reactions were a tell. I peered at her. "Sonya is with MJ and Amelia. Your father should be walking in any second. Why?"

"Just because."

In my incessant stare, her gaze dragged away.

"It's not like you to be away from the girls. From John," I said.

"How do you know that I didn't just need a break?" Her tone was indignant. "Aren't you ever just *tired*?"

A rush of empathy bowled me over. Mae was in the thick of parenting young ones.

"Oh, honey. With work and the kids, I know you must be pulled in different directions. I get it."

With two older girls and two younger girls, with a span of ten years among them and a gap of five years in between my second and third daughters, it had taken almost three decades for me and Quinn to become empty nesters.

And because our early years had been lean with Quinn in the army and then as a basketball coach, when my hobby of mommy blogging had surprised us and evolved into a business, I'd leaned into it for financial support. It had splintered my attention, and I, too, had had trouble managing my time.

Mae had discovered as I had that time wasn't infinite. Time couldn't be saved and then be cashed in. Time was fleeting, and when raising children, time spent on work meant it wasn't with them, and vice versa.

The glass ceiling was so much lower as a mother, and hitting one's head on it was a shock to the system.

"Oh, Mom. I can't even explain." She searched my face. "I just feel like I'm a horrible person right now."

"Stop, Mae." I wrapped an arm around her. Turning toward me, she nuzzled in, and I tucked her into me like a joey. She might have been thirty-two, but in that moment, she was still my little girl.

The days are long, and the years are short. It was a statement mothers passed down to one another. And while as a younger mother, I'd snorted at the flippant way veteran mothers had said this because they'd been done with the baby and toddler stages . . . it was true.

Still I searched my mind's cupboards for the wise thing to say, because I didn't want to come off as judgmental. And because I didn't believe she was telling me the whole story. "You're not horrible. And it's okay to admit that you're tired. But . . . I feel like this is a smoke screen. You look more nervous than upset. So what's really going on?"

Her shoulders sagged, and for a moment, I thought that the truth was forthcoming, but her next words were screeching, breathy. "I missed you, I guess. And everyone was here, and I had major FOMO, you know?"

I shook my head, disbelieving. Her words were making sense, but she could barely keep my gaze.

"I mean, it *is* Boston. This is where it all began," she added.

My insides softened. Mae remembered how nostalgic this stop was to me. I had grown up in Boston—first with my parents, and then with my brother, Samuel, when my mother had died.

"And Louisburg is just down the road," she continued with a whisper.

"Yes, that's right." Despite the rush of heat that was doing its thing to my neck, I froze my smile. "Well, I just wish you'd told me you were coming. I would have gotten you your own room."

"Dad knew." Her cheeks caved in pure admission. "I didn't want to bother you with it. With this tour, you've been so busy."

My breath left my body, and guilt replaced it. "I'm not too busy for you, or for either of your sisters. Nothing is more important than the three of you."

Her mouth opened, then shut, as if she was deciding against what she'd wanted to say.

Her hesitance unnerved me, but I decided not to push. Mae never did keep her secrets for long, and time was ticking. I looked at my watch—I had less than two hours to get ready and review my talking points. "Well, I love that you're here. That the whole family's here." My voice croaked with this part truth because our family would never be whole without Libby. I pushed on with a smile. "You can bunk in with MJ; she's got two doubles in her room, and she'll be glad to have you around. Unless you want to jump in with Amelia and Theo?"

"With their newlywed PDA?" Her face screwed into a frown.

19

"You were the same way with John, especially that honeymoon year."

"I know." She sighed. "John and I are definitely out of that phase. Honestly, I'd rather stay with Amelia and Theo and all their PDA than with MJ. With her deadline and all, she's up all hours."

"Deadline? I didn't realize she was under deadline." MJ was an independently published mystery author, and she hadn't said a word about work. My mom antennae detected another concern. "Up all hours, you say?"

Mae's face stilled—another tell. She was like a duck, all calm up on top and paddling like heck underneath.

"Honey?" My heart was in a free fall into my belly. MJ was usually my most transparent daughter. Her emotions weren't only on her sleeve, but on her face, in her body language, in the words that valiantly leapt from her tongue. "When I asked her if she was under deadline, she said no." I didn't force my girls to come to my events, especially when they had their own responsibilities.

But this wasn't about the deadline—more that MJ hadn't disclosed it. She usually told me everything.

A familiar dread started in my gut. Nothing bad happened on its own. It was usually preceded by warnings, by sirens blaring just below one's conscience.

"You know MJ; she probably just didn't want you to worry either." Mae bit her lip, and the wrinkle between her eyebrows deepened. At that moment, the hair on the back of my neck stood. If my two eldest had something odd going on, what were the chances that the next person down our family tree did too? "And Amelia?"

She slapped a hand over her mouth, and her brown eyes rounded in panic. "I'm not saying a word."

"Mae, this is ridiculous. You're not fooling any—"

A knock sounded at the door. It was followed by a trio of voices.

It was the rest of the most important women in my life. My heart should've been thrumming with excitement. Instead, what hovered above me was the thing I'd continued to push aside time and again. Dread. That despite my accomplishments, I wasn't enough. There were still secrets and plans I wasn't privy to or included in. That I couldn't seem to keep my people in check.

"It's Sonya! Why aren't you answering? Is Quinn in there with you?" said my best friend from the other side of the closed door.

"Coming!" Sighing, I turned to Mae. "Our conversation isn't finished. It's obvious we need time to catch up. All of us. Later."

When I opened the hotel room door, Sonya, MJ, and Amelia burst in like a mishmash cloud of colorful clothing and contrasting scents. But instead of overflowing with the usual banter and the occasional squeal of laughter, their faces froze into prim smiles.

"Is that my Tessa Mae?" Sonya seemed to startle awake, bounding toward Mae with open arms. Sonya was the first person I'd met in Louisburg. She had been a neighbor turned best friend and then had become my executive assistant. Then, a godmother to my girls. Ten years my junior and Korean American, she treasured the title of Ninang Sonya. Sonya and I had fought our wrinkles and gray hairs together (with her using her au naturel methods and with me taking advantage of Retin-A, Botox, and regularly scheduled hair appointments) while the girls had grown into their adolescence and tumultuous teen and young adult years.

She was the sister I'd wished for, a family in all ways—when Quinn and I had relocated to Annapolis, Sonya had agreed to come along with us, moving into a place just down the street so she'd still have her space.

To my girls, Sonya was another mother. When times had been hectic, when my and Quinn's conquer-and-divide method had lacked an extra caring heart and two hands (and a car), she had been there.

She had been the third in-case-of-emergency number for all the kids' schools and in their cell phones.

Mothering was never done in a vacuum, and Sonya was my safety net. She filled in when I ran late, picked up the balls I dropped when the business was at its busiest, especially as of recently.

Not a day had I worried about her relationship with the girls. My trust for Sonya was implicit. But when she had hugged Mae just now and she'd whispered something in her ear, red flags had waved in front of my eyes.

But a buzz snatched my attention, and five out of five of us dug or searched for our phones. My gaze landed on mine; it was vibrating on the hotel desk.

I thumbed to my messages and read it. "It's Quinn. He's parking the rental. He'll be up in a bit."

Sonya clapped once, resetting the room like a teacher. "All right. We should all get ready. Celine, you especially. Girls, follow me, and leave your mom be. Otherwise we won't get her onstage in time. For all the amazing she is, she is far from prompt."

Of course, the girls halted their banter. They loved Sonya, adored her, as I did. She was the only friend who had come through the tumultuous recent years. When others had fallen away because I wasn't great at keeping in touch, even before she'd been my assistant, it was she who'd made up the distance. She was the one who had pushed me over the line of doubt when I had hesitated to file for my incorporated status eight years ago. Sonya had suffered through my brainstorming of every chapter of each of my books.

My suspicion about her covert whisper, that small sign of intimacy with Mae that I wasn't a part of, melted away. Sonya loved my children. She loved me. I was lucky to have her to once more round up the kids. If Mae needed her more than me right now, then that was okay.

"Yes, go." I laughed, and the tension inside me was alleviated. "I definitely don't want to be late. Those Steppers are ruthless."

The four began to file out of the room, but in the quiet, my conversation with Mae returned. "Wait. MJ, can you stay, please? I need help with"—I scrambled for an excuse—"my socials."

A smile lit up her face. "Ooh, yes."

Sonya gave us a stern look. "Not too long."

"Yes, ma'am." I winked at her.

"Gimme." MJ approached me with an outstretched hand just as the door closed, gesturing to the phone in my hand. I handed it over. "Okay, what's going on? Did you need help doing a video? Or a photo shoot? The view from your balcony is divine." MJ went to the sliding glass door and put a hand on the door handle.

The bright sun lit her profile. Each of my children was unique in how they expressed their DNA. Amelia with her cat eyes and dark skin. Mae with her father's curly hair and freckles and delicate neck. MJ's petite stature and full lips that belonged only to my mother. And Libby . . .

I gasped at the natural progression of my thoughts.

"Mom?"

My eyes swung to meet MJ's curious expression, and the reason why I'd kept her back rushed in. "Right. So, Mae . . . she told me that you were under deadline."

She blinked slowly. "Yeah. And what else did she say?"

"Nothing else. But that you're hard at work." Raising a hand to her impending interruption, I racked my brain on how to speak to her. There was a push and pull between asking for information and demanding it from an adult child. MJ was thirty, and she could very well do what she wanted, but I was still her mother. And, the ground felt shaky today, with the secrets Mae was keeping and the elevator Steppers. "I appreciate that you're here despite your work. But I was wondering why you lied to me when I asked you if you were under deadline."

She shuffled to the desk and leaned against it, looking down. Her fingers drew circles on the desktop, and as the seconds passed, my thoughts meandered to the worst-case scenario.

What had I missed once more?

Eyelashes fluttering, she raised her gaze to me. "You won't get mad?"

"MJ, this is more angst than any of your books put together. Just tell me." I smiled to assuage her worry, though my insides coiled in anticipation.

"I . . ."

She paused, throat working, before saying, "I wanted to spend time with you. I guess I just . . . missed you. And since my sisters were going to be here, too, with Amelia canceling her trip to Tokyo . . ."

My thoughts thundered to a stop with her mention of Amelia, tabling my initial thought that MJ was still lying—the pause had been a tell. My words came out like wisps of fog on a frigid day. "They canceled a trip?"

Amelia and Theo had married a year ago, shortly after she'd graduated from college. The wedding had been like a lighthouse's foghorn in the dark, cloudy night sky of Libby's death, navigating our family back to one another. Preparing for it had been my girls' first steps back toward laughter and get-togethers, and under an arch of greenery at Quiet Waters Park in Annapolis, Theo and Amelia's bittersweet ceremony had marked a milestone in our collective healing.

Sitting in that front row during the ceremony, I had also taken a cleansing breath.

She would never be alone, I'd told myself. Not only did Amelia have her sisters and her parents and Sonya, but she now had Theo, and his whole side of the family too. At her worst nights, and on her best days, she would have someone to turn to.

And who would be a better fit than Theo Loren, who was equally as free spirited, and who wanted to see the world with her. Tokyo had been a bucket list destination for them.

MJ's jaw fell open at her revelation. "Um . . . ," she started. "It's no big deal, though."

"That's not true. It *is* a big deal. She and Theo have been planning forever for this trip. Does your father know about this?" He'd been aware about Mae coming to Boston, though he hadn't informed me. If he had known about Amelia, why wouldn't he have dissuaded her?

MJ's gaze was rooted to the floor.

Alarm rang through me. This day had been like an onion, with every moment peeling back to the bitter truth that I didn't have a handle on my family. That plans and discussions and decisions had been made without my knowledge. "MJ? What the hell is going on? With you, Mae, and Amelia—and your father?"

"Oh my God, will you look at that!" She spun a nonexistent watch on her wrist. "Mom. You have an event in an hour and a half. How about we talk about this later?"

A knock sounded on the door, and we both turned our eyes to it.

MJ jumped up, relief playing across her features. She lumbered to the door and pressed down on the handle.

Sure enough, Sonya was on the other side of the threshold with a curious smile. "What's going on?"

"I'm gonna head . . . out." MJ slinked out the door.

Sonya's eyebrows arched up at me.

"Something is up with the girls, and I can feel it in my bones." I headed to the vanity and rested my palms against the top. "And I don't like it. Not a single bit."

My friend stood behind me, eyes boring into mine. "I hate to say it, but you've got to try to forget that for now. It's almost showtime."

Thirteen years of this. Thirteen years of content creation, of coaching groups and individuals into finding their career passions. Thirteen years of networking, of navigating myself through and around people and, most often, away from home. Thirteen years of helping people plan their dreams, of connecting them to experts. Of blowing air into a balloon that had grown so big that it had lifted our entire family in status and wealth—so that I was the breadwinner—and work life and family life had become one and the same, only to leave me exactly the way I was feeling now: a little out of breath.

Celine Lakad Coaching had been and continued to be for a good reason—to help others find their professional true north within the chaos of their lives. It was for something bigger than myself.

I wouldn't stop now. I couldn't, even if I wanted to—even if exhaustion had settled itself into my pores. Even if at the moment I felt like a fraud. A performer, a mother who had lost touch. It wasn't for lack of trying to be the best mom. When things had changed—when Libby had died—I'd tried even harder to make her death mean something. To fuel me, at the very least—at the most, to mute the voice in my head that reminded me that I could have done more, done better.

Lakad meant *walk* in Tagalog, and my newest book, *Just One Step*, written after Libby had passed, was my life's work. To everyone else, it was a series of steps to achieve their greatest passions one step at a time. To me, these were the steps I had taken to move on from Libby's death.

I couldn't not go out there, even if my instincts were pushing me the other direction, to find out exactly what was going on with my family.

Otherwise, losing Libby would have been for naught.

Sonya's reassuring hand on my shoulder brought me back down to the moment, and I lifted my eyes to her reflection in the mirror. "All right. Showtime."

Chapter Four

These were the facts:

Libby had been a child who had routinely gotten strep throat. Once, in high school, it had escalated to rheumatic fever, which had left her immunocompromised. Two years ago, strep had returned in the form of toxic shock syndrome. It had taken her so quickly that Libby herself hadn't been alarmed until it was too late. When Quinn and I had arrived at her bedside in Louisburg Hospital, she had been in the ICU, and by then, she'd been septic.

Then she was gone.

What had been a pack of four by my side—Tessa Mae, Maria Josephine, Elizabeth Abigail, and Amelia Lou—had become three.

Just one step is one step forward.

I repeated my book's message in my head in the shower and then once more while looking into my vanity mirror while applying my mascara in my robe. One word after another. Like the prayers said with each mala or rosary bead, this sentence had been my way of pulling myself from what had been the darkness of Libby's death—from within myself so I could care for and earn for my family.

Blinking at my reflection, I said it now to calm my running thoughts about my girls, my fear that because Libby's death had come from left field, I would miss the next curveball. Yes, I would need to follow up. But right now, right this second, the way forward was to mentally be present for this book event. Five hundred people had paid their hard-earned money to see me, as I had been reminded by that group of women in the elevator. Celine Lakad-Frasier had to show up.

But why?

The question arose in my subconscious, and it swirled through the synapses of my brain, though not for the first time.

As with every time it did, an imaginary me stuffed the thought into an overfull cupboard of concerns and shut it before they all toppled down and out.

Not showing up was a ridiculous notion to even entertain. This business was my life. More so, I had to believe my own advice that so long as I continued to take steps, all would be okay.

I listed those steps now:

Get ready for this event.

Trust that my girls are telling me the truth.

Trust that my husband isn't keeping something from me too.

Quinn and I had done what we could to survive the first weeks after Libby had died, and that had been to tend to our daughters, once more dividing and conquering. I'd stayed with one daughter while he'd bunked in with another, and our paths had crisscrossed as we'd switched and consoled two of the three at a time. But when some of the dust had settled and we'd found ourselves alone and together in our Annapolis town house, the silence had been all-consuming.

We'd lost touch.

Now, two years down the line, things were good between him and me. His team was winning, my business was thriving, and our town house had slowly begun to show signs of our partnership. Our schedules were hectic, but we were talking. We'd made love.

Surely, if our girls were in crisis, sick, or in need of help, he would have told me.

As if the universe had heard my inner ramblings, a knock sounded on the door, followed by a beep. The door popped open, revealing my partner of the last thirty-five years. All at once, my body exhaled, melting like snow on a warm day.

My voice shook from the mishmash of emotions. I stood. "Quinn, hon."

As he seemed to read my mood, his forehead creased, and he parked his things. "What's wrong? I thought you'd be all ready by now."

I opened my mouth to speak, though nothing came out; my jumbled thoughts clogged my throat. My heart pounded with dread.

I'd mentioned it to my primary care doc once, this emotion I couldn't nail down, like I was missing something, or forgetting something. It was followed by shortness of breath and an aching chest. The first time it had happened was at Libby's funeral reception, soon after I'd locked up the piano. I'd thought I was having a heart attack, and to my gratitude, Sonya had noted my panic and scooped me up before anyone had seen. It had since occurred occasionally, without a discernable trigger.

Stress, Dr. Simpson had called it, in addition to high blood pressure, for which I took medication now.

Since the book had been published, these episodes had come every few days. Sometimes more than once a day.

It made no sense, seeing that I should've been on top of the world.

"I'm here." Quinn rested his hands on my shoulders, and his thumbs grazed the line of my jaw. His thick eyebrows dipped in worry. I reached up to cup his cheeks. His skin was warm, the wrinkles around his eyes and mouth so familiar and comforting. His salt-and-pepper beard was soft under my touch. "Breathe," he said.

At his instruction, my chest rose and fell. *Inhale . . . exhale . . .*

He swiped at the tears I hadn't been aware of. His blue eyes scoured my face. "Talk to me." Voice gruff, it vibrated through his fingertips and onto my skin.

"Our girls . . . they're keeping secrets. I can tell." I swallowed, gathering my wits. "And you. You knew that Mae was coming, and that MJ had a deadline. That Amelia canceled her trip to Tokyo. Why didn't you say anything to me?"

His expression softened. "Why? Because this is an important stop of the tour. And they wanted to be here too."

"If that's all, then why not just say?"

"Because . . . first let me get you some water." His departure from my side was sudden and a little heartbreaking, and I wished for his arms around me, to help steady the last bit of my nerves.

Quinn handed me an open bottle of water, which I gulped down like I'd run a half marathon. "Quinn? Why didn't you just tell me?" I asked.

"Because it wasn't necessary to say." He shrugged, and his wavy hair flopped lazily over to one side, except for strands that curled over his forehead.

Quinn was the perfect specimen of the silver fox, and the butterflies in my belly reliably stirred. It was criminal that despite age, stress from his all-consuming job, and the last two years of us winging it with our parenting and our partnership, he was that much more attractive. Without trying, and unknowingly.

But he never had answered my question in full. "I would have wanted to know."

His gaze dropped to the floor, and in the brief silence I understood that the piece missing in the puzzle was sitting right in front of me. Dipping down to catch his eyes, I said, "Wait. Did you ask them to come?"

He nodded once.

"But why did you do that?" My shoulders slumped. "They're busy, and they have their own lives. You should have consulted me." Keeping abreast of the girls didn't mean the same thing as occupying their time. It didn't mean having them choose between their set plans and me. Ultimatums didn't work; it hadn't worked with Libby when I'd asked her to move to Annapolis with us. It had been one more point of contention between us.

He inhaled and seemed to hold his breath. "They're adults. They came here of their own free will. They could have said no. They agreed this tour stop is important."

"But in comparison to Amelia and Theo's trip to Tokyo? And MJ's deadline. And asking Mae to miss work?"

"Some things are, yes."

The dip in his tone turned up my body temperature, not out of need, but out of frustration. Quinn was again playing devil's advocate, a trait that had once drawn me to him so long ago—that he could see all sides to a problem—but these days, it grated at me. Because he couldn't just let the conversation move forward. Everything became a discussion. And then there were moments like this when I was right, and yet he couldn't acknowledge it. "You always do that."

"Do what?"

"Take the opposite side, just for the hell of it."

"There aren't sides to take here. I asked for them to come, and they chose to be here."

"Then why the secret?"

He shrugged once more.

My husband was too casual, too flippant, when his body language told me that he had something to say. It was in the way he clasped his hands together, like he was trying to contain the words within himself.

"What the hell is going on?!" The words erupted from my chest, and my lips trembled from the force.

His chin dropped to his chest in clear disappointment at the flare of my temper. And instead of firing back, as he normally would have, he remained silent. Which emphasized how I'd overreacted.

Remorse filled me. "I . . . I'm sorry. I shouldn't have yelled."

The truth was, it hadn't been all silent in our town house after Libby had died. Quinn and I had fought, over everything. We'd argued with the energy of two parents who were mad at the world, who were incensed at their fate. Once, we'd spent a better part of what should have been an intimate dinner in silence after an argument on the benefits of veganism. Another time, one of Libby's bills had been routed to the town house, and we'd debated for hours as to whether we should open it.

Then, one day, after a night of him sleeping on the couch because of an argument I couldn't recall, we'd retracted our claws, and we'd set some rules. One of which was to rein in the yelling.

"I told you this tour is too much," he said now. "It's too much, too soon. Your stress level—"

"Don't start on that again. Quinn, there's no such thing as living a life without stress." I sat back down at the vanity while a tide of unease rose inside me. This tour was a good thing. Was it stressful? Some parts of it were, yes. But stress wasn't a good enough reason not to work, to reach people, to make a difference. To keep going.

Our conversation fell into the depths of silence. Our communication style these days, if described, would be *it's complicated.* A better comparison would be that it was like a sinkhole—just beyond the darkness of everything left unsaid were the rushing waters of change.

Common sense would dictate—even Celine Lakad-Frasier, the encourager and coach, would advise—that Quinn and I should talk this through. That we should attempt to dig deeper into the reasons why we had gone from loving to contentious in a matter of seconds and that, perhaps, after two years of slipping in and out of fights, it was high time we go to couples therapy.

But doing that would take stopping. It would mean that we would have to commit to actual appointments together when it was virtually impossible with Quinn's practice-and-game schedule and my event calendar. It had been easiest to deal with things on our own.

He ran a hand through his hair. "You know I think you're brilliant. That you're everything, really. You know I'm proud, right?"

I nodded, though this felt like a precursor to something more. There was a *but* coming.

"But." He sipped in a breath. "I'm just tired of fighting, you know? This is tough."

"Finally. Something we can agree on." Snippets of our three decades came to me in a quick clip. How in the beginning of our relationship and parenting, we had cherished our time together. We'd had date nights set on our calendar. We'd taken a few minutes after the girls had gone to bed to talk about our day. We could channel a message with a quick glance between us, once even thwarting a sneak-out attempt by Mae. She'd been fourteen and hell bent on going to a party. Quinn and I had been sound asleep, both awakened by the squeak of her window.

We'd turned to one another and, in the dim bedroom light, shared a look. And we'd shot out of bed like rockets.

Now it was like pulling teeth for us to work as a team.

A knock sounded on the white, ornately paneled door, followed by the voice of our precious youngest daughter, Amelia. "Ma? Dad?"

Quinn spun his head toward the door and snorted. "Her instincts are always on point."

After a quick swipe of a hand over his face, which he seemed to reset to neutral, Quinn paused for me to give him the signal. I patted under my eyes for the stray tear before nodding.

Quinn opened the door, and on cue, we presented smiles to our daughter. She was carrying two to-go cups of coffee.

"Daddy! Yay, you're here." She rolled on her tiptoes and planted a kiss on his cheek.

Quinn gently wrapped an arm around her. "Hi, sweetheart."

"I wanted to bring you both your usuals." Her gaze jumped from me to Quinn and back. "With half-and-half for you. Black for Ma."

I accepted the cup of coffee. "Thank you, sweetie."

"Ninang Sonya also told me that you're to be in the greenroom in a little more than a half hour."

"Got it."

"She mentioned doing a quick live video before the event. Get everyone in the mood—have them feel what it's like in the greenroom. With Dad."

"Eh. Not sure I'll do that." A crooked smile bloomed on Quinn's face. "Your mom's the brand."

I curtailed the annoyance that threatened to rear its ugly head. Quinn's statement was full of mirth, but behind it, I heard resentment.

Quinn hated social media. He thought it put distance between people. He believed it a crutch, an excuse, and inauthentic. A distraction. It made no sense how a man could be so open minded in so many ways but completely against the digital age.

Gone were the days when I used to blog quietly at the computer. Media—whether a phone or a professional DSLR, a video camera or the content calendar—was part of our lives. Content planning happened daily, but the more Quinn was around it, the more he pushed it away.

My opinion? This refusal to participate was all due to how it affected our dynamic. Our entire marriage had been about him—supporting him in his endeavors and getting him to his dream. And with my career and its initial slow-rise trajectory and then the sharp incline of the last several years, the tables had been turned undeniably my way.

But instead of pointing this out, I chose the kinder route—Amelia needn't see the ugly side. "Aw, people love to see you on the feed, babe. It's because you're so handsome." I winked at Quinn, for levity.

"That's right, Dad. And the more people love the feed, the more books Mom sells, the more they come to see her. Besides, you're part of hashtag team Celine! We all are." Amelia shot her father a mischievous grin. "You can't avoid social media like a boomer, Dad."

"Did you just call me a boomer? I'll have you know I hang out with Gen Zers all day!"

"Yeah, but you're paid to yell at them." Amelia stepped back out. "Okay, lovebirds, forty minutes." With a final grin, she shut the door.

Silence engulfed the room at our daughter's departure, and an understanding passed between us that it was time to table our conversation. The clock was ticking.

"All right. Guess I should freshen up." Quinn set his coffee down on the dresser and brought his bags next to the bed, then unloaded his toiletry bag.

Quinn was a tall man. He took up so much space, even in a large stadium. There was no missing his wide frame on the sidelines, his booming voice, and his smile that made it all the way up to his eyes, crinkling the sides of his face. With his quick unpacking, the energy in the room rose.

While I continued on with my makeup, Quinn took his turn at the shower, spending a mere five minutes, not nearly enough time for me to think through the last thing he'd said—that things were *tough*—while attempting to decide on the eye shadow combination for the evening.

An eye shadow brush was halfway to my lid when Quinn's reflection appeared in the mirror. He was shirtless, with a towel around his bottom half. Any semblance of coherent thought went poof when a vision of an uninhibited version of us flashed in my memory.

A full-body flush swept through me.

Then the body in the mirror turned. The face, my husband's face, blossomed with an all-encompassing smile. "I see you looking at me."

Was he flirting with me? My eyes snapped back to my reflection, cheeks reddening from the whiplash of my emotions.

He came closer from behind, and soon, the heat of his body was palpable through my clothes. I turned, and in a smooth motion, he fixed us so I was sitting on his lap.

Yes, he is, in fact, flirting. And he was half-naked, and now the heat was everywhere. My toes tingled with it, and my belly buzzed with butterflies gone awry.

"Quinn. We've got to get downstairs." My voice came out like a wheeze, and my entire body lit on fire. It had been a few months since we'd last made love. Everyone assumed that with how successful we had both become, due to the image we'd presented on both our personal and professional socials, our sex life was on point. But it didn't take just solitude to tumble into the sheets. It took us being in the mood—and, well, we were working on it.

"Let's make them wait," he said, his answer a growl.

Chapter Five

A growl. Dear goodness.

Tingles ran down my spine. "But the people."

"Who cares about them?" A hand steadied me by the waist, and another slipped under my shirt. His lips found their way to my neck, against my pulse point.

My heart thumped at double speed, and I shut my eyes.

"I've missed you." He spoke into my skin, sending a current through me, and my heart soared with hope. That the rough patch of the last couple of years was simply that, and we were on the path to getting back to the way we had been. "I'm sorry for fighting."

"I'm sorry too. I've missed you too. After the tour, we need a week alone together." I cupped his cheek and kissed him, and to my toe-curling relief, he moaned back in reciprocal pleasure, sparking all my nerve endings. Thirty-five years, thirty-three of those married, and the connection was still there—thank goodness! Slideshow images of us frolicking and emerging from the sheets just to eat and shower rotated in my head.

Then, the hand that had been gloriously stroking my inner thigh slowly withdrew. Quinn sat back, inhaling. His gaze dropped. "I have something to tell you. I wanted to tell you later, but since we're here, and alone . . ."

I straightened, though my brain was still in a vacation resort somewhere. "Hmm?"

"I had a change of plans—I made them a couple of weeks ago. And before I tell you all about it, promise me you'll listen."

But my brain was still stuck on the fact that he'd had the flexibility to change plans when postseason was weeks away. "Okay?"

"Wait. Let me get dressed. I can't think like this." He stood abruptly, and I all but fell off his lap. He headed to the bathroom with a handful of clothes—he was stalling, composing himself.

Meanwhile my imagination took flight: Had he been fired? Had he lost another player from a school transfer? Was it him . . . oh my God, he'd had blood work the other day for his yearly physical—was he sick? Or, it was the girls. I *knew* it was the girls. One of them was sick, or something was wrong with one of my granddaughters!

Finally, Quinn emerged in jeans and a dark long-sleeve shirt.

He hiked his hands on his hips. "I took leave from work. I'm going to Sampaguita."

Stunned, I said, "Not what I expected." Questions racked up in my head, vying to be asked first, all prevented by this roadblock of being sure my ears were playing tricks on me. "You took leave?"

"Yes, it's been in the works—"

This was another secret. "How long in the works? You never take leave. You said so yourself that there's no such thing as off-season."

"And I'm going home. To Sampaguita. And I want you to come back with me."

"Our home," I started, "is in Annapolis."

Addressing only part of his statement was the easiest, because the second part, about going back to Sampaguita with him?

No. Hard pass.

"Three ninety-nine Lexington Road, Louisburg, Massachusetts, is still owned by the two of us. You and me. And it's full of—"

My hands shot up. "Stop. I can't." I would soon need to face a conference room full of people. Smiling and encouraging and charming to boot.

He raised both palms to me. "Okay, okay. Look. We can talk later. After the event, all right? I'm sorry. I shouldn't have brought it up right this second, but we were having a moment."

We can talk later. Mae and MJ had said something similar. And now Quinn.

Seconds later, my phone buzzed with a text.

Sonya:

28 minutes.

I looked up at my husband, the time reminder turning the page of this moment to a new chapter, for now. "We're *definitely* going to talk about this later."

Chapter Six

Twenty minutes remained before my stage entrance. And while my makeup was flawless and shoes comfortable, with my team clucking around me in preparation, inside I was everything but settled.

Nothing felt right. Everyone was keeping a secret from me and then acting as if nothing was amiss. Mae was commenting that the conference room was packed. MJ was taking greenroom photos to send over to my social media person. Amelia and Theo were on the couch on video chat. And Quinn . . . Quinn was on the phone with a smile on his face—he was talking with one of his assistant coaches, as if he hadn't dropped a bomb that he'd taken leave to head back to Sampaguita.

The image of our old home filled my mind. The creaking boards; the miniscule, dark kitchen; the backyard of blooming jasmine. Bittersweet emotions flooded me—nostalgia from precious memories of growing our little family until Amelia graduated from high school, and the inky-dark sadness of Libby's death.

We'd left Sampaguita two days after the funeral reception and never returned. There had been no reason to—the most important thing that home had housed was no longer there. My time had been better spent putting one step in front of the other, replacing my grief with purpose, with writing and coaching.

I couldn't go back there and risk the drag backward into grief. I wouldn't.

"Ma." MJ waved from the couch, where everyone had piled on. Held up against her lap was her iPad. "The girls are on video chat with Ate Mae now. Do you want to talk to them?"

"Of course I do!" My insides lightened—my apos! I rushed to Mae's side and gazed at my beautiful granddaughters: six-year-old Joanna and four-year-old twins Jocelyn and Jacqueline. All three were sporting their dazzling grins. Somehow they'd all found space on John's lap. John was grinning ear to ear.

"Hi, Lola Celine," they said in staggered unison; it was a symphony to my ears. Forget my motivational speaker, coach, and bestseller status; nothing was better than lolahood.

"Hello, girls. I love you and miss you. And you too, John." I pressed a kiss into my hands and then blew it toward the screen. Flying kisses. My baby girls pretend-caught them. "I already have pasalubong. I have magnets from all the airports for your fridge."

"Did you have your meeting?" Joanna asked.

"Meeting?"

"Not a meeting, baby. A book tour," Mae interrupted.

"No. You said meeting." Her lips pursed into discontent.

The interaction gave me pause, and my eyes slid to Mae.

She clapped. "The time. We should go."

"Yep, Mom, you should get ready. Don't you need to go through your notes?" Amelia jumped up, taking Theo next to her.

My notes. *Focus.* "Yep, I do. Thank you, Amelia."

"Okay, say *I love you* to Lola," Mae instructed her girls. "Tell her to break a leg."

My grandchildren yelled out their greetings, buffering my whiplash emotions. Children were amazing. Children were a joy. And they were young for only such a short time. One of these days, I would take my apos on a fun vacation, just us. Like all the day trips with my girls when they were little, when Quinn had been deployed or on temporary duty.

Libby flashed in my memory: her dragging her feet behind the rest of us, arms crossed and with a scowl on her face. She of the four had hated to leave home. All she'd wanted was her piano and a quiet afternoon. She'd been perfectly content skipping through Sampaguita's backyard.

At the memory, my chest retracted as if punched, and I pressed my hand against it.

I was breathing. I was fine.

But not everything is, my conscience reminded me. MJ was on deadline. Amelia wasn't going to Tokyo. Mae was here instead of with her family. Quinn wanted me to return to Sampaguita.

And my granddaughter's words: *Did you have your meeting?*

Sonya interrupted my thoughts. "Fifteen minutes, Celine."

Looking up, I saw the room was empty except for Sonya. She was tapping on her iPad, presumably to look through the schedule. Reliable, focused, Doc Martens–wearing Sonya.

Sonya, who knew the ins and outs of my relationships with people and our family dynamics. Of my complicated relationship with Sampaguita because it was so entwined with Libby.

Libby had been twelve when I'd started to travel to different conferences, with Mae and MJ in their late teens and Amelia a carefree elementary schooler. Up to that point, I'd been all my girls' primary caregiver—but especially with Libby, who clung to me around strangers, was my shadow for any given errand, and considered me her confidant. Predictably, she'd had the hardest time adjusting to my work schedule, and she hadn't been shy to say so. As she'd grown into her teen years, Libby and I had clashed over big and small things, culminating when she'd chosen to remain in the home and not follow us to Annapolis six years ago. Libby had felt abandoned by me. I'd felt abandoned by her too.

I knew children were meant to grow up and leave their families to start their own, but I'd thought—I'd assumed—that since Libby hadn't been romantically attached, she belonged with us still. Also, Filipino tradition encouraged the unmarried to live with other family members—with parents, especially.

"Celine? Thoughts?" Sonya held up an earring in each hand. "Dangling? Or stud?"

Tonight, Sonya wore the barest of makeup, and the overhead lights created a shadow on the lower half of her face. My view tilted slightly, taking in that her smile wasn't quite right, on the verge of artificial.

I caught my friend's eyes in the mirror. "What's this meeting about?"

"What?" Sonya set the earrings down and sat next to me. "What are you talking about?"

"Why does Quinn want me to go to Sampaguita?"

"How about I get you some water?" Her voice shook slightly, and I knew.

Sonya was in on it too.

"Get my family back in here."

"But we have thirteen minutes. And . . ." Her gaze flitted around the room, as if searching for assistance. "We can talk later."

There went that phrase again. Whatever this was, I wasn't going to sit and wait for it. One step forward, no matter how hard it was.

I turned to face her. "I won't start my event until we have this meeting. Call Quinn and my girls. Now."

Chapter Seven

"This is a what?" I screeched, touching my forehead, warm from the overhead lights. From inside bubbled confusion and hurt.

It had taken a short five minutes to get my family back in the greenroom, where we'd all taken our seats, set up in a haphazard circle, after which I had been told something that happened only in reality television.

"A family meeting," Quinn repeated. Leaning his elbows on his knees, he looked as dire as he had watching his team lose by twenty during the playoffs last year. His eyes darted around the room, to our daughters, who all looked as guilty as hell, their gazes on the floor or in the middle distance. "I planned a family meeting because we think that it's time for all this to end."

Yep, it sounded just as ridiculous the second time as it had the first time. I snickered in disbelief. "So an intervention. To halt a book tour."

The room exploded with explanations.

"It's more than just a book tour. It's everything." Quinn spoke with his hands, as if he was at a whiteboard drawing a play.

Across from me, Mae spoke up, wincing. "It's not an intervention, Mom."

"I mean . . . technically, it is." MJ crossed her arms tightly in front of her.

"I'm sorry, Mom." Amelia's hands were clasped around Theo's, knuckles white. "I'm really, really sorry."

Sonya's leg was bouncing so the heel of her boot was a metronome.

In the background, beyond this room and down the long hallway, was the faint sound of music and the loud murmurs of five hundred people waiting for me to appear.

A headache started at my temples. None of this was good. I could only imagine the tweets, the posts, and the complaints flying among the audience. It had been my choice to address my suspicions before my event, and now I regretted it. Because what Quinn was saying was ridiculous. We were not canceling the book tour with only two stops left.

"This is not a laughing matter, Celine." Quinn's voice rose above the rest.

Was I laughing? As I came back down to the present, sure enough, my lips were pressed into a smile. "I mean, it is, when all this isn't necessary."

"But it *is* necessary. We are imploring you to cancel the rest of this tour, and to come back to Sampaguita."

I scanned the room, evaluating each family member's serious face for a crack of a smile, a sign that this was all a joke. All were stone faced. "So wait. *Wait.* You're telling me that Amelia and Theo canceled their Tokyo trip, that MJ's here writing on deadline, and Mae left without the family so you can convince me to cancel a book tour? A book tour, where I'm signing books?! Which is a good thing?"

My children's heads bobbed in unison.

"This is the twilight zone."

"Don't minimize this," Quinn shot back.

My head swiveled toward my husband. "What the hell is that supposed to mean?"

He inhaled, his chest rising with effort. "You're in denial. You've been in denial, and it's high time that we talk about this. About *her*. About our home. All of which I wanted to discuss with you. But, in truth, everyone in this room has something to say, and that's why they chose to be here. Are you willing to listen for each of us to speak? Will you please listen to us?"

I stood, the word *no* at the tip of my tongue. Not only was Quinn's claim unfounded—I wasn't in denial; in fact, I dealt with Libby's death each and every day—but this was also a betrayal. How long had my family been talking about me when they should have been talking *to* me?

It was then that my girls raised their gazes to meet mine, unwavering and in solidarity with their father.

My heart tore.

I'd let them down.

I'd been on the other side of that disappointment when the meticulously crafted pedestal my own mother had occupied had crumbled, when I'd realized one day that my mother had had enough of the role.

The idea that my children would lose hope in me, in my love, gave me pause.

"Fine, I'll listen." I sat back down. Despite every part of me that objected, that refused to be part of this emotional hostage situation, I could not turn away from my daughters.

"Mae, do you want to go first?" Quinn asked.

"Sure." Her voice wavered, though she sat straighter in her chair. She produced her phone from her pocket. "Um, MJ, Amelia, and I came up with a little something." Eyes darting up briefly to each of her sisters, she began.

"Dear Mom, we're sorry for cornering you like this. We know it doesn't feel good to think that you're the last person to find out about things. We know it's uncomfortable. But it's the only way we can tell you how we feel." She cleared her throat, and she raked her teeth against her bottom lip. As she shifted uncomfortably, I had the inkling to stop her right then and there. What she was about to say was going to be big, and I was no longer certain that my heart would be able to take it. But her next words darted out. "We feel like we're losing you."

"Wh . . . what?" My body jerked back like it had been tackled by a 250-pound linebacker.

She continued. "You've always worked really hard. You put yourself in everything you do a hundred percent. We don't doubt how much you care for us, and we know you always have our back. And when you started Celine Lakad Coaching, we never felt like you weren't there for us. When you were home, when you were with us, you were present. Emotionally. But things are different now.

"Right after Libby died, we all just tried to take care of each other the best way we could. We all hit our low points. With me blowing up at John, MJ hiding out in her writer's cave, and Amelia never coming round. You and Dad were all over us, wanting to know our every move because you were worried for us. And that was all okay. As much as it was hard, we knew that we all still had each other. We went to therapy as a family, and we all unanimously benefited from it. But then you stopped going, and work became your life. Work consumes you, Mom, more than ever. Do you remember falling asleep on the park bench while watching the girls on the playground a few months ago? Then, MJ had a doctor's appointment that you said you would be able to make and then forgot. And when Amelia and Theo were planning their wedding, Amelia had spent an afternoon going over the photographer's plans with you, and yet that night, you texted her because you wanted information about the photographer."

Had all those things happened? As Mae continued to mention more instances when I had been apparently out of it, I couldn't definitely remember. A rumble began in my belly as I waited for a moment to say something. Because this was unfair, right? It was cruel to keep track of people's mistakes and hold them against them, when no one was perfect.

"But those are little things compared to what we really worry about," Mae said. "You snapped at Amelia because she was wearing one of Libby's necklaces. You had lunch with MJ at a café that had instrumental piano music on their playlist, and you simply walked out of the café because you couldn't take listening to it. And the one time you were helping me and the girls bake, you had to step out several times. I knew it was because you were in tears.

"But what's standing out to us most is the fact that you haven't said Libby's name. We checked with one another, and none of us had heard you say it. We try to talk about her. We want to talk about her, but we can't, not fully, because you haven't been able to. And the house—there's so much in Sampaguita that we miss. There are so many things in it of Libby's that we love. In all the times we tried to broach the topic of visiting, you avoid the topic altogether.

"We miss her, Mom. And we miss you. It's like your body is here, but your heart is not. Like *you* are not." Her voice cracked, sending shooting pains through me, and I pressed a hand against my lips, to keep myself from whimpering.

It was true; I didn't speak of Libby aloud, nor did I say her name—though I didn't have to, because my daughter was alive in my heart. She was in every crevice of my imagination. She was everywhere: in my dreams, and part of my everyday reality. She was the first person I thought of in the morning, the last before I went to bed. Her death would always be a marker in my life. Before her death, I had been a mother of four with an optimistic outlook. My zeal for life had been almost innocent, where I had seen nothing but good—in me and Quinn moving from the fall to the winter of our lives doing exactly what we loved, and in watching our children achieve what they desired. Then, after her death . . . I knew too much about what could go wrong. My eyes had been opened to see that tragedy was possible.

Libby's name was sacred. To say her name would unlock the Pandora's box of every mistake I'd made with her. I wasn't going to do it since we were on the road to healing. We were so much better than before.

So for them to say that *I* wasn't here?

How could I have been so productive and done so much in my career since Libby's death if my heart wasn't here?

"Mom." Mae pulled my attention back to her face. "MJ, Amelia, and I are ready to go back to Sampaguita. And we want to do it tomorrow. We want you to come with us, and cancel the rest of your book tour, and see a therapist. We have someone you can see, and she's ready and on call. Will you, please?"

"So you all planned to go to Sampaguita too?"

My girls nodded. "And we want you to go with us."

I shot a look toward my husband, and anger sparked inside me. I was being blamed for not being present, and yet my family had purposely kept their Sampaguita plans under wraps. Hypocritical much? "I'm sorry, girls. I'm sorry you think I've checked out. Lord knows I'm just trying to do my best. I've *done* my best. And I'm sorry for the things you said I did. Falling asleep on lola duties, and then leaving a restaurant, and all that."

"That's not what we mean, Mom. We know you're trying. It's just . . . we've been trying to talk to you about this," MJ said in a low voice. "But you refuse to hear."

Amelia's forehead creased. "It's that we can't seem to reach you. Like right now. You're hearing that we're unhappy with you, but it's not about that. It's us worrying about you."

I shook my head, plowing through whatever my daughter had said, which couldn't register amid the anger that was glowing bright. "And why now? This is my career. This book tour? It's a big deal. Couldn't you all wait to talk to me later? There are only two stops left."

"Actually," Sonya chimed in, and my neck snapped to her. After a brief glance at Quinn, she said, "I think that I should go next."

49

"Are you serious?" I raised both hands in exasperation because Sonya was supposed to be my best friend. Above all, she was supposed to have my back.

Sonya avoided my eyes, and took a folded piece of paper from her pocket. "Celine, there's no one I consider a sister more than you. We've known each other for twenty years, and I've been at your side the last thirteen years as your assistant. I believe in who you are. You've coached hundreds of people who didn't know what their next step should be. But in this case, in your case, you haven't been your own coach.

"The last two years brought on a lot of change to Celine Lakad Coaching. We've become more professional, more brand than personal, which is fine. The company is moving up in ways that meant we had to add a half dozen people to the staff. This year and next year are packed with events, which is all great too. But you haven't stopped. Before Libby died, you took vacations; you took weekends off. You saw friends for lunch or brunch. But I haven't seen you take a real day off in two years.

"The exhaustion is all over your face. At the Denver stop, you lost track of the talking points in the middle of your event. I see some of the texts you send, sometimes in the middle of the night. And . . ." She heaved a breath, looking up and meeting my eyes. "Your panic attacks are back."

"Wait a sec—" I interjected, a hand out in warning.

But it was too late. Mae's, MJ's, and Amelia's eyes rounded in shock.

Only Sonya and Quinn knew about my panic attacks. It had been my choice not to tell my girls. My reasoning had been simple: I didn't want to worry them. I didn't want to saddle them with this information, because losing Libby had been equal to the rug being pulled from under their feet. I'd also known that the panic attacks were temporary, and they indeed had gone away a few months after my routine work schedule had been reestablished. They would go away once more.

"No," Sonya said. "I don't want to enable this any longer. I'm scared. I feel helpless, and if this meeting is the only way I can help you, then here I am. You have two more stops, and we can always reschedule them. Will people be disappointed? Yes. But you are more important to me. So here's what I'm asking. What I want is for you to see someone, talk to someone, ASAP. I also want you to take a break. If you don't agree . . . then I can't help you any further, as your assistant."

My heart thudded, and my breath hitched. "You're giving me an ultimatum."

She nodded.

My anger turned into incredulity, and I responded with a snort. "Come. On."

"I mean it. It's the only way you'll listen to anyone. You're as stubborn as they come, and you don't do anything that doesn't have a result, a consequence. Well, that consequence is my two weeks' notice. I just want you to get help. I believe it's time to take a knee. And I think that going back to Sampaguita is a good first step."

"Sampaguita, again?" I half laughed. "This focus on getting back to that house . . . why? Why now? Do you want me to take a break? See a therapist? Fine. I will, but after the last two book tour stops. You can whisk me away to some private island. I can do virtual therapy—it's all the rage. But no Sampaguita."

"My turn," Quinn said, voice serious and gruff. He, however, didn't take out a phone or a piece of paper. He simply sat up in the chair and clasped his hands on his lap. "I had hoped that I wouldn't have to take my turn. That you would have agreed with the girls or with Sonya. But here I go, I guess." Remorse descended in his expression. "Sampaguita is in trouble. The roof is in bad shape, and there are a couple of leaks in the house. Birds have taken residence in the fireplace. The jasmine is everywhere."

On instinct, I inhaled, and though my logic told me otherwise, the scent of jasmine filled my senses. What followed was the memory of

Sampaguita's brick front walkway, the dark exterior of the home, and the moss-green door. The sounds of giggling coming from the third-floor dormer window. The myriad of shoes toed off at the front door, and the thundering footsteps from above that caused the house to shake and the floors to creak.

"Robin, our property manager, has been nagging us about these problems for months now, but you haven't wanted to hear it. Every time I speak of it, you shut down, just like you did earlier today. Well, a couple of weeks ago, I received another call from Robin. A developer is interested in the home, but not in its state, and definitely not with all of the things in it. *Our* things.

"We've left that house in limbo the last two years; we're paying the mortgage on it, though it's unused."

"We can afford it, Quinn."

"This is not about the money. This is about you pretending day after day that the house doesn't exist. And I'm done keeping up that charade for you. Because I miss her. I miss Libby. And her stuff's sitting there, gathering dust. The piano, her books, her favorite apron. Those are our daughter's things. Those are the only things we have left of her."

"Hence why it needs to stay there. It's fine where it is. Everything is safe, where it should be." I snatched my gaze away from my husband's stricken face and trained it on the floor, willing away the tears that were welling up in my lower lids. *Stop it,* I commanded myself and girded the sob threatening to break through. There would be no crying, no ruining of makeup, because the crowd was still out there, in that conference room, and it had taken forever to get my face this way. Because work was what I needed to focus on. Not the past, which I could not change.

"Celine. I can feel you clamming up. Please look at me."

Finally, after a beat and with a splayed hand against my abdomen to keep steady, I did.

Quinn ran a hand through his hair, then rested it on the back of his neck. "I haven't forced the issue of going back to the house because

I wanted to respect the speed of how you were grieving. And I kept hoping you would finally suggest going back. At the year anniversary of her death, at All Souls' Day, at the two-year mark. I thought for sure when this tour was set to stop in Boston that you were open to going back. To return to it and to me."

Confused at that statement, I frowned. "What does the house have to do with us, Quinn?"

"Everything." He folded his arms over his chest, now perched at the edge of the chair so he had no choice but for his legs to cross under him. "Sampaguita was the last place Libby lived in, the last place we all lived as a family. With you not being able to talk about it or her . . . a whole chasm has dug itself between you and me, without a way to cross it.

"*I* want to talk about the house and Libby. Do you know how hard it is not to be able to talk to your best friend? Instead, I've become a prop in your great big Celine Lakad Coaching world, where our conversations are transactional, and our public appearances are for the benefit of your followers. And yet, we haven't made love in six months."

My cheeks burned; our children were hearing him admit that our sex life was a massive fail, in addition to the fact that Quinn was unhappy. My voice dipped; I infused humor into my tone to dispel the growing tension in my chest. "Quinn, seriously, did you have to say that aloud?"

"And yes, that too," he kept on. "This . . . pretending that we're okay. The girls know. Without me telling them, they guessed it."

Against my better judgment, I scanned the room and my daughters' faces, and all were nodding.

"I knew that one time weeks ago when I dropped by at the town house and the guest bedroom was being used," MJ said. "Dad's house shoes were at the foot of the bed."

Mae raised a finger bashfully. "And I thought something was up when you didn't go to one of Dad's home games, which you never miss."

"I could tell by the way you just didn't touch each other like you used to, you know? Like how Dad used to pat you on the butt randomly, or when you used to hug Dad from behind just because," Amelia said. "I don't remember the last time you two did that. Like normally, if you were in the same room, you wouldn't be caught sitting across one another like this. You would be right next to one another and, every once in a while, place a hand on each other's knee."

Amelia's nose scrunched in what was classically her method to keep herself from crying, and it brought me back to a time when she had been self-conscious about her nose. Amelia had my nose, whereas the other three had Quinn's, and she'd compared herself endlessly to them. When she had been in middle school, I'd caught her at her vanity mirror assessing her profile. Since then we'd had more than our share of talks about body image and self-confidence and identity.

My heart dipped at my foolishness. Of the four, Amelia was the most socially aware. How had I thought that she wouldn't notice that things were off between me and Quinn? That each one of them wouldn't, for that matter?

I squirmed in my seat. All my and Quinn's business was out in the open. My character, my behaviors—they were being thrown into the ring by the people I loved. My prior actions, my current reactions, how I ran my business, how I acted toward Quinn . . . how long had they been talking about this?

"You've been judging me. All of you." My voice came out as a whisper, body running cold.

"It's not judgment. It's worry. As you can see, we have different concerns, but it all boils down to our fear that you've gone too far into denial."

"My goodness, what do you think of me, Quinn?" I stood; I was done listening to all of this. This was all insulting, to say the least. "I'm not in denial. I know she's dead."

"Not in denial that she's dead." His voice lowered. "But that we're all still very sad, that *you* are sad, and that nothing is ever going to really fix it. That work, that writing this book, that going on tour and never saying her name isn't going to make that fact go away."

"You have no idea how I feel." I jabbed a finger in the air. I *was* coping. Work, the book, the tour—all of it was part of my moving on. All those things helped me and led me to this book tour.

How was this in any way bad? It didn't compute.

He reached out with both hands. "So tell me, then. Tell us how you feel. See a therapist; we can all go to therapy together. Work through getting Libby's things back to Annapolis. Let's do something about Sampaguita. I believe that if you can do that, we can finally be on our way back together, back *home* together, all of us."

"No." The hurt and anger turned into full-throttle objection and resentment. "I can't believe that you all did this. For the record, I have never stopped you from going to Sampaguita on your own. I don't know if you haven't noticed, but I've been a little busy."

"That's the problem. You're *too* busy."

The music changed in the background, and the thumping bass sped up.

"I . . . I'm sorry?" A giggle burst out of me, and I pressed my hand against my chest, to keep it from turning into maniacal laughter. The audacity of this man. "I'm so, *so* confused right now. What do you mean, I'm *too* busy? You have been busy most of our marriage. In the past, there were deployments and TDY with the army." I counted out my fingers. "And in the last decade, all the away games for all of the teams you've coached. And who was there to take care of our home, to manage our children, Quinn? It was me."

"Here we go again. I don't need a reminder that I was and have been away from home. I know you've done the lion's share of taking care of the house."

I would never let him live that down, as most military spouses wouldn't with their service members. Maintaining the homestead was something only others who shared that same experience could fathom. The worry, the responsibility, the pride that society often forgot about.

"So to the point," I countered, "an intervention to address my mothering and Sampaguita is so damn hypocritical. Because you could have had every opportunity to flourish, to shine, without me once complaining how you were *too busy*. No one has ever stopped you from doing anything. If you really wanted to go to Sampaguita on your own, you would have." I shook my head. Already, our argument was going astray. This was one of the problems about being with somebody for three decades. There was so much to pull from beyond our current problems, so many years of unresolved feelings—hell, even the resolved feelings could be good fodder for more argument—and if we weren't careful, we could end up in 1992, arguing over the fact that he hadn't introduced me to one of his exes.

"Please, if I had gone on my own, you would have been angry." His voice deepened. "You've shut me out, Celine. I know that some part of you hates me for what happened with Libby. Hell, I hate myself. Had I not taken that meeting instead of checking in on her, then maybe things would have been different. But instead of telling me off, or screaming at me, you've closed the door between us. And I'm tired. I'm tired of waiting."

Snippets of that night returned to me. Libby's flat affect in our last family video chat, her red cheeks and eyes. Her complaint of a sore throat and prolonged fever, a mention of a rash. *It's fine, Mom. I'll go to urgent care if I feel worse.* Then, Libby's request for Quinn to swing by Sampaguita since he'd be in Boston for the weekend. For some quiet company.

But something had come up in Quinn's schedule. He'd notified me that he wouldn't be able to make it.

I could have traveled up to Louisburg. My daughter hardly ever asked for company, and the time together would have done her and me some good. Our relationship had shifted, so we'd been out of sorts. My moving to Annapolis had changed our dynamic. Partly from physical distance, because Libby and I had been best face to face when I hadn't quite come off as such a nag and I could read her body language to get past her aloofness. But it had mostly been because my heart had still been recovering from her refusal to move to Annapolis with us. My assumption had been that she'd realize how lonely she was living solo in such a big house and change her mind. Instead, not having us there had forced her to come out of the safe barrier of Sampaguita. She'd made friends. In addition to her life as a gig girl, doing freelance work creating jingles and music for podcasts and video productions and small businesses, we'd learned after her death that she'd given piano lessons and become a microbaker.

The things one found out after a loved one died. In Libby's case, there'd been nothing salacious. What had come out from the woodwork was how kind and thoughtful and industrious our dear daughter had been.

Perhaps that was even worse, because those things weren't secrets. And yet, I'd had no clue of her endeavors and hobbies.

On that night when Quinn could not make it to Louisburg, there had been an available seat on a plane to Boston from DC. The thought had occurred for me to hop on that flight, but I hadn't bought the ticket on the spot. Something had snagged my attention, and by the time I had gone back to purchase it, all flights had been booked.

I'd checked in with Libby—she'd said it was fine. That she had a friend to call.

What mother would've allowed for that to happen? What mother would have not purchased the first ticket out?

Me. I was that mother.

"What do you mean by *you're tired of waiting*?" My husband's words caught up to me.

"I fell in love with you, above all things, because of your heart. In the way you embraced others. In the way you shared your life with others, and even through your business. Celine Lakad Coaching was built from your heart, and your need to help others. The last two years, you leaned into it; you continued to help others. But you haven't helped yourself. And you are so important to me that . . . that . . ." His voice croaked.

Alarm bells rang in my ears; I shook myself to clear them and took steps toward the door. "I don't want to hear anything else. I'm going to go out there and do my event. We can talk about this later, okay?"

"Celine, if you go out that door, if you don't even try . . . Sampaguita, our daughter's things, therapy. If you go, that's it. This is over."

My feet tangled, though I caught myself, arms jutting out to steady my body. I glanced back at the group, who were all on their feet. "What do you mean? Are you talking about a separation?"

"Is that what you want?"

"No." My answer was a whispered breath, with fear constricting my vocal cords. Because Quinn, my husband of thirty-three years, was looking at me with the same gaunt expression as he'd had at Libby's funeral reception. Like he'd lost someone.

"Then please. Come with me." He stretched out a hand and beckoned for me to return to the group.

Chapter Eight

The tingle of déjà vu came over me, and I was nineteen, staring, mouth agape, at Quinn and his outstretched hand after he'd said, *Please. Come with me.* Except over thirty years ago, he hadn't been in a sweater and slacks but had been in jeans and a flannel shirt, with his hat to the back, standing next to his truck. His green duffel bags were in the cab; it was everything he owned. We were in front of my brother's house.

I don't know, was what I answered, though my hand automatically reached out to take his into mine. It was a rough hand, though instantaneously, my body relaxed. *Kuya Sam is going to kill me,* I went on. Because my big brother was like a papa bear. *I bet he's watching us through the window.*

His gaze flicked up for a beat, a smirk on his lips. We'd met through Sam; he and Quinn had been college friends and were five years older than me, and he was in Boston to see his parents in transition between duty stations. *I'll speak to him. But it's you who has the final say. It's just for a weekend. Small road trip, drop off some of my stuff. And you'll be back in class by Monday. What do you say, Celine? Let's do this.*

We'd spent an amazing month getting to know one another. It had started with short visits at the house while he'd hung out with Sam. Then it had evolved to meeting up for coffee while I'd studied, or a trip to the bookstore. Nothing romantic had happened between us in those small outings—though there had been *moments*. An accidental bump of our hands, a hug that had lasted half a second too long. Random phone calls that had gone on into the night, to my brother's chagrin since we only had one line in the house.

But this offer—to tag along as he drove down to his duty station in Fort Hamilton, New York—was on a different level. It was a thrilling proposition. My first instinct was to answer with a resounding yes.

I had only one problem: Rex Maldonado.

Rex Maldonado was my high school sweetheart. Known and loved by my family, he was a mainstay figure. We had loose plans to finish college and marry at the end of my senior year. It was the kind of plan that young people made, with heart eyes and with all the hope in the world. It was the kind of plan that I—a woman who was going to community college, a woman who didn't really have a clue what to be when she grew up—clung to.

Rex and I had not been intimate for a while—our last visit had been three months before, for Christmas, and even then, it had been a week of family festivities. But he was my first love.

At that moment, Rex was at school in Vermont for a computer science degree, without a clue that a Quinn Frasier existed or that I'd been spending my free moments with him. I hadn't said anything because we were just friends and he would be gone soon.

Or so I'd assumed.

In hindsight, my "commitment" to Rex had fizzled at first sight of Quinn, at first conversation with him. I loved Quinn's brain, his quiet but strong nature, and his sense of community. In thirty days, Quinn had upended everything I'd known to be true. And I'd chosen him.

Let's do this.

But now, as I looked at Quinn's outstretched hand, what he wanted was for me to go back instead of moving forward. He and my girls and even my best friend, Sonya, had schemed and betrayed me, using my Libby's death, using Sampaguita, as bait. As motivation.

It was wrong, so wrong.

I didn't know what twisted my insides and caused me more pain—Libby's death, or this intervention. Because my family should have known better. They should have known me by now. That it wasn't just about a daughter dying, but about my culpability in it.

It had been my fault that she'd died.

My work had been my savior from that one strand of truth. My work kept my mind from exploring the fact that my appearance could have changed the trajectory of her health. That so much time had been wasted between us because of differences that would have not mattered an iota today.

A sob choked out of me, but I stomped it down with my two-inch heel. "No, Quinn. I'm going to see my readers."

After spinning on my heel, I marched out of the room, leaving the sounds of my family yelling at all octaves behind me. My eyes were on the multicolored carpet, my lungs struggled to take in air, and my vision wavered. The bass-heavy music in the auditorium faded, and a piano instrumental was mixed in.

"Celine!" a woman's voice called from behind.

My body was yanked back by the arm, by Sonya. Her cheeks were wet with tears, eyes glassy. "Please . . ."

But I had no empathy for her. "Please? Please what? How about please tell me how you expect for me to talk to you after all that. You're my best friend, Sonya."

"It's because I care about you." Both of her hands were on me now, clammy and firm. "It's because I *am* your best friend that I have to ask you to make the choice. To choose your family, and yourself."

I pressed my fingers against the throb in my temple. Damn piano. The tune was incessant, though familiar. Where had I heard it? It was lively, almost chipper. "Look, no matter what I choose, I need to go out there first. You of all people should know this." After brushing her away, my body surged forward.

Still, Sonya kept up, stomping in a way that felt timed to the beat. "Those people out there? They don't matter. But I'm afraid if you don't choose correctly now, things are going to change. Between you and the girls, and with Quinn. They're counting on you to choose them; don't you see? And this I know, Celine Lakad-Frasier: if you go out there now, you'll forget what that meeting was all about, immersed in the spotlight and with the people."

"Believe me, I'll never forget that meeting." The double doors to the conference room were in sight, and the music was exponentially louder. One of the doors slammed open, revealing a woman wearing all black and a headset. It was one of my publicists, Callie.

The piano instrumental blared through the doorway.

The room tilted minutely as my brain sang along with the tune.

A memory dashed in, of Libby at fifteen at the piano, a lamp up above casting a glow. She had been picking at the keys, though her eyes had been trained out the window, toward the front of the house. It was a Friday night, and her older sisters were at the movies with Theo and John, and Amelia was running around in the house. That night, we would all find out that Amelia had purposely erased some of MJ's documents because they'd gotten into an argument—but right then, Libby's somber expression caused me concern.

I asked her if something was wrong.

It's not bad that I don't want to go out, is it? she said.

No, sweetheart, it's not, though it's also good to get out every once in a while. But ultimately, it's your choice.

Good. Because staying home is my choice. I like it here. Then, she'd smiled, wide and contentedly. *Do you want to hear something? It's new. I call it "Petals Fluttering."*

It was *this* same tune, now playing on the loudspeaker. It didn't make sense. Pressing a finger against the side of my face, I rubbed at the opening of my ear, to snap out of what had to be an auditory hallucination. But the same tune remained.

The hairs on my arms and the back of my neck stood on end. My thighs wobbled at the sensation, and my chest swelled with foreboding.

My first days after Libby had died had been just like this exact unsteady moment. Like the world had stuttered in its rotation, and my insides had whiplash, so my nerves were shot; I couldn't trust anyone, not even myself.

I'd worked so hard to get away from this feeling. One foot in front of the other, I'd amped up my productivity to move my life from uncertainty to concreteness. Writing was concrete; social media was concrete; speaking to others was concrete. And now, here I was, back to square one because of this damned intervention, once more reminding me that life continued to turn out differently than what I'd tried to plan. And that despite all my best efforts in the last two years, I was not living up to anyone's expectations—not as someone's mother, or friend, or wife.

Would I ever get away from this? From the pain, the remorse, the regret?

And would I be able to continue to live my life if I *couldn't* move on from it?

Because if I had a chance to do it over, I would.

An escape hatch of a thought opened up to me. "What if . . ."

"What's that?" Sonya asked, steps away from the double doors. "You said something?"

I leapt into the idea with my full self; saying it would give a moment's reprieve from reality. "Do you ever think, *What if?*"

An eyebrow lifted. "What if . . . what?"

"What if I had chosen differently?"

Reading my mind, Sonya gasped ever so softly because my words were blasphemous. They were a betrayal to my family. And the idea alone was against everything I stood for. My life's message was movement forward, of leaving regret at the side of the road. Of taking charge of one's life instead of lamenting history.

But now that the words had been cast into the world and my imagination had taken over, the weight on my shoulders lessened, if but a smidge. And I wanted to feel more of that peace. Just for now. "What if I hadn't gone on that road trip with Quinn."

"You don't mean that." Disappointment clouded Sonya's expression. It laced her tone.

"I do mean it. Had I seen well into the future, and known what I know now, would I have chosen the same? If I had stayed home, this would have never happened. None of this would have happened."

"You can't think like this. By doing so, you're putting the blame on yourself. None of Libby's death is your fault." She inhaled, then blew out a breath, glancing up at Callie. Callie was beckoning me forward, into the conference room. "Which makes it all the more important that maybe we should go back to the girls and to Quinn."

From inside the conference room, chanting began.

Just one step. Just one step. Just one step.

"No," I answered back, peering at her. "Not only am I pissed at you right now, but you know as well as I do that it's too late to cancel this event. Do you expect for me not to go in there? Honestly?"

Hesitation flashed in her expression. "We hadn't actually planned to talk to you until after this event."

"Then the decision's made. I'm going in."

Sonya turned to me, face ashen. "Are you really okay? Can you do this?"

"Yes?" Though I was still slightly off kilter and light headed with my swirling thoughts about the present and what could have been, the sound of the crowd grounded me. Thirteen years of traversing the stage—I *could* do this. "This is my choice."

"I'll figure out something to say to Quinn and the girls, but . . . all right." Sonya tugged at my clothes to straighten them, lips pursed while she inspected me. "No more thinking about the what-ifs, at least for now, okay? Remember who you are. You're Celine Lakad-Frasier, encourager. You wrote *Just One Step*. You're loved by your family, no matter how it all feels right now. And I love you."

I nodded, despite being unable to say it back. Anger still coursed through me, and it would be a long time before my mind could ever purge the intervention from my memories.

What my family had done to me had been an example that love sometimes showed itself in the most painful of ways. Then again, my love for Libby had been limitless, and I hadn't shown it enough.

The MC's voice rang above the crowd and the music. "Thank you, everyone, for your patience. The woman of the hour is here. Your own Celine Lakad-Frasier!"

Sonya tugged on my wrist, then signaled for me to follow her to the platform stage set up in the conference room. Her message resonated in my head:

You are Celine Lakad-Frasier. You wrote Just One Step.

The playlist restarted, and the piano instrumental that sounded like Libby's piece spilled out of the speakers. It caused me to falter midway toward the podium and microphone, though I recovered, plastering on a smile for good measure.

This is not Libby's song.

I wish it was Libby's song.

What if I had chosen differently?

A glare from the spotlight blinded my vision. With the chords of the piano vibrating through me, and with those errant final questions floating in my subconscious, I tripped on my own feet, catching air, and my body tipped offstage.

Chapter Nine

Twenty-Two Years Ago

Christmas wasn't Christmas without ensaymada, unless, of course, they didn't get made.

So I worked quickly, shaping the sweet butter-and-sugar rolls for the second rise, then lining them up in deep pans. A half hour in a warm kitchen, then another thirty minutes in the oven, and my work would be done. Tomorrow's Christmas breakfast would be set, and the rest of the menu would be gravy. The whole kitchen could have gone up in smoke, but so long as the kids had their ensaymada, they were as happy as clams.

Screaming ensued from somewhere in the house, though the human source was unrecognizable. I looked up from wiping my hands on a dishrag and listened intently before moving toward the noise. Mothering three had taught me that I couldn't jump at every yelp and argument—or else nothing would get done. Also, I was eight months pregnant, and even if I willed my body to sprint, my belly would surely protest.

Then came a wail.

There was only one person who wailed these days (except for me, inside my chest as all mothers did from time to time), and a second later, that little person walked into the kitchen.

"Mommm." Knuckling her tears away, three-year-old Libby walked in with her hair in a tangled mess. Her pajamas were askew, misbuttoned because she was a big girl now and refused help getting dressed. "They won't let me in."

"Who won't let you in?" I considered kneeling to get on her same level—nothing helped more when trying to sort something out with toddlers than looking into their eyes while speaking with them—but thought otherwise. Rising from such a position would require my husband's assistance, and he was unavailable, currently serving holiday brunch at the military dining facility in his dress greens along with the command staff. It was an event that our whole family normally would've gone to.

But the belly.

The belly ruled everything at the moment.

"Ate Mae and Ate MJ. They won't let me play with them in the attic."

Sighing, I brought Libby and pressed her against my side belly. Amelia—because in my heart, this baby in my belly was a girl too—shifted inside me and thunked back on Libby's cheek, making her giggle.

"What are they doing?"

"Writing a script." Except the letter *r* in *script* skewed to a *w*. "They said . . . they said I was a bother."

I pressed my lips together, making a mental note to talk to the older two with yet another request to include their baby sister. Empathy coursed through me—as the current youngest child of two much-older sisters, Libby was often physically left out of their activities. Emotionally, it had been hard for her to keep up with Mae and MJ's conversations and inside jokes.

I didn't like being excluded, either, though years as a military wife had given me tools to cope when feeling left out or left behind—from gathering my strength to speak up to being the person to include and invite others. Sometimes, it meant buoying up my own self-esteem by working on my own thing.

"Well, you know you're not a bother, right?" I tilted her chin for her to meet my gaze.

She sniffed, eyes glassy. "No?"

"Nope. In fact, you came at the perfect time. You can help me bake or . . ." My eyes darted around the kitchen for another option, and through the open door, the electric piano, tucked in the corner, came into view. It was a piano that had been gathering dust—Mae had thought she'd be a pianist, though she'd given up the endeavor after a year of piano lessons. Libby had occasionally tapped on the keys, though it had been unplugged, the cord secured, when she'd grown into toddlerhood.

An idea sprang forth. "Or, we can make music?"

The seconds passed, during which her eyebrows twitched in decision. "Music."

"Great."

After glancing at the clock—I had some time before the oven needed to be preheated—I held my daughter by the hand and led her to the living room. The power button lit when I plugged the piano in—done with great effort, grunting, and tiny beads of sweat.

Immediately, Libby pounded on the keys, and the chords screamed through the tiny speaker.

"Whoa." My hand shot out to lower the volume, and I laughed. "Hold on. Let's grab you a chair."

"No chair." Her chin just cleared the keyboard.

"Okay then." A smile burst out of me. My girl had some fire under her sometimes quiet nature, and pride shot through me. She would need it since she had two older siblings who were closer in age and thick as thieves—and then she would be eclipsed by her soon-to-be-born baby sister.

I pressed down on the middle C key. "This is C."

"C," she repeated, tapping on the same key. I called out the other notes while pressing on their corresponding keys, and she followed until she lost interest. Her fingers nimbly explored the keyboard while she wore a wide, toothy grin.

The room brightened with the echoing random notes, and though her little fingers were clumsy and playful, I had a vision of her, older, playing Christmas carols, writing her own music, perhaps.

"Am I doing good, Mama?"

"So, so good." I raked my fingers through the strands of her dark hair, soft to the touch. It was growing thicker by the day, and soon she would need to tame it back much like her sisters. My heart ached at how fast time was flying—the girls were growing by feet and leaps and bounds. Next year, Libby would start prekindergarten.

Years had gone by in a flash. For me too. For a beat, I yearned for time to stand still because I couldn't seem to catch up, especially with being pregnant once more.

Quinn and I had wanted more babies, so that wasn't it—it was the fact that everyone was doing something, being something, gaining something. But I had remained the same.

Shaking my head to rid myself of those thoughts, because they were wrong and wrong timing, I focused my gaze on the bookshelves above the piano and savored the sound of Libby humming to the piano notes. I knew my value. Mothering was important. We bore these children; we would shape them, intentionally and unintentionally. I'd wanted this. I *loved* this, but right now . . . something was missing.

Was it all right to want more, if one had everything they'd wished for? I had found a partner who was loyal and hardworking, who loved me and the family, who was idealistic and cared about the world— check. Lived in a home and community that were safe—check. Had become a mother, full stop, when it wasn't possible for everyone— check. Was currently raising amazing children—a million times check. I didn't have a perfect life by any means. A bigger income, perhaps a husband who didn't have to deploy, or a normal blood pressure with this pregnancy would be great, but overall, my life was pretty damn good. I was lucky, blessed, and all descriptors in between.

But this want, this waylaying energy, was growing by the week. Its source didn't seem to be the same location the rest of my physical self drew from. Worse, I didn't know *what* I wanted.

This energy was humming now, standing with Libby, even if my logic told me that what came after pregnancy was newborn mamahood, and all my energy needed to be saved up for those sleepless nights. My own mother came to mind—rest in peace. Had she felt this way? Had her aloof attitude toward me been due to her own silent and hidden wants?

If only I could've asked her how to direct this energy. I needed sage advice and perspective. All the mothers in my circle of friends were in this same boat—all were simply trying to keep their kids alive, fed, and safe while attempting not to fall into the vortex of laundry and budgets and dishes.

My eyes were drawn to a row of embossed leather spines, to the classics passed down to me by my father. One stood out. *Little Women.*

My head tilted just so, as if a spotlight had shone right on the title. It had been years since I'd read the book, and it had been a favorite growing up. But one character's name came to me in a whisper: Marmee.

Marmee had four children.

Marmee took part in her community.

Marmee was a military spouse.

With effort, I reached upward, and my pointer finger hooked the top of the spine so it tilted downward. It toppled forward, right into my arms.

I sat on the couch and turned to the first page. The mishmash of piano notes faded away.

Let's see what Marmee can tell me.

Chapter Ten

My eyelids slammed open to the phone faceup on the pillow next to me, and the image of a turning page and a singing toddler flitted away. Heart beating wildly, I took in my current surroundings: a bright, sunny hotel room; a flat-screen TV on a dresser against the wall; a desk with my iPad propped up; shoes next to the front door.

Holy shit. It was all a dream.

I shut my eyes to ride my adrenaline down to more acceptable, non-heart-attack levels. Thank goodness. The intervention, the incessant piano playing from the conference room, and then a flashback to Libby playing the piano the first time and me finding *Little Women*—it had all been in my wicked nighttime imagination. A dream within a dream, even—à la the film *Inception*.

Indigestion. It must have been the indigestion from . . .

Hmm.

I couldn't remember what from. Then again, what had happened after I had gone onstage?

My heart skipped a beat. *Hold up.*

Wait. When was my event? What day was it?

I turned to my back, hair trailing across my face. As I swiped the strands and the sleep from my eyes, my brain woke all the way up, and it was then I noticed the intricate chandelier above the bed. To my left was an archway leading into a sitting room, where a purple tufted couch was situated.

I was in a suite.

Except . . . my team hadn't reserved suites.

Then, next to me came a snore.

I twisted my head to the right. The lump under the blanket rose and fell.

When had Quinn started to snore? And what time had we gone to bed?

A clip of me ascending the stage stairs flashed in my memory, along with the incessant piano playing the same tune over and over.

Along with me falling.

My heart rate spiked. Had that been part of the dream, or had that been real? And if it had been real, what had happened in the greenroom? A void existed where there should have been tangible memory of Sonya giving me a final pep talk before I went onstage. Or something as simple as putting on my lipstick. There was only the memory of the intervention, and because Quinn was asleep next to me, there obviously hadn't been an intervention.

I frowned as I tried to open the cupboards of my mind, only for the handles to fall off.

Or maybe I was still dreaming.

I wiggled under the blanket. The sheets were cool against my bare thighs, which was good. It meant I was awake. But this was also . . . odd. Pajamas were my clothing of choice for bedtime, even in the summer months.

The moment didn't feel right. At all.

Another snore rumbled from Quinn, and it dragged me from my runaway thoughts. "Jeez, chill," I whispered.

Yes, the moment was off, but everything was fine, obviously, because my husband was here, as loud as he was. And thank goodness, because talk about drama. Talk about heartbreak. I couldn't believe that dream Quinn had coordinated an intervention. That asshole.

He was going to hear about it as soon as he got up.

I reached out with a foot . . . to warm skin. The contact brought instant relief, and I heaved one deep breath. Once, I'd dreamed it was the first day of school and I was tardy and running to class. Except my legs moved in slow motion, and I could not feel the ground under my feet.

This leg? It was real.

But when I shifted my foot lower, my heel rubbed up against definitively copious amounts of leg hair, sending shivers up my spine.

Quinn had, enviably, very light and fine hair on his legs.

I shot off the bed, belatedly draping the useless floral half comforter these hotels insisted on decorating with around me, because—to my shock—my body was barely covered by a thin and silky nightie.

"Oh my God. Oh my God."

Nothing was adding up. I must've still been dreaming, right? My brother had told me time and again that calling out one's nightmare during the nightmare actually could wake you up. And waking up sounded good right about now. "Wake up, Celine!"

Yes, fifty was the new forty and all that, but surely my heart couldn't take any more of these surprises.

The lump quit snoring. It shifted, and from the top of the comforter peeked out dark hair.

I blinked, then blinked twice at the sight. My jaw dropped. *What the hell.*

Not only was the hair dark, but it was straight. Straight and dark, not curly and red.

Then, the comforter shifted lower as the body turned, revealing a shirtless, fit man with golden-brown skin, a chest with a smattering of dark hair, and a distinct tattoo of his frat insignia on his left pec.

A tattoo that had brought me to maniacal laughter when it had been shown to me the first time—because who did that?

Not Quinn.

"No, no, no." My voice cracked; my gaze went to the ceiling, where it found solace in the ornate ceiling medallion from which the intricate chandelier was hanging—my goodness, this was a really fancy hotel.

"Ten . . . nine . . . eight . . ." I whispered the countdown like a prayer. Surely, at *one*, my body would jostle awake, next to Quinn, in a modest hotel room with standard light fixtures and a popcorn ceiling. Maybe . . . maybe it was actually before the tour—weeks before, even—and this was simply a stress dream. I would have a laugh while recounting it to Sonya, and she would suggest a massage. And all would be well.

My gaze slid to the sleeping body once more, which was now starfished on the bed. To the man's sharp jawline and rounded nose, which made him one of the most photogenic people I'd known. To his thick, dark eyebrows and prominent Adam's apple, which I'd once found sexy.

It couldn't be him.

"Rex?" My voice came out like a shriek.

"Mmm?" As he stirred, the comforter crawled toward his waist, exposing his abs.

"Oh God." Panic flushed through me, and I stepped back; the corner of a desk poked me in my silk-covered behind—this was wrong. So, so wrong.

How had we ended up in bed together? And when?

I tried my memory again, scrounged up clues. There was the elevator, and Mae and MJ and Quinn, and the intervention, and then . . .

Nothing.

And had that been last night?

"Did I pass out?" Lowering my hand, I scanned the room for any signs of debauchery. Alcohol, drugs, anything that would have impaired me enough to call a boyfriend from over thirty years ago. Because that would've been the only reason for me to do something so far fetched.

But the room was neat. Two matching suitcases stood next to one another in the corner of the room. Not a single accidentally dropped piece of clothing in sight. On the vanity table was makeup perfectly lined up in a row, not in a haphazard pile in a makeup bag as it normally would have been.

It wasn't just neat in this hotel room. It was Rex neat. It was deep-clean-his-car-once-a-week neat. It was everything-has-its-home neat.

"This is . . . I don't understand." My cheeks burned; I vacillated between laughing and crying. A giggle burst forth, and I clamped my hand over my mouth.

Then, upon looking up at my reflection in the mirror across the room, at my left hand over my mouth, at what was missing from my ring finger, I screamed.

"My ring!" My simple gold wedding band, which had remained on my finger every day for thirty-three years, marred and scratched by time and rough use, was missing. I'd worn it through all my pregnancies—even through Amelia's labor, when the hospital had threatened to cut it off because my fingers had been so swollen with hypertension. My attachment to my wedding band was so steadfast that I'd refused to replace it even when we could have afforded the upgrade. My husband had bought that wedding band with his lean army paycheck, and that meant more to me than the clearest diamond.

"Where is it?" I checked all my fingers once, and then twice more to no avail, then hobbled to the vanity. There, I searched amid the makeup, sending things thumping to the carpet below.

There are only two reasons why you don't have your ring on. Either you took it off because you and Quinn are over . . .

"But the intervention was a dream," I said aloud.

Or maybe it wasn't? Maybe there *had* been an intervention, and he and I had split up, and I'd called Rex.

Or you were never married to begin with, my conscience continued.

My knees buckled, and I eased my body onto a chair. Because that was ridiculous. I had memories. Of our brief ceremony with the justice of the peace, of me in a simple white eyelet dress and with an antique pearl clip in my hair, and of Quinn in his Class A uniform. Of each of the five homes we'd lived in, with specific details to boot. Like how the second house had had a stove with only two burners and an oven that couldn't fit a turkey for Thanksgiving dinner, and the fourth had had carpet in the bathroom. If all that hadn't happened, how did I remember all these things?

Then, another thought descended like curtains on a stage. *Where are my girls?*

I looked for my phone, which would have had their picture on the home screen, but it was still on the bed, next to Rex's hand. Dammit.

I did have another test.

Swallowing my curiosity, I peeled away the blanket and lifted my nightie—it was lavender and delicate and decidedly not machine-wash friendly, and why would I have bought it in the first place?—and felt my belly. It was taut.

Taut. Not soft.

At my rising panic, I inhaled and exhaled. *Keep going.*

My fingers crawled down my torso.

I'd had my tubes tied years ago, and the only external evidence was the one-inch-long scar just above my pubic bone. As benign as it looked, it would get aggravated during the winter and itch like hell, and no ointment could soothe it. The scar itself was raised and could be felt with a slight touch.

I explored the area with my finger, and even widened my search to the other side of my body, but my skin was smooth throughout.

"No surgery." My conclusion came out breathy, my heart rate accelerating as I traversed the branches of my decision tree.

No surgery meant that I hadn't had my tubes tied.

Did that mean . . .

Holy shit. The room tilted, and I steadied myself on the chair.

I hadn't given birth. Or, I hadn't had my tubes tied after I'd had babies. I hadn't had babies with Quinn. *I think?*

No. There had to be a logical explanation for this.

"Hey, baby, what's up?" Rex's low voice pulled me from my racing thoughts. He was sitting up, hair messy and tufted in places. He rubbed his eyes with a knuckle.

Except this wasn't the young Rex who'd been my boyfriend. This was my current Facebook friend Rex, now a man with a full head of salt-and-pepper hair and lines etched into his forehead.

And he'd called me *baby*. Like he knew me. Like I'd chosen to be here.

I tightened the blanket around myself and dragged my gaze to the ground. Either I was asleep and dreaming or I was drunk, or high, or both.

Because I didn't wear nighties, never took off my ring, and would never cheat on Quinn.

Quinn.

Oh God.

I have to get out of here. Whatever this was, this Rex, in any state—solid, or liquid, or gas, or a figment of my imagination—was not someone I should be alone with.

"What are you doing way over there, Cece?" Rex's lips were pursed, and he was assessing me.

Cece. No one called me Cece—well, no one but Rex. "What . . . what are *you* doing here? In my bed?"

An eyebrow plunged. Then, his lips quirked up into a grin, eyes lighting up with mischief. Out of nowhere, I predicted what he would say next . . .

I think you know what went on in our bed.

"Oh, you *know* what went on in our bed," he echoed.

"But I'm a married woman." My voice was a squeak, and once more I heard his answer.

Does he know about me?

He snorted. "Does the other guy know about me?"

I coughed, choking on my own spit. *How did I do that?*

My Rex had been predictable as much as he was neat, and he'd been proper to a fault, as buttoned up as he was.

This had to mean that this was a dream. A whole scenario concocted in my subconscious, where I even picked the lines. And I had amnesia. Both, at the same time. Maybe the person in this bed was Quinn, and to him I was confused.

I blinked back the panic that was at full throttle in my throat, my thoughts swirling on how to manage this.

"Looks like you need coffee stat. Want me to call Sonya?" Rex kicked off the sheets.

Relief rushed through me. In my attempt to piece together this entire situation, Sonya had slipped my mind. And if there was a fixer and explainer, it was her. "Sonya! Thank God. No! Don't get out of bed. I . . . I'll go find her." I showed him the palm, more to block the view of his body as it climbed out of bed. What if he was naked? And if so, how had he gotten naked?

Gah.

Focus, Celine. Sonya was nearby. Of course she was. She always took the room across the hall.

I waddled to the door.

A chuckle came from behind me. "Are you planning on walking out like you're headed to a toga party?"

"Yes, it's fine. No biggie." And I hightailed it out of the room as fast as my legs could take me, then exhaled as the door clicked shut.

But in the silence of the clear hallway, a piece of the puzzle slid into place. Rex knew about Sonya, which meant the reverse had to be true.

Did my girls—I was unconvinced that I was childless—know about him as well? If so, then what had happened to Quinn?

It was as if a laundry basket filled with mismatched black socks had been upturned in front of me and I was being timed as I tried to put pairs together. So I threw myself at the door across the hall and pounded it to silence my head.

The door opened with a flourish; Sonya was already speaking. "I'm amazed you're up this early, but it's a good thing because we've got a list of stuff to cover before we catch our plane to Milwaukee. First of all an interview with *Entertainment Wee*—" She turned back to me, and her jaw slackened. "What are you doing? Why are you wrapped up like a mummy?"

"I . . ." My words froze on my tongue, because Sonya, my Doc Martens–wearing, cruelty-free-skin-care-using, slowly graying Sonya, was . . . not. She sounded like her but was dressed in heels and leather pants—were they real?—and her lipstick was red.

After blinking to clear my head of shock, I closed the distance between us and reached up to touch the strands of her healthy tresses. They were silky in between my fingers, without a split end in sight. This dream was in Technicolor.

At my continued silence, Sonya patted her head, then rushed to the hotel vanity. "What's wrong with my hair?"

I swallowed and said the easiest thing that came to mind. "There's color in it."

She turned her face left and right in front of the mirror. "I mean, yeah. Is it starting to fade? Dammit." She inspected her roots in the mirror. "Maybe it's the deep conditioner last night that stripped it?"

Deep conditioner?

As if seeing me for the first time, Sonya rested a hand on her hip. "Did housekeeping not stock your room with a robe? I'll call them right now." She picked up her phone and spoke into it in quick bursts, so unlike the gentle disposition Sonya showed to everyone.

Sonya's face softened, and she put down the phone. "Did you and Rex have another fight? Listen—if he's got an issue being second while you're on this tour, it's really his problem. We've talked about this. He can't always be in the spotlight. Just because he feels jilted from not being nominated."

Rex worked with computers. "Nominated for what?"

She snorted. "Exactly. He's got a chip on his shoulder. Listen, even Leo waited for his Oscar."

"Leo?"

"DiCaprio."

I needed to sit. And made to do so on a velvet tufted wing chair. My fingers left prints where the fabric gave under my touch.

Did people in dreams leave tangible marks such as this? With my right pointer finger, I pressed against my left forearm, and my skin gave, then bounced back. And, I'd felt the sensation of touch in both my finger and my forearm. "Am I awake?"

"It's obvious you need coffee." Half laughing, Sonya buzzed around the bedroom. "I'll make hotel room coffee for now, since breakfast won't be here for another half hour—you don't mind, right?"

"No. I don't." Maybe my body needed caffeine. Maybe the coffee was going to snap me out of this weird dream. Maybe . . . "Sonya, I woke up with Rex sleeping next to me."

She nodded as she poured water in the back of the one-cup machine. "And? Did something else happen?"

"I mean. Yes. You have highlighted hair."

After fussing with the coffee maker, she turned to me. "You okay, babe?"

Babe? Did she just say *babe*? "I . . . I think I'm confused."

"Confused about what?"

"This . . . all this. You. Rex." The more I said his name, the more my insides lurched. "How did I end up this way?"

The coffee maker beeped its completion. Sonya tore open two packets of sugar—I hadn't put sugar in my coffee in years—and my eyes were drawn to her fingernails, which were painted.

My memory took me back to the eve of Mae and John's wedding, when I'd rushed out for a last-minute trip to the nail salon. I'd asked Sonya to come with me, to which she'd answered, *Never in this world will you catch me in a nail salon and all those noxious fumes.*

The light-headed feeling returned, but I shot to my feet anyway. This dream was overwhelming, and I wanted out.

Sonya frowned. "What are you doing?"

I backed up toward the door. "You're not you. And I . . . I'm not me. And that man in that other room isn't my husband. And where are my daughters?"

"Daughters? Husband?" She arched an eyebrow, snorting. "Unless you married someone else behind my back, you have been happily—I take that back: somewhat contentedly—partnered with Rex for the majority of the last thirty-seven years, and the only children you have is your staff, who you nag to death." She did a double take. "Wait. That was a . . . serious question?"

My vision hazed over, and my legs scrambled for footing. I shot my arms out for balance. The walls were closing in on me . . . and my head . . . my head swam with thoughts. It was heavy with memories of the past, of that fork in the road. Of that one day when my choice had been made, when I had taken Quinn's hand and agreed to a road trip.

My words, said to Sonya in some moment in time, returned to me. *What if I had chosen differently?*

And here I was, unmarried, without children. With Rex.

My body tipped askew.

Chapter Eleven

"I think she's in shock," Sonya said, beyond the bright light shining in my right eye.

Shock was not it. To me, shock meant blunt emotions; it meant standing frozen when a decision needed to be made. Shock was not my MO. When Libby had died, there had been the initial debilitating sadness, but that hadn't lasted long. When a whole family depended on you, shock took a back seat to scheduling the funeral, consoling others, and rearranging your professional schedule.

Shock was when I'd woken up next to Rex. But I was past that. Confused? Yes. Surprised? Absolutely. But now I was in survival mode. *Survival* meaning figuring out how the hell to wake up from this dream because it was lasting a little too long.

"Pupils look good." The light shut off, and the face of the person holding said penlight—the hotel doctor—came into view. She had blonde hair that framed her face and wore a white doctor's coat with the name Dr. Green embroidered on the right breast pocket. "Celine. Do you know what today is?"

"Like I said, the day is not the problem. It's everything and everyone else." I was sitting up in my hotel room bed. After my bout of dizziness, Sonya had elicited help from Rex to tuck me right back into bed and called Dr. Green.

"Can you be more specific?"

Three pairs of eyes blinked back at me. Sonya was at my bedside, arms crossed and visibly bothered. Rex was across the room, leaning against the dresser, outfitted (thank God!) in joggers and a T-shirt.

I pointed at Rex. "For one, he's not my husband."

Rex grumbled. "Not for the lack of trying. You're the one that doesn't want for me to put a ring on it. Then again, it's not like we've been together *together*."

Straightening, I asked, "You mean we haven't been . . ."

"Having sex?" He glanced at Sonya and Dr. Green. "Again, not for the lack of trying. You're either too tired or too busy. Doc, do you have any advice for that?"

Relief came out of me in the form of a cackle. Rex and I hadn't slept together—last night, anyway.

Dr. Green cleared her throat. "That . . . sounds like something you and Celine should talk about privately."

Sonya took my hand into both of hers, encasing it with care. They were smooth and warm. Again, I noticed that her hands were solid, and she was holding *my* hand, which meant I was solid to her too.

I thought back to the dreams I'd had in the past—had I had a sense of touch? Turning over her wrist, I glided my pointer finger over where her pulse point would be and felt the thrum against my finger. "I can feel your heartbeat."

Sonya's face crumpled. "Oh, sweet Celine." Her long eyelashes fluttered upward to the doctor. (Were those eyelash extensions? Holy . . . they were!) "Dr. Green, what do you think?"

"It could be a lot of things. Exhaustion. Dehydration. It could be something neurological. As of right now, she's okay. Vitals are fine. I don't think this is a stroke, or low blood sugar. But I do think that a trip into your doctor sooner than later is necessary."

"Hello?" I waved a hand. "I'm right here."

Dr. Green smiled. "Celine, you need to see someone for a full evaluation. Perhaps a specialist. In my opinion . . ." The doctor peered into my eyes. "You're under a lot of stress."

"You think?" Laughter burst forth. "Of course I'm stressed. My best friend's wearing leather, and I'm wearing silk, and he's . . ." I waved at Rex's general vicinity. "Here."

"I told you this tour was going to be too much. Don't you see she's hit the wall?" Rex crossed his arms. "Babe, you've been working nonstop for thirteen years. Then you went viral, and what had been a normal life for us just went kaput."

"What do you mean, *normal?*" The mention of what was normal to him intrigued me, because maybe the answer to what this place was lay within that history.

"Normal meaning living in LA."

My back straightened. "Los Angeles? We live in California?"

He arched an eyebrow and gestured at Sonya, seemingly waiting for some backup. "Um, we moved from Louisburg so I could pursue my acting career, remember? And it was going so well, and now . . . well, now . . . I'm on tour with you for your debut book."

"You mean my fifth book."

His expression darkened, and his voice lowered. "*Just One Step* is your first book. And you were already exhausted coming into this tour, but you insisted on moving forward."

I gathered all the facts I'd learned thus far, in this . . . situation, like a mama duck scooping up her runaway ducklings. I was unmarried to my IT-guy-turned-actor high school sweetheart, childless, a business owner, a viral success, and a California resident. I was on tour for my debut, not my fifth book. And apparently, based on a look around, my finances were in much-better shape than the other Celine's.

Not the other Celine . . . the real Celine. This Celine—me, now—was the dream Celine.

I pressed my fingers against my temples to grind that fact in.

"All right." Sonya stood and led Rex out by the arm. "You need to go."

"Why do *I* need to go?"

"Because you're not helping." With a final wave, she shut the door.

After a moment of silence had passed, Dr. Green said, "There is some credence to what he said. Stress can be debilitating. It can . . . alter perceptions, change perspectives."

While I assessed Dr. Green's face, and tried to read her message, the intervention came to mind once more. Sonya and Quinn had been concerned about my stress level, forgetfulness, denial. And now with this discussion about perceptions and perspectives . . . what were they insinuating? "Are you suggesting that I'm having a mental break?"

Dr. Green cleared her throat, as if in discomfort. "I'm not your primary care doctor. I can't make that assessment. But certainly, it's a consideration that something is happening within this stressful time in which people and situations are not familiar to you. A situation that may be helped by a mental health specialist."

"No." I shook my head. "No, I don't think so. I feel great. I am fully a hundred percent aware." Sure, my body was a little off kilter, but my mind was not.

Dr. Green glanced at Sonya. "I'm not sure what else to say."

"I can take it from here. Thank you for coming in last minute," Sonya said.

Dr. Green got on her feet. "Anytime."

"You'll keep this confidential?"

"Absolutely. This establishment is adept at dealing with high-profile clients." Dr. Green patted me on the knee. "Let me know if there's anything else you need. But this doctor orders a lot of rest, with an urgent follow-up when you return home."

My head bobbed in a habitual nod, though rest was furthest from my mind. My next step was finding out how to wake up from it.

Sonya stood and walked Dr. Green to the door. With bent heads, they spoke, during which Dr. Green reached out and touched Sonya's arm.

Touched her. As in, Sonya let her.

My eyes widened. That . . . that was all wrong too. Sonya valued her personal space and especially didn't allow strangers to get inside her bubble.

"Take me back!" The demand shot out of me, for anyone: the world, the universe, Mother Earth, God. Or someone else in my awake world. Because the lede had been buried, and perhaps if I just said it aloud, whoever was playing with those levers that woke people up from dreams would pull mine. "I actually didn't mean what I said!"

"What didn't you mean, honey?" Sonya shut the door but kept her distance.

I opened my mouth to recount my what-if moment and thought better of it. Giving voice to it would mean that this current situation was real, that in wishing for it during the intervention, I'd conjured this entire experience. That Dr. Green was right and perhaps I was having a mental break.

No. There had to be a simple solution to all this, maybe as simple as a nap to perhaps jump into the dream cycle. So instead I said, "It's nothing. Maybe the doctor's right. I should take the day off today. I'll go right to bed, take the next couple of days off if I have to."

"Mmm." She nodded, deadpan. Her hands were clasped together in front of her torso, like she was a kindergarten teacher attempting to discern her student's concerns. "Sleep is good, but I want to discuss our plan with the team."

"Our plan."

"There's still a tour going on. Your final two stops are Milwaukee and New York . . ."

Milwaukee and New York? Those two were the same final stops in my real life. My brain began to note how this dream was comparing to my awake life. Color me impressed that my dreams were creative.

"Mae, MJ, and Amelia will surely have ideas on how to take you off your tour," she continued.

"They exist?" At the mention of my daughters' names, my heart leapt into my throat, though only for a moment. I lifted my sheet and pressed a hand against my belly, confusion descending. A laugh bubbled out of me, as well as relief. My imagination was clearly having fun with me.

"Yes, they very much exist. Um . . ." Sonya darted to the in-room refrigerator. "Let's refresh your water. You have to be completely dehydrated."

A frantic rapping began at the hotel door. Sonya opened it, and through it came the most glorious sight.

My little women.

My daughters. Mae, MJ, and Amelia, all in casual outfits. They looked exactly the same, like my daughters, aside from their marked hesitation as they hung around by the door.

My heart seized in relief. "Oh my God. Your beautiful faces." Light-headedness be damned, my body hurtled out of the bed. After steadying myself, and fully appreciating that Sonya had handed me decent clothing earlier, I threw my arms around them. Their perfumes and shampoos mixed and mingled. Apparently in this dream, my sense of smell was on point. I detected MJ's favorite strawberry scent, Mae's shea butter bodywash, and Amelia's favorite perfume.

For the first time today, my soul was enveloped in comfort.

My heart skipped a beat. If three of my daughters were here, what were the chances that the fourth was too? I dared a whisper into the circle. "Where's Libby?"

"Um . . . Libby . . . who?" Amelia asked, the first to step back with awkwardness in her expression.

My chest caved in after what felt like a blow to the heart, my hope dashed. Swallowing the tears that threatened to usurp the moment—*get behind me, tears!*—I feigned a smile, though underneath I cursed this dream for not giving me at least that one thing. "Oh, n . . . no one. But I missed you three so much." I squeezed MJ's and Mae's shoulders.

Belatedly, I realized that the two were stiff under my touch. I looked up; their gazes were not on me but on the floor, and their lips were pressed into grimaces.

I peeled my fingers from their shoulders as the truth dawned into full clarity. That while *my children*—MJ, Amelia, and Mae—were huggers who kissed cheeks freely, who never thought twice about showing their physical love toward me, these women were not. Not my children, that was.

My arms dropped to my sides, and as if to drive the point home, all three politely walked past me, toward Sonya, as if she was their protector.

It was a familiar sight, to have my girls stand by her in solidarity. But right now, I wished they'd remained next to me.

"Celine, please sit." Sonya ushered me by the elbow to the wing chair and pressed a water bottle into my hand. My girls—my team, that was—took the first seats they could. Amelia all but sat on MJ's lap in the tufted chair next to the hotel room door, as if yearning for a quick escape. "Now that the team is here, we should strategize on how to manage the tour in the short term. Time is of the essence."

"Right." There was no avoiding this conversation. This was a movie intending to play out despite my lack of interest. "I can make it easy for everyone: I need to take a nice long nap. A Tylenol PM, and a room, just mine, and blackout shades, and this will all be done."

Worry flashed in Sonya's eyes despite the gritted smile on her face, and she cleared her throat. "Exactly. Our hope is rest for you. But we need to discuss the details." Her eyes darted to the team. "So for a bit of reintroduction, you've got MJ for social media and partnerships."

MJ raised a finger in acknowledgment.

"Mae for event coordination. Then Amelia for all of your marketing and merchandizing. Now, ladies, I'd like to hear your suggestions for what we can do for the way forward. Because we have some decisions to make. Celine, Dr. Green has suggested that we postpone the tour or perhaps cancel it and bring you back home to Los Angeles."

I responded with silence because my brain was processing the fact that my daughters were working for me—and with them sitting next to one another, could they not tell that they were related and, furthermore, related to me?

This dream was so rich in detail.

It's a consideration that something is happening within this stressful time.

Dr. Green's words lingered in my periphery, and I shoved them back and away. I was not having a mental break. The stress of the tour had not been unique. And with a team behind Celine Lakad Coaching, I had help.

Sonya continued, hands clasped in front of her. "I've already spoken to Dr. Simpson, and she's expecting you."

Dr. Simpson was my primary care doctor. "And then what?"

"I . . . don't know. That's not for me to decide. It's between you and your doctor." She slid her gaze to MJ. "What's your plan with messaging, MJ?"

"Yes, um." MJ cleared her throat. "There are already rumblings on socials that you seemed distracted in Denver a couple of days ago. And in last night's event, with how late you were to arrive onstage."

I clocked the similarities with my awake life: Sonya's report of my unusual behavior in Denver and that I was late to the event due to the intervention.

A part of me was impressed at how consistent my memory was even in this dream.

"We're going to have to straddle being able to say just enough. In my opinion, we should be honest with your mental health. That you need to take time off. I started writing the official post." MJ lifted her phone and thumbed through, reading. "My dearest friends. It is with my deepest apologies that I need to take a knee for the next two events. I have to be honest. I have hit a wall, and I'm tired. My mental health isn't, for the lack of better words, healthy—"

"Wait wait wait," I interrupted. MJ was being presumptuous. She hadn't been here for Dr. Green's initial evaluation. "How can you say that this is about my mental health when this is just about me being tired?"

"Um." Her eyes darted to Sonya.

"I told them that that's probably the case, Celine," Sonya added. "You're not understanding what we're seeing here. Your facial expressions alone. How surprised you are at what is a given. That you and Rex were sharing the same room, for example, and that they"—she gestured to my girls—"quote, 'exist.'"

My first inclination was to correct Sonya, to explain that this wasn't about my mental health as much as the fact that I was asleep. But arguing this fact, when they were part of the dream sequence, was a recipe for frustration. The whole *doth protest too much* could be used against me. "The message is fine." I waved a hand in the air. "Whatever we need to do so I can get some alone time. Thank you, MJ, for the post. It sounds just like me. I'm impressed." It had been in the last couple of years that I'd relinquished control over social media, and sometimes, despite the posts gathering enough traction, they hadn't been written in my voice.

MJ's jaw dropped minutely. "I mean. I've written your posts for six years now."

"You have? But what about your novels?" Belatedly, I wondered if my daughters in this dream still had their same connections, hobbies, and passions.

MJ shifted, clearly uncomfortable. "I am . . . still writing . . . but this job is my focus. In any case, we can rewrite this statement. Just like your book, you have full editorial control. I'm just . . . drafting for you."

"You drafted my book too?" That was impossible. No one drafted my books for me. I'd agonized over every blasted word in each one of my books. Once, I'd spent a whole afternoon on a three-sentence paragraph. "Even the actual method of how exactly to take steps forward? Did I agree to that?"

"Moving on," Sonya prompted. "Mae?"

Curiosity made me sit back in the wing chair. The Celine Lakad in this dream seemed less attached to her message.

But Mae had taken out her iPad and scrolled through, humming, and my attention slipped away from my thoughts. "We can put you on a plane to Los Angeles within the next three hours, and you can be home by dinnertime." Her smile was encouraging; it was the same kind of smile she gave her children when they threw their tantrums.

With the mention of home, more questions arose. Namely: "Where are my apos?"

A hesitant smile played on Mae's lips. "Uh, your what?"

"My grandchildren. Your children. Where are they?"

"I don't . . . have . . ."

"John, how about John?"

"John's back in LA." She cleared her throat, and her expression turned sheepish. "And we're far from making decisions about kids. We can barely pay off our student loans."

"No apos? That's so . . . sad." A pain started in my chest, and I pressed my hand against it. Life without them was unimaginable, and my face warmed with the start of tears. "I'm sorry; it's just . . . they are the light of our family."

It's not real, I reminded myself. *It's not real.*

"Let's keep moving on." Sonya jumped in, frowning. "Amelia?"

As usual, my youngest child spoke with her nose in the air. "We're going to suffer some losses. There are the ticket sales we'll have to refund. The loss from merch. People will be upset, so we'll see some backlash from fans. But really, nothing is more important than your health, Celine. Whenever you're better, we can always schedule a shorter tour. I, however, believe there's no rest to be had here at the hotel. There are too many people here for the event. I think you need time away. At home."

"Oh, Amelia." My youngest daughter was still so sweet despite her pretentious attitude. She'd been maligned by her sisters, called difficult and spoiled, but how was a youngest sibling supposed to act when there were shadows of each sister hovering over her?

She'd had to make her own noise. And because this Amelia wanted me to take care of myself, I nodded. It wouldn't hurt to agree—I would wake up soon enough. Might as well play along.

"Okay."

"Okay?" Sonya's face lit up.

"Yes, maybe a week off is a good idea. But I don't want to go to Los Angeles." The idea alone was wrong. California wasn't my home. And though Rex and I were together in this dream, the thought of me going with him was equivalent to adultery.

"I mean . . . where would you want to go?" Mae asked.

I tested the waters. "Do I happen to have a town house in Annapolis?"

"No," answered Sonya, concern clouding her features.

"Then I don't know. Anywhere. Just not where Rex is."

The girls shot glances at one another as Sonya took her buzzing phone out of her pocket. "Mae, can you come up with a small list of retreat destinations? Or private vacation locations?" She pressed the phone against her ear. "Hello. Yes, I will call you back in a few minutes." Hanging up, she continued on as if she hadn't been interrupted. "Someplace peaceful. How does the beach sound, Celine? Or the cape?"

"Sure, wherever." Not that it would matter. At some point my real body had to wake up.

The three stood and bade us goodbye with the promise to return in an hour with some options. As the room quieted, Sonya's phone rang once more. A growl escaped her lips as she spied the caller ID.

"What's up?" I asked.

"Incessant, nagging person." She did a double take toward my direction, then heaved a breath as if making a decision. "I'm sorry. You asked me to deal with this person, but she only wants to deal with you. And I fear that she's going to make a stink about it."

None of what Sonya was saying sounded familiar, though her tone was disconcerting. "Who is it?"

"It's your tenant at your rental in Louisburg."

"My house?" I had to turn over each new bit of information on my tongue for it to sink in.

Her eyebrows knit together. "Yes, the one you and Rex bought two decades ago. Don't you remember? You wanted to be within an hour of Boston but far enough away to start a different life. It was where we met. You moved out a couple of years ago when you decided to follow Rex to LA. This person rents the second house out back."

Two years. Another milestone similar to my awake life. But one detail stumped me. "There's a second house on the property?"

Sonya sighed, impatience radiating off her. "I mean, yes. You've always had that extra living quarters. Anyway, the house is in escrow, and hands change in a week. It was a quick close; the house sold as is, and though your tenant was compensated for having her lease broken, she's still very upset that she's had less than thirty days to move out, and apparently her oven's still not working. Elizabeth hasn't stopped calling—"

"Who's Elizabeth?"

"The tenant."

Elizabeth Abigail Lakad-Frasier. My third-born. Who died.

I held up a hand. "Wait. Elizabeth? Elizabeth is in Sampaguita?"

"Sampaguita?"

"Don't you remember that the house was named Sampaguita when . . ." After pausing and piecing together that it had been me and Quinn who had given the house its name, I moved on. "What does she look like?" My voice was short of shrieking; I was already standing. My eyes scanned the room for the dresser that held my clothes.

If this Elizabeth was my Libby . . .

My heart pounded against my chest, loud and heavy. "Tell me, Sonya. What does Elizabeth look like?"

Sonya's arms extended outward as if to catch me. "I . . . I don't know. All I've done is talk to her on the phone. Whoa, wait a minute—what are you doing?"

I was pawing at the phone in her hand. My vision focused; my breathing slowed. I needed to know if Elizabeth was Libby. If my daughter was alive. "Give me your phone. Call this Elizabeth back."

"All right, all right. I'll dial her up right now." After a couple of presses of her thumb, she handed the phone to me. The speaker amplified the ringing line.

The phone picked up immediately, and every single cell in my body held still, waiting for a greeting.

"Finally. Honestly, it shouldn't take this long for me to get ahold of my own landlord." The woman answered without pretense, voice echoing through the speaker, discontent lacing each and every word. Her voice was familiar and wonderful and painful all at once. I envisioned the woman in my mind immediately, one hand resting on her hip, the other holding the phone against her ear. She was most likely pacing, which had been her way to shrug off frustration. I would have bet money that she had an apron on, with her hair in an intricate braid.

The tears that I had been able to hold back throughout these last few hours spewed forth. Because it couldn't be, could it? Could a dream conjure up such a clear impression of my daughter's intonation?

Sonya responded by placing a hand over her mouth, a clear sign of worry.

"Hello?" the voice said. "Did you hear anything I just said?"

"I heard it." My voice shook. "Is . . . is this Elizabeth?"

"Yes, this is Elizabeth. You called me, remember? Who's this? This isn't Sonya."

"No, it isn't. It's . . . Mo . . . I mean Celine."

"Finally! I have been waiting long enough for you to call me back. Thank goodness. I have so much to tell you."

Me too, dear Libby. Me too.

Chapter Twelve

Louisburg, Massachusetts

I sat in the back seat of the hired car, and my eyes fought the urge to shut. Exhaustion had settled in the last couple of hours, from convincing Sonya that Louisburg was my choice destination for my weeklong vacation, to informing the rest of the team and Rex—to his outrage—to arranging for a car service and packing for my retreat.

Both Rex and Sonya had fought my decision to head to Louisburg alone. They'd been concerned by my crying jag, confused about my motivations to head back to a town and home with an angry tenant instead of a beach or spa retreat.

But I was an adult and had made my choice. I wouldn't allow myself to be alone with Rex one more second and had even refused his company. There had been no question that Louisburg was where I would stay when there was a chance that my daughter, or her image and likeness, would be there.

It was true what people said about those who were left behind forgetting the little things about the loved ones who'd passed. Nuances about personalities and mannerisms blurred with each day. The photographs and little snippets of video we had of Libby just weren't enough to really capture her essence, and that short phone call earlier today had given me so much more of who Libby was than all my memories of her combined.

Seeing my daughter took priority, and I would not risk that for a nap.

Thirty minutes later, the car passed the city-limits sign of Louisburg, population 15,789.

As the rideshare entered the town, I braced myself for the influx of pain. Two years ago, the Lakad-Frasier family had driven away from this town with one less family member. Since then, I'd had no incentive or motivation to return.

Or, there had been none—until now.

Still, I scrutinized my view out the car window. The narrowness of the streets, the color of the sky, the way the leaves shimmered with the slight gusts of wind. Was it true to life? Different? Odd? Was it pixelated like *The Matrix*, which was a movie—truth be told—that had gone over my head the first time I'd watched it? Were there secret portals that would lead me back to my consciousness?

Once I got to Sampaguita and saw Libby with my own eyes, I was going to do whatever possible to wake up to where my children were. Where Quinn was. For as much as I wanted to see my daughter again, she wouldn't be real.

When the car turned down Lexington Way, my tummy somersaulted, and my heart raced.

I remembered my and Quinn's return from the hospital without Libby. We had driven down this road, both carrying the burden of losing our child. In the pit of my belly had been a burning rage. In my heart, a chasm of emptiness. And upon opening the door of an empty Sampaguita—that was, empty of Libby but full of her stuff—I'd been desperate to turn back time.

Up until recently, on the hardest of nights, the same questions had invaded my psyche.

Why didn't she tell me how sick she was?
Why didn't I follow up?

Why did I believe her when she said she was fine?
Why didn't I just push my way in?

Maybe my subconscious had been tired of all my questions, had decided to have pity on me, and had given me this dream to ease some of my regret. Perhaps this was my brain's response to the intervention—like a practice run of visiting a dream Sampaguita before I did so in real life.

No matter the reason, I was engulfed with anticipation and trepidation, because to get to Libby, first I would need to enter the home that I'd actively avoided for years.

My body froze when the car halted in front of Sampaguita.

I peered at my former home with its cracked pathway and overgrown front lawn. Staked into the grass was a **SOLD** sign, and though I knew that the changeover would occur in a week—and that this was all a dream and that, in both cases, this shouldn't matter to me—my stomach gave way to the nostalgia nonetheless.

Toys used to litter the front of the house. A Hula-Hoop, a bicycle, an occasional book. Signs of the girls had been everywhere, from the chalk drawings leading up from the driveway, to every light in the home being on. Even up to when Quinn and I had moved away, when our children were all grown—we'd kept their DIY mosaic stepping-stones, made during one long summer day, which were dug into the yard, along with garden flags with insignias of their colleges.

Those had been the good times, when my biggest worry had been how to balance being a mom and starting a new career. When the logistics of growing a family had been straightforward problems to tackle, such as what times pickups and drop-offs were. Or what the right uniform was for that afternoon's extracurricular activity. Or whether we had enough money to cover fixing the finicky furnace. A trip to McDonald's had been a surefire way of putting smiles on four out of four of my girls' faces.

"Ma'am?" The driver peered at me through the rearview mirror. "This is the house, right?"

I took stock of my body, my breathing. So far, so good. I felt . . .
okay. "Yep. This is the house."

I popped the door open and met the driver in the back. He
unloaded both my suitcases. "I can pull it up to the door for you."

"No, thank you. I'll do it myself."

The driver grimaced at the shabby front facade. "I can stick around
until I know you're okay. It doesn't look like anyone's here."

Raising my hand over my eyes to block out the sun, I considered his
offer. Was I really ready for this? Who knew what was on the other side
of the door. Ghosts and poltergeists. Spirits in limbo. A vast emptiness.

None of it can hurt you. It's just a dream.

Right. I needed to get to Libby before I woke up. My heart sped
up, urgency kicking in. "No worries. I have someone waiting for me."

"All right, ma'am. Good luck."

"Thank you."

I grasped one suitcase handle in each hand, gripping tightly, and
strode up the walkway toward the dark-green door. As I neared, my
anxiety heightened, magnified by the memory of the hundreds of times
I'd taken this path. Before two years ago, the thought of home, of
Sampaguita, had conjured images of only the good, the sweet, the fun,
a result of all our family memories. Libby's death had eclipsed all of that.

But when the scent of jasmine hit my nostrils, my thoughts quieted.

The flowers were in bloom. They bloomed from spring to fall without fail, and without fear, as hardy as they were.

I needed to have that same fortitude, to see this through. To be
willing to face this house in hopes of seeing my daughter. I missed
her—her face, her voice—and I would take any version of her if but
for a short amount of time.

A glimmer from the dormer window on the third floor caught
my attention. For a beat I expected MJ's reflection through the glass
because of the many hours she'd spent writing and reading in front of
that window, lit by her desk lamp. As I climbed the one step to the

porch, I scanned the window on the right side, where Libby would have normally been, playing at the piano.

That, too, was dark.

My heart dipped.

What if Libby wasn't here after all? What if my subconscious had decided that that was a dream too good to have?

There's only one way to find out. I placed my hand on the knob and paused.

Libby's funeral reception came to mind, along with the numerous times this door had squeaked with every entry and exit of visitors. That day, I had become so frustrated that sometime in the middle of the reception, I had shaken the door, intending to take it off its hinges.

It hadn't been one of my shining moments. Nor had threatening to slam the fallboard on the fingers of one of Libby's friends. Or throwing *Little Women* into the fireplace.

Marmee. I missed her, too, though it hadn't hit me until now, seeing this home where I'd felt most like a mother. When the joy of motherhood, and not simply the survival of motherhood, had been at the center.

Had Marmee fallen into the same kind of anger and desperation after Beth had died? I wished I knew.

What I *did* know was that Marmee wouldn't have stood here like I was now, hesitating and contemplating going into the house at all. She would have stepped in despite the expectation of facing whatever was on the other side of this door. And if there had been a chance it was Beth, she would have barged right on in.

But I wasn't Marmee, and it wasn't bravado running through me but this twisted mix of nausea and a gut-wrenching fear. Of possibly walking into a living museum of what had been two years ago, of something that would remind me of my culpability.

I had never even taken down Libby's macramé wall hanging. Her piano was still there, locked up.

So I held my breath and turned the knob; the door squeaked as I stepped into the foyer. For a beat I kept my eyes shut, like I was a little girl watching her first horror flick. After another count to three, I opened my eyes and gasped at the sight, chest caving in. "Holy . . ."

This wasn't Sampaguita.

The lights were off, and the house was dim, but it was evident that absolutely everything in this house was coordinated and modern, clean, and organized. These front rooms could have come right out of an Ethan Allen catalog.

"It's so . . . pretty." I toed off my shoes out of habit. On stockinged feet, my legs were lead filled and clunky on the way into the front room. In our Sampaguita, where Quinn and I had raised rambunctious girls, we could never have nice things without suffering some kind of consequence. Each piece of furniture had been purchased at different times, creating a home that was eclectic and cozy, shelves brimming with knickknacks.

There wasn't a single personal memento on the walls, on the mantel, where photos of our extended family had resided. The couch even had coordinating pillows—something I hadn't braved until all the kids had been out of the house.

In this dream you don't have kids.

Right. Of course nothing would look the same. When one didn't have kids, they led a different kind of life, without mosaic stepping-stones and college banners, without the random frames of photos and school pottery projects on windowsills.

This house was definitely not Sampaguita.

Relief spilled out of me; I reached out to steady myself on the back of the sofa and released a breath. The tension in my jaw loosened. I'd been unknowingly clenching everything, anticipating the worst, like coming up on Libby's things still left in the same place as the day she'd died.

I'd once read that dreams reflected the fears in a person's consciousness, and this whole dream must have been my subconscious playing out my what-if scenario.

The Elizabeth on the phone must have simply been the character my subconscious knew to lure me with all the way here, to show me what it would feel like to walk into Sampaguita. Which hadn't been so bad after all.

"Well, I've learned my lesson." My voice echoed through the space, firm and determined. When I woke up, I would find a way to a middle ground with Quinn, my girls, and Sonya. I would listen. Negotiate and meet them halfway in a calm manner. Those moments before I climbed that stage had been rife with so much drama and tension. These few hours—however real time had passed—had given me perspective.

Sonya, my real-life Sonya, had been right. We couldn't live in the what-ifs.

"Anytime now, okay?" I said to the ceiling, to whatever or whomever, to my sleeping self. "But until then, I guess I'll get settled."

I dragged my suitcases all the way in, turning on a lamp on one of the sofa tables, admiring the details of the inlaid wood by running a finger against the grain, only to catch a glimpse of an upright piano tucked into the corner of the room. The fallboard was up.

I froze, my hand still on the table, with me bent at the waist.

It was Libby's upright piano—the same piano that Libby had thrived on, gifted to her by our next-door neighbor, Mr. Loren. The same piano I'd locked up.

A fresh surge of pain washed over me, along with new questions. What was it doing here if there was no Libby? Mr. Loren had given the piano to Libby when she was just starting middle school. He'd said that she reminded him of his own daughter, who'd loved the piano. He'd had it delivered one day and refused any offer for payment.

And why was the fallboard up? Rex and I supposedly hadn't lived here in two years.

"Petals Fluttering" played itself in my memory, or was it off in the distance? I couldn't tell, and with it, my skin tingled.

"It's just a piano." I dared it to turn into something more. To come alive. For two years I'd winced whenever I'd heard piano music, so much so that I'd skipped listening to certain songs. But now that I was here, staring at it, it was anticlimactic. It was just an object. It didn't have to hold me hostage.

Though my heart was still in my throat, I declared, "Moving on."

Toward the rear of the home, next to the back door that led to the backyard, was a table with a sign that read WELCOME, PLEASE SIGN IN. On a clipboard was a sign-in sheet. Written up top: *The home is pending, though feel free to tour it. Should you like to be on the waiting list, please put a star next to your name.* It was signed *Robin Noriko, Realtor.*

Seven names were scribbled on the list in various forms of penmanship, all with stars next to them.

The last bit of fear and tension left me. I hadn't known what to expect walking into this house. An answer? A way back? A poltergeist? But what was facing me now was evidence that this home wasn't mine. That in my what-if scenario, this home was simply one that Rex and I had moved on from. This home wasn't steeped with sadness because there had been no tragedy.

A door slammed open from somewhere on the first floor, making me jump back. My backside bumped up against the table, and its legs scraped against the wooden floor. A quiet shriek escaped my lips.

I jammed my hand into my pocket for my phone and backed up slowly. My thumb hovered over the power button. Multiple presses of the power button supposedly would send an SOS straight to the police. It was the kind of information I'd forwarded straight to my girls, just in case.

My mind ran through the possibility of who was in the house. It could be my Realtor, or another agent who'd decided to enter through the kitchen side door.

Then, a woman's voice echoed from the mudroom. "Yes, I understand . . . no . . . all right. I get it. Give me a few days for another sample. I'll try to get you something sooner . . ."

My entire body went slack. Perhaps it was the way sound traveled. This house was old. Could it actually be—

"Hey . . . yes, I'm home now . . ."

Home.

Only six people had lived in Sampaguita. Me, Quinn, Mae, MJ, Amelia. And . . .

"I'll see you in a bit. Yeah, making tea."

Then came the click-click-click of the stove, the rustle of grocery bags, the opening and closing of cupboards.

All the while, I hovered next to the back door, my mind struggling through logical thought. Usually I was so good at managing decision trees. But since this morning, since I'd woken up, I'd felt like a child on her first tree-climbing experience, unsure of the next step. Up one limb, down the other, crossing over to an intersecting limb of another tree.

I'd rushed coming here because of the possibility that I would see Libby. Totally unthinking, and out of instinct.

Seeing this empty house, how different it was than the Sampaguita in my awake life, reframed my expectations. This dream was what it was: a stress dream, and nothing more.

But hearing her voice . . .

Then, I watched Libby—my dead daughter, Libby—walk through the kitchen door, wiping her hands on her jeans. She raised her most beautiful face to me.

Stumbling backward, I fell.

Chapter Thirteen

The searing pain in my tailbone when I landed on my bottom sent a jarring thought through me.

I must have died falling off that stage.

I was dead, and this place, this state of being, was purgatory.

It made sense now: The blank spots in my memory. That this world wasn't quite right. Knowing people and yet not knowing them at all. That feeling of being in limbo, in the in-between.

My Catholic parents had told me about purgatory with a mix of awe and wonder—that it was the precursor to the afterlife, to heaven. That purgatory was a place for atonement, a time to feel the pain and remorse and earn our keep. Until then, we would get glimmers of heaven, to keep us hopeful.

This had to have been why, despite science and logic, Libby's face was inches from mine, and she was touching me. Touching. Me. With warm fingers.

"Oh . . . holy . . . shoot." Hands on my elbow and with bent knees, Libby helped me back to standing. "Are you okay?"

"I . . ." My tongue was frozen, brain in a full stop while I scoured Libby's face. From her broad forehead, to her golden-brown eyes rimmed in black, to the smattering of freckles over the bridge of her nose. To the angles of her cheekbones and strong jawline. Her hair was in a french braid, though wisps had fallen out in the attempt at wrangling back her coarse hair.

I reached up and palmed her cheek. There wasn't a lick of makeup on her face.

My daughter.

My daughter.

Tears filled my eyes; my throat was clogged with them. "Libby?"

Libby's eyebrows knit together, but I pushed on. My brain continued to calibrate, eyes darting over her face, what she was wearing, how she stood. My hands fell on her shoulders, squeezing them as I relished the strength of her posture.

I threw my arms around her and squeezed her tight. The faint scent of lavender, her favorite scent, filled my nostrils. Hot tears slid down my cheeks as I clutched her to me because it had been forever since I'd held her. More than a couple of years. At the hospital, she'd been connected to all those wires . . . "Oh my God. It's you; it's you. I can't believe it."

"Whoa. Um . . ." Libby pried me off her body. "Not Libby. Celine? Uh . . ."

At the sound of my name on her lips—not *Mom* but my first name—my body snapped back as if it had been restrained by a car's seat belt after going at a high speed. As Libby stepped away, the truth settled in the cold space between us. It was transmitted through the confusion in her eyes.

Libby was uncomfortable. Not only because she'd never been the type for big bear hugs. But because to her, I was not her mother. Much like I wasn't the same Celine to Sonya, the girls, and Rex.

No. My chest constricted, pressing against my lungs, and the record skipped on my decision track once more. If this was purgatory, and I was dead, shouldn't the person in front of me have been my daughter?

If this wasn't purgatory, then what was this place?

I needed to get out of there, away from her presence, to process all this. "I'm sorry. I don't know what came over me . . . I need some space." And on shaky legs, I strode out the front door, to the porch, gulping air.

I bent at the waist. *Inhale . . . exhale . . .*

I couldn't do this. Yes, I'd hoped Libby would be here, but now, as I faced her, it was all too much. My heart hurt. It had already been broken, but I'd done my best to mend it, to superglue parts, to tape up others temporarily just so I could keep going.

I thought that by seeing her today, it would heal the rest of me, but not knowing where I was and having Libby be here and yet not be *her* was a cruel joke. My subconscious was a jerk.

Ultimately, it didn't matter what this place was. Whether it be a dream or a hallucination, a mental break or purgatory, this wasn't where I belonged. I had to find my way back home. Where my family was waiting for me. This I knew: wherever Quinn, my girls, and Sonya were, there was real support, real love, and my real life.

Let's do something about Sampaguita. I believe that if you can do that, we can finally be on our way back together, back home together, all of us.

Quinn's words flew in, his voice clear and soothing. As if he'd nudged me by the chin to look up into his eyes, his ultimatum became my road map. My breathing and heart rate slowed. My thoughts cleared at the next steps that materialized in front of me.

The house was changing over in less than a week, but before we turned over the keys, the house needed to be emptied.

At that moment, I was filled with certainty that getting this home through escrow was the way home—and therefore my next step. I couldn't be distracted, no matter how good Libby had felt in my arms. No matter the joy of seeing her alive.

Footsteps sounded from behind me, and I shut my eyes for a beat. *This is not your Libby.*

"Celine, I don't know what happened back there. But are you okay?"

I turned to Libby, who was hovering by the doorway a few feet away. "Yes, thank you. I'm fine. I guess I'm just a little . . . overwhelmed, and I shouldn't have hugged you like that."

She smiled. "Aw, it's okay. It's nice every once in a while to get a hug. But, I did want to mention that my name is Elizabeth, not Libby."

A fresh set of tears threatened to flow. Of course I'd known that Elizabeth and Libby wouldn't be one and the same, but having it confirmed . . .

Focus, Celine. "Right. I'm sorry, Elizabeth. And thank you for understanding my, um . . . actions. Now, how did you get into the house? I thought you were living in the house out back?"

As the question left my mouth, I laughed. Because Libby wasn't actually alive. And oh my God, I was having a conversation with Elizabeth like she *was* alive.

Stress can be debilitating. It can . . . alter perceptions, change perspectives.

Dr. Green's words flitted into my thoughts once more, and this time, they settled into the dark crevices of my doubts, rattling my insides. Sweat formed under my arms as I scrutinized the neighborhood in front of me, the random car riding past. The bright sun and the amazing details that made up my surroundings.

It was incredible, the details. I could fall for all of this if I wasn't careful.

Elizabeth eyed me. "I do still live out back, but that's what I was trying to contact you about. The logistics have made it difficult—" From the kitchen, the kettle whistled. Lifting a finger, she walked back into the house. The whistling quieted, and as she returned, the way her body moved, how smoothly her muscles and joints worked together, and the smell of lavender stunned me in one fell swoop.

It conjured up that endearing phase when Libby had wanted to learn how to make soap and essential oils had filled our home, followed by a dining room table full of misshapen bar soap. Every local friend and neighbor had received soap in their mailboxes that year.

Libby had had a way of showering people with her gifts. From soap, to song, to her baked goods. Her kindness.

"Anyway," she continued, "what I hadn't mentioned on the phone was that because of some issues with the little house, I actually live here. Here, in this main house."

Chapter Fourteen

"You've been living here all this time?" My head spun with thoughts, starting with images of Elizabeth roaming these rooms like a ghost.

Not the same house. Not the same person. Not even real, my logic reminded me.

"I've lived here about three months." Her voice dipped. Then, beeping came from the kitchen. She hiked a thumb behind her. "Can we talk inside? You look like you need to sit, or hydrate. Or eat. I've also got something that needs to go in the oven."

"Sure." Not seeing the harm, and because I was wobbly on my feet, I followed her in. But as we approached the kitchen door, I halted. The idea of me and this Libby look-alike mingling in a kitchen was not something I would entertain. I could barely cook in my Annapolis kitchen, with every baking gadget or utensil a reminder of my daughter.

What she'd said earlier caught up to me. Elizabeth lived *here*. Which meant that part and parcel of me staying here would mean sending her back to the little house, and handing over the keys to the new owner meant displacing Elizabeth. I would be throwing out someone who looked like my daughter.

But it had to be done. Home was my target.

As she crossed the threshold, Elizabeth turned. "Coming in?"

"No."

Her eyebrows rose. "No?"

"No, and you need to leave." I trained my eyes on the bridge of her nose. If we locked gazes, my mind would change. But the truth was I couldn't be around her. This Elizabeth was a stranger, and I couldn't forget it.

"Okay." She clasped her hands in front of her. "I . . . I'm sorry. Did I say something to make you mad?"

I still didn't meet her eyes. "I think it best that you take your things and head back to the other house."

"All right, that's no problem, but for the record, I've been a great renter for two years, you know, even when things started to break. The furnace, the oven. The refrigerator was making this awful noise. I emailed Robin a million times, even texted about repairs and stuff, and finally she told me that I should use *this* house for what I need since it was going to be sold. I didn't like the idea at first, but when the oven went out, I decided not to wait. Obviously, I can't work without an oven. I'm a baker, and it was in my lease application."

Tamping down my shock from all this information, because I needed to remain focused, I answered coolly, "I had no idea that this all happened. Three months is a long time, and I thank you for your patience."

"I suppose I could have forced the issue, for her to fix things," she continued, and her smile turned sheepish. "But I honestly kind of enjoyed it here. Then the house went up for sale, and it sold just like that." She snapped her fingers. "And then Robin wanted me to move out in less than a month. Do you know how hard that is? For all I've done for this house the last three months. It sold so quickly because it's spotless. I've taken care of its general maintenance. Did you know that Robin barely came by? I bet she charged you a monthly fee to check in on the house, but guess who made sure birds weren't just making nests on the eaves? So really you should be thanking me . . ."

Her assertiveness had me raising my eyebrows. This Elizabeth had the same stubborn attitude as Libby, and I fell right into mom mode.

"I should be thanking you? Did I charge you extra to live in a bigger place?"

She gritted her teeth. "Okay, look. All I'm saying is this . . . I might need more time to move out. I get the whole *changing keys in a week*, but I don't know if I can make that deadline. I have a place, but it needs a little help."

"You need to go in a week. No extensions," I shot out. A great probability existed that I could become more attached and confused as the days went by.

I was starting to feel it already; I didn't want our banter to end.

My head and my heart were in battle, and in all cases it would be me who would lose.

She raised both hands, eyes wide. "All right. Don't call the police or anything. Can I at least show you what I've done to the place? I'm quite proud."

I waved the air in front of us. "Fine." She was clearly stalling, but a part of me was curious.

Elizabeth took the lead through the living room. She pointed out a chair she had repaired with Gorilla Glue and the wooden furniture to which she'd applied wood polish. She gestured at the stairway—Quinn had been adamant about carpet on the stairs of all things, to keep someone from falling—and said, "I pulled up the old carpet and even sanded the stairs down and reconditioned the wood."

"I see." The first floor indeed seemed in good shape; she'd painted the baseboards too. "You did it on your free time?"

"Who has free time? No." She half laughed. "I like taking on small house projects. And I figured that it was my way of making up for the rent staying here."

As I walked up the stairs, my mind flew back to the real Sampaguita. Libby had renovated a few things in the house too—she'd painted the bedrooms and changed out light fixtures—though she had never taken me on a tour like Elizabeth was doing now.

In the four years we'd lived apart, I hadn't visited Libby in Sampaguita like I should have. When we'd celebrated holidays, it had been Libby who would take the trip to Annapolis. It had been easier for one person to travel rather than the whole family since most of us lived in the same general DC tristate area.

But because Libby hadn't been a fan of travel, her visits had been limited to the big events.

It hadn't concerned me, the lack of these visits by us or by her. Those pockets of time, I'd thought, were opportunities for growth. To miss each other, to not get upset with one another. Absence made the heart grow fonder and all that.

I had thought we had all the time in the world.

A rush of grief caused me to trip up the stairs.

"You okay?" Elizabeth gazed upward at the dim hallway bulb. "There's really not enough light here. That's one thing that I wish I could have changed."

"I'm fine, thank you. But, you're right," I said, only to choke up when I reached the landing to a hallway that seemed to have been frozen in time.

Framed photos of my parents and Sam hung on the wooden walls. The smell of wood polish was in the air, but underneath it all, I swore, were signs of my family. A mix of scents from the different bath and body products from the hallway bathroom, the faint trace of wood-smoke from the fireplace that remained lit from late fall through early spring.

A dent in the wall from my girls careening through the halls without a care. There'd been a time when I'd thought that the ceiling would come down with how rowdy they'd been.

All those who stereotyped boys as being wild and girls as being meek would have been bowled over by my girls, who had their own unique shrill screams and could wrestle with the best of them.

I smiled at the thought.

"Whoops." Elizabeth shut the door of what had been my and Quinn's bedroom and blocked the entrance. "It's kind of a mess. I'll get my stuff out of there. But look what I did to the hallway bath." She ushered me down a few feet, passing two other furnished bedrooms, to a bright spotlight where the sun's rays were streaming through the window. "See? I repainted in here so it's all white."

I stepped inside, and despite my best effort, I was impressed. "I can't believe that you did all this . . . in three months? How could that be?"

She let out an awkward laugh before the doorbell rang. "Wait right here." She bounded out of my sight.

I followed her down anyway, not wanting to be alone. Enough of the unexpected had happened today, and the house itself felt like it was in the in-between—not quite the real Sampaguita, and not quite this world's.

Elizabeth stood with her back to me at the exit off the kitchen. "Thank you, Mr. Loren. You're so generous."

"It's no trouble," the man answered.

"Mr. Loren?" It was my longtime next-door neighbor and the grandfather of Theo, Amelia's husband.

I rushed at him—belatedly remembering that since Amelia was not my daughter in this world, this meant she actually wasn't married to Theo—only to encounter his cold expression.

With a frown, he said, "Ms. Lakad. I was just dropping something off." His eyes darted to Elizabeth. "Now if you need anything else, please let me know."

"Will do." She looked from him to me and then back again. "Okay, good evening."

With that, Mr. Loren turned to walk away, spearing me with one last glare.

For as many years as we'd known one another, not once had Mr. Loren ever frowned *at* me. If anything, he was wry, sarcastic, and coy. And he'd always called me by my first name.

It hurt, if I was being honest. Curiosity tugged at me at what his real relationship with Celine was like, but I pushed all that away. This encounter wouldn't matter when I was back home, when I could call the real Mr. Loren.

Perhaps I could even speed up the moving-out process. "So, how long will you be before your stuff's out of the house?"

"An hour . . . maybe two." She looked away.

Guilt coursed through me, shortly followed by incredulousness at my guilt. My emotions had already run amok, when my focus was to remain logical. "That's fine. I appreciate it. And I appreciate you taking care of the place. I'm going to reach out to Robin to get this all straightened out."

I avoided her eyes and, on the way up the stairs, grabbed my suitcase as well as Robin's phone number from the front table.

In what had been Mae and MJ's bedroom, I threw myself back on the bed and exhaled. Finally, some quiet, some peace in what had felt like a whirlwind day, a whirlwind life. The room was shrouded in shadows from the branches of the tree outside the window, and if it hadn't been for all the things to be accomplished right this second, I would have fallen asleep.

I dialed up Robin, who picked up after two rings. "Celine? God, are you okay? I just read the update." Her voice trilled like a hummingbird's, and though she was unfamiliar, her casual nature put me immediately at ease.

"The update?" Apparently the day wasn't done with showing me all the things I was unaware of.

"Yes, um . . . you just posted it on your Facebook."

It must have been the update that MJ had been planning to send out. "Oh yes . . . that update. Thank you. I'm feeling . . . okay. But I'm at the house here in Louisburg."

What sounded like a cross between a yelp and a slew of mumbled words came from Robin—though indiscernible, it was probably an explanation of why Libby was living in my home. "We met," I finally said, to cut through her chatter.

"You did? I . . . I apologize. I don't know what state the house is in, but I can put you up in the B and B. They actually just renovated, and it's quite beautiful."

Robin kept going as I considered the option. I could surely just leave. No one was holding me here. And yet, in this world and in my real world, this house was mine, even if only for another week. And of all the places to go, this was the only place that was safe. I knew these walls—this town, even. And while the floors creaked, and there were memories buried in every crevice, never once had it been unsafe.

Call it pride or stubbornness, but it also shouldn't be me who had to go.

"I'm staying, Robin. So can you grab the estate planner and meet me here at the house, as soon as you can? We need to discuss escrow and the estate sale. And you need to facilitate moving my renter back to her home."

"Yes . . . yes, of course. I'll contact Nelson now, and I'll text when we're on our way."

"Thank you."

"Absolutely, I . . ." She paused. "I will take care of everything, I promise."

"Good. I hope so, because I need to get back home."

Chapter Fifteen

Looking up at the white ceiling, I groaned. "Nooooooo."

Was it foolhardy to think that a nap would have transported me back to my life? Yes, but I had been all in anyway. Before I'd opened my eyes, as soon as consciousness had descended, my whole self had been filled with hope that I had finally woken up from my dream.

Alas.

I hefted myself to sitting and set my sock-covered feet on the wood floor. Looking at my watch, I saw I'd napped for about a half hour.

It had been accidental. After hanging up with Robin, I'd decided to remain upstairs for some much-needed peace.

But with all the little noises throughout the house—Elizabeth's footsteps up and down the stairs as she presumably started moving her things, the back door opening and shutting, and the occasional sound of her voice as she spoke on the phone—I hadn't been able to do anything but lie back on the bed and listen. Much like how I used to watch her sleep when she was a baby and take note of how her nose wiggled in her deepest slumber.

Admittedly, though it wasn't my Libby downstairs, all the commotion had acted like white noise, and sleep had taken me before I could protest.

Somewhat rested and clearheaded now, I stood. Robin and Nelson would be here soon. So after I freshened up in the hallway bathroom, I climbed down the stairs.

The first floor was empty except for the heavenly scent of fresh-baked bread. On the kitchen table, ensconced in a small basket covered by a plaid napkin, were several slices of sourdough.

Warmth emanated from the slices, and I pushed on the outer crust. It was incredible—the details of my imagination—that the crust flaked like it normally would. I tore a slice in half and placed it in my mouth.

It was perfect, absolutely perfect: melt-in-your-mouth soft with a crunchy outside, and just the right amount of sourness that was both subtle and divine. Boudin couldn't touch this, because Libby's bread was not pushed through an assembly line. She took time to inspect each loaf; I'd once caught her speaking to her dough. The overall result, each and every time, was bread that brought joy and a smile, much like it was right this second.

While I was here, I should ask for fresh bread every morning, much like when we used to live together in Sampaguita.

Short of taking another bite, I was startled back to the present by the thought, to a house that was not Sampaguita. And I would not be flirting with ideas of staying any longer than I needed to.

I stuffed the rest of the bread in the basket, no longer hungry.

The phone buzzed in my pocket with a text.

Robin:

Nelson and I will be there very soon.

Celine:

Ok

I scrolled through the other messages I had missed in the last couple of hours. They came from unfamiliar names. The previews all showed similar supportive messages such as I'm here if you need me and I hope you're okay, though I swiped past to Sonya's.

I'd promised to check in multiple times a day.

Sonya:

What do you think of the announcement?

She'd screenshotted the message that had been posted on all my social media accounts:

> @CelineLakad: My dearest friends. After much delib-eration with my team and after my own soul-search-ing, I'm sorry to say that I must cancel the rest of the tour. I have to be honest. I have hit a wall, and I'm tired. My mental health isn't, for the lack of better words, healthy, and I'm taking a time-out. My hope is that by doing this first hard step, the next ones will be that much easier. Yours, Celine.

I inhaled, pondering the message. It felt too . . . vulnerable. Sure, I'd shared much of my life in thirteen years, but recently, I'd tried to draw a line between my personal and professional lives. Then again, in this particular case, this message was the least of my worries.

Celine:

It's fine.

Sonya:

Fine meaning?

Celine:

Fine meaning that I have a meeting in twenty minutes with the estate planner to get this place ready.

Sonya:

You're already scheduling meetings. Wasn't your goal out there to rest?

My goal is to get out of here.

Celine:

Yes, and I will. How's everyone?

Sonya:

Good. Rex in the air, heading to LA. The rest of the team will be on their way home for remote work until further notice.

Sonya:

Check in after the estate planner meeting.

Celine:

Ok.

A knock sounded on the back door. Elizabeth stood on the stoop and waved hesitantly. "Hi, sorry. I still have a couple more loads to bring back to the house. Do you mind if I keep this door propped open?"

"Sure." And because it seemed like the right thing to do, I added, "Thanks for leaving a few slices of bread."

"You're welcome. My starter is a beast. She's fairly new, only a couple of years old, and I named her Wilhelmina. She seems to like the kitchen. Your kitchen, I mean. She doubles just like that." She snapped her fingers, her cheeks reddening. "Sorry, just bread-making talk. I'm kind of a nerd about it."

In any normal conversation, that would have been my cue to comment on her bread, but my tongue tied at my response. Not because I didn't know what to say but because there was too much trying to make its way through.

That I had been a bread-making nerd too. That it had been me who'd taught her how to mix up her first starter, though her bread making, much like her piano skills, had blown past mine in record time. And that I wanted to hear every little thing about bread making that she would care to share.

But this wasn't a normal conversation.

At my silence, she gestured up the stairs, and her footsteps bounded up and above me. Seconds later, she came down with her sheets folded against her chest. Avoiding my eyes, she went out the door and down the path to the second house.

I was being cold, but it was necessary.

Her figure disappeared behind a bank of trees, where a small structure had been built by the previous owner, and though in my real life we used it for storage, here it was apparently another home.

I went to the window and spotted Elizabeth's shadow against the second home's bright indoor light. My gaze traveled across the acreage, across the rolling grass that dipped below my line of sight. My heart swelled in my chest; the backyard was magnificent. My view unfocused for a beat, and I saw my children running past with balloons during a birthday party, laughing. A piñata hung on a nearby apple tree, and the charcoal grill piped a savory, mouthwatering scent.

It had been easy to make the decision to move to Annapolis when Quinn had been offered his coaching job. As beautiful as Sampaguita was, the upkeep had been overwhelming for the lack of time we'd had, though it wasn't that I'd loved it any less.

When Libby had refused to move with us, the house had become a point of contention.

It doesn't make sense for you to move, Mom. Dad's traveling half the year with the team. At least we'll keep each other company here, she'd said the night Quinn had come home with the head-coach opportunity.

I don't know, Libby. I'd looked around, at the kitchen that begged to be updated, and at the backyard that would need professional landscaping if Quinn wasn't around to do it. *I'm looking forward to having something small and modern. I feel like this is the next phase of our life.*

Libby had blown out a breath, disbelieving. *You mean the next phase of work. It's always new, better, bigger, further.*

I'd chosen not to engage on that point. Libby, of all my girls, had not been impressed with Celine Lakad Coaching. She'd been most open when we had been one on one, when we'd gardened and cooked together. When we had taken grocery trips. But I'd never questioned why she'd resisted the business, eager to keep the peace.

Living with adult children was tricky. And though Sampaguita had been a spacious house, it had never been quite big enough for me to ignore Libby when she had been upset with me. Which had been often.

Well, you're going to love Annapolis. The city's beautiful, historic. There's so much to do. The Chesapeake Bay's a stone's throw, I'd pushed on.

I mean, the river is right down the street here too, Mom. Anyway, I'm not moving with you.

W-what? I'd glanced at Quinn, whose mouth had been agape. I hadn't considered, not even for a second, that she wouldn't move with us. *You're only nineteen.*

Old enough to know where home is. And this is home. She'd leveled me and Quinn with a steady gaze. *This is where I belong.*

Outside, a bird darted across my vision, dashing the scene away. It had been the first of similar situations in the coming months when I'd begged Libby to come to live with us. The fact that she'd continued to decline had been like arrows to the heart and the ego. I'd missed her presence and questioned what exactly about Annapolis, or me, she had been rejecting.

Now, I found myself standing next to the piano and wiped a hand against the top reflexively, halting next to a book opened faceup. A quick glance at the title in the upper-right margin stole my breath.

Little Women.

The last of my daydreaming fizzled away, and what replaced it was a pounding heart and a slew of questions. I stepped back, conjuring the scent of singed leather.

Where had that book come from? It hadn't been on the piano earlier today.

Or had it been?

I took one dainty step toward it. Without touching, I inspected the edge of the hardcover, and sure enough, it was made of leather.

It couldn't be the same book I'd thrown into the fire, because there had been no funeral reception—there had been no funeral.

So it's not real, I reminded myself.

Then what was the point? What did the book want? What did any of this mean? Message received—my life would have turned out differently had I not gotten into Quinn's truck—but there had to have been more to all this than showing me that lesson.

"Just stop." I couldn't allow myself to fall into a spiral of questions. This wasn't useful, this examination of why I was here, when my present, my real family, was just on the other side of this task I had to do, which was the estate sale.

Everything else was a distraction.

I shut the book and stuffed it into the nearest bookshelf.

The rumble of a car's motor took me from my thoughts, and I went to the front door, opening it in time for two people to come up the walk: A petite Asian woman with a short bob, Robin, who, in my real life, was the property manager Quinn and I had hired to watch Sampaguita after Libby had died. And then Nelson, I presumed—a grandfatherly Black man with gray hair and a slower gait. Both had paperwork tucked under their arms and carried hesitant expressions on their faces. After a round of handshakes, they stepped inside and took their seats in the living room.

Robin wrung her hands in her lap. "I know that must have been a surprise to find out that Elizabeth was staying here. We had issues with the second home, but you'd been adamant about not investing more into the house since you were going to sell it as is."

That didn't sound like me at all. "I would never have said that. I would have done everything to fix that second house."

"I have all of our correspondence that shows your instructions." Her words came out methodical and careful. "And Elizabeth was perfectly fine with this arrangement, until the house sold. I apologize you had to field all those phone calls."

"Well, I want whatever is broken to be fixed. I don't care how much it costs. I asked her to move out."

"Yes, of course. I'll call someone as soon as we're done here."

"Now what of these plans for the estate sale? Can I be updated on that?"

Nelson cleared his throat and pushed up his glasses. "We've got a day of inventory and three estate sale days. On the last day, we'll donate what's left over."

"Then, that afternoon, I'll grab the keys from you, and that is that," Robin added. "You're scot-free."

"Can we speed up the timeline?"

Nelson shook his head. "At this point, no, since I have the crews scheduled out."

Exhaling slowly, I nodded—it sounded straightforward enough. Less than a week of focus, and then home. This place would simply be a faraway memory. *Scot-free.* "Okay. I can help with the inventory."

"Great," Nelson said. "We've already done quite a bit of advertising in town and online marketplaces, and there's interest."

"Everyone is super keen to come to Celine Lakad's home," Robin commented.

We all turned to the sound of Elizabeth stepping in. She halted at the threshold. "I just wanted to say I'm done."

"Elizabeth, I'll be sending over someone tonight for the furnace and the oven," Robin stated.

"Good." She brightened, dragging her gaze among us, and said, "All right, then. I'll see you all . . . around."

Once Elizabeth was down the path, Nelson said, "She's the best baker around. Bread, pastries. Not cake, though. Cakes, you'd have to go to Angelica's."

Robin hummed. "Elizabeth can do a lot with a home and a countertop oven. Not only is she out there at the farmers' market every week, but she takes special orders. She's quite ambitious, even if she wants to stay small."

"That's . . . neat." We were veering off topic, and talking about Elizabeth was conjuring up nausea in my belly.

How had I allowed that chasm to grow between Libby and me so I didn't get the chance to support her, or guide her, when I was a coach myself? I'd excused our long stretches of minimal communication, knowing that she'd been keeping in touch with Quinn, with her sisters.

I shifted in my seat. My clothes felt too tight; it was too hot in the house. Every time Libby came to mind, which included when Elizabeth was around, I wanted to come out of my skin. I'd worked so hard to slough off this weight of guilt. My entire business in the last two years had been dedicated to moving on.

But every minute in this experience was setting me back.

Robin smiled at me expectantly, and it brought me back from my thoughts. "Why don't I come by to grab you tomorrow for the farmers' market?" she asked. "Or you can take a bicycle on the bike path. The market has grown since you left here a couple of years ago. Everyone goes."

"That's right," Nelson added. "Even Coach Q. swings by and picks up doughnuts from Lou Donuts for the staff."

I stuttered on the next word. "Quinn?"

"The one and only."

My mind swirled with wonder. How and when had Quinn made it to Louisburg, and had our paths crossed? Then again, did I want to know? Enough surprises and twists had come my way since this morning, and riding this trip to the estate sale as far under the radar as possible was paramount.

The corners of Robin's lips twitched. "I can drop off my bike later on today along with some dinner, so you don't have to worry about heading out tonight. It's the least I could do, for understanding. And for being patient. Plus, it's supposed to be gorgeous this coming week. Spring's blooming; it's such a magical season."

Laughter bubbled through me. The only kind of magic I wanted was a good night's sleep. In fact . . . "Could you bring over a bottle of wine too. I'd like to enjoy this magical spring with a glass of it tonight."

Robin beamed. "Will do."

Chapter Sixteen

Robin came by as promised a mere hour after our meeting to drop off her bicycle, a steaming to-go container of chicken alfredo, and a beautiful bottle of prosecco. That night, I ate my first meal in Louisburg, alone.

"You're forgiven, Robin," I said to the empty kitchen chair across from me and tipped the bottle of wine to my lips. Everything was delicious. The food, the wine, and the empty room. My extroverted nature had been put to the test today, and my plan for the rest of the night was to revel in my solitude.

Because today . . . today had been weird. And I hadn't had time to process. Like, I was back in my old kitchen. And no one was who they were supposed to be.

Holy shit.

A burp bubble climbed up my throat, and it erupted from me like a hot gust of air from a geyser, echoing into the empty room. I slammed my hand against my mouth and giggled.

"Need noise. Oh, music!" Earlier today, I'd realized that there were no televisions in this house. How had Libby—excuse me, *Elizabeth*—lived here for so long without a TV?

So, my phone was my only option for any kind of noise. But my thumbs were clumsy. The screen was too small, and I kept going from one app to another—they all looked the same to me—and then the phone rang. Not on my end, but on someone else's end. I pressed at the screen frantically. I didn't know who half my contacts were, and I was supposed to be *resting*. "Shoot."

Finally, and thank God, the phone hung up. I found and pressed on the music app.

I toggled to an eighties playlist—at least I still had good music taste in this world—and it filtered through the phone speaker. "Yes. Perfect. Just perfect."

I stood and swayed to the beat, the phone in one hand, the bottle in the other. How long ago had it been since I'd just let loose?

Not since forever. Not since Libby had died. Not since I hadn't been able to help her or save her, or be the mother I should have been. Not since I'd utterly failed.

It wasn't supposed to be this way. Mothers weren't supposed to outlive their children. I was supposed to go first. What was the point of me, if I couldn't keep my daughter alive?

Tears sprang to my eyelids, but I swiped them away roughly. "No no no. No crying."

There would be no crying, no feeling sorry for myself. I didn't have a right to cry when I could have done something about it.

"I am fucking Celine Lakad-Frasier, and I need to take a fucking step up. I'm gonna get rid of every single thing in this damn house. Don't worry; I'm coming home, babies." With the faces of Quinn and my girls—my real daughters—in mind, I lifted the bottle high up in the air, because it only made sense to do a toast.

But when I tipped the bottle up to my lips, it was empty. When I turned the bottle over, not a drop leaked out. *Ruh-roh.*

I needed more . . . something. I wanted maximum shut-eye and fast. Because now that I was thinking about my family, I missed the hell out of them. And I didn't want to think about that, or the fact that someone who looked like my dead daughter was literally in my backyard.

"Dead daughter." I choked on the words, and nausea gurgled in my belly. This was wrong. All wrong.

I spun around in the kitchen, stumbling, then steadying myself to look for another bottle of wine, or liquor, or something, but the only thing out was the leftover pasta alfredo.

"It's your fault, pasta. You're foiling my plans." It had absorbed the little amount of alcohol this bottle of prosecco had held.

I tiptoed around the kitchen, my playlist still in the background. If I was a bottle of alcohol, where would I be?

I checked the refrigerator—nope. The cupboards—nope. The pantry—nope. Tapping my chin, I scanned the room, slowly this time, ignoring the hazy outline of my vision, then spotted one cupboard that had been missed.

As I pushed a chair up to the refrigerator, Sonya's voice was in my ear. *Don't do anything reckless* had been one of the things she'd said before I'd left Boston. Climbing a chair wasn't reckless, was it?

No matter—my body got up on its own. Reaching up to open the cupboard, I was rewarded by a bottle filled with amber liquid. Bourbon.

"Eureka!"

I didn't have to go far. I simply sat on the chair, and twisted the cap. The pungent smell wafted to my nostrils, and heat invaded them. My mouth watered but not in a good way.

But this magic bottle was my key to rest. I thought I'd been tired before. This . . . this was exhaustion.

I tipped the bottle up to my lips, pinched my nose with the fingers of my other hand, and, with my eyes shut, took a swig.

Chapter Seventeen

My vision focused on the popcorn ceiling above me.

"Dammit." Groaning, I pushed myself up to my elbows, and then to sitting. The sun was menacing and bright through the back windows, causing me to squint. My tongue was thick and dry from dehydration, my breath disgusting, my eyes sticky from sleep and tears. Pressing my fingers against my eyelids, I steadied my breathing, which had gone erratic.

Because I was still here.

Tears ran down my face; snot dripped from my nose. I swiped the backs of my hands against my cheeks, and my mascara and eyeliner smeared against my skin.

Had I believed that one deep sleep would take me back? Not really, but a tiny part of me wished it had. Inside, I knew my going back had everything to do with this house, but damn, did I miss my family.

Why couldn't this be like any other story? In every book and movie, and even in fairy tales, everything went back to normal once the lesson of the story had been learned, once the theme had played out in its entirety.

I took the thin blanket that was draped across my lap and dabbed my face with it. The fabric was cool against my cheeks, and it allowed me a breath. When my heart rate finally slowed, I felt the cogs of my brain crank on.

I could do only the first step, right? And at the moment, it was to get up.

With a ragged breath, I pressed my entire face against the blanket to mop up the mess of last night, the events of which I didn't quite remember. If Sonya were here, she would simultaneously laugh at my pathetic hungover state and be horrified that a perfectly good blanket had been ruined by my makeup.

Blanket? I lifted my face from the sheet, now riddled with yesterday's foundation, mascara, and lipstick. I didn't remember grabbing a blanket, or lying down on the couch.

Then, my eyes traveled to my phone, sitting faceup on the coffee table, next to a glass of water and a bottle of Tylenol. Two slices of bread were nestled in a small basket, which tacked down a note with a phone number with the scribbled message:

Text when you're up
—E

Elizabeth.

When was she here, and how did she get in? Then, yesterday's chain of events replayed in my head, and I realized that she hadn't returned her key.

Anger raged through me at her intrusion. I'd told her to leave. The audacity to enter my home without permission—it was unacceptable.

She would get more than a text; I would take those keys from her in person.

Robin's words returned to me: *The market has grown since you left here a couple of years ago. Everyone goes.*

Not only was Elizabeth going to be at the farmers' market, but perhaps Quinn would be too. Maybe seeing him would keep me focused, would help me work faster.

The thought boosted me off the couch, into the shower, and then into casual clothing. After, as I picked up the shameful evidence of last night, I noted that this house had Sampaguita's quirks. That the water pressure was lackluster, and that certain parts of the floors creaked. And if the kitchen door was open and one was sitting at the kitchen table, there was a perfect view right to the front door, which had been handy when keeping track of four children, especially with my escape artist, Amelia.

Small bits of comfort. I'd associated more bitter than sweet memories with Sampaguita—more of Libby and her death than of our good times as a family.

When I finally stepped outside, the May air had a chill—I noted it was unlike the heat and humidity in my awake life—but the sun was high. Flower buds had begun to burst through the bushes around the house, and though there was the occasional gust of cold wind, the sun's warmth won out, beaming down upon my face.

It felt so real, this world's sun, that after walking the bike to the path, I shut my eyes to bask in it for a moment. My headache had dulled from the Tylenol, but a tinge of hangover nausea lingered in my belly even after the two pieces of bread, and the fresh air was a kind of salve.

Doubt descended: Maybe it wasn't a good idea to seek out Elizabeth. This was the opposite of what my goal had been, and that was to avoid her. I could very well wait for Elizabeth to get back from the farmers' market to grab my keys, or text her, as she'd suggested.

Then again, wasn't it better to speak to her out in public, to prevent our conversation from becoming intimate?

And then there was Quinn . . .

Also, I needed food.

So, after a couple of deep breaths, I straddled the cruiser. It was an older bicycle—it had seen better days, from the looks of its dents, but was equipped with a Nantucket-style basket in the back.

It had been years since I'd ridden a bicycle, and the saying was true—the knowledge of it returned after a couple of starts and stops. Soon, my back straightened with confidence, and I was on my way.

But with every block that passed, my senses heightened. Perhaps it was from the lingering effects of the alcohol that the birds' chirps took on an echoing quality. The rumble of the cars driving by, the occasional shout of a child from somewhere, caused me to gasp and jerk the handlebar.

This world was in HD, in stereo surround sound. Or was life always this *in your face*?

This is not the real world.

Right. It wasn't. I had to ignore it and focus on pedaling.

Main Street greeted me with the farmers' market sign at a closed-off intersection. Gobs of people came and went with packages and bags in their hands. White tents lined the street, their pointed tops meeting the lowest branches of trees. The scent of fried goods lingered in the air.

The market was just as I'd remembered it—I had to constrain the nostalgia roaring through me.

It would've been about this time that my girls would have taken off from my sides, dark hair cascading behind them, armed with their allowances, leaving me in the dust. They'd have their pick of sweets and treats. A chocolate bar, a freshly made cinnamon roll. Sweet, crispy, and warm kettle corn. A palm-size shiny apple. I'd never bothered checking what they'd bought, so comfortable in what was being sold, so at ease with them among our neighbors.

My focus when the kids were little had been to be the best mother, which had meant making sure they had healthy food on the table. That we stuck to the correct bedtimes. Organic or GMO? When did we get them out of their booster seats? Were sleepovers toxic?

Those years had been easy for me; yes, I'd been tired, but my instincts had usually been correct. But that phase of mothering was so different than the kind of mothering that was needed when the girls became young adults and fully fledged adults. The skill set for that kind of mothering was something I'd had to learn.

One would think that working with the public, with other mothers, and the sheer amount of coaching would make me a natural. But it was quite the opposite. My tendency had been to instruct my girls as I'd used to, even as they had become adults. Mae, MJ, and Amelia had been flexible, and would lovingly call me a nag, but Libby'd pushed back. She'd asked the hard questions about everything. Despite her introversion, she'd fought for her way of approaching life. When I'd started my career when she was in late middle school, she'd questioned the time I'd spent with other people. She'd refused guidance regarding going to college. And true to her personality, she hadn't moved with us to Annapolis.

I had to let go of that resentment—I knew that—but being in this faux world wasn't helping the cause.

But walking my bike through market-goers, in search of Elizabeth's booth and Quinn's face amid the crowd, I soon got lost in the sights and sounds around me, as if I was still a little girl myself. Unlike my ride into town, this HD experience was less assaulting. My nose detected where the homemade tea tree oil soap ended and where the sweet smell of the doughnut shop began. My ears picked up the crinkle of someone wrapping up a bouquet of flowers and the hollow slap of a palm on melon. I witnessed a vendor's concentration in the way he bit his lip as he counted out change, a mother's open-mouthed surprise in finding her child under a picnic table.

"Celine!"

I halted at the sound of my name, and seconds later was flanked by two women who threw their arms around me. They had matching polo shirts with embroidered logos at the top: Louisburg Flowers. Above the logos were their names, with the dirty-blonde, blue-eyed, fair-skinned woman as Deb and the brown-haired, dark-skinned woman as Lena.

As they spoke, familiarity descended. They had been at Libby's funeral reception, at the piano. Not knowing what their impression was of me, I kept a neutral smile. "Hi, Lena. Deb."

"We had no idea you'd be back in town. My goodness, it's been a couple of years." Deb grabbed ahold of the bike's handlebar, the move so sudden that I jerked the bike back.

Deb's eyes widened, and she hiked a thumb toward a tent. "I was just . . . going to bring it under the tent while you shopped. Like we always do."

"Right." Heart calming, I tilted the bike her way. "Sorry."

"You're among friends. You can let go."

I blew out a laugh; if she only knew that letting go was just one thing I'd had to do the last day and a half.

Deb walked the bike to the shop's tent, then kicked out the stand.

"Thank you," I said to Lena.

"No problem. This way you can take your time. So? What brings you back?"

"I . . . decided to take a break from the tour."

Her expression softened, and she glanced at Deb, who'd just returned. She plucked a leaf out of her hair. "I thought I heard a rumor about that. Well, you did the right thing by coming home."

"Because even if you moved, this is home still." Lena nodded. "And perfect timing, too, for the May Day social."

This I remembered. The May Day social was a private event usually held in someone's home. It had been another reason for select neighbors to get together for drinks and appetizers, and for the kids to dance around the maypole.

It had also been a runway for spring fashion and gossip, or so I'd heard.

I'd never received an invitation—not until my first book had been published, and then the invites for town events had come in droves. Though, out of pride and stubbornness, I'd sent regrets. Instead, the family would make a day of it, leaving town for Tallulah's Tulips so as not to trigger my FOMO (because admittedly, it came around with a force). Being around those glorious blooms, picking our bouquets, and then splurging on ice cream had become a day to look forward to.

"Do you think?" Lena waggled her eyebrows at Deb.

Deb brightened, turning her face to me. "You should come, Celine."

"Who, me?" Betrayed by my aforementioned FOMO, my voice squeaked with delight. Because it did *still* make me curious what went on during the event.

"Yes. I mean, you went every year, and I bet the only reason why you didn't get an invite was because the committee didn't know you were around. Just come with us. Everyone will be thrilled."

At the mention of *everyone*, my logic entered the chat with a ruler in her hand, reminding me that this all wasn't real and the most sensible thing to do was avoid strangers. It would be like strolling into a lion's den with a tray of raw meat, when my efforts should be spent doing inventory of the house to get out of it. "Oh, I don't know. I've got so many things to do with the estate sale."

"Right, the estate sale! We were planning on going." Deb glanced at Lena with an expectant smile. "And we can help! We can work on the house with you, to free you up so you can come to the social. How about it?" Her palms were pressed together as if in prayer. "You can't clean all day and night."

Grasping for straws, I looked away. Last night, in fact, had been a bust. I'd been lonely and pathetic drinking all by myself, and then having to be put to bed, by Elizabeth of all people. . . my cheeks burned at the thought of it. Talking to Deb and Lena, even if they were strangers, had eased my mood. But giving in to this charade was bad. Bad for my psyche. It needed to think I wanted out so it would have no choice but to get there—a basic rule of manifestation. "I appreciate the invite, but . . . no."

"Phooey." Deb frowned, backing up as a family gathered around their tent. "But I'm not giving up."

"So, what are you shopping for today?" Lena asked.

"Food. I need lunch and dinner I can stick in the refrigerator. And, I'm looking for Elizabeth."

She tapped a finger against her chin. "Some new businesses popped up the last couple of years . . . three booths to the left, the Jensens have every wrap you can think of, and they're so delicious. You can have that for lunch, and Poe's Farms has these fantastic salads. You can grab that for dinner and pick up some chicken? The market's grown so much. And oh, Elizabeth's booth is now catty corner, on the left. Though, with the bonus housing, I'd expect a discount . . . I'm just saying."

I kept my expression even and pleasant to cover up my swirl of curiosity. These ladies seemed to know everything about everyone, and temptation tugged at me to ask about Quinn. But I didn't want to misstep. They surely would be able to detect that there was something different with me.

Lena continued on, "Elizabeth's great. We love her, though I do worry that her next place won't be as nice as yours. Who am I kidding—it's a crap hole. Anyway, oh"—she pointed out another booth—"fresh lemonade. That's another addition this year."

As Lena pointed out people and updated me on their statuses, it became clear that the town I'd left in my real life was still in some ways the same as this version. My head swam with information, though one thing stuck out, and that was Lena's comment about Elizabeth's next home.

But that wasn't any of my business, right? This all wasn't real. And moving was something everyone had to face at a point in their life. Military and basketball-coach life had subjected us to several moves before we'd settled down in Louisburg.

And I'm tired. I'm tired of waiting.

Irritation wiggled into my mood as Quinn's words popped back into my head. How much had I waited for him in the last thirty-plus years? From the macro level of him finally getting his dream coaching job, to the micro level, where I'd had to miss him every day he was physically away from us.

And now to suggest that I wasn't present emotionally?

Of course I'd made a life for myself in the interim. What else was a person, a woman, a wife, to do in their wait, but to surround themselves with things they were passionate about? And in my case, it was helping people; it was networking and communicating with others. It was inspiring them with things I'd learned along the way. And that passion had grown into a business. God forbid I asked for him—for everyone, including my children—to support me.

Damned if I do. Damned if I don't.

Lena threw her head back and laughed, bringing me back to the present, and I imitated the gesture, because it was either that or cry. For despite the anger I had over the intervention, I would take all that over this confusing dream world.

A sob threatened to break through my fake laugh, so I said, "I should go and do my thing. You know how it is."

"Sigh. I guess I have to help Deb. If not, I'll be in the doghouse tonight." Lena gritted her teeth in jest. "How about me and Deb come by this evening to help with the house?"

"You really don't have to."

"We said it, so we meant it. And we can bring some fresh flowers to brighten it up for when people come for the estate sale."

I had a feeling that the two would show up at the house whether or not I conceded. "All right, fine."

Lena beamed, rubbing her hands together. "Great! I've got the perfect idea for an arrangement."

After telling them when I would be returning for the bicycle, I walked deeper into the farmers' market, grounding myself in the sights and sounds. Elizabeth had stepped away from her booth, so I did my food shopping first. Soon I had a reusable bag of salad and fruit in one hand and a plum to snack on in the other. In the serenity around me, I searched for Quinn above the heads of people. Soon, my heart rate slowed.

I could get used to this pace, the meandering, the short side conversations, and the nontransactional smiles.

Quite the contrast to the hustle and bustle of the airport, to being shuttled through an event space in order to lessen distraction, to keeping to a schedule planned out to the quarter hour. To the sheer amount of emails that needed my attention.

Sometimes work had been so busy that I hadn't stepped out of my house unless it had been for an errand. Not that those things were all negative. Work fueled me. Work gave me purpose. It saved me from my low moments—had I not had work when Libby had died, who knew how else I would have coped?

But everything in this dream, in this . . . whatever this was . . . was all beautiful.

A woman pushing a stroller went past, and the toddler—he couldn't have been older than two—caught my eye. He smiled open mouthed and gleefully giggled, and he poked his head to the side so we could make eye contact. I turned, waving, captivated, seized by the thought of my own granddaughters when they had been that young a mere few years ago.

But I was jostled forward in a soft collision, and I dropped my bag of food. "Whoa."

"Crap. I'm so sorry. I wasn't looking," said a man, hands steadying me by the waist.

My lungs ceased expanding—that voice was as familiar to me as my own. Out of instinct, my body softened in his hold. "It's fine. I'm good."

"No freaking way. Celine?"

Straightening at his frigid tone, I turned and faced my husband, who was wearing flannel.

Flannel.

Quinn hadn't worn flannel since his younger years, in our twenties. These days he wore polo shirts. Oxford shirts with quirky ties. Khakis with sweaters of the schools he represented. Coachwear, basically.

And when my eyes traveled up to his face, I encountered a different version of Quinn. One who was still wearing glasses—Quinn had had vision-correction surgery years ago—was clean shaven, and had sideburns.

Maybe it had been too long, or perhaps this new world had reactivated my libido, because this look? It was . . . sexy in this rugged way. This had been Quinn's fit as a soldier, minus the sideburns, per army regulation. Was it okay to feel this way about my sort-of husband when my real one and I were in a fight?

No matter, because to see him was pure relief. "I'm so happy you're here. I wasn't sure if you would be." I threw my arms around his neck and was hit with an unfamiliar scent—the cologne was more musk than citrus. He smelled all wrong, but I didn't care. My best friend, the man I loved, was in my arms, and in this world, he'd never uttered that ultimatum. In this world, the tragedy of losing Libby wasn't between us.

With him here, it was all going to be fine.

Quinn, however, didn't bend down to reciprocate. He didn't grab me by the waist to lift me up into a hug—and yes, even during our tough times, he'd still swept me off my feet, literally. It had been a consequence of our differences in height.

His voice was firm. "Stop this. Let go."

Chapter Eighteen

"But you feel so good," I whispered into his neck. Also, his cologne was growing on me by the second. "And you smell so good too."

Every part of me knew that this wasn't my Quinn. But he'd been my person for three decades, my love and trust in him so deep that in my hug, I channeled the apology I wished I'd said in my real world.

Finally, his hands settled on my waist. My heart leapt at the strength of his hold.

Then, in one firm push downward, he peeled me off him. The cold air between us sucked the breath out of my lungs, and I was met with disdain in his eyes. "This is inappropriate." His voice was like gravel, sharp and unsteady. Glancing around us, as if worried we were being watched, he added, "What are you doing back in town?"

Taken aback, I scrambled for my explanation. "The stuff in our . . . I mean, the house . . . it sold. I'm here for the estate sale."

"Ah." His eyebrows lifted for a beat. "Cutting the last of the ties."

Ouch. A pain lanced through my heart. Though it was unclear what he was referring to, my mind went straight to Libby and Sampaguita. To the implication that I would be callous enough to just let go of them, even if letting go of this world's Sampaguita would bring me back home—hopefully.

In my silence, he took two steps forward. "Well . . . I've got to get going." It was only then I noticed that he was holding a box. "Doughnuts for the staff."

"I . . . I heard you were coaching for the high school."

"I've been coaching at the high school for years."

"Right. I . . ."

"I've gotta go. It was . . . interesting seeing you." Quinn brushed past me before I could respond. By the time I turned, he was already darting across the street, shoulders slumped in the chill.

"Quinn?" I croaked out a plea. Watching his back disappear down the street jump-started my fight mechanism. I didn't want to let him out of my sight. Quinn was my person, no matter the drama he'd had with this Celine or our intervention in real life.

Deb and Lena were ready for me when I reached the tent. Deb was holding my bicycle up, and Lena helped me pack the food into the basket.

They'd been watching. What more did they know?

Then again, getting to Quinn superseded my curiosity.

"Thank you." My voice came out as a screech.

"No worries. Go. We'll see you tonight."

I pedaled the cruiser shakily toward the high school, spotting Quinn's flannel shirt and distinctive gait as he climbed up the hill. I knew that march anywhere. In uniform, coming down a parade field after a deployment. His walk up the driveway after a day's work. How he stalked the baseline like a caged animal during a game. Quinn had long, fervent strides, exactly as he was, serious and intentional.

His ambition, his optimism, his calling to coach and help people. He loved me, despite that ultimatum.

I loved him, though I should have told him more often. Especially at the intervention.

"Quinn!" I screamed, finally, in between ragged, regretful breaths from my awful bicycling skills.

I should have acknowledged his emotions in Boston.

I should have agreed to visiting Sampaguita.

He turned left at the next block, so I sped up and careened around the corner, spotting the redbrick sign of the high school parking lot.

To my surprise, he slipped into an alleyway.

There was a stream of light in between the two homes where Quinn was pacing when I braked. After stepping off the bike and leaning it on its stand on the sidewalk, I followed him in. Equal parts grateful that he'd stopped and frustrated that it had taken me chasing him across half the town, I could barely catch my breath.

"What are you doing carrying on like that?" He stuffed a hand in his pocket, though his face was animated, like he was trying to contain himself.

But he was unsuccessful; he was red faced, blustery. Upset . . . affected.

"You were the one who walked away . . . ran, really." I swallowed a breath, though my antennae shot straight up. There was something else going on between this Quinn and me. And while it still was odd to think of me as someone else, this fact was intriguing, and I wanted to know more. "I wasn't done talking—"

"Let me guess. You're home a few days, and you missed me. You want to hang out. But see, I know how this ends. Just when things'll start to get somewhere, you'll decide that this is all too much, and it's time for you to go back to Rex. Well, I'm done with that. I'm done being second."

My body reared back at his words, and I covered my mouth with a hand. "We were something?"

He dug a hand through his hair as frustration radiated off him. "Didn't you think we were?" He waved the air in front of him. "Never mind. I can't do this with you. I'm simply appalled that you think things between us are good, enough that you can just hug me like it's any old day. Well, we're not going to do that. We've given this town enough fodder."

Words escaped me for a beat. Through his contorted expression, it descended once more that in this life, I kept people at arm's length. But . . . "I chose Rex."

How had we gotten here if I'd been with Rex for thirty-seven years, according to Sonya, and it was Rex who I'd awoken to yesterday morning? The domino effect of not going on that road trip with Quinn was just starting to take shape. The repercussions of that choice weren't just about me being unmarried and childless, but how it affected the choices of other people.

"Yeah, no need to rub it in," he snapped back.

"I'm . . . sorry," I said, knowing it didn't encompass the magnitude of my regret. Because at the heart of it, I didn't know this world's Celine and what she'd done. "I . . . I must have been horrible."

"You say that so empathetically." He snorted sardonically. "And look, guilt's not going to work on me this time either. I've got to go. I'm late, and just . . . don't follow me. Let's try to stay out of each other's way, okay? This is a small town, but there's enough room that if you see me, just pretend that you didn't."

"You don't mean that. We've got to talk about this."

"You made it perfectly clear when you left that what I was offering you wasn't enough."

"That wasn't me." As the words came out of my mouth, I knew it was a poor excuse. It was the truth, but poor nonetheless. But making up with Quinn was a nonnegotiable. During the intervention, I hadn't listened to him, acknowledged him. This time needed to be different. "And I'm sorry, and I love you."

"No. We're not going to do this." He scoffed. "Let me make this memo clear. I don't want to speak to you. Please, leave me alone."

Then, he strode out the alleyway, leaving me stunned and in silence.

The pain came seconds later, like the accidental grab of a hot pan out of the oven without a mitt. It seared through my skin, into muscle, into bone.

What was imprinted, as I stepped out into the sun, were some undeniable facts.

In this world, I had not gone on that road trip with Quinn.

Rex and I had stayed together, but I'd sought Quinn anyway, and lost him.

And I stood to lose Quinn in my real world too.

"Watch it!" A shout, followed by a trilling bell and the screeching tires of a bicycle, startled me out of my thoughts, and I jumped back with a yelp.

Elizabeth skidded to a stop. She wore a long flowing dress and sandals. Her chest rose and fell, hands white-knuckling the handlebars. "Crap! I almost got you."

"Yeah, you did. You scared the living daylights out of me!" My tone came out more biting than I'd intended, but dealing with Quinn moments before had boggled my thoughts. Now, having to face this woman who looked like my daughter was a reminder that neither world was perfect, or even close to it.

Her eyebrows lifted, almost daring. "Sorry. I mean, you did just wander out without looking both ways. You were so intent on watching Quinn walk up the street. Coming from the same alley, to boot."

I peered at her. Her tone was suspicious. And, belatedly, I remembered that I had a bone, or a key, to pick with her. "And you just *happened* to show up. Like last night, when you somehow entered my home without permission."

"If you're implying that I'm following you around, trust me—that's far from the truth. I was making a bread delivery, to Anne Frasier." She spoke thin lipped, the way Libby used to when she was unhappy with me. "And for your information, the only reason why I walked into your house last night was because you passed out at the kitchen table. Before you say anything . . . there are no blinds or curtains against those back windows, and it wasn't hard to see you with all the lights on. Excuse me for trying to help you out, and for making sure you were alive. I thought it would have been a better wake-up on the couch." She jerked her bicycle so the front wheels faced away from me.

My face flushed from shame, from the image of me splayed out across the kitchen table in a drunken stupor. Very rarely had my girls seen me in that state. I drank, yes, and when they'd all come of age, we'd drunk together. And while Elizabeth wasn't anyone I needed to impress or mentor or guide, the fact that she'd seen me so bad off . . .

I couldn't let anyone see me as a hot mess.

But Elizabeth helping had been thoughtful, and something I'd have done myself if the situation had been reversed. My current indignation slipped.

"Well . . . thanks," was all I could say, mortified at this whole situation. "But I want my key back."

"You're welcome, and I'll be more than happy to hand it back when I get home this afternoon." She straddled the bicycle, hitching a foot up. Her back was to me, and she turned around in her seat. "But could I share a little observation?"

"About what?"

"About Quinn."

My eyes widened, and I crossed my arms. "Okay?"

"He comes by once a week and buys the same exact bread—sourdough baguette. He never switches it up. But he buys all kinds of specialty jams and spreads and isn't afraid to try new flavors and textures. So long as the bread is the same. Know what I mean?"

"Not really." My mind scrambled for purchase on what to focus on: Quinn hating me, what our relationship was about, or how to feel about Elizabeth advising me. All the while resisting this urge to spend more time with her.

She shrugged. "That he never does give up what he knows he loves. So don't give up on him."

Startled, I raised a hand, to stop her from pedaling off. "What do *you* know about me and Quinn?"

"Just what everyone knows."

Everyone? "And that's . . . ?"

"That you both are . . . complicated. But I've got to go. I'll be by with your key later." Then, without another word, she pedaled off, leaving me to my thoughts and another question in the bucketful I'd accumulated since waking up here: Who was I in this world?

Chapter Nineteen

I decided to start my decluttering in the attic after returning from the farmers' market.

Frozen at the threshold, I scanned the room, which was filled with boxes and containers. Up above, the light fixture flickered a dim yellow; the room was stuffy and dark, with the boxes blocking the sunlight from coming in through the windows.

Nervous energy brimmed from my pores. The memories this room held were like the journals I had loyally written in before my writing had become public, stacked and tied together and hidden in my sturdiest cabinet. They were precious, sacred, and of an innocent time.

Sampaguita's attic had been the girls' practice stage for whatever production they'd coordinated. With enough actors for a play—and, in Quinn's eyes, for a three-person pickup team with a fourth in rotation—my girls had created plots and conflicts and acted out stories. There'd been an old trunk that had held all their tangled, wrinkled, and well-loved costumes. Amelia would take the lead in creating the stage, though the other three girls would contribute. They'd gather props from all around the house and from flea markets to manifest the script MJ would pen. Mae had taken charge of the total production like the mother hen she was, even as a child. And Libby and her quick wit had topped everything off with sound effects from her piano.

In that attic, it had been quintessentially the four of them, individually and collectively authentic. Cooking downstairs in the kitchen, I'd tracked their progress from the stomping, the yelling, and the maniacal laughter that would filter down through these old walls.

I hadn't seen the attic in Sampaguita in years, and I had refused to go into it after Libby had died. Like the piano, it was too precious. The room belonged to them. *Them* meaning all four of them, with Libby included. Disturbing it meant fuzzing out the memories, stepping over the footprints, and smudging out their thumbprints.

"But this is different," I now said aloud to myself. "This is not Sampaguita. You can go in."

After my short conversation with Elizabeth, and during my ride back to the house, I'd decided to declutter this room to find out more about this world's Celine. What made me, what caused me to go back and forth between Quinn and Rex. Why I was all right not fixing up the second house out back for Elizabeth.

What about me pushed everyone away? Or hedged between two people? What of me here was the same as me in my real world?

And surely, what was in these boxes would give me a clue of what had mattered to me. Who and what I loved, and who loved me.

Ultimately, this was a task that would take me home.

It would, however, mean that I had to cross the threshold.

I can do this.

With one big breath, I stepped into the room with my eyes shut, then exhaled after opening one eye. And . . . nothing happened. My heart didn't break; my lungs didn't cease breathing, though the sheer amount of boxes pressed all around me like ghosts.

The only way to do this was to work quickly.

I went to the farthest stack of Sterilite containers and pulled them all so they were on the ground. Upon opening the first container, my heart leapt—it was full of Christmas ornaments. And right on top were acorns painted red and dusted with glitter—from my childhood.

Christmas was my most favorite holiday. I'd hoarded everything that my girls had made over the years and displayed them on their own special trees, lit bright with white lights. The season meant hope. It meant songs at the piano, and ensaymada, and reruns of old movies. It meant one of the girls' plays on Christmas Eve when they were little, and sitting with Quinn, watching them in their chaotic splendor.

My thoughts meandered to last Christmas Eve, a contrast at our town house, where somber holiday tunes had played from Quinn's playlist, and it had just been me and Quinn at the dinner table. Mae, MJ, and Amelia had had plans for the night, and we hadn't seen them until Christmas Day.

For all the years you raise children, you never really think of the day when they will be gone, be it just one night, or the rest of a lifetime.

I stood straight and set my hands against my hips, to gather my wits and the ball of tears threatening to spill. *Breathe in, and out. Inhale . . . exhale.*

Maybe I *couldn't* do this. Maybe this was too much.

But when I looked down, I caught sight of a handprint ornament, similar to the ones made by the girls in their classrooms. I plucked it from the container, anticipating whose of my girls it was.

When I turned over the ornament, I saw it had *Celine, first grade* written on the back. My body slacked, mood declining. After setting it aside, I unearthed more ornaments wrapped haphazardly in packing paper and Bubble Wrap. None were from my girls.

The obvious descended, and it was a snapback to the reality that I was not in Sampaguita.

This was a life without children.

I refocused. An assumption thus far: since Celine had kept her childhood ornaments, she must have been somewhat sentimental.

I dragged the container to the corner of the room, and approached the next plastic tub. When I peeled off the cover, gold Christmas decorations greeted me, from tinsel to glass balls and ribbon. The next tub contained coordinated red ornaments.

I moved on to the next box, and lo and behold—green ornaments. The next tub revealed silver. Another box had blank wreaths. Another contained neutral-colored sofa pillows. A box of knit blankets. A set of white dinnerware.

None of the contents in the tubs had any personalization, despite the brand names—I apparently had champagne taste. Nothing here represented my current history or things I loved. Like a cookie-cutter furniture room had been packed up and stored, only to be unveiled next season.

The ladies from the elevator in Boston came to mind.

But are you guys getting a different feeling about her content? It's so curated these days.

After covering up a tub and taking a seat, I dug out my phone from my pocket and swiped through the home screen. I hadn't yet checked my social media accounts. It was no longer my habit after employing a team the last couple of years. There had been a freedom in it, in not reading the immediate feedback of my followers and just focusing on my actual work.

I clicked on Instagram, and a grid of perfectly coordinated photos loaded. The same filter had been applied throughout. One of every few photos was of me, in perfect makeup and hair. Graphics of quotes were scattered across the grid—quotes of my speeches, I realized.

The overall aesthetic was pretty, resembling the last couple of years of my real feed. As I scrolled farther, going backward in time, it seemed that this curated feed had been going on for a while. I checked the dates randomly, tracking back to over five years ago.

It made sense, how this world's Celine would have come to the conclusion that a branded image was important much earlier than I had. In the beginning of my real-life social media habits, the photographer and designer had been me, myself, and I. Which had meant that my photos had been candid and messy, or random, or hadn't adhered to any kind of theme.

My thumb clicked on a selfie, and it loaded. I paused and examined it. Something about it didn't look right. The photo had been taken two years ago, and yet, where were my wrinkles?

Zooming in confirmed it: the deepest of my wrinkles, the ones in between my eyebrows—my thinking lines, as Amelia had called them once—had been brushed out.

Then I read the caption.

Have you ever had a hard time concentrating? Whenever I do, I automatically reach for Thoughtspiration by Matilda Scents. It's the perfect combination of lavender and lemons that clears the mind and refocuses the intentions.

Interesting. I didn't have anything against ads. They were part and parcel of being a brand and another source of income, but . . .

As I clicked through to the other photos and read through their captions, I discovered that half of the photos were ads. For teeth-whitening strips. Lash-defining mascara. A spill-proof travel coffee mug. Hand-cut leather earrings. Two years ago, I had been photographed in front of a Mercedes-Benz.

"Wow."

In this world, with Rex, without my family, I was an influencer of a different sort. The kind that focused not on entrepreneurship, but on image.

When did that happen? How did that happen?

In this life, posts were scheduled daily. It was mesmerizing, almost addicting, to trace the current of events, from megainfluencer to author. My book? *Just One Step: A Memoir of a Late-in-Life Influencer.*

I covered my mouth with a hand, struck by the difference. While my real-life book was a self-help, a step-by-step guide to achieving one's dreams, this world's *Just One Step* was a chronicle of my life.

I stood from the plastic tub and swiveled my head, toward the boxes yet to be searched. What was the chance that there was a copy of *Just One Step* in here? My writing habits in my real life included a myriad of notebooks, random binders, and calendars, sometimes half-used. Add to that an array of different-colored Post-its that I'd eventually gathered together to store on a shelf. I never threw any of my writing away.

There was only one way to find out.

I tore through the first box at my feet. In it was a book light that was still packed in plastic and Bubble Wrap. In another, an unopened diffuser. A disassembled ring light. A home-manicure UV light and its accompanying nail polishes that looked to have oxidized. Journals that hadn't been unwrapped, all from recognizable, posh brands. Brands that had pitched to me in my real life, too, though I'd declined. I'd been discerning with my advertisement. Only products I found connection and value with were considered.

Back to the Instagram feed, I scrolled down and halted, with a thumb, at one of me holding up a diffuser as part of a paid ad. It wasn't the same brand as this diffuser.

In this life I was a brand influencer in the truest sense.

This Celine and I both had the same drive, but our focus differed. Having children had steered me toward being a coach, and without children, this Celine was a personality. Both were valuable careers. Both required so much work—it was evident with all this stuff in the attic.

But what did that say about me when my love life in both worlds was on the rocks? When I had avoided dealing with a home and its issues? And my social media was full of curated images?

It says that you're not who you say you are.

The foreboding words from my conscience triggered my heart rate. Moving quickly, I repacked packages and pushed away my dreary thoughts. Every minute in this place was dragging me to emotional spaces I'd successfully avoided, and more than ever, I wanted to go home.

Chapter Twenty

"Achoo." I sneezed for the third time in a row from the dust in the air.

"Gesundheit," Nelson said, through the speaker on my phone.

"Thank you." I rubbed the back of my hand against my nose, which itched still. "But as you were saying?"

"Yes . . . we're already scheduled to come out tomorrow to start sorting the house inventory. I fully empathize that you don't want to go through the attic, and you certainly don't have to."

"Do we have to do the estate sale? Why can't we just donate everything? That way, we can turn in the house sooner than later."

Robin, who was also on the call, hummed in disapproval. "We can certainly turn in the keys earlier, but I'm not sure canceling the estate sale is a good thing. Nelson—"

"Yes, ma'am. Ms. Lakad, I oversee a very honest and hardworking group of people. And we have been planning and advertising this estate sale for a couple of weeks now. To cancel it altogether . . . that doesn't look good for me."

I growled, though my conscience sided with Nelson. He hadn't said it, but his company took a percentage of the sales, and by canceling, I would be depriving him of those earnings.

But this isn't real, a dissenting voice reminded me. This all wouldn't matter in the end.

And yet, with empathy coursing through me, I could not put Nelson in that situation. "No, you're absolutely right. I guess my next question would be, when's the earliest you can get here?"

"Tomorrow, early afternoon. And it will be fast and furious until the estate sale."

"If you're uncomfortable at the house, I can still book you at Louisburg B and B," Robin said once more.

"I appreciate that, but no thanks," I said, because familiarity still ruled above all.

We bade our goodbyes and hung up, and I looked around at the now-messy attic. Might as well pass the time and clean up.

With a trash bag in hand, I picked up garbage, filling the bag up to almost halfway before the slam of a car door brought me to the window. It was Elizabeth, loading boxes into the trunk of a small sedan. She must have been taking a load to her new place.

Questions arose as naturally as the sunrise: Where was she going to live? Was it a safe place? Would she have a roommate? Was anyone else helping her move?

Questions that stemmed from my maternal instinct for Libby, still so ingrained despite my logic warning me away.

I should've backed up from the window in case she saw me, but for the life of me, I could not drag myself away. She was doing that thing where she scrunched her lips to the side when she was frustrated. I'd completely forgotten that she did that.

I was enamored by it, committing it to memory and then locking it with a key.

My phone buzzed in my pocket with a text.

Sonya:

Have you responded to your primary doctor?

I grumbled. Sonya's steadfastness (a.k.a. stubbornness) had not skipped this world. Because I'd ignored my doctor's voice mail—she'd called sometime in the morning.

Celine:

No hello, how are you?

Sonya:

I knew it. Please email her back so she can set you up with an appointment. You need to speak to someone.

Celine:

I'm speaking to you right now

Sonya:

Don't make me regret dropping you off in Louisburg

Celine:

Technically no one dropped me off

Sonya:

Even more reason to speak to your doctor! You can vent.

Sonya:

It's important.

I bit my bottom lip in deliberation over how to write this next text.

Therapy was lifesaving, true—but it hadn't worked for me. Yes, it had been a good outlet in the beginning, right after Libby had died. But at some point, I simply had needed to get on with doing *stuff*. Sitting and stewing and verbalizing my feelings had served me nothing but another bowlful of pain.

I created too much content. My words were everywhere, from my blogs, podcasts, interviews, conferences. They were quoted, highlighted, repeated.

Frankly, I had gotten sick of myself.

I left Sonya on read and resumed cleaning up. While I was stuffing a second garbage bag, the doorbell rang.

Still in my thoughts, I headed downstairs and opened the door without looking through the peephole.

An avalanche of flowers and arms and high voices cascaded around me.

Lena led me inside with an arm linked with mine—it didn't escape me that I hadn't invited her in, but okay. "We know we should have probably texted, but we were on the way home . . ."

"And we thought, *What the hey? Why not come over a little earlier?* We wanted to make sure you were all right." Deb was bringing up the rear with yellow flowers wrapped in paper. "And we put together a bouquet for you."

"Lilies and gerbera daisies. In yellow, of course." Lena pulled out a chair and all but pushed me down to sit.

And truly I didn't have the energy to object. "Thank you. That's so sweet."

"So." Deb sighed into the chair in front of me while Lena stood behind her, arms crossed. "Are you okay? With the whole thing with Quinn."

"I'm . . . okay, I guess." I opted for honesty, at the risk of sounding clueless. "I was surprised at how he reacted toward me. He was really mad."

Deb's face softened to a *what did you expect?* "You left him in a bad spot. Yes, it's been years, but he thought . . . we all thought . . ."

Lena laid a hand on her shoulder. "What she means is—"

"No," I interrupted, at the edge of my seat. "Go on."

Deb glanced upward for a beat, and a message passed between them. "That you guys were getting back together, when Rex left for California."

Rex went to California without me. Another piece of the puzzle slowly clicked into place.

"Those six months were probably the happiest I had seen you and Quinn. Then Rex came back, and you reconciled with him. Though we still don't know why."

No wonder Quinn hates me, I thought.

Lena snorted. "Deb, that's not fair. Celine shouldn't take all the blame. It takes two to tango. Quinn wasn't innocent either." Lena's gaze caught mine. "You wanted to explore the world and travel and see where your business would take you, and Quinn didn't want to budge from Louisburg. If you hadn't left for LA, you would've had to settle."

Elizabeth's words from earlier came back to me. *He only buys one kind of bread.*

Deb's right eyebrow lifted. "Anyway, love doesn't solve everything, honey. We know this for a fact. The logistics have to make sense too. Not to say, though, that we don't sympathize with the both of you. But you can't make things better in just one day. You probably almost gave him a heart attack."

"The feeling was mutual." I shut my eyes for a beat. "It was a lot."

"Are you planning on trying to be friends?" Deb asked.

"I don't know." His rejection had been a lightning bolt to the spirit. And would it matter once I was no longer here?

"Well, it doesn't mean that you should just stay here, in your house. You've still got to live. So you should still come to the social."

I peered at their not-so-innocent faces. "I already said no."

Deb flashed Lena a look, then chirped a "Please?"

"Still a pass." I pointed at one woman and then the other. "There's an entire conversation happening between the two of you. Don't think you're fooling anyone with it."

"What Deb's trying not to say is that we sort of committed you to doing a book talk." Lena grimaced.

"You what?"

Deb said, "C'mon. This is your thing. It'll be easy peasy. You love talking about your book. I mean, it's Louisburg. Your family. They're going to love you."

Lena cleared her throat. "There's also one more thing."

A cackle burst out of me. This entire experience was a whiplash of emotions, down to these two in front of me, who were much-needed comic relief. I settled into my chair. "Tell me, then."

"The social is at Anne Frasier's house."

"Nope, nope, nope." I waved a hand in front of me, still laughing, except it had turned maniacal. Quinn's aunt Anne Frasier was a critical woman, and one could only imagine what she thought of me in this world if Quinn and I were on the outs. And if the social was at Anne's, then Quinn, her only nephew, was sure to be there.

Yes, I was curious about Quinn's life here. Would I have preferred that he and I were cordial? Absolutely. But to subject myself to more rejection wasn't on my list of things to do for the day.

"I'm reading your mind, Celine. Quinn won't be there. You know how he hates those parties." Deb pressed her hands together in prayer. "So please? I've already told the group chat. If you back out, they're never going to let me live it down."

"Which group chat?"

"Our friend group, who else?" Lena said. "There are now twenty-seven in the group. Twenty-eight because Nigella Church has two phones and can*not* seem to pick just one to use. Anyway, so many of our friends bought your book, and we thought, *What would be a great way to welcome you back to the community?*"

A *hell no* was at the tip of my tongue. The crowd would surely know that something was amiss with me: I hadn't even read the memoir!

But I was facing two women and their begging eyes. They'd brought me a gorgeous yellow bouquet. Being around them lifted my spirits. And, I needed to pass the time somehow, and why not in this world's Celine's work?

Harrumphing, I peered at them, crossing my arms. "What am I going to get out of this?"

Clapping ensued.

"We said we would help, so why don't we start a little early?" Lena spun her watch around her wrist. "We can stay a couple of hours to do whatever you need."

"And I can grab food. You can keep what you got from the farmers' market for another day. I want something deep-fried." Deb patted her belly. "I'll have it delivered."

"All right, then." If there was one thing that soothed my soul, it was work. "Let's get this going."

Chapter Twenty-One

I was up by eight o'clock the next morning sorting through a closet for a coat to wear to the May Day social when my phone, plugged in in the other bedroom, rang. I hefted myself to my feet. Rex's picture was on the caller ID.

Welp. It was back to whatever this reality was.

Rex and I had texted back and forth a couple of times last night while Deb and Lena and I had decluttered much of the attic. I'd filled the screen with details about the estate sale but let his phone calls go to voice mail. It was one thing to text, but another to put myself in a conversation in which I would not be able to make small talk. His issues were with this world's Celine, not me. And while he was surely racked with worry, speaking to him might inflame the situation rather than quell it.

Knocking sounded from the front door (thank goodness for the distraction!), so I climbed down the steps. The hour was too early for Nelson and his crew. Deb and Lena wouldn't be here till much later to pick me up for the May Day social.

I peeked through the peephole—I was learning—and my heart lurched. Elizabeth was on the other side of the door.

Elizabeth had passed my back windows several times while Deb and Lena had been here last night in what I'd assumed were her moving trips, and each and every time, I'd physically turned my back to her. It had been to squelch my need to help, to inquire if she was doing well, to ask her inside, or to ask for my key back. It had felt like dangerous territory.

But there was no way to ignore the actual person on my front porch, even if every part of me screamed in protest.

The doorbell rang once more.

But it's Libby.

The whisper, the pleading, was from inside me.

"Dammit." Ignoring my logic, I opened the door to Elizabeth holding up a key.

"Hi. I just wanted to drop this off. I saw that you had company yesterday, so I didn't want to interrupt." Elizabeth wore an apron, and her braided hair was held up by a bandanna.

"Thank you." The key was cool in my palm, and I willed my swirling thoughts to simmer down.

Close the door, a part of me instructed.

"You're up early. No wine last night?" Her lips quirked up.

Her statement knocked me unsteady, and I laughed. Maybe I'd been primed by last night's easy company, or maybe at that moment, I was coiled up so tight. Libby had had this same humor, a little off the cuff. She had been the middle child who'd broken the tension among her three type-A sisters. "No, not even a single drop."

"Good . . . good," she breathed out. "Well, okay, I've gotta get back. I've got a full list of things to do. Thanks, by the way, for sending over someone to fix the oven and heat. They're both working now."

"Oh good. I'm glad."

Tell her goodbye, my logic prompted.

"Which is good because I had a huge order set for this afternoon," Elizabeth continued.

"For the May Day social?"

"Yep." Her head tilted. "You got an invite? You just got into town."

"Lena and Deb said it would be all right."

Her lips wiggled into a grin. "I see."

"Uh-oh, what's that for?"

"Lena and Deb are, like, the greatest people but are hands down the biggest gossip hens in town. They probably want to show you off. I mean, you are a celebrity." Her eyes gleamed. "So what are you bringing to the potluck?"

"Myself. Deb said that she would whip up something extra and we'll count it as my contribution."

She smirked. "You want to sign off on what Deb Masterson has made? She tries, but sometimes, she doesn't quite succeed. Her efforts are better spent gardening." Her gaze traveled up and down my body. "And is that what you're wearing?"

"Please. Don't hold back," I quipped, though the banter was whisking me to our better times. People had taken Libby's quiet nature as apathy, when in fact, Libby had been as opinionated as they came. Her humor had been so under the surface that one had had to pay acute attention. "If you must know, I have several outfits in my suitcase, so that's not an issue. But I didn't realize that the potluck was serious."

"But . . . didn't you go to these when you lived here?" She frowned.

"Yes, um. I guess I forgot how serious it was."

Her expression eased. "So serious that people have placed their orders with me for weeks. Everyone wants to bring something different. I have a running list to make sure that no two clients bring the same thing. I've been baking nonstop. I mean, I bake nonstop anyway, but even more so close to May Day."

"Then I guess I should stop by a bakery."

She snorted. "Good luck—shelves are cleaned off." She looked down, biting her lip. A second later, her face lit up. "I have an idea, if it's okay with you. My oven's in use at the moment. But if yours is available, I know exactly what to make so you have something to bring."

"Oh, I don't know. I wouldn't want to impose." It was a coward's answer, and I looked away so as to not get caught in a lie. The truth was that the more I spent time with Elizabeth, the more I could fall for this whole . . . facade. I was already having too much fun with her on my front porch.

"Okay." Elizabeth's face fell in disappointment, and holy wretched feelings, my maternal instincts clamored for attention.

I wanted to give her everything she asked for. And despite how Libby and I had grown apart when we'd moved to Annapolis, I had wanted to give her everything back then too.

But pride had gotten in the way. Pride, and maybe a low-level wound that had refused to heal. She'd felt I'd chosen my work over her, and I'd felt disappointed—disrespected, even—as someone who'd raised her.

Why did humans do this to one another? Why was it our nature to push away rather than pull people close in times of struggle? If I'd reeled my child in, Libby could have lived. No perceived obstacle would have been between us, and I would have rushed to her side. Hours of my help might have made a difference. What could a day have done? A week when she'd first come down with symptoms?

Now, looking at Elizabeth, I shoved my logic to the side. "Actually . . . I change my mind . . . but only if you have time. I don't want to put you out."

"No . . . no worries at all." A smile lit up her face, and it smothered the embers of my regret daring to light up. "I'm grateful that I got to stay in this house for so long. It's the least I could do." She hiked a thumb over her shoulder. "I'll go grab my stuff, and I'll be back."

Then Elizabeth was gone, a shadow streaking as she bounded toward the little house on the stepping-stone path as Libby had done, like a frog on lily pads. The air around the backyard was so hazy from pollen that without stepping out, I could smell the jasmine perfuming the air.

A knock startled me out of my thoughts, and I came to with Elizabeth staring at me from the other side of the window, gesturing for me to open the back door.

She carried a grocery bag of items and waved a handwritten card in the air. "I'm so excited for this."

"What's on the menu?"

"Ensaymada."

"Ensaymada." The word lodged itself in my throat. I hadn't eaten ensaymada since my real Libby had died. It had been our staple at Christmas breakfast, and she'd learned how to make the soft butter-and-sugar rolls after seeing a Filipino food documentary. Hello, she'd had an actual Filipino American mother with her own recipe, but kids sometimes didn't listen to their parents.

"Well, I thought . . . I'm Filipino, and you are too. Why not ensaymada? Not quite as elegant as sans rival, but anyone who knows will know." At my silence, her eyebrows plunged. "Though, if there's something else you preferred, I can make that instead."

"No, I . . . that sounds perfect. It was one of my favorites."

"Was?"

All I could do was shrug, to brush off the temptation that burned bright. How every part of me wanted to let Elizabeth into some of the memories I carried of her and our family. Like that after Libby had died, I couldn't bear the thought of eating ensaymada—because it was wrong, a betrayal of sorts. "I guess it's because it's been so long since I've had it."

"Well, get ready to be blown away. My recipe's pretty damn close to authentic, if I say so myself. I worked on it for a very long time."

"I believe it."

In truth, I'd seen it, for this exact recipe. Week after week of making batches of ensaymada that had been delicious to us but had failed Libby's expectations. Our family had had more than our share of gluten in that recipe discovery. It had been at times frustrating for Libby, but for us it had been a treat.

"All right. We should get started. That is, if you're ready," she said.

My hands were clasped in front of me, and my fingers hung on as if for survival. "Um . . . we?"

"Yeah." She grinned. "You and me."

"I thought *you* were going to be making it." My cheeks burned. Baking was something I hadn't done in forever; I'd felt no joy in it after Libby had died. "The last time I baked was with yo—" Clearing my throat, I started over. "The last time I baked was a while ago. Years."

"Then you should definitely help. There's nothing more therapeutic than getting your hands into dough."

I tore my eyes away from her sincere, beseeching expression in an attempt to separate myself and my feelings for Libby from Elizabeth. But it was futile, because my mouth was already answering for me, eager to spend as much time as possible with someone I'd missed so much. "Okay . . . fine," I said before my mind changed.

"Yes." She pumped a fist at her side.

At the sight, I smiled from ear to ear.

She led the way into the kitchen. "There's an apron hanging behind you."

I donned the apron and parked myself at the kitchen counter while Elizabeth took out mixing bowls. "There are hair ties right there, in that drawer, if you wanted to use one. I stash extras because of my big ol' mane."

Sure enough, when I opened the drawer, I was met by sparkly hair ties, and I picked one up to inspect it. These were the same ones Libby used to wear on her wrist. They were heavy duty; Libby had been picky about the brand and type, and it had taken months of experimenting, of her and her sisters ruminating over their hair needs.

How had Elizabeth come to her decision? Who had she consulted?

Did everyone come round to what was meant for them at the end of the day?

"Everything okay?" In front of me, Elizabeth had halted with a spatula in her hand.

"Yes. Just thinking that this is so cute."

"It's the little things. And I like these because I can find them, since I have a habit of taking them off everywhere. Are you ready?"

I tied up my hair. "Yep, I'm ready."

She pointed to the recipe, propped on a cookbook holder. "Go ahead and mix the yeast and water and sugar, to proof it."

I ran the water to warm it for the yeast, added sugar, and sprinkled the yeast on top. It always fascinated me how instantaneous the reaction was, with the grains blossoming in the water. How a combination of things, stagnant on their own, came alive when combined.

"So, how's the decluttering going?" Elizabeth asked, weighing the flour on a scale.

"Good. Nelson should be arriving with his team in a couple of hours. And with some help from Deb and Lena, we got a lot of things accomplished yesterday. But it's been . . . tough."

It was the best explanation of my feelings, which had been like a lint ball in the dryer, jostling and catching only pieces of each moment because I was literally incapable of taking it all in. The bits of information I had been learning about Celine, the significance of this house. Facing Quinn. And now, Elizabeth—here with me, baking a bread so integral to our family—who was very much alive.

This moment felt so astoundingly close to what life had been and also so far removed from reality.

Elizabeth blinked up at me. "I can relate. I'm a creature of comfort, and moving, packing, decluttering, is all tough for me. And I have a tinier house to go through, and I'm moving not that far away. Everyone says it's just stuff, but it's not *just* stuff. It belongs to me, and I want it to stay safe." She shifted her feet. "Did you find anything interesting in the decluttering? Something that surprised you?"

Everything. Absolutely everything. But most of all: you.

I gently tucked the thought away. This moment had to stay light and easy, for my own benefit. "Why? Are you thinking of first dibs at the estate sale? I don't know what to tell you, but Deb and Lena have their eyes on certain things."

"Those two." Elizabeth laughed, throwing her head back, and the sight of it squeezed my heart. She did it with such gusto, with energy, red cheeks, a hand on her belly, all of it.

"I know, right? They're a hoot."

"They're going to be in your shadow the whole time you're here."

"Eh, I don't mind. Honestly, they've kept me laughing, and time flies with them."

"Do you need extra help? I've got two hands."

I snorted an objection. "You've got your own packing to do."

"Yes, but . . . um, let's hold that thought for a little bit." She gestured at the foaming yeast. "The yeast is calling our name."

Elizabeth buzzed around the kitchen, clearly comfortable. Light on her toes and talkative, she spoke of the different types of flour as she began to mix the dry ingredients together, then combined it all with the liquids into a glob of dough.

She scooped the contents out in front of me, on the floured countertop, then pointed to the heel of her hand, giving me basic instructions on how to knead the dough. Then, she demonstrated. "Now, your turn."

"Pass."

An eyebrow arched.

There were many things I avoided in association with unpleasant situations. A skeevy interaction with a high school teacher had taught me to be wary of people who demonstrated the same behaviors. A video of me dancing at a bachelorette party had taught me to avoid tequila at all costs.

It was part of a human's survival to key into their instincts to keep away from trouble. The one thing I'd told my girls time and again was to listen to their sixth sense. A message, a sign, that would tell them if they were safe or unsafe.

When Libby had died, so had a whole host of things I used to do. I'd stayed away from pianos, from certain books, from making bread. Any of these things rendered me shaky, uncertain. I had been fine with helping a little bit here and there with this bread-making session. But to touch the dough?

"Really, I'm good." I showed her the palm.

"It's super easy. I promise." Elizabeth gestured to the dough with an encouraging smile. She waved me forward.

My brain and heart jostled for attention. My brain insisted that it was unsafe and dangerous to play with my imagination and memory.

But my heart insisted that this was simply bread making with a character named Elizabeth who just happened to look like Libby, and to experience it in this context was nostalgic.

"Then you can really say you made it." Elizabeth waggled her eyebrows. "Give all those hens a run for their money."

See? It's only bread, Celine. Nothing more, nothing less, the angel on my shoulder said.

After a final bit of hesitation, I relented. "Okay, fine."

My body softened the moment my hands touched dough, switching on its muscle memory, in remembrance of the many times I'd baked with Libby. I pushed and folded and turned, feeling the gluten stretch and strengthen under my touch, angst lessening with each movement.

This wasn't so bad.

"Wow. You're a natural. You said it's been a while?" Libby was cleaning up, and she peeked down at my work.

"A long while." I felt my lips part into a satisfied smile, a full smile, because the dough was becoming a taut ball; I was giving it life.

Life, when inside I'd felt stagnant.

In this world, I'd been able to walk into this house, go into the attic, and knead bread. Because it wasn't real life.

And in this world, my worst nightmare—Libby dying—hadn't happened.

In this world, whether imagined or real, I wouldn't have to experience the kind of pain that struck without notice and left a heavy weight on my shoulders. There was no pain here because Libby had not died.

She was right in front of me.

Okay, so not Libby, but Elizabeth. But was it close enough? Could I twist it somehow so that for the time I was here, she could *be* Libby?

I pushed harder into the dough and reveled in the idea that I could live, even if for a few days, with the freedom of a heart without pain. It meant not wondering every single day what I could've done better. It meant finally ascending that second rung in Maslow's hierarchy, which I hadn't achieved in so long. It meant having confidence that when my eyes opened every morning, I would be greeted with hope, and not regret.

Though Elizabeth was not my daughter in this world, she was still fun, insightful, and kind. She was still here. And why couldn't I celebrate that?

"Wow." Elizabeth gawked at the smooth ball of dough, waking me from my thoughts. "It's perfect."

Surprise flooded my senses. "I guess it's like riding a bicycle."

"This is fantastic." She pushed a greased bowl toward me. "Now for it to rise. It won't take long, just until it's doubled in size. Maybe an hour at the most."

"Great." I was out of breath and speechless, because this was more than great. All this time, I'd assumed this was a dream of what could've been, had I chosen differently.

I had been wrong.

This could be my second chance with Libby.

Chapter Twenty-Two

There was a hitch to all this, however. I didn't believe in second chances. Clamoring for a second chance was simply a waste of time, when the most important movement was forward. It was *Just One Step*'s message, preached in every page of the book and discussed in all my coaching sessions.

But what if the second chance was handed to me? Was I supposed to throw away the opportunity?

Too many nights had been spent with me wishing to have more time with my daughter. To smooth things over with her. Things had never been perfect between us—our personalities had been such that we'd conflicted in the smallest of ways. When I'd insisted she wear her red sweater, she'd dress in a tank top.

To be in the same spaces with her but not be in conflict, to get to know her—it was tempting, almost hopeful. Whether Elizabeth knew why I was doing it was beside the point. *I* would know. And I could finally say I had done my best.

The slam of the oven door brought my attention back to the kitchen. Elizabeth had just placed the dough in a cool oven to rise. She rinsed her hands at the sink. "While it's doing its magic, can I help with anything?"

"Sure." I shoved the devil off my shoulder before he objected. I could certainly make something up for Elizabeth to tackle. "Only if I don't keep you from your own stuff at your house."

"I'm on track with everything. From the moving and the baking. I might have to pop out sometime to start on something, but I have at least this hour to spare." She stood a foot away.

My insides brightened at the proximity. "How about I show you what I have and haven't done?"

"Sounds good!"

We both climbed to the third floor and walked through the open doors of the attic.

She gasped at a room that didn't look any better after Deb and Lena had gone through it. "Wow."

"I know. It's a little overwhelming." I pointed out the boxes in one corner. "Those are tagged, but this whole area back here? I'm kind of afraid of what I'll find."

Elizabeth peeked into one of the boxes, and as she did, I allowed myself to examine her profile. Her cheeks were pink, probably from the walk up, and her skin was smooth—I wondered if she was still loyal to her Korean skin-care products.

"For the three months I stayed here, packages continued to come, probably once a week," she said. "I've been putting them up here, but I didn't realize how many there were. Oh . . . oh." She lifted up a box for a phone-activated personal-home-security system. "Now this . . . this is handy."

Over the last day, I'd parsed out, with the help of social media and the attic storage, that housewares were Celine's favorite things to rep. "Getting product definitely has its perks. But thank you, for putting it all away."

"The new owners are going to have a field day with whatever else trickles in. Though I suppose you can get Robin to forward the packages that the mail system misses."

It was the perfect segue for the questions that had trickled in since I'd arrived. I jumped on it like a pool on a hot summer day. "That's true. Speaking of forwarding packages, you said that your new place isn't that far. Where will you be staying?"

"Nearby." Her voice was airy and casual.

Her answer was so typically Libby, a mix of private, defensive, and coy. "Hmm, would you like some of this for your place? How about this . . . diffuser?" I lifted up a sealed box.

Her face lit up with a smile. "Seriously?"

Though I attempted to contain my excitement, I all but shoved the box into her arms. These were all just things. Objects. Maybe even imagined objects, but that smile was priceless, and I wanted more of it. "I'd rather it go to someone I know than any old stranger."

"Well." She bit her lip. "How about I come back and work throughout the week, and I'll let you know if there's anything I like? Then it'll be up to you whether or not you want to give it or sell it. I do feel like some of these things are pricey."

"The rest of the week?" The sentence lodged itself in my throat, a reinforcement that we would see each other every day. That I would get more time with Libby.

With my daughter.

Not . . . , the devil began, but with an imaginary turn of the volume to zero, I didn't hear him.

"Sure!" She brightened. "There are a million rooms in here. And the closets are full."

I inhaled a deep breath to ease the anticipation and the fear in my chest. That perhaps I might be in over my head.

But I stuck out my hand anyway. "You've got yourself a deal."

"Awesome." She took my hand in hers. It was warm, unlike the last time I'd held Libby's hand.

Libby had been surrounded by our family when she'd passed. There'd been time to get everyone up to Boston in the ICU. And up to the very moment she'd left us, I'd rubbed her hands to try to keep them warm.

My eyes pricked with the beginning of tears.

No. There would be no crying. The tears would keep me from enjoying the company of Elizabeth, as superficial as our time together would be. Because it would truly end sometime.

There was no such thing as forever.

I cleared my throat and infused lightness into my voice. "How about we start on the first floor?" Big enough not to crowd her, but small enough that I could feel her presence. I stepped down the stairs. "You take your pick."

"Sure . . . um . . ." Hesitance laced her tone, and I knew—because this was Libby to her core—that she'd detected something was wrong, that she'd wanted to comfort me. When we got to the first floor, she said, "How about I do the living room?"

"Great. Just group like items together best way you can. I'll get started in the study." Offering her a smile, I stepped away, to move the moment forward, and to allow myself some breathing space.

"Okay. I'll let you know when the dough's risen."

"Sounds good."

I stepped into the study, and once I was alone, my body fully exhaled. Sitting on one of the boxes, hands propped on my knees, I bit against my cheek to keep from crying. "Dammit. Stop it," I instructed—demanded of—myself. "Just one box. Just one step."

But the tears spilled over my cheeks. My will had no control over this ball of grief overflowing from where I'd locked it up.

It had been necessary to keep it all inside. Everyone relied on me. My family, the public. They looked to me for strength, and like everything I focused on—I had become an expert at it.

Now I had this second chance. This should make me happy, so why couldn't I sink into the joy of it? It was fruitless to think about the other shoe dropping. It was a waste of time, of my last precious moments with Libby.

What was wrong with me? To have achieved every goal, every wish—even this impossible one of having Libby back with me—but still fall apart?

I didn't know how long I sat and stared at the middle distance, except that Elizabeth humming brought me out from my haze. It was a start and stop of a tune, but it repeated itself over and over. It was familiar, and I tried to place it as I fell into the rote task of sorting through the shelves of decor and books.

With the light that streamed through the windows, I was hit with a wave of nostalgia, for Christmases in this—or my version of this—room. The large tree that at times hadn't had a ton of presents under it. The cast-iron stove that had piped out delicious heat, and the mistletoe hanging from the door's archway. Songs being played on the piano by any one of my girls—but most of all by Libby.

Footsteps sounded from behind me, and I turned. On Elizabeth's face was a tentative smile. "It's time to do the shaping and the second rise."

"Okay. How did everything go on your side of the house?"

"Productive. After we finish up baking, I can work on getting stuff out of the kitchen cabinets."

"Maybe we should be giving some of Nelson's estate sale commission to you."

"Hey, I'm not too humble to say no to a payout." We were halfway through the living room when she said, "I've been meaning to ask. If you come across the book *Little Women* . . . could you pull it from the sale? It's actually mine."

My legs slowed to a stop. "That was your book?"

"Yes. It's here? I wasn't sure if it got lost in all my packing."

I went to the bookshelves and slipped the book out. "I put it away."

Her lips curled into a grin, and she took the book with both hands. "Oh, yay. I love this book. I got it from the secondhand bookshop. When things don't go well, reading about this family gives me hope, you know? Even through their bad times, the family stuck together."

I was struck silent. She was right: despite all the family's struggles, the faults of the Marches, the book ended with a happily ever after.

"What's that grin for?"

Was I grinning? "It's just that I used to read *Little Women*. A lot actually."

"Used to? Why no longer?"

The image of the book sizzling in the fire flashed in front of my eyes. "I guess I fell out of love with it."

"That happens. I'm a moody reader, so I need to be in the exact headspace for a book. We get what we give when it comes to books, you know?" She spun toward the kitchen. "Let's get to the dough. I'm always so paranoid it's going to overproof."

I followed her into the kitchen, where the air was now permeated with the heady smell of rising bread. But what was cultivated in my thoughts was what she'd said about getting as much as you gave.

Was it true in relationships too?

One could invest the time, the energy—in motherhood, wifehood—and still could end up with misunderstandings, roadblocks, and rejections. So perhaps it wasn't about time or energy but quality?

And when did forgiveness and grace weigh in? When did acceptance for someone's mistakes come into play? If no one was supposed to be perfect, then why had I felt the pressure?

The moment reset with the bowl's clatter on the counter. With a magician's flair, Elizabeth uncovered it and said, "Ta-da."

Her enthusiasm flipped my mood to a crisp, blank page. "What do you want me to do?"

"Prepare the pans." She gave me instructions, and I lined the pans with parchment.

She began to hum the same tune once more, and I realized what it was: her song, "Petals Fluttering," though in its beginnings.

"That tune you're singing, what is it?" I asked.

"Just a little something I'm working on." Flour dusted the air as Elizabeth spread a generous amount on the kitchen counter.

"Do you write music?"

"I dabble here and there." She handed me the bowl. The dough had risen almost to the rim. "Want to do the honors?"

"The punch down is the best part," I said, at the exact moment as she did.

Inside, I gasped. This saying had been an inside joke between me and Libby; though it wasn't laugh-out-loud funny, we'd said it so often that it would still bring us to stitches.

We looked into each other's eyes, though hers were filled with mirth. "That's funny; it's what my mom used to say when we made bread. 'The punch down is the best part.'"

"Ha. Great minds." I looked away, not wanting to reveal my awe. The rules of this world felt arbitrary. But I couldn't dwell on that. I punched down the dough and tipped the bowl forward, plopping the dough out onto the table.

Elizabeth gave instructions on how to shape the rolls, spreading butter and sugar so every bite was perfectly sweet, and I followed her lead, watching her hands as they worked the dough swiftly and gently. Her expression was relaxed even in her focus; this was her happy place.

It eased the worry that I hadn't realized I still carried for my daughter. Libby hadn't finished college like her sisters, and she hadn't had what could be considered a steady, normal job. I'd staked so much on the milestone of having reliable employment that even as I'd resigned myself to letting her be, I hadn't actually believed that she could be content, and make money to boot.

Ironically, here I was, someone who had checked all those employment boxes but hadn't smiled for a while.

"Why don't you come with me, to the social?" I asked. In the pans was evenly spaced rolled and shaped dough, though one could tell my rolls from the way they were sadly uneven.

Elizabeth opened the oven door. "I didn't tell you? I'm going to be there. I'm part of the serving staff. But really, I just want to keep up with gossip. Mimosas equal loose lips." She threw her head back in a cackle. "And Anne Frasier pays well and in cash."

"Good ol' Anne Frasier." My lips curled as irritation rode up my back.

"Ooh, there's something in that tone."

I waved it away. Perhaps my issues with Anne hadn't bled over to this world, and starting a rumor would not be wise. Still, every part of me knew that I could trust Elizabeth. "Let's just say that she likes to share her opinions about me *with* me."

"Ah . . ." She slid the pans on the rack, shut the oven door, and then pressed a finger against her chin. "This sounds like every townsperson in Louisburg. I can't tell you how many people think that they can tell me what to do. For some reason, they think I'm helpless. And yet, they're all showing up with my desserts on their silver platters. How does that work?"

Pride swelled in my chest. "I love that."

"Love what?"

"That . . . the attitude, the confidence."

"Well, you can't survive a small town without it. That and knowing exactly who everyone is."

"I actually have to give a book talk at this social. I may need you for information about my audience."

"I'm there for you. And now I'm *really* glad you're bringing ensaymada. All eyes are going to be on you."

"Thank you for looking out for me."

"Easy peasy. But as soon as the baking's done, I'll get out of your hair. You and I have to get ready." She crossed her arms. "You know what? It's going to be nice to see another friendly face at the social."

I felt myself glow from the inside out. My daughter had called me a friendly face. She was looking forward to seeing me.

It made all the confusion of this experience worth it.

Chapter Twenty-Three

Later on that day, armed with a disposable pan of ensaymada and with Deb and Lena next to me, I charged up the sidewalk to Anne Frasier's colonial. The house's facade was magnificent, with bold round columns and a wide front porch. Green shutters banked each window, and greeting us was a red door showcasing a live wreath. From the backyard, music filtered, along with chatter.

"She already planted the season's perennials," Deb mused, glancing at plants that lined the walkway. "And it wasn't us who did it. How dare."

"Deb," Lena pleaded. "Hush."

"She'll be back," Deb grumbled. "Toronto's has horrible design."

I tugged at my summer dress, not quite pressed due to the lack of time. Elizabeth had stayed well past the ensaymada baking, having coffee and partaking of the imperfect rolls while Nelson and his team arrived and began their work for the estate sale. What had started as her giving me an overview of town gossip had turned into her sharing her microbaking business adventures.

To be honest, she could have been talking about her hair ties, and I would have been there for it. Had Elizabeth already not planned to work the event, I would have canceled. Every minute spent with her was like unwrapping a gift, with heightened anticipation at what I could learn.

The consequence, however, was an unpressed dress and a slightly topsy-turvy brain—I hadn't properly prepared for this talk, except for skimming a downloaded copy of this world's Celine's *Just One Step*. I'd had just enough time to read the chapter headings and the first and last chapter.

As with my social media, *Just One Step*, the memoir, had nothing salacious or shocking in it—a relief. The memoir recounted my childhood, which had been exactly like my real world's, and then picked up with my and Rex's move to Louisburg, where my business had begun.

Quinn wasn't mentioned, nor was our apparent on-again, off-again relationship, and if formatted a tad differently, it could have been read as a self-help book. It contained advice on how to withstand the rise and fall of fame as an influencer, and hints on how to get started with the business.

The positive: despite my unpreparedness, I might be able to pull this talk off without trouble. Enough similarities existed between coaching and influencing.

Even more positive: Elizabeth would be there to watch it.

The last time I'd looked out into a sea of an audience to find Libby's eyes staring back at me was years ago, when she'd surprised me at a blogger summit in Boston. It was after Quinn and I had moved out to Annapolis, and Libby and I had been trying to manage this new normal. Of me attempting to push down my resentment that Libby had chosen not to move out with us. Of Libby intending to show us that though we were living apart, she supported me still.

Except that night, we'd bickered. We'd gotten into discussing Sampaguita's maintenance, which she hadn't followed up on. I'd reminded her that part of our agreement of her staying there rent-free was her ensuring the home's care. Libby had accused me of not trusting her.

Looking back, I realized I'd known my gripes were inconsequential, and still I'd wanted to be right.

This time? This time, my pettiness would take the back seat. Elizabeth would see me only at my best.

As we climbed the steps to the house, my heart startled to a gallop. Shadows mingled inside—the house was packed. Usually, I was seized with energy at the idea of speaking to a crowd. Public speaking was my forte. But I had Anne Frasier to get through first, which was the equivalent of climbing a barbed wire fence.

"Maybe I shouldn't have left Nelson by himself at the house?" My voice croaked.

"Nope. Let him do his job. His team will be way more productive if you're not around. Besides, he's run all of the estate sales in the county, and he knows what he's doing," Lena said.

"All right." I blew out a breath. One step at a time.

I entered after Deb, and was hit with a greeting by one person while another simultaneously took the tray of ensaymada away. Hugs from impeccably dressed strangers, another pushing a flute of champagne into my hand. All the while, my eyes conducted a systematic search for Elizabeth, but she was nowhere to be found.

I was relieved to see Deb and Lena flank me with their own drinks in hand. And amused by the way they commented on every person they passed, and sometimes not so discreetly. It allowed me to roll out my shoulders, though it would take this full glass of champagne to relax me.

Lena held up her flute. "Here's to today."

"Today." I clinked my flute against hers, my chest bursting with anticipation. "And Anne Frasier."

"Hear, hear," Deb said, and we all took a drink. "Now let's go find the host and set you up for the book talk. Ready, Celine?"

My nerves were still raw; in order to do well, I needed to chill. "Can I meet you two outside? I want to find a quiet corner and practice a little." Breathing would be good. Not passing out would be better.

"Keep your phone on you," Lena instructed. "In case we can't find one another. These things can get a little wild."

I nodded, gulped another swig, and then decided to head toward the quiet of the front rooms.

Anne Frasier's home was still as beautiful as I remembered, if not more, decorated with fine art and elegant furniture. As a widow and recipient of a sizable inheritance from her side of the family, she had the freedom to commit her money or her ideas to whatever she chose. She was, I realized now, the ultimate influencer without a social media handle attached to her name. An endorsement from Anne was all one needed; her money sweetened the pot. And it showed by how many people were in this house.

If only she had bestowed the same empathy she had for her philan-thropic projects on me. Instead, what she'd done was pepper me with unending interrogative questions:

You're pregnant? You should be putting your feet up.
You're pregnant again? You do know how that happens, right?
The way you expose your life on that blog!
Is this really the time to be traveling? Your children need you.
Are you and Quinn spending enough time together?

They'd been the kind of questions that had plagued me in all my decisions. She was the devil on my shoulder incarnate.

The sitting room drew me in. It was opulent, with old-world details that had been enhanced by modern carpentry and design, even more intricate than in my real world. The built-in bookcases were lined with leather spines. Standing in its midst, I could almost hear the chatter of my girls for all the times they'd visited.

They always did fuss over Anne's things. MJ would tilt her head to the right and read the book spines at her sight level. I swore that Anne had paid someone to rearrange her books just so she could hear MJ's surprise at finding a new title.

But it had been Amelia who'd caught her eye as her favorite, prob-ably because she most resembled Anne herself, a lover of art. Amelia had spent one summer with Anne in Europe, during which she'd been bitten by the travel bug.

The memory that Amelia and Theo had canceled their trip to Tokyo because she'd been worried about me triggered an ache that started in the middle of my chest. I pressed my hand against it. This experience was like peeling back layers of wallpaper in a remodeled historic home.

I missed my husband and my girls. All of them. I would even settle for the ones in this world who didn't think I was their mother at all.

"Fancy meeting you here," said a voice next to me, and I turned, gaze meeting Elizabeth's, as if conjured. She was wearing a black A-line dress, and her hair was coiled into a chignon. She was expertly balancing a tray of mini quiches.

My body melted at the sight of her. "You look so pretty."

She curtsied. "Why, thank you. You look beautiful too."

My daughter thinks I'm beautiful. My grin widened to the size of the study. "Thank you. Not bad for scrambling in the last minute."

"Did you have any doubt? We're awesome." The doorbell rang, and Elizabeth glanced behind her. She lowered her voice. "Oh my gosh, everyone's so excited to meet you. I keep hearing people say your name. Anne Frasier's been hyping you up."

The jitters surged in the form of nausea, and my voice cracked when I said, "Great."

"Something's wrong." She inspected my face.

I made a *pfft* noise to blow off the notion. Giving in to the nervousness made it worse. "Nothing's wrong. Everything's perfect."

She frowned. "I know we haven't known each other that long, but I can tell you're totally fibbing. Okay, so see that counter over there?" With her chin, she gestured to the dining room table, burgeoning with food. "I easily made half of those desserts."

"That's amazing."

"I know. It's so satisfying that it makes my serving these people not such a big deal. But all that to say . . . this house is filled with the snobs of Louisburg, and it might seem like a lot. But what you've done . . . your work? It makes a difference."

"I'm just an influencer," I snickered. The Celine in this world was a brand. There was no real message behind her name, just pretty photos.

"Just? What you've done is inspire a whole lot of us to aim for more. Don't minimize that."

The knot in my belly unwound from Elizabeth's sincere tone. I dragged my eyes down to the floor, to keep my breathing steady. Elizabeth believed in me. She looked up to me. And I hadn't realized that it was something I'd needed to hear from her. After clearing my throat, I said, "I appreciate that. Lately I've been wondering if the things I was doing were even worth it."

"Are you kidding? They are." She laid a warm hand against my wrist, and confidence shot through me. "You know what makes me feel better? Venting. Don't you have a team or manager? Why not give them a call?"

"That's a great idea." I'd tried to speak to my family before each event; touching base with them had been grounding.

While I dug through my purse for my phone, she took a step back. "I'll give you some privacy . . ."

But I couldn't let her walk away. At the moment, Elizabeth was that grounding force too. "Wait. Do you want to meet my team, by chance?"

A grin burst from her lips. "Really? Sure."

"All right. This might take a little bit of coordination, but . . ." I texted Sonya.

Celine:

I'm about to do a short talk

Sonya:

Say what?

Celine:

At a neighborhood social. To the point: it starts in a few minutes.

Can you put the team on FT so I can say hello?

Sonya:

I don't understand. You've never done that before.

Dang you, this world's Celine.

Celine:

First time for everything. Please.

Sonya:

Okay hold one.

The phone rang in my hand seconds later—it was a video chat request, and I accepted it. Four boxes appeared on the screen, and one by one, faces materialized: Sonya, Mae, MJ, and Amelia. One hundred percent of their expressions showed confusion.

"We're all here," Sonya said.

"Hi, everyone," I called out, then shared the camera with Elizabeth. "I have someone with me too. This is Elizabeth."

My screen showed both our faces, and Elizabeth waved. "Hi. I live in Celine's house out back."

Kindly, the other ladies waved back. As they did, realization descended like East Coast humidity in July. All my daughters were on this call. "This is a miracle," I whispered.

Thank you, cell phone engineers. Thank you to whatever put me on a ride here to this world. Because this was a moment I'd never even thought to dream about. To hope for. To ask for.

On the screen, Sonya's smile faltered by a smidge. "What's wrong, Celine?"

Worrying Sonya was the last thing I wanted to do. She would surely fly out here the next day and whisk me away if I appeared off. "Nothing!

I wanted to mention that I'm at a social for an impromptu book talk and signing, and I guess I just wanted a pep talk."

The faces in front of me seemed to relax.

"Oh, you've totally got this, Celine," MJ started. "We believe in you."

"Yep." Amelia nodded. "But don't forget to give the audience some time to ask questions. They love that."

"Since we're not there, have someone keep track of the time. We know how you sometimes veer off topic. But you're amazing, Celine; you can do it."

"You *have* been doing it. Be yourself," Sonya said.

Elizabeth raised a finger. "I agree with all of you. I think you're going to kick butt, Celine."

Heat radiated through my chest, but it wasn't from the compliments. It was from knowing that for the moment, everyone was fine. That my girls were here. That they supported me, and life reflected what it used to when there hadn't been a layer of sad smothering us.

I choked out a response with relief. "Thank you. I feel better already."

"I mean, she also had a glass of champagne," Elizabeth continued, and we all laughed.

It seemed so normal. So, so normal. The only thing—person— missing was Quinn.

My heart squeezed. He would have loved to see this. Tears would have sprung to his eyes, and he would have sobbed. My real Quinn, that was.

This world's Quinn? Who knew how he would have thought or reacted. And I would never know with the boundary he'd drawn between us.

At least I had this time with Elizabeth.

"Okay, well, I've got to go. I'll update you when I'm done."

Chapter Twenty-Four

Soon after I had hung up with the team, Lena scooped me up in a flurry, leaving Elizabeth to work the last of her shift. We wove through the grand home, past the staircase, and into the family room in the back, where the potluck was set up. We exited onto the back porch that looked out onto the green backyard that was littered by people. In the farthermost corner stood the maypole, encircled by toddlers in pastel clothing. Flowers bloomed from planters next to groups of strategically placed chairs. To the right was an outdoor kitchen on a stone patio, where another food table was set up.

Unsurprisingly, everything was beautiful out here, too, but one thing was missing: a playground set. Though Anne Frasier had been so meticulous about her yard, she'd had a fancy swing, slide, and monkey bars erected in her backyard for the girls to play on.

In this world, Anne didn't have my girls to buff out her crabby nature. Which left a foreboding feeling that perhaps, the old woman was surly a hundred times over.

Lena nudged me from the right, and I turned to where her gaze had landed, to the legend herself, on her throne, a high-backed wicker chair. She was surrounded by a gaggle of ladies who looked upon her with adoring eyes. Anne Frasier, if the same as the one in my real life, was the OG it girl, and since she was the host, my priority was to greet her.

I would've rather spoken to a stadium full of people than dealt with Anne. There had never been a moment's peace with her; she'd wrestled me for the last word, and in my world it had been expected for me to comply. I never could figure out: Was it because of age? Or race? Or experience? A combination of the three? No matter; it had been like having a mother and grandmother all at once. I had both been glad to have familial support and then immediately regretted the vulnerability of needing it.

Anne Frasier never just listened. She dispensed advice constantly, even if unsolicited.

Whether or not that would translate into this world, my memory surely could not set my preconceived notions aside, traumatized from all the ways I'd had to defend myself.

Of course we'd had our good times. We'd shared laughs, and when I'd had trouble with the girls, she had swept in with her Volvo to provide my girls much-needed distraction. But for the most part, she'd been a pain in my side. Because some days, I just hadn't wanted to banter, and discuss, and argue. Some days, all I'd wanted was to be loved on, and Anne Frasier had not been for private or public displays of attention.

At my approach, people made room, and at a foot away, Anne Frasier looked up at me through her wire-framed glasses. The expression on her face remained unchanged: deadpan and unaffected and, in a slight way, bored.

Still, I rallied, smiling with all my teeth and concerted effort. "Anne, it's great to see you. The house is just beautiful. Thank you for having me." I bent down and kissed her on the cheek. She smelled exactly the same, with the mix of her makeup and her French perfume and the bourbon neat she'd surely drunk before this event had even started.

Having been part of the family for three decades, I was privy to her secret. She loved her bourbon; she'd attributed her long life to her one drink a day.

My opinion? The heavens just weren't ready for her.

"Celine." Her voice cracked with rancor. Anne's face bore the decades with a regal grace. She still wore makeup, had her hair styled. Large pearls dotted her lobes, matching the string around her neck.

Then, with a wave from Anne, everyone scattered around her. "Sit," she said.

I complied, because there was no declining, though I braced myself for whatever was coming my way. A tongue-lashing for how Quinn and I had fallen in and out of love, maybe? A critical one-liner for how horrible my book was?

Instead, she said, "I hear you sold your place."

It took a beat for me to register her statement. "Yes. I'm turning the keys over in a few days."

"Does that mean that you won't be by anymore?"

"I . . . I don't know. I guess it all depends."

"On what?"

On whether the estate sale will really be my exit, I thought, then reworded it in my head so it was applicable for this world, or the one I left behind. "On whether or not I have something to come back to, I guess."

"Just because you've sold the house doesn't mean you have to move on. Though, you are the expert at that."

Ouch. She hit the target on the first try. She didn't even fire a courtesy warning shot.

"But I understand." Her voice resonated, though it wavered at the very end of her sentences. "Sometimes, it feels better to forget the past. There's some peace in turning your back to it. But the past is never really gone for good, and to pretend that it won't affect the future? It's better to face what you're afraid of. Understand, child?"

I nodded, as one did in front of Anne Frasier, though her advice sounded like the kind slipped out from fortune cookies. My brain resisted her words and chalked them up to someone who simply liked to spew advice whenever she felt like it.

Anne was just so . . . *strong*. From the first day I had met her, on that defining road trip with Quinn, when she'd peered at me over tea, she had been on me and unrelenting. That day, she'd asked me what my intentions were for Quinn. My intentions! I'd said we were friends, because that was what we had been. She'd responded with a huff, turned to Quinn, and said, "Don't you think she's a little too young?"

I'd answered with, "Better than a little bit too old, I think."

I had come from a home in which my strong mentors had been my brother and father, so we'd started off on the wrong foot and both stubbornly kept at it. She'd continued to try to mother me, and I'd snapped back with snide one-liners.

At her recent comment, I answered with, "I understand," to move the moment forward.

She pointed across the field with a shaky finger, to a group of people gathering under a tree. "Looks like they got everything set up for you. The book you wrote—it's good."

I sat back, surprised, fighting to suppress a grin, refusing to give her the satisfaction that she'd pleased me. But my mouth was a traitor and did it anyway, even if this version of *Just One Step* wasn't quite mine. "Thank you. I appreciate that."

"I just wonder if you're being too hard on yourself."

I felt my smile wane but refused to let it slip. "What do you mean?"

"You speak of everything being under your control, and that's how you got to where you are today. Child, so much is not in our control. Sometimes the situation is the way it is because of the choices other people make. Or, it's because of the unexplained."

This time, this zinger carved a little mark through my layers upon layers of well-worn skin. As if she knew that I actually didn't belong here. *Well, damn.*

"Thank you for your feedback, Anne." I stood, clamoring for space. My respect for this woman's age and stature would be the only thing that would keep me from saying something back, like: *Next time, you write a book.*

I set off into the backyard, and the cool, shaded grove welcomed me with a slight wind—and my friends with bottled water at the ready.

"You survived." Deb patted the back of one of the chairs and gestured for me to sit.

"Barely." Because I still wasn't out of the woods. Predictably, what Anne Frasier had said had settled in the pores of my skin.

"Don't you worry. This talk is going to cheer you up. People are so eager to hear from you. Look." She gestured to a trickle of well-dressed individuals headed our direction, some with the hardback book in their hands.

I squinted at the gaggle and witnessed Lena stepping out, elbows bent at a concentrated ninety-degree angle. Her dress billowed behind in her urgency.

"Deb. Celine." Her chest rose and fell, words constricted by her deep breathing.

"What is it?" Deb twisted open a bottled water and handed it to her. "Here, sweetheart. Drink before you pass out."

Lena swigged and, after a protracted swallow, said, "He's here."

"Who?" I scanned my notes. More people meandered to the chairs and sat, chatting, heads bent.

It was almost go time.

"Quinn." Deb swallowed a breath.

"Okay, so?" Would it be awkward for him to be here? Absolutely. But this was his aunt's house, after all.

"He usually doesn't come to these things, but lo and behold. And there's more." Lena flashed Deb a look.

Deb snapped to me. "Would you like more champagne, dear?"

"No. Water only, or I'll start slurring my words. You don't want to see that." More so, my attention had to be on point, since I'd read so little of this book. Tipping the water bottle to my lips, I chugged down half its contents, making me tear up. "But you say there's more? What more?"

"You'll see soon enough," Lena whispered, rubbing my shoulders. "But it's time to start. You've got this."

"I do." I swallowed the last bit of water, befuddled at her angst but confident and ready to take on this book talk. Up toward the house, Libby was looking on, though holding a tray. She wiggled her fingers in a wave, and it gave me that last-minute boost.

Until I took my spot and turned to the crowd, to find Quinn standing in the back, with a beautiful woman next to him. Inches from him. Practically draped over him.

My jaw dropped for the start of my greeting, but nothing came out of my mouth. The woman looked familiar, but most importantly, what was she doing with and to Quinn? "Oh, hell no," I whispered.

A body sidled up next to me. It was Deb, who, with a frozen smile, urged me—and all but tipped another bottle of water on my lips—to drink. The slide of liquid woke me from my trance, and I coughed.

"Hello . . . and welcome," I started, somewhat recovered, and my brain went on autopilot. I'd done dozens of book talks over the years, and over a hundred general presentations.

But my attention remained fully on Quinn and that woman. On how they matched. Him in gray on gray: a button-down oxford and trousers. She in a taupe gauzy knee-length dress. How he'd given her his napkin, and she'd dabbed her lips with it. How she'd handed her lipstick to him, which he'd slipped into his trouser pocket.

Jealousy roared through me like the ocean's waves.

Our marriage had endured many ups and downs, but I'd never been the jealous type, secure in what we'd built. So this emotion, this *I want to halt this class and challenge this woman to a duel à la historical romance novels*, was new. And it singed.

So much that I entertained only three questions after my presentation before getting on with the signing. Once I was seated with Sharpies at the ready, Elizabeth came front and center to my table.

"Okay, so I don't have a book just yet, but I wanted to say . . . keep calm."

"So you know too."

She nodded, biting her lip.

We need to stop your father, was what was poised at the edge of my tongue. Instead, I said, honestly, "What the hell is going on, Elizabeth?"

"Just remember. He buys the same bread every time."

"What does that even mean?"

"That *this* doesn't mean anything, and just give it time. Until then . . . breathe."

I nodded, then mimicked her as she took her own deep breaths. She stepped aside, gesturing the signing line forward.

And yet, the signing didn't clear the red from my vision. Afterward, I tugged Deb and Lena away from the crowd. They would be straight with me. "Who was that woman with Quinn?"

"Nora," Deb said.

"Who's Nora?" And yet, the memory came. Of me signing a book at Libby's funeral. *Nora. N. O. R. A.*

"They're on, and off. And on and off." Lena gritted her teeth. "Not sure which they are at the moment."

"They're dating?" My voice turned up. This was unacceptable. He . . . he was my husband.

Um, no, he isn't, not in this life.

I pressed a knuckle against my lips.

"Yeah, and she's here probably trying to cozy up to the queen bee." Deb gestured toward the backyard porch.

"Which is smart, unlike Celine over here, who looked like she was being scolded while sitting with her. I don't think I've ever seen that woman smile around you." Lena grimaced. "Sorry."

"No offense taken." Apparently I had never earned Anne's preference in this life either.

"As much as he doesn't think so, Quinn is our most eligible bache-lor in town and the only heir to Mrs. Frasier. It would behoove anyone who wanted to be in his good graces to get along with the old lady. So, I don't blame her."

"But is it serious for Quinn?" I asked, as if that made a difference. My temperature was ratcheting up by the minute. Whether or not this was real, there was no room for . . . other people.

I searched for my husband in the crowd. A piece was missing in the puzzle of his and my story. Not just what had been told to me—that I'd chosen Rex time and again, or that Quinn had been inflexible. There had been something there when we'd spoken in that alley. He'd stayed for my book talk; that had to have meant something.

"I don't know. He's very quiet about these things, apparently," Deb said.

"Should we go on a stroll and look for them?" I arched my eyebrows in a dare. If I was in this world anyway, why couldn't I make this work? Why couldn't I make the most of this time and try to get him back?

In both worlds, my relationship with Quinn hung in the balance, and I teetered toward losing him. In my real world, I planned to agree to his ultimatum the first chance I had. Getting back together with him in this world made sense, didn't it?

To hell with these boundaries Quinn had drawn between us. He had come to my book talk to show off this woman. Game on.

"Ooh," Deb cooed. "This is why I like you so much. Let's go on a stroll."

Lena shot off a list of cons, including the fact that we were acting like teenagers, while my gaze skittered over the tops of heads and found the redhead who I'd exchanged vows with, who I'd raised children with, and who was the love of my life.

He was under the shade of a tree farther down in the yard. With Nora. They were standing close. She smiled up at him.

And I turned into a ball of flames.

Deb hummed next to me. "I see them."

"They *are* cute," Lena added.

"Hush, Lena." Deb tapped her forearm gently with the back of her hand.

"I'm just saying. She's a nice person, Nora is."

Nice or not, this world or another, married or on the verge of divorce, that was my husband. And to the gasps of my friends, my body launched itself toward Nora and Quinn. I barely felt the cool wind against my face, nor did I register the emotion on Quinn's when he met me halfway.

A foot apart once more, I could see the panic in his eyes and visually trace the part of his Cupid's bow that didn't quite line up.

How many times had he and I been this close to one another in the last couple of months—I could count on only one hand. The last time, the alley; the time before then, when he'd begged me to come to Louisburg.

Well, I'm here now, babe.

"What are you doing, Celine?" His gaze darted past me, and a smile materialized on his face—a fake one—that didn't even attempt to make it up to his eyes. His Adam's apple bobbed as he cleared his throat.

"I'm . . ." In the pause, I recalibrated. And thought. Rex and I were supposed to be together. Quinn had his own life. And there were phones everywhere. With cameras. And social media apps. Sonya materialized in my conscience with her quintessential disappointed shake of the head. Because this trip was supposed to provide me rest, not catapult me into folks' socials. I cleared my throat and said, "We need to talk."

"Okay." He relaxed. "Not here."

"When?"

"I'll call you."

It was a brush-off, and this, above everything that had happened thus far, cracked this outer shell that I'd erected upon arriving in this place. If there was one thing that had been consistent in the last thirty years, despite the changes in our lives, despite the fights, despite Libby . . . it was that Quinn would be there. He'd show up.

"No." I shook my head. "Tell me when. And where."

He inhaled, impatience written on his face. "Tomorrow. I'll come to your place. I'll tell them you hired me."

"Hired you."

"Yes. You've forgotten that I do odd jobs on the side too." He snickered. "I'll say you need things hauled out of the house."

"Who's 'they,' and why does it matter?"

He blinked ever so slowly. "They don't have to matter to make a ruckus."

Sure enough, faces were turned our way. Nora was behind him, hands on her hips. *As if.*

But I got it. Small town and all.

"Right. Okay." I took one tentative step back, then another.

But before I turned, Quinn gestured for Nora to follow him.

The only thing that kept me from lunging at the couple was my dearest friends, who held me back and chatted away like I hadn't just provided everyone with a good dose of Celine Lakad soap opera.

Elizabeth met me at the top stair of the back porch. "You couldn't have just waited for him to choose the same bread?"

Chapter Twenty-Five

I decided to walk back home after the social along the winding walking path that teemed with pedestrians and bike riders. With the clack of my flats against the pavement mirroring the beat of my heart, and tucked into my light coat, I tried to purge the image of Quinn and Nora from my head.

Though with too many glasses of mimosa and straight-up champagne consumed in the last couple of hours, I was tipsy, and hopelessly spiraling.

"It's not real," I told myself, repeating it twice, and then a third time.

But why did it feel real?

Why did it hurt so bad?

If it wasn't real, how was I able to feel the chill against my cheeks? Or the firm pavement under my feet?

How could I feel the thundering beats of my heart against my chest?

My default excuse for all the surprises I'd come up against was that all this would go away soon. That something else was waiting for me on the other side. That my real world was waiting for me.

But what if everything was actually the other way around, and this was my life?

The thought halted me, and I bent at the waist, hands on knees. My vision swam, hazing at the edges. Because if this was real, then was my other life a dream?

If this world was real, then what were my memories drawn from?

But if the other world was real, and I was really soon going to leave this one, then what would happen to Elizabeth?

"Petals Fluttering" drew me from the mush in my brain, and I straightened. I'd halted exactly in front of my house. Nelson's two vans with his company's logo on their doors were still parked in the driveway. The windows were lit by the warm indoor light, and Elizabeth's profile showed she was at the piano.

Understanding descended: the piano's fallboard had been raised because Elizabeth had been using it. It was also the reason why her copy of *Little Women* had been opened faceup on the top of the piano.

But as the notes traipsed the distance to my ears, warped and garbled by the cold air, I didn't recoil as I normally would have. Instead, my anticipation heightened for what would be the complete melody.

But what was Elizabeth doing in my house? She'd left Anne's house after her shift because she had more orders to bake. She hadn't told me that she was coming.

At the moment, her profile exhibited true concentration, forehead scrunched in worry. She continued with the same repetitive melody but couldn't seem to get past it.

Libby had been a whiz on the piano. Usually, her fingers flew just as hummingbirds popped from one bloom to another, frenetic and hurried. Quite the opposite of Elizabeth at this moment. And quite the opposite of how she had been in the rest of the home. Libby had dawdled; she had been slow to jump to action. And yet, when it had come to her baking and gardening, and when she had played the piano, it had been done with an energy powered by a source that none of us—me or Quinn—could tap into. Much like when MJ got into her zone of work. It bordered on obsession, where all her frustrations and joy were channeled into this one hobby.

Currently, it was clear that Elizabeth was struggling.

And I knew the next note. I knew the next few notes, actually.

I pressed my hand against my heart. To my surprise, it beat steadily despite the piano playing. There was no panic attack to be found. It must be because this wasn't Libby. Or maybe because it wasn't the full song.

Whatever the reason, it allowed me to watch her for a few seconds longer.

Elizabeth bore that undeniable Lakad-Frasier profile, with Quinn's slight hunch in her shoulders. When Libby had been younger, I used to press a hand against her spine as a reminder for her to straighten her posture, much like my own mother had done with me. To stand tall and to take up space.

If only I'd realized that that was the most inconsequential thing I could have picked on. That there would've been more to worry about in the future, rather than her posture.

I swallowed against a building bubble of regret. So much of motherhood was this—the managing of the decisions one had made, wishing that some things could have been done better. And, finally, absorbing all the consequences from those decisions made by me and by my children. Wiser mothers might have said that we shouldn't have to take responsibility for the decisions our adult children made, but they must have never lived with a brick-heavy knowledge that they could have made a difference.

That *I* should have made the difference.

"She's working on that thing again." A voice came from my right, startling me out of my ruminations. I must have not heard the man come upon me, and my instincts pressed me against the fence. The boards gave minutely with a creak.

"I'm sorry." He lifted his hands as if in surrender, and his wind-breaker swished as he did so. "It's me, Jaime." He came out of the darkness, and my breath unhitched.

"Mr. Loren," I breathed out. "I apologize; I wasn't expecting . . ."

As the words left me, an unexpected giggle wormed its way out of my esophagus. Because nothing had been what I had expected the last few days, and right then, my body and brain were weary of it. Of all the thinking, the assessing, the assuming, and the questions. I would need a vacation from this supposed vacation.

An eyebrow arched. "Are you okay?"

"No, not even a little bit." I composed myself. The last time we had seen each other, he'd given me the side-eye. And since I'd had my fill of fake pleasantries, I asked, "How can I help you, Mr. Loren?"

He stuffed his hands in his pockets. "I . . . I came outside because you looked like you weren't doing well out here, hunched over at the gate."

"Thank you for checking up on me. I'm fine."

He nodded, though he didn't make a move to leave. His eyes darted to the window as Elizabeth growled, hefting herself to her feet. "She's composing something new, for the Laundromat down the street."

So, she sold jingles here too. "That's great."

He hummed another tune. "I forget the words, but that's the jin-gle for the cell phone company. Elizabeth's pretty successful, with the jingles and the baking, but she donates most of what she earns for whatever the community needs."

"Wow." Pride bubbled out of me like the fizz from a shaken can of soda. This news was a surprise, and yet, it wasn't. After Libby had died, the details of her life had emerged like the buds of newly sprouted plants. Like all the Kickstarters she'd funded. Or the charity member-ships she'd belonged to.

Libby had been a good person. Generous. Thoughtful.

I should have told her that more often. I should have told her every day.

"Anyway . . ." He crossed his arms. "That's why I'm upset that you're selling the house. I apologize for our earlier greeting."

"You mean snub."

"Snub," he said, voice weary. "You're right . . . it's just that she does so much good. And it's been nice to have her across the street. My grandson, Theo, is a bit of a rolling stone, and Elizabeth, she's as close to me as a granddaughter would be."

Knowing that Elizabeth had Mr. Loren in this world soothed a worry that I hadn't realized I was carrying.

"I'm glad you care so much about Elizabeth, Mr. Loren, but I don't know what to say. The house is sold. And Elizabeth assured me that she has a place lined up."

Despite my words, a niggle of a worry began. In truth, I really didn't know much of those details.

"I understand. And I know it's not any of my business, and that I'll see her enough times in town. But there's nothing like being right here. Anyway." He took two steps back. "It's getting cold. And you should go in too. You don't have a warm-enough coat on. May can still surprise you."

"Indeed," I whispered, tearing my eyes from the window, feeling like a sponge, heavy with today's happenings. "And thank you, for your honesty." As he disappeared into the shadow of his home, I strode up the walkway with his words on my conscience, and turned the knob and stepped in.

Several voices were engaged in chatter and echoing throughout the house. In the living room, Nelson was inspecting a stack of plates while checking something off on his clipboard.

"Hi, Nelson. How's it going?"

"Ms. Lakad. We're almost done here. Tomorrow, two of us will be back bright and early. You won't have to worry about keeping strangers in check."

"Thank you."

"It's our pleasure. It helped that we were fed. Ms. Elizabeth handed out a few cookies for us. She came in about a half hour ago."

"That was nice of her."

"Hey." Elizabeth emerged from the kitchen carrying a reusable grocery bag. "I dropped off some dessert and packed up my ingredients to bring back to my place. I didn't think you'd be here so early." An eyebrow plunged downward. "How are you doing?"

"All good." I was unwilling to rehash the commotion. "But, I heard you on the piano just now."

Her face flushed red. "Sorry. I should have asked . . ."

"No, it's fine." When the words came out of my mouth, I found that I meant them. It *was* fine. What followed was curiosity. "Mr. Loren mentioned that you're working on a jingle?"

Her eyes darted downward. "Yep. Though it's giving me a bit of trouble."

"Do you usually work on this piano?"

"I have a setup in the little house, with an electronic keyboard. My home office, if you will. When I'm stuck, a full-size piano usually gets me going. It's the whole feel and the sound of it that unlocks something. Before I had access to this house, I asked Pastor Lim at Saint Paul's Episcopal for an hour or two on their spare piano in the nursery."

In her words, I detected vulnerability, and I hesitated to commiserate.

You don't want to understand.

Those were words out of Libby's mouth during one of our fights. She'd been upset after I had sent her a listing of full-time remote job opportunities. *Mom, none of these jobs interest me,* she'd lamented. *I'm perfectly happy baking and writing music.*

I just don't understand, Libby. Don't you want stability?

Mother, it's not just that. You don't want to understand.

My Libby and I had avoided talking about her work after that. Any conversation about career progression had become a source of tension, a launch point for arguments if we hadn't been careful, all stemming from this idea of what work was. What defined work. Libby couldn't understand this nebulous world of coaching and motivational speaking—she'd thought it wasn't legitimate, based on popularity. And I couldn't accept this gig-girl way of life.

So, I had never been privy to her struggles and triumphs; she'd kept it all from me. I'd realized only in hindsight, after she'd died, that my opinion about her jobs had clouded our relationship.

But today I saw how Elizabeth's baking fed our community and how her generosity continued to affect those around her. And what had *I* done? What had *I* accomplished? In this world, I was an influencer for products I hadn't cared about. In my other life, I couldn't coach even myself.

I'm ready to understand, Libby.

Inhaling a breath to stay in the moment with Elizabeth, I said, "I know exactly what you mean, especially the whole unlocking part. A different perspective always helps. When I get stuck, sometimes I use a different pen, or a completely different notebook, or I change the scenery." I internally snickered at how ironic this change of scenery had been. "How can I help? I do a little writing myself." Knowing Libby's love for making music, I didn't want to barge into helping her with finding her notes. Even I knew how personal that was.

She grinned. "I know you write. You do a lot of writing. All that content on your socials and your blog. Your podcast too. Pretty good content."

"You've read my stuff?"

"Yup. I mean, you're Celine Lakad. You put our little town on the modern map. And you don't have time to help me come up with a jingle. But thank you for asking."

"I can make time." I was begging, but I wanted to help ease her frustration. "Since you're helping me declutter and all. We can even brainstorm."

I knew I'd said too much when she started to slink toward the back door; clearly, she didn't want to be pushed. "I . . . I'll think about it."

The oven dinged, and it lifted the awkwardness as well as Elizabeth's expression. My nose detected something sweet in the air. "Yum, what's that?"

"Hold on." She rushed back into the kitchen, and I followed, rounding the corner of the room.

"It literally smells like a bakery in here."

My feet stuttered to a stop upon entering. The dinnerware had been pulled out of the cupboards and stacked on the kitchen table. Pots and pans were tagged with prices, and matching utensils were placed in separate boxes.

The last time all my dishes had been laid out like this was the day we'd moved in, and it had felt like having our underwear out on the clothesline. From the sippy cups and the cartoon-branded melamine children's plates to the mismatched Fiestaware from decades of accidental breakage, the phases of our life, from the struggles to our final family success, were written in the scratches in the silverware.

At the moment, I felt neutral. Perhaps because nothing in these cupboards had been purchased by me, and because our family had shared good memories in Sampaguita's kitchen.

"I put something in the oven to warm up for Nelson and the crew. I was just about to tell him to take it out once the alarm rang. Might as well do it now." She set down her bag and slipped on an oven mitt. Grunting, she carried the pans to the stove top, the smell drawing me to her side.

"Chocolate babka," she announced.

"That is . . . beautiful." The braided bread in the pan begged to be sliced.

"Thanks. It's a new recipe for me. I figured Nelson wouldn't mind being a guinea pig." She peeled off the mitt. "It'll need to cool for a few minutes, then turned out to be sliced." She glanced at her watch. "So another half hour or so? That extra loaf is for you. It keeps well in the fridge if it's wrapped in double plastic wrap."

"That's thoughtful of you." The idea of pastry in the morning made me yawn, because it brought up the subject of sleep, which sounded perfect right about now. I'd lost years of my life with all that had been crammed into a day. "Sorry. I guess I'm more tired than I think."

"I feel you." She smiled. "I'll head home and stop by in the morning. I'm curious to see how this estate sale pans out. Nelson's advertising is everywhere. He's got that magic touch in getting people to show up."

After watching Elizabeth walk down to the second house, and while thinking about magic and her on the piano earlier, I peeled the red price sticker off its cover.

Whatever was going on, I still had my maternal instincts, and I'd bet this piano would be just the thing to trigger her muse.

Chapter Twenty-Six

Got that magic touch . . .

Elizabeth's words ushered me into slumber and into my subconscious, and I dreamed of my gaggle of girls. Each memory was hazed with a filter like old Polaroid photos, and each scene passed like the horizon on a road trip. I cycled through the pangs of regret, of joy, and of hope, through the different stages in their lives. Each photo was with the four of them, proceeding in chronological order, like a stop-motion compilation. My heart leapt with every familiar scene, like of the four of them holding on to each other's hands at Disney World. All four sitting poolside, feet in the water, squinting as they smiled, the sun in their eyes.

In the background I heard music—piano music.

In the dream, I was an observer. Despite my attempt to grab each photo or memory, my hand passed through the transparent images. I wanted the film to slow, to stop at certain images, to allow me to fully remember the context. But the images continued to flip, skewing slightly, and then the girls became women, and became not quite my daughters. The last photo was of the four of them, arms linked, sporting wide smiles. In it, they weren't sisters, but friends.

Chapter Twenty-Seven

A ring tore me out of my dream, and I woke, with a gasp, to my phone buzzing. I palmed the nightstand for it. "Hello?" I asked, voice croaking.

"You sound hungover."

Sonya.

I blinked myself awake, though just barely. It had been a fitful night. "I am. Sort of. More like hungover from drama."

"You texted that the book talk went well. You didn't mention any drama. Do I need to put Callie on this?"

"No. No publicity rehab needed. It's all drama in my insides."

"Do you want to talk about it?"

At my silence, she said, "Today marks the fourth day you're there, and you haven't spoken to your doctor once. You are what medical people call noncompliant. You sound more tired than ever when you're supposed to be resting. I'm starting to think this was a bad decision on my part to let you go on your own."

"I chose to go on my own." I sank into the pillow, and tried to explain my state of mind as truthfully as possible. "And the estate sale begins today, so good things are happening. But I miss the whole team. It feels wrong, for us to be apart from one another too long. Would it be possible . . . for all of you to come here?"

"I can get on the next plane, but to mobilize the whole team when there's no tour isn't the best way to manage our staff. You've got Mae in LA, and MJ in Upstate New York. And Amelia in some RV somewhere."

"Amelia's in an RV?"

"Hashtag full-time RV, remember? Anyway, to get them all to Louisburg just to hang out? Not sure if that's wise or if they'll even agree."

"I know I sound needy . . ." I was aware that these feelings were bleeding over from the day before, with having to face Quinn and Nora, and the FaceTime and the dream of my girls all in one place. Not to mention, there was no way for me to explain my perspective—namely, who I was in this world. "Have you ever felt out of place? Did you ever feel like you didn't belong but desperately wanted to?"

"Of course I have. You know that. We're Asian women in business. You and I have been othered."

"Then you understand when I say that I need my people. Without you all, it's harder to face the day, when everything feels so confusing. Having you here, I think, will help focus me on what I want, for the future. Will you bring them? If we need to make it more official, you can come up with an itinerary of things to talk about."

"I'll think about it and feel it out with the team. If it helps you for us to be there, that is a big consideration. Have you made an appointment with your therapist?"

"No."

"Celine." Her voice dipped. "You need to talk to someone."

"I will soon. I promise. And I swear I have people I can talk to here. There's also you, which is like ten people in one."

"But we're not a replacement for—"

"I know. Okay? I'll get on it." I didn't want the conversation to turn. "But thank you, for considering."

"You're welcome. But listen. Therapy could be good for you. Everyone should have therapy, in my opinion. How do you think I've dealt all my life? Just talking to my ever-growing shoe collection?"

The thought stumped me. The Sonya I'd known had been a minimalist. "You have a shoe collection?"

"What are you talking about? You've been in my closet. The mere fact"—she heaved—"the mere fact that you don't know is something that really disturbs me. I just feel . . . I just feel like you're really not yourself, and as your closest friend, I want you better. Please. Let me schedule one virtual appointment? I'd wanted you to do this part yourself, but apparently you avoid these tiny details. Say yes."

"Fine." If negotiation was what she needed, then I was all in. "Yes."

"Good." She sighed. "So what time does the estate sale start?"

I checked my phone, and my heart rocketed to my throat. I scrabbled and grabbed clothes out of the suitcase. "Shoot. Nelson, the estate sale planner, is going to be here any second. And I need a shower. Who knows when Quinn's coming over."

The doorbell sang in the house. At the same time, Sonya's voice was urgent, bordering on shrill. "Wait. Quinn? *The* Quinn?"

"Yes, that Quinn. I'll explain later." I didn't wait for a response and hung up. I peeked out the window, and Quinn's truck—the truck we'd taken that first road trip in—was parked out front.

My first thought: Holy moly, that truck was still kicking.

My second thought: Shoot. I wasn't dressed. My pajamas were wrinkled, and my hair was . . . who knew. And a woman my age couldn't just willy-nilly show herself without a bra on.

But I didn't want to reschedule this talk.

I padded down the stairs, grabbed a folded quilt from the stack in the corner, and wrapped myself with it before I opened the door. The bright sun was a shock, though it was nothing compared to Quinn. He wore a beanie and a puff vest over a plaid long-sleeve. He also smelled of his cologne, which I was now officially a fan of.

"Morning," I said, breathless.

"I can come back." He darted his eyes away. "I'm sorry. I assumed you would be up early, with the estate sale and all."

"No, you can stay." I couldn't let him out of my sight. "I forgot to set an alarm."

"Listen, I know that we used to be . . ." His voice trailed off. "But it's been a couple of years, and I moved on the moment you told me that it was over. And it is. Because Nora and I . . ."

Her name was like nails to a chalkboard. And though I couldn't do anything about Quinn's ultimatum in my real life, getting this Quinn away from Nora was my priority.

This was why I'd wanted Sonya and my girls next to me. Their pep talks dashed the nervousness from my heart. I needed one now—this was my husband! I wouldn't fail in showing him how much he meant to me.

"Quinn, I know. Just . . . I'll head up to change. Give me ten minutes, max." I pointed to the kitchen. "Make yourself comfortable. Elizabeth made a babka, and it's in the fridge."

To my relief, he stepped in. I stalled on the stairs until he slipped off his shoes and padded into the kitchen. Then, I took the stairs two by two.

In my bedroom I executed the fastest change since our children were tiny. Like those days of throwing on a bra in the last minute before I had to shuttle them to school. Now in jeans and a T-shirt, I combed out my hair and pushed it back with a hair band. Brushed my teeth, slathered on sunscreen. After a back-and-forth with myself about makeup, I swiped on gloss and dabbed on concealer.

I still had no plan, no proposal, no speech. Quinn and I weren't married; Rex was in the picture. He had Nora. But we had a whole history.

And I loved him.

I bounded down the stairs, all the while praying that he hadn't left. "Quinn?"

"Still in the kitchen," he answered back, and relief coursed through me. When I turned the corner, he was standing at the counter. He'd pulled out two mugs from the sell stack and picked out mine—a chipped Massachusetts Starbucks mug—and his, a mug from the Basketball Hall of Fame. On the counter, the coffee maker dripped, and the scent of coffee filled the air.

It was a scene of déjà vu, right down to the mugs, except my Quinn would have been shirtless. I would have wrapped my arms around him, his skin blazing hot, and he would have turned and planted a kiss on my forehead. Then he'd have poured me a cup—with nothing in it but perfectly brewed java—and we'd have shared a few quiet minutes catching up from the day before.

The memory took the breath out of me.

Because those small moments had happened up to when Libby had died. He and I *had* been good together, as friends, as lovers. Our movements had been automatic, honed after years of circling one another with four children in tow. And I'd taken it for granted.

I'd chosen work over him. Over my girls and Sonya.

I was startled out of my thoughts when Quinn turned with eyes that showed zero love.

Not an iota.

"Thanks, for starting the coffee." I willed the moment forward. It could be our last chance to talk. For me to find out what had happened, and for me to tell him that I missed him. That I loved him. And that I was sorry.

He shrugged. "Easy enough. I know you can't function without it." A chill radiated off him. "So, what did you want to talk about?"

"I mentioned there was babka, right?" I threw the refrigerator open and reached in for the bread, then unwrapped it on a breadboard. For my sense of conviction, my thoughts hadn't quite organized themselves in my brain. What should I lead with? What was most important to mention if he was going to give me only ten minutes?

The scents of chocolate and sugar bloomed in the kitchen.

"Celine, seriously."

I sliced a small piece, my back to Quinn, my intentions still in a jumble. Then, from my right, a hand reached out and gently took the knife away, then set it down.

Quinn stood a foot away. "I don't have time—"

"What happened to us?" I blurted out, the words ricocheting against the worn cabinetry.

His entire body sagged. "Not this again. You know exactly what happened to us."

"Explain it. The whole thing."

He sniggered. "Have you been so busy that you've forgotten the last two years?"

"Two years." It dawned on me then that in this world, my crisis point was our breakup.

"And I've had to hear about you every day, because this damned town can't stop talking about you. To them, I'm the person you left behind. I'm the person who didn't want to go with you. But you and I know different. You and I know that it was your choice to leave too." He ran his fingers through his hair. "I shouldn't even be here. Nora . . . Nora's great, you know. She's nice. And we just started to get to know one another."

"Is it serious?"

"Serious?" His face screwed into a frown. "No. Not even close. And who are you to even ask that, when you have Rex?" He set the mug down, looking unsure. "I don't know why I keep doing this. Why we keep doing this. You made your choice thirty years ago, and then you made it again two years ago."

He started to walk out the kitchen just as the coffee maker beeped. His footsteps thudded through the front room, and paused at the foyer.

The silence, during which he was most likely putting his shoes back on, was glaringly accusatory.

A thought occurred: What if losing him here superimposed itself in my real life?

I couldn't let him leave. Not like this.

He was my closest connection to this house. To everyone, because everything started with him and me.

"Wait." I caught his wrist before he walked out the door.

He turned with resignation in his expression.

"It's obvious I've made a lot of mistakes with you. We keep doing this because I think something connects us here, or somewhere else. And I know it's unfair for me to ask . . . it was good of you to come this morning . . . but please stay."

I let go of his wrist; it fell to his side with a swish. Because he didn't make a move to go, I kept on.

"It's true; I went back to Rex, but Rex and I are not together, not in the way you think. And I'm sorry. I'm sorry for hurting you. I can't make any excuses for that. But I'm only here a few days, and I guess I just want you to know that I'm trying to be better. I'm trying to do things better."

I wanted to say more to my husband. To tell him that he was my only love. But words could not fix his last two years, in this world and in the other. Me telling him I loved him right this second would only inflame the situation, and he wouldn't believe me.

But if we could spend time together . . .

Much like with Elizabeth: If we could just make our time together good, just as so much of my previous life was in this one, maybe parts of this life would transcend to the other. Maybe, it would make my other life better. Even if I couldn't fathom no longer having Libby in my real life, the memories I would have built, with her, would remain.

My heart was doing its thing—it shook in my chest, unsure what to latch itself to: this world or my other one. How important was it to have a foundation, a home?

It was crucial, and I didn't have it.

But maybe I could create that foundation myself, if just temporarily. Perhaps I could actively make this moment mine, this house mine, this person in front of me mine.

Outside, Nelson's vans rumbled and parked curbside. Quinn looked from them to me and back. The moment was a fork in the road, and it was Quinn's decision to go or stay.

I was not above begging. "Please. I'd like the help. And the company."

Nelson sauntered up with his clipboard. With him was one of his team members; each had a cup of coffee in hand. "Hey, Quinn."

"Hey, Nelson. Tony."

"You helping us out today?"

Quinn looked straight at me and, after a hefty pause, said, "Yep. I'm here."

My heart leapt in my chest, though I kept a straight face. It was a step.

Chapter Twenty-Eight

Shoppers arrived on the dot at ten o'clock. While Nelson and Tony managed the first floor, Quinn and I focused on cleaning the second floor.

He was currently breaking down the last of the boxes across the room from me, though he was in my periphery. It allowed for me to take him in, to watch him, as I swept the floors.

Quinn was different in so many ways in this life that I couldn't help but spy as he worked. Or maybe some of these characteristics had always been there in my real life, though I hadn't noticed or paid attention. For example: The way his body moved, the expressions on his face, the sounds he emitted while humming a thought or lifting a heavy box . . . he seemed more rough around the edges. His default smile was nowhere to be found; instead, a permanent scowl was imprinted on the furrowed lines on his forehead.

Then again, in our early years he'd been quick to temper and spoken bluntly. He'd been in the infantry, around too much testosterone with not enough supervision. But a wife and four daughters had since softened him.

"I can't believe there's so much stuff." I threw the topic of conversation between us, hoping to erase the silence he was clearly intent on imposing. "I can't even remember how long it's been since I moved in."

"Almost twenty years. Around the same time as me, when I got out of the army to help out Aunt Frasier. Two months after, actually."

"What a fluke, right?"

"That's one way to call it."

"You say that like I've been torturing you all that time."

"Pretty much." He glanced at me, hands on his hips. "No, that's not true. We had our own lives, and there were no issues with us living in the same town. It only made sense for you to move to the suburbs from Boston—real estate was cheaper. But when Rex left for LA, when I finally got you alone, I thought that you and I, that we were it. That it was meant to be for us to have lived in the same town. And since then . . . you being here doesn't feel quite as comfortable." He scooped up the broken-down boxes. "I'll be back. I can haul these to the recycling place."

No, don't stop talking.

Inside, I begged for him to keep going. He couldn't stop telling our story now. I slung the garbage bag over my shoulder and followed him downstairs. There were at least a dozen shoppers in each of the common rooms, taking me aback. Outside, cars stalled in front of the house, jockeying for a parking spot.

As Quinn dumped the flattened boxes onto his flatbed, one fell out of reach and dropped to the ground.

"I'll grab it," I said.

"No worries; I'll do it."

I picked it up off the ground anyway, eager to help.

"I said I would pick it up," he grumbled.

"It isn't a big deal."

"Okay." He sniggered. "You do what you want, whenever you want." He turned and went back inside; the screen door flapped behind him.

I raised both hands belatedly, belly souring.

What just happened?

It echoed how Quinn and I had been in my other life, when he and I couldn't seem to match up our conversations, so they would end in one big disagreement, with either him or me left standing alone and absolutely confused. It had to change for us to make up in both worlds.

The question was how to draw out his thoughts.

"Damn," a voice said from afar. Elizabeth stepped off the path from the little house. She was fresh faced, was wearing overalls, and had her hair in a braid, and I did a double take at how much she resembled Quinn. Even as she drew her face down in remorse. "Sorry. I saw that there were boxes available, and I was going to grab some. I didn't mean to walk right up to that."

"It's all right." Resignation settled in around me. "It's not like my and Quinn's business was ever private."

"Nope, definitely not here. This town's too small for that." She heaved a breath, and stuck her hands into her pockets.

I winced. "Are people talking about us?"

"News travels fast." She nodded. "With the whole encounter at the social. And especially because his truck is parked in front of your house."

I rested a hand on the side of the truck, at the beginnings of rust, and warmth rushed through me. Lots had happened in this truck. Our first road trip. Later on, Mae, quite possibly. In my real life, Quinn had his permanently parked in a storage garage. "He's owned this thing for forever."

"We know. We hear it puttering down the road every day." Her smile waned. "You okay, though? That conversation—there weren't a lot of words said, but if looks could kill."

"It was fine; I deserve it." The words came out casually, though they hurt nonetheless because of how true they were. It was obvious that I had many things to fix, to reconsider, to improve.

Elizabeth frowned, stepping closer. "No, it's not fine. And you don't deserve it. If he wanted, he could leave right this second. You're not tying him down."

But maybe I had—not with actual rope, but with obligation, bound by our previous life. Maybe, our vows had somehow bled over like permanent marker through onionskin paper.

Like this house, which I had ignored.

And Libby, who I'd let down.

With the sun in my eyes, I squinted up at Elizabeth. "You're a lot wiser than your years."

She laughed, grabbing a stack of broken-down boxes. "From your mouth to my mother's ears."

"Your mother?" My heart sped up, and I jumped in to help her grab extra boxes. This was the second time Elizabeth had mentioned her mother, and a whole new set of questions began to unfold in my head, starting with: Who was she?

"Yeah. She thinks I'm still a child, and that what I want for myself can't possibly be right." Sarcasm marked her tone as she trudged up the path, looking once at me. "She and I are not the same kind of person, and I think she kind of wishes I was."

The similarity between Elizabeth and her mother and Libby and me leapt up and all but clocked me in between the eyes, so much that they watered. I blinked the tears away while attempting to keep up on the path.

"That can't be true." My voice came out like a wheeze, because was that what my Libby had thought? That I wished she was different? "You're a wonderful person. You're thoughtful and kind. And you work so hard."

"Thank you. To clarify, I know my mother loves me, but I've never met her expectations."

Defensiveness rushed through me. Had I given her that impression? That she was the kind of person who had to meet expectations to be my daughter? "You are totally enough, Elizabeth."

"No offense, but that sounded like one of your quotes on your social media." She snorted. "For real, though. You don't know my mother. Anyway." She heaved a breath when we got to her door. "This is me. Thank you."

"I can bring the boxes in."

"No worries. I'll take care of it." She all but blocked the door, and gestured for me to set the boxes on the ground.

Which I did with a sinking feeling. This whole conversation harkened back to the way my Libby had often held me at arm's length.

It had hurt me then, but I'd accepted her boundaries.

Now I wished I'd tried harder, or somehow made things better between us. Would I have gotten to her sooner when she was sick? Would she have been comfortable to turn to me first when she was in trouble?

I didn't want Elizabeth to have that same experience, with her mother, or with me.

But, she had the choice to keep me around.

Clasping my hands together, I stepped off her porch. "If you need any help at all, I'm right next door . . . for whatever you need."

"Okay," she said, though she waited for me to walk away before she entered her house.

I'd give her some space, for now. There was still Quinn to contend with.

Chapter Twenty-Nine

I had barely stepped into the house when Deb and Lena called my name from across the living room, and seeing them unwound my spinning top of thoughts. They both beamed, bearing armfuls of loot. Their energy was contagious; we waved and laughed as if we were separated by a chasm and not by a tide pool of people, and through hand and arm signals and a slew of giggles, it was understood that I would need to brave the channel.

The rest of the shoppers weren't quite as lighthearted. Someone in the corner raised a beveled candy dish against a window, inspecting it for cracks. Another plugged a toaster into a socket to verify it was working. I overheard another person ask Nelson for the certificate of authenticity for an antique highboy in the formal dining room.

Through and around, I navigated myself around shoppers, waiting for the panic to settle in that people were touching my stuff. A few days ago I couldn't fathom even walking into Sampaguita, much less sifting through its things, and here I was traipsing over them.

It was as if the stuff had reverted to just that . . . stuff. It had lost its meaning in this world. I had more to think of. Like people.

It was apparent that many in the estate sale knew who I was. A couple requested an autograph. Another person asked for a picture. A few waved shyly as I passed them.

Almost to where Deb and Lena were standing, I was halted by a shopper. He was holding silver candlesticks. "I've been looking for you. Hon!" He raised the candlesticks in the air. "I found her, hon."

A woman neared, eyes rounded in glee. "I was hoping you would be here. I wasn't sure, seeing that you've taken a break. It's okay to not be okay."

She had said all the right things. The words were correct, but the sentiment was off. Her tone was placating, and it was clear she didn't mean it. It wasn't helped by her insincere smile.

I mirrored it (though aimed for affable) and sidestepped my way around them. "Yes, just a small break. Well . . . I hope that you're enjoying the estate sale. Have you taken a look at the kitchen? Lots of great stuff in there."

"But wait." She held me back by the elbow, and the air around me sparked with warning.

I twisted my elbow from her grasp, though still with a smile on my face. "I'm sorry, but I do have to get going."

"I heard you were at the May Day social yesterday." Her face switched to glee. "I'm bummed I missed your book talk. I've watched all of your videos. I love your makeup tutorials, and of course your absolutely amazing advice on moving on."

The last part of her sentence sounded menacing, and my heart dipped. *Oh no, Celine, what did you say?* I had no idea what this woman was referring to. "Which video?"

"You know, the one where you equated losing your diamond earring to grieving for a person?" Her voice escalated to soprano.

She was angry. At me.

"I . . . I'm so sorry." Had I really done that? Equated a loss of a thing to a loss of a person? Stunned, I was speechless. Present me might've created a set of steps to achieve personal success, but I would've never gone as far as trying to guide someone through loss, knowing that coping with grief and loss was personal and unpredictable.

But hadn't I preached in the same way? Had I thought I was right, that my way was the correct way? Had I been equally presumptuous in my real life?

A pressure on my lower back snapped me back to focus, and I inhaled, replenishing the oxygen that had escaped my lungs in the last seconds, and turned my face up to Quinn. Next to him was Nelson.

The relief that coursed through me almost knocked me off my feet.

In my thirteen years in this business, this was my first experience with an aggressive fan.

"Ready to go?" Quinn asked, and I nodded, despite neither being ready nor knowing where we were going. "Thank you for your questions. Nelson can help you check out."

Then, Quinn guided me by the waist in the opposite direction, to the back door, outside to his truck. He opened the passenger-side door and helped me in.

I gulped in air after the door slammed shut.

The truck rocked when he climbed into the driver's seat. Turning to me, he said, "Are you okay?"

"Yeah, I . . . I don't know how I froze. She caught me off guard. Thank you for stepping in."

"It's no problem. She didn't have a right to grab you like that."

"I think that people assume they can because I'm so accessible, I guess." My body temperature had dipped, and I wrapped my arms around myself. Rationalizing the situation kept me from shivering.

"It certainly poses problems sometimes. It's the thing that broke us up."

The shock hit me right in the chest, and I snapped back, "Excuse me?"

He looked at his rearview mirror. "More people are driving up. Let's get out of here. You good with that?"

"Yeah, sure." I buckled my seat belt, still reeling from his last comment, from this day.

He backed up and wove around the traffic that had developed in front of the house. It was only when we were out of the thick of it that I heard U2 on the radio.

He blew out a breath. "There's a local farm nearby that has a food trailer walk-up and a couple of tables. Fine with that?"

"Yes." Then, in the silence that had extended to what felt like an hour, I said, "What did you mean back there, about fans breaking us up?"

He groaned. "Just . . . we don't need to talk about it. There's no purpose to rehashing everything over and over. You already told me that you were leaving in a few days."

"Then why are you here with me right now? And why would you say something like that?"

"Because I still wanted to make sure you were safe, dammit. And I'm a glutton for punishment, apparently." Then, he glanced at me, with a hint of a smile on his face.

I laughed, and it was enough to release the tension in my chest. I buried my face in my hands to keep myself from crying.

He rested a hand on my shoulder. "Talk to me?"

"I can't believe that I uploaded a video comparing losing a diamond earring to losing people."

His face crinkled into a wince. "I haven't seen it. But no video gives her the right to come at you that way."

"Still." I thought back to my real-life work, the motivational quotes I posted like *You can achieve anything you set your mind to* and *Channel your worry to the next step*, the workshops on time management and vision planning, my speeches about dreams and the grit. Was it all just toxic positivity? And who made me an expert? Had I spent thirteen years pumping up people's egos and calling it coaching? "Lately, I've just been feeling like . . . everything that I've done has been just useless, or for nothing at all. Done for money and never really helped anyone."

It surely hasn't helped me.

"What? No. Booo."

I cackled. "Did you just boo me?"

"Because what you said deserved a boo." He leaned an elbow against the window, driving with one hand. "Don't tell anyone. But even if I'm supposed to be upset at you, I'm actually one of your biggest fans. Count me in as someone who's proud of you. You don't have to be perfect to try to be better or to try to spread good, and that's what you've done."

"But that video . . . and other things I'm sure I've done . . ." And now, thinking of my relationships in my real life, all of which were in turmoil, I added, "And all I've given up . . ."

"The fact that you were concerned about the hurt you caused and not the fact that she put her hands on you already says what your intentions are. And while intentions aren't always excusable, I believe that for you . . . you want to do better, and you will."

His words landed on my shoulders like his counsel had done in the past: heavy and sincere. This was us. Our conversations could veer, but somehow we could find the middle of the crisis point. And it was a relief that even in this upside-down world, we had that.

"Our work happened to us," Quinn said after seconds of silence, answering my question from earlier. "Because our work took us to different physical places."

"I don't believe it. People make long-distance relationships work all the time. You said you thought that we finally found one another. If so, why didn't we let it stick?"

"We laid it all out in our last conversation. You said that you had too much to do, and you couldn't do it in Louisburg. I asked for a compromise—I just couldn't do a permanent move, not with what I wanted, as a basketball coach, with Aunt Frasier at her age. And you wouldn't or couldn't meet me in the middle. I gave you an ultimatum then, and you called my bluff and left." He heaved a breath. "I look back now, though, and maybe it was for the best. Work drives you."

"That's not fair." My protest was an automatic reaction because Quinn in my other life had said a version of this. It had been his chief complaint. "Work matters to me."

"I know it does." He clicked on the blinker and made a right turn. "You've told me a million times. But it doesn't mean that I have to live with it. I know you're in the business of talking, of storytelling, of being out there, but sometimes, I feel like you need to really listen."

I shook my head, and half laughed. "I object?"

He gave a double take, a grin on his lips once more. "You object? Object to what?"

"That claim that I don't listen. I'm an expert listener." I guffawed as he turned into a gravel lot where two other cars were parked. Next to it was a food trailer with its window up. Lights were strewed around the trailer, while portable torches marked the edges of the eating area.

"This is cute," was all I could say, still buried by his last comment.

"Mostly sandwiches. You'll like it." He shifted in his seat. "Look. I know I'm making it like us breaking up was all on you, but I wasn't compromising in some ways too. I didn't take what you were doing seriously, and you knew it. It was good you let me go. I would have held you back."

"Then why are you so angry with me?"

"Because we still split up. Because you still left. And I knew when I saw the house's for-sale sign that you were going to come home to say goodbye. But that wasn't the thing that set me off. It was because when you finally *did* show up, you did it at the eleventh hour, and you just thought . . . you just thought that things would be cool between us. That's not how it works. Just because you tell yourself things are good doesn't mean they are. But . . . I want to be done being angry. All we're doing is giving a show to all these people."

The May Day social came to mind, and I groaned. "And they are definitely watching us."

"I mean, you *are* Celine Lakad."

"And you are Quinn Frasier, most eligible bachelor and heir to Anne Frasier's estate."

He snorted. "Nooo. Please tell me you didn't hear that from the grapevine."

"From Deb and Lena themselves."

He ran a hand through his hair, his cheeks turning pink. "That is embarrassing. And this is the perfect time to change the subject. Let's eat, shall we?"

We popped out of the truck and walked up to the counter. It was a standard sub place, and my tummy growled at the smells emanating from the truck's exhaust.

"Meatball, no cheese?" Quinn turned to me, crossing his arms.

"That's right." My cheeks warmed. "You remembered. And let me guess, you want a hot turkey with provolone."

"Always." He grinned, then ordered and took out his wallet to pay.

"Here, let me." I reached for my purse, belatedly realizing that it was sitting in the bedroom closet. "Crap, I forgot it at home."

"It's okay. I've got it."

With a ten-minute wait for the sandwiches, we took the nearest bench seating, across from one another. He caught me up on his coaching job at the local high school, and his side jobs to make ends meet.

"Make ends meet? But I thought you were an heir?"

Arms crossed, he grinned. "I expect Aunt Frasier to be kicking for a very long time. Until then, I don't mind earning my keep. She spoils me as it is."

The thought that Anne would think to spoil someone made me cackle.

"What's up?"

"Nothing . . ."

"No, tell me." His smile slipped a smidge.

"Anne just seems to have something against me."

His eyebrows plunged. "I don't know why you think that. She thinks very highly of you."

"Really?" I peered at him, appraising his comment. "Because she's always told me what to do."

His expression softened. "It's because she cares about you. If you weren't important to her, then you wouldn't get a second of her time."

"Why would I be important to her?"

"Well, because you were important to me." His gaze dropped. "And she's a strong mother figure. I imagine that if you were a mom, you would be the same exact way. You and your YouTube videos."

The reminder of my fan encounter caused me to groan, and as he laughed, temptation tugged at me. I wanted to tell him that I *was* a mother. That he was a father, and that maybe I'd misjudged Anne Frasier, and he was right.

"I'm happy," he added before I could respond. "I like what I'm doing. I thought I wanted to coach college ball, but I love high school ball. It allows for me to stick around and keep an eye on things with my aunt. And, though it took a while, I finally got over you."

"I'm glad you're happy, Quinn," I said, even if it was a half lie. Of course my wish was for Quinn to have everything he wanted—but that should've included me in his life. In both lives.

"How are things with you?"

"At the moment? Life is in flux." I lowered my gaze and chose my next words carefully. "But every day is a surprise."

"I read that you're on a break."

I nodded. "I need it."

"I'm glad that your tour supported it."

"They didn't really have a choice."

His eyes roamed my face. "Are you getting help? Do you have resources?"

The fact that he was still able to put aside our strife to talk about my needs—it was so Quinn; he was a good man in every way, in this world and my real one. I wished that I'd remembered that during the intervention and, instead of fighting him, that I'd simply listened.

Mollified, I said, "I do have my resources. Though I'm still really debating how to access and who. But right at this second, I'm coping."

"Can you share what happened?"

To summarize this whole experience was like trying to fit a week's worth of clothes into a backpack. "In short? I explored a fork in the road, and it wasn't what it was cracked up to be. And I'm here to sort through what I could have done better. Then, maybe find my way back to that original road."

He nodded contemplatively. "Have you accomplished what you were hoping for?"

"To figure out what I could have done better? I think so. To get back to that road—that's a little more complicated."

"I'm a basketball coach—you're really making me work with these vague sentences."

I laughed. "I know. But the details aren't as important as the fact that I'm figuring out that no matter what I do, I won't have everything." I bit my lip to keep my voice steady, and threw in a subject change, to lighten the mood. "Though what I did find was someone living in my house, and an angry ex-boyfriend."

"Ex-fiancé," he corrected.

I gasped. For all the gossip Deb, Lena, and Elizabeth had shared with me, why had not one of them mentioned that Quinn and I had been engaged? Lacking a more clever response, all I could say was, "Oh."

"Meatball and turkey are up!" called the cook from the trailer.

He stood, and as I followed behind him, I slapped a palm against my forehead. No wonder Quinn had been angry. He and I hadn't just had a fling.

Damn, Celine, you really did hurt him.

Chapter Thirty

When we arrived back at the house an hour before the end of the estate sale's first day, it was lit up bright against the shade of the trees. Fewer cars milled in front of the house. As Quinn parked his truck, its headlights illuminating the side yard, I caught sight of Elizabeth entering the little house.

Our family in our real life collectively had moved four times before Quinn had transferred from active duty to the Guard and then had settled down in Sampaguita. Each move had been a struggle, and while Elizabeth had declined help from me, my instincts told me that she still needed it.

"Do you know where Elizabeth's moving to?" I asked.

He half laughed. "Now, how would I know that?"

"I just thought . . . with it being a small town and all."

He pulled up the emergency brake. "Louisburg's not *that* small."

"I beg to differ—we'll see how much of today's excitement makes the rounds by tomorrow." Quinn had yet to move to get out of the truck, right hand on the gearshift, so I stayed put too. The tension between us had gone, and our ride back had been filled with easy small talk. "I set her up with boxes earlier, and I've seen her take trips out with a carful of boxes. But I haven't seen others around. I just thought that maybe she would want some help."

"I would assume. She's sure to have furniture."

"Well, I offered help earlier, and she said no. But I was thinking . . . would you ask her if she needs help? I can pay you for your time."

He raised an eyebrow. "You don't need to pay me."

"I'm not trying to insult you. It's just . . . you gave the reason to everyone that you were here to work, and I want to help her . . ."

"It's no worries—I'll offer help. I'm curious myself where she lands." He popped the door open, and I met him at the front bumper. "But why would you think she'd say yes to me, when she said no to you?"

"I just have a feeling."

All my girls had been daddy's girls. They'd wanted to please their father as much as they'd wanted to mother and dote on him, and Quinn would have done anything, within relative reason, for them. Quinn had especially doted on Libby—he had been able to get behind her stubborn walls, and she'd pulled and challenged Quinn's empathy.

Perhaps that thread of connection was here too.

"Okay. Let's do it. Should we go now?"

"No time like the present." I lifted up my sandwich. "And we've got bait!"

We skirted around back to the little house. Then we knocked on the door, our bodies shadowing the threshold.

The door opened with a whoosh, and Elizabeth met us with a curious expression. "Hey, you two. Um, are you okay, Celine? I came by at the tail end of the commotion at the house."

"Yes, I'm much better now. Thank goodness Quinn was around. We took off for a bit, for a breather."

"Good. Nelson called in for backup. There's more of his people in there to help with crowd control." A tentative smile blossomed on her face, and she readjusted her shirt. "So what's up?"

I lifted my sub. "Need company for dinner?"

"And some help with your boxes?" Quinn added.

She waved the notion away. "That's not necessary. I'm good, really."

"The house has to be vacated in four days. Are you really good?" Quinn raised his palms. "I've got extra hands—and a truck and a hand dolly and some time."

Hesitation danced across her features, and a shoulder lifted. "I mean . . . really? Are you sure?"

I sneaked a peek up at Quinn. It had worked, and it had taken a mere thirty seconds.

"I'm here working on the house, so it's no extra effort for me to come around back, especially for the big items."

"Wow, then, okay. I mean, if you don't mind him coming back here, Celine."

"Celine?" Quinn asked.

I started at the question, realizing that my face was still turned toward Quinn, and he was, in fact, looking at me too. "Nope." I snapped my head back to Elizabeth. "I don't mind at all."

"Thank you. This is . . . thanks." She stepped back, widening the entrance to her own moving chaos. Boxes were stacked in one corner, and currently she was packing up the kitchen.

In my real life, this little house was a storage area. Lawn and garden equipment took up residence in it but not much else. *This* little house was adorable, with high ceilings. The walls were painted white, and long curtains banked tall windows, giving the illusion that it was larger than eight hundred square feet.

The house had one bedroom, one bath, and a kitchen that looked out into the living room. There were very few things on the walls: a scenic picture here and there, the very same macramé wall hanging from her real life. And in one corner were musical instruments with a mic setup.

The whole place smelled like chocolate. "What are you baking?"

"Brownies. I was going to bring them over in a bit." At the island, Elizabeth cut up brownies into tiny squares. It was a homing signal, and I beelined toward the chocolate.

I gestured at the brownies. "May I?"

"But of course. In my opinion, the dessert should come before the main course."

I handed her the sandwiches. "We can cut these up too. There's no way I can finish up a footlong."

"Want to point out what I can work on while I wait?" Quinn grabbed a box from the corner.

She pointed to a closet door. "You can start with the linens."

I busied myself by putting another box together and taking in more of the little details of my daughter's life. Pictures on the refrigerator. A cookbook on every surface. Two industrial mixers on a stainless steel cart in the corner of the room. Cat-themed items.

My Libby had loved cats, too, and I didn't remember a time we hadn't had one when the girls were little. "Do you have a cat around?"

"Nope." Elizabeth grabbed plates from the cupboard. "Robin said no pets. But there's that cat café down the street I go to where I can get my fix."

"A cat café in Louisburg?"

"Yeah." She smiled. "It's super cute. And they have pastries and coffee, and chairs that are so comfortable. And the most important thing: cats."

"You can adopt the cats too," Quinn called from the hallway.

"Yep. One day, one day. Maybe sooner than later." Elizabeth brought plates to the coffee table. "Everyone ready?"

Quinn and I took seats on the couch.

"I hope you don't mind, but I cut the sandwiches into even smaller pieces. I love them bite sized."

"That's fine with me." I passed out the napkins.

Once we were settled and we had loaded our plates, we took the first bites of our sandwiches, and collectively groaned. It brought us all to laughter, and for the first time in what felt like forever, my soul eased. To be just an arm's length away from the two people I missed deeply, in different ways, filled up a hole in my heart. Because when I'd lost Libby, I'd lost Quinn too. It hadn't been Quinn's fault—we had all buried a bit of ourselves with Libby. But I hadn't helped our relationship by escaping to my work.

But here we were. The three of us. Like a little family.

This is your family.

The thought came from the recesses of my brain, and I looked down at my food and chewed in earnest. Because I couldn't allow myself to think this. My family, my real one, was elsewhere. I couldn't forget them.

"Can I be honest about something?" Elizabeth wiped the corner of her mouth with a napkin.

Quinn and I nodded.

"You both got here right on time. I was starting to feel over-whelmed. Not with the logistics of moving. But with the idea of getting to know a new place. I like it here. This house has been good to me."

"Take it from someone who's moved several times," I said, gently, "but your new place will feel like home soon enough, especially as you unpack. And I can help with that. After today, I'd rather not be around all those strangers, so you can count on me for as long as you need, for anything."

Before my conscience warned me that my promises might be shallow, I pushed it out of the picture. This was my chance to show her unconditional support.

Quinn took a sip of water, then said, "I'll leave you my number, and you can text, anytime, for help. Or even just to talk."

"Thank you." Her cheeks reddened. "Celine, there *is* something I'd like to talk to you about, and I'm wondering if you would be willing to negotiate." Elizabeth bit her bottom lip, so reminiscent of the times when my girl had wanted something so painfully.

"What are you interested in?" I asked without looking at her straight on, because Libby had never liked being under pressure. "And I can see if we still have it in the house."

"It's the piano. It has its quirks, but it does make such a beautiful sound." She glanced up briefly. "I know she's still there. I . . . um . . . asked Nelson to let me know if someone was interested in it, that I was going to talk to you about it."

I ramped up the effort to contain my smile. "I'm so glad you asked me for it because . . ."

"Because why?"

"I already told Nelson not to sell the piano, and I took off the for-sale sticker." The idea that Elizabeth would be bringing it along with her in this life filled me with hope. Knowing that she would continue to play, that the music would continue—if not in my world, then here—felt like enough.

Both her eyebrows lifted. "Really? I . . . I don't know what to say."

The expression on her face was not what I had expected. There was a trace of hesitation there, in the way her smile was a tad short of gleaming. "There's nothing to say, because the deal is done. The piano's yours. And until we move it, you can have your key back so you can play on it whenever you'd like."

She pressed her hands against her mouth in a silent squeal. "That would be amazing. Do you mind if I come in late tonight? I'm on a little bit of a deadline."

"Absolutely. Come anytime."

"Thank you . . . I'll pay you back. Or, we can barter. Just set your price."

I shook my head. "No, there's no need for that. Moving the piano to your new place will be cost enough."

"I insist." Elizabeth's face had gone serious, voice flat.

I was befuddled at how this conversation was slowly going sideways. With my Libby, it had been the same—I'd unknowingly say the wrong thing, and soon she was excusing herself from my sight. The mood in the house had flipped on its head; I scrambled to switch it back. "Okay, sure. I'll . . . come up with a value tonight. And I'm good with bartering, especially with fresh bread."

"Everything is better with bread," she said, seeming to exhale, and my own body relaxed.

"But let's talk about the real logistics here. Are you moving far?" Thank goodness, Quinn switched up the mood as easily as turning the dial.

"Not at all far. I'm staying at the Thornes'. They have a little house out back, too, and—"

Quinn grumbled next to me, setting his sandwich down.

Quinn and I . . . in my real life . . . hadn't been fond of the Thornes. They had been our backyard neighbors, with our five acres butting up to their ten. Over the years, while living in Sampaguita, we'd had a few passive-aggressive interactions with them—about trees and property lines, and then about fencing costs—issues that hadn't been large enough to take public but had still strained the relationship.

Though in my opinion, it had had everything to do with Nate Thorne and Quinn himself. Both had been too alike for their own good.

Her gaze darted between me and Quinn; and it brought me back to all those moments when Quinn had sat Libby down, to try to discern how to be her best support.

"Is there something wrong with the Thornes?" Her voice lowered.

"They're nice enough, but . . . I don't know." Quinn shook his head. He looked to me, for my opinion.

"Did you sign a lease?" was all I could answer with. I couldn't speak for this world's Celine. But one thing still was true: my trust was with Quinn's perceptions of people. He had a knack for picking up behaviors and attitudes that could be masked by charisma and flair.

"Yes, but we're doing a month to month."

Quinn shifted in his seat and rested a hand behind his head, discomfort radiating off him, mirroring my thoughts. "Month to month is pretty risky."

Elizabeth took a bite out of her sandwich. "I'm not worried."

She was frustratingly unbothered. My Libby had been fine with going with the flow, sometimes minimally preparing—for the things that didn't matter to her, that was. Then again, it had seemed to work for her. Whereas even with all my planning, I'd ended up in this other world.

"Why are you grinning?" She popped a brownie in her mouth.

Had I been grinning? It was probably because I was figuring out I knew less than I thought I did. "It's just that . . . you're pretty headstrong."

"I've been told that time and again." Her face fell, and guilt washed over me that I'd insulted her. She was her own person. She would make her choice despite what Quinn and I said.

When did a mother's guidance stop? When would this end, this feeling of responsibility?

"Headstrong isn't always such a bad thing, though," I added to try to lighten the moment. "I've been told that life could go a lot smoother if I listened now and again."

Quinn snorted. "I know all about that."

I balled up and threw a napkin at his smug face, only for it to plummet at my feet.

"I think you'll make Celine and I feel better if we can take a look at the place. Between the two of us, we know a few things about houses. Are you open for us to take a load out tomorrow?" Quinn asked.

The butterflies in my belly awoke. The teamwork between us—it was still here. I'd always joked that in the thick of parenting exhaustion, there had been some things that could light up my libido: One was seeing Quinn do chores. Two, when we were both in sync in our parental duties. And three, quite reliably, was when he'd leaned against the doorway with his arms crossed and forearms on display.

My face flamed with the start of desire. Then, I imagined myself jumping into a cold lake. In this world, I still had Rex. And this man in front of me wasn't my same Quinn.

"Taking a load out tomorrow sounds . . . okay. We can do that," Elizabeth said.

It was a nuanced win, but I would take it.

Chapter Thirty-One

That night, sleep was impossible. For hours, my eyes scoured the ceiling, tracing shadows made by the moon and streetlights. The faces of my girls ran across my memory; my granddaughters' laughter came and went like the sound of the occasional wind blowing against the old windows. The smell of Quinn's cologne. Sonya's chatter. It all intermixed into a glob of faces, names, occasions, dates, and places. Of my life. Of both lives, now.

Time was slippery; it was fickle. It was gone by the time one noticed it. In the last week, time had been almost inconsequential, because the people, devoid of the superficial details, were who they were, and I was who I was. Over thirty years ago, there had been a fork in the road, and while it would have led me to different milestones, the people on the road remained. My love for them remained too.

Tomorrow was the last day of the estate sale. After that, the last day in the house—and time *would* be consequential. Time would tell me if my guess had been right, if I would return to my real world.

But what would that mean for this world? And what was I supposed to do, knowing that while I was back with Quinn, with my three daughters, Elizabeth was elsewhere, in some other time.

Because I wasn't sure if I could let go. Not again.

My phone, nestled in my crumpled blankets, rang, and I picked up without looking, lost in thought. "Hello."

"*Finally.* God, I've been so worried."

Rex.

"Hi." I threw the covers over my head. Fully cocooned, I had the semblance of protection. This conversation was overdue, but it wouldn't make it less difficult. Because I would not be able to pretend that we were a couple, even if this world's Celine had chosen him.

"We need to talk," he said.

"Okay. Did you want to go first?" I offered, remembering Quinn's words once more, about listening.

"Okay, um . . . this is the hardest thing I've had to say, but . . . I don't think I can do this anymore. The last few days of you being there and then not keeping in contact really hit me over the head. Look, we've been together a long time. Thirty-seven years, give or take a few months from our break. But to tell you the truth, we just haven't been the same since I moved to LA." He half laughed. "You never did take to LA."

I smiled at his candidness despite the way I'd avoided him. And though I didn't have firsthand knowledge, I could imagine that living in Southern California would have been another fish-out-of-water experience. For me to have gone meant that I'd loved and respected him. "I still tried."

"Yes, you did, and I was . . . am . . . grateful. But the months we were apart, when you and Quinn had gotten together. Gotten *engaged.* I know, I know," he rushed in. "I don't reproach you for that. I all but pushed you together. But it was clear to me then, as it is to me now, that you and I . . . well . . ."

My eyes filled with tears, though I didn't know where they were coming from—except that Rex's voice was so kind and sincere. And because in the span of my splintered lifetime, I hadn't chosen him twice. "We were together so long."

"I know. I don't regret a single day of it. We gave it one hell of a try."

"Yes, we did, didn't we?" To admit that, to accept it, and then to say it now allowed me to push off the covers. Rex had been referring to our thirty-seven years in this life, but it also applied to our young adult years in my real world too. Our romance had ended, but I had not had a single regret about it.

For that, I decided to say my piece—my true piece that spanned both worlds, which I hadn't been able to express those years ago. "Rex, you're a good person, and you were always so kind to me. You were my first love."

"It's one thing to be loved and a whole other thing to be in love." He inhaled. "Ideally, we're both to that one person. But it's okay that it's not me for you, or you for me. And I don't know . . . but maybe there's someone out there for me still."

"I don't have a single doubt about it." His Facebook profile in my real world came to mind, including his long-term girlfriend, and a smile crept onto my lips. "There will be more for the two of us. We're just getting started, right?"

"Absolutely. Me and my CPAP machine and arthritis in my left knee." He laughed.

"Young at heart is a whole lot better than feeling too old to live."

A lengthy pause descended on the other line. "And this was why I fell in love with you. When you say stuff like this."

The mood circled once more to serious, but this time with hope. We discussed my return to Los Angeles in order to pack up my things, and to manage our shared assets, even if in the back of my mind, I wondered if any of that would happen at all.

We soon hung up, with me cuddled into my sheets, relief tugging me into slumber . . .

Until the sound of a piano playing tickled my thoughts, waking me. The set of notes stopped and started and back again.

Libby.

No, Elizabeth.

Her name registered in my thoughts without a single bit of fear, hesitation, or sadness, unlike a few short days ago. Instead, what brought my eyes open was the obvious struggle she was having getting her jingle down. Already, a picture was forming itself in my mind, of Libby with a frustrated look on her face, her strong fingers laying down the keys in the effort to draw out the words. A grunt and a curse word to herself. And then starting from the top once more.

She was working so hard.

She wasn't giving up.

Another wave of regret hit me, this time accompanied by the melody from downstairs.

Libby had *always* worked hard, though I'd never given her credit for it. Her tenacity was on display downstairs at this very minute, and she'd had that tenacity when she had been alive. But I'd had this vision of what that was supposed to look like, and because she hadn't matched that vision, and because we could not transcend our quiet disagreements, we had lost time and each other.

The thought hefted me to my feet, and I padded across the rough weave of the carpet and out the bedroom door. The lighthearted echoes of the piano traipsed up the staircase and into my heart.

Elizabeth sang, "*In a bit of a rush? On a deadline to crush? Lucky Four Laundry to the rescue! Bring all your special attire . . .* argh." She growled. "Do people even say *attire*? What's wrong with me? And that chord just didn't sound right."

Upon hearing her exasperation, I had the inkling to rush down to offer my help once more, but I hesitated. She'd been clear earlier that she didn't want my help.

Then again, it was worth asking. I couldn't just stand there in the wings, especially when I knew what this melody was supposed to sound like.

So I stepped down the stairs quietly.

"I'm sorry," Elizabeth said even before I reached the bottom step. "I know it's late."

"It's all right. I said you were welcome, and I meant it." I turned the corner. Elizabeth's fingers were clasped on her lap. "The jingle sounds so cute already."

"Pfft. Cute does not equal complete." She returned a wry smile. "It's due to my production partner in the morning, and nothing is sticking right now. I'm just not feeling it."

"Can you get an extension?"

"I could, but I have other projects lined up. If I don't get this going, I'll be backed up with my other work, and then it becomes a spiral."

"Okay. Well . . . I can try to help."

"I'm good." Her chin dipped to her chest in a kind of resignation. "You've done so much for me already, with me staying here, you helping me pack, and this piano." She stood. "I should really get out of your hair. I didn't mean to wake and bother you."

It's fine, Mom. I'll go to urgent care if I feel worse. I didn't mean to wake and bother you . . .

Elizabeth's words created a tsunami inside me. There had been three conversations between me and Libby from the onset of her fever until she had been admitted to the hospital. Three opportunities for me to get on the plane immediately. Three plus countless moments when I could have told her that her work mattered, that I loved her despite all our disagreements. All those times I could have listened.

I approached her and placed my hands on her shoulders out of emphasis. "You're not a bother. You've never been a bother."

She stiffened under my touch.

"What I mean is . . ." I cleared my throat, dropping my hands to my sides. "I'm here, and I can help. I heard some of the lyrics. Go ahead; begin the intro, and play what you have."

I sat on the piano bench and encouraged her to take my side. Seconds later, she followed suit.

As Elizabeth queued up the introduction, a memory flew in of a family sing-along during Christmastime. The other three girls had stood around the piano in their pajamas, belting "Joy to the World," with Libby playing with as much glee.

Elizabeth now sang: *"In a bit of a rush? On a deadline to crush? Lucky Four Laundry to the rescue!"* She lifted her hands from the keys. "That's all I have. All I need are two lines. Two simple lines that for some reason I can't nail."

"Hmm." I bit my cheek, though nothing stood out to me either. "I haven't been to Lucky Four Laundry. What kinds of images come up for you?"

"Speed, definitely," she said. "The machines are always whirring; customers are in and out in a few minutes' time. They're a close-knit work family."

I hummed the tune and rolled these ideas around in my head. "How about: *In a bit of a rush? On a deadline to crush? Lucky Four Laundry to the rescue! Not a moment to spare . . .*"

She whispered, "Not a moment to spare, something something care."

"What other word rhymes with *spare*? Fare, mare, lair, dare . . ."

Elizabeth dropped her face in her hands and began to cry.

Stunned, I wrapped an arm around her shoulders. She'd shown me so little of her vulnerability that it caught me off guard. Everything inside me wanted to fix it. To keep her from hurting. "I feel like you're really close. Do you think . . . ," I hedged, wondering if my suggestion would offend her. "That we should change that A major chord to a C major?"

She sniffed through her tears, forehead folded in thought. "I can try." Then, she rested her fingers on the keys and, after a pause, played the tune. "Oh . . . that . . . that might work."

"I'm sure you'll have to play around with it a little . . ."

"Thank you. And I'm sorry for bawling like that. Deadlines. It comes to a head, and this is how I deal with it." She swiped the back of her hand against the tears on her cheeks. "But I'll get it."

Except I knew my daughter. Something else was wrong. "What else is on your mind?"

After a long pause, she blew up into her bangs. "Truthfully? I'm going to miss this house. There's something about this place. It's cozy and private. The jasmine in the backyard. This feels like home; this feels safe. Here, I can exist and be who I want to be."

"You do exist. You can be who you want to be anywhere you live. It's okay to be attached." And as I said so, as I tried to convince Elizabeth, the thought seeped into my own conscience. I hadn't said these things to my Libby. When Quinn and I had moved out, I'd imparted the opposite. I'd taken her refusal to move with us to Annapolis personally, convinced that she should have been able to move on, to do different things, to be with us, her family.

I hadn't listened to her.

"And, I believe in you. In your ability. In your talent," I implored.

"You're just saying that. You barely know me."

If only you knew. "I've witnessed the good things you've done and the difference you make. I know you're having trouble right now, but it doesn't bear on who you are. I just know that the words will come, and that all the good feelings you felt in this house will follow you to your next home. Because all the people who you care about will be right behind you as you make it home."

A pause settled between us, in which her breathing calmed. "Thank you. I really needed to hear that."

"Just telling it like it is."

"Speaking of feelings . . . right this second, I'm having a massive case of déjà vu."

My heart thumped. "Yeah?"

"Yeah. With the two of us here at the piano."

I bit my lip to keep myself from spewing forth the truth, from declaring that yes, there had been so many times with us together, side by side exactly on this bench. The temptation was so strong because I wanted to unload this burden of being the only one who knew of my experience.

Her face turned up to me. "I think it's because my mom and I used to sit at the piano, when times were still good. We'd take a piece and split up the keyboard and make a game of it, to try to coordinate our hands." She smiled, though it slipped a second later. "I miss it, how we were so close. But when we get together, sometimes there's this disconnect, like we're not tuned in to the same frequency."

Her words landed like bricks on my shoulders, and I tried to keep focus despite the discomfort and heaviness threatening to flatten me. "If you feel this way, I bet she feels the same way too."

"I know. But it doesn't solve the situation, does it? Sometimes I think, are we just too different? Is it too late to change who we are to one another?"

"I hope it's never too late to change." *Because I'm trying to change right now,* I continued in my head. "Otherwise I've surely pissed off a lot of people." We both smiled, and an idea sparked. "But until things are better between you and your mom, I'm right here."

Her eyes glassed over. "Really?"

"Absolutely. So, if you needed help or if you wanted advice—whatever you need, even just to sit by you. From now until . . ." I swallowed against the start of tears, because herein was the part that was unknown. What would happen when the keys were turned over, with me, Elizabeth, or this world? "Whenever."

"I'd like that." Elizabeth's face crumpled further, chipping against the final barrier that I had put up around me. I hadn't wanted to fall for this whole world, to believe it in totality, but when Elizabeth leaned her head on my shoulder, much like she had when she had been alive, that thin gap between the two worlds filled in.

My daughter was here, when all I'd wanted the years before she'd died was for her to need me like she used to. And yet, despite the joy that was surging through me, there was a seed of grief germinating inside. A reminder that the time between us was unknown. For all the assumptions of what needed to be accomplished for me to get back to my real world, I actually didn't know anything at all.

But that this moment, right now with my daughter, was real.

Chapter Thirty-Two

Things changed literally overnight. In opening my heart, in taking responsibility for the role as her mother in this world, I began to see Elizabeth as a fully fledged human being.

Like cliff jumping, where there were no take backs after leaping off the rock, I was all in to care about this woman. I would see Elizabeth as my own, treating my grief over Libby's death like history to learn from.

It didn't matter if Elizabeth didn't call me Mom, that I wasn't her mother. It was just semantics. This fact didn't negate that our relationship would continue to grow, because we were both present to work on it, for however long I had in this world.

The next morning, Quinn and I drove to Elizabeth's future home. We were in his truck, with the radio playing classic rock, with boxes between us and under my feet. In front of us was Libby's car, weighed down with boxes. One couldn't see through her back windows with it packed to the brim.

Elizabeth had ended up sleeping in Sampaguita last night. I'd offered the family room couch so she didn't have to make the walk down to her place. She'd been gone by this morning, the evidence of her stay marked by her folded blankets and a raised fallboard.

I was singing along with the tune on the truck radio, enjoying the sun's warmth against my right cheek. A lightness had come over me, now that I could finally enjoy Quinn, this moment, and everything I had in this world.

"You're in a good mood." Quinn peeked over at me. We each had a hand on the box between us, to keep it from falling forward.

"How can you tell?"

"You're a mic short from going full karaoke."

The tops of my cheeks warmed. "It's Guns N' Roses. How can you not?"

"Not arguing that the selection you chose to showcase your vocal skills isn't epic, but I haven't heard you sing since . . . God, I don't know when. So . . . what's up?"

"Things are . . ." I searched for the most accurate thing to say. "Working out."

"Things? Like the estate sale?"

"That, and helping Elizabeth move. That the piano has a home. And that you're here, and we're talking."

"All good things." Quinn nodded, and as he did so, the occasional streak of silver shone from the red of his hair, waking me from my lingering doubts. "I guess it hasn't been so bad hanging out with you these last couple of days."

"So you're not helping just because I asked?"

His gaze slid over to catch mine. "You know that's not the only reason why. But this also means that you'll be on your way soon."

My breath caught in my throat. I'd been flying so high since this morning that I hadn't quite gotten to the details of what my future would be. What I did know was that being around all my people was paramount. "Do I have to be on my way soon?"

His eyes widened. "What are you saying?"

"I don't know." It had never felt so good to say this truth. "But going away doesn't feel like it should be part of the plans."

"And how about Rex?"

"Rex and I agreed that I'm not much of a California girl. I like my winters cold, with snow that requires shoveling and warm boots and hot chocolate."

"Really?"

"Yup."

"Wow . . . when you said things were over with Rex, I didn't truly believe it. I mean, that's over three decades." He clicked his blinker on and made a left turn onto a gravel path. The truck bumped and swayed, jostling the box between us.

"It *is* a long time." I looked out the window as we passed rows of apple trees to our right. "But even Rex acknowledged that there's so much more up ahead, and that maybe we should be looking for that."

No words came from Quinn, but in the silence, he reached across the top of the box and took my hand into his. "This okay?"

I sipped in breaths; I was awash with giddiness. This was what jumping with both feet into the present would bring: happiness.

Still, I remained composed, because these were all just baby steps. "How about Nora?"

"I told her that I still had feelings for you at the social."

"You did? But you weren't even really speaking to me."

"I know." He laughed. "But I couldn't pretend. Everyone could read it on my face. At least that's what Aunt Frasier told me."

"That lady." At the mention of her name, her words came back to me: *Just because you've sold the house doesn't mean you have to move on. Though, you are the expert at that.*

I pushed her foreboding words away; her negativity would not be allowed. She might have cared for me as Quinn had suggested, but she was also acting as a protective mother figure. And I wasn't pretending now. Now, I was accepting this life as mine. Entwining my fingers tightly with his, I said, "But, I'm glad she set you straight."

The hand-holding lasted a glorious few seconds, until Elizabeth began to slow, then parked next to a bank of trees. Through the line in the woods was a home that appeared to be smaller than the secondary home at Sampaguita. It was under the wide canopy of trees, so the structure was shaded, looking sinister and dark.

My gut sent me a warning that this place was not an upgrade from Sampaguita. Glancing back at Quinn, who was peering through the windshield, lips pressed into a line, I saw that he, too, wasn't impressed.

"Maybe it's not so bad on the inside," he said.

Elizabeth stepped out of the driver's seat, and her trunk popped open. Her lips were splayed into a smile, and she hopped and clapped in place.

I laughed at the sight of it. "She looks excited, so maybe you're right."

Quinn jumped out of his truck. I grabbed the box that was at my feet and followed Libby to the path into the trees.

Under the canopy, it was dark and markedly cooler. Creepier, in my opinion. Then again, I wouldn't be the one living here.

"So, the vibe is a little different, as you can see, but it's private, and the inside has a lot of potential," Elizabeth said over her shoulder and climbed the porch of the one-floor cottage.

"The front's adorable," I mused, though the facade could use a lot of elbow grease. The formerly white siding had moss growing in places. Looking up above, I determined it wouldn't take much for an errant branch to fall straight onto its roof.

But, I was here to neither judge nor impose, but assist. Just as I should have immediately supported Libby in staying at Sampaguita, in trusting her judgment, Elizabeth deserved my support.

"I know!" Excitement exuded from her voice. She stomped her shoes on the welcome mat out front and stepped in, turning on the light.

As I entered, my eyes widened at how rustic the cottage was. Not rustic as in the shabby-chic, cozy kind of a cottage, but in a cobwebs-wherever-you-turned kind of way. The wooden floors had large gashes and stains; the light fixtures were dim and few—she would need extra lighting right away. The kitchen had one tiny countertop, and the oven—the oven was half the standard size.

"Not bad, right?" she cheered, though I heard her telltale tone of fake optimism. "Let me show you the bedroom." She opened the door to a tiny room that already contained some of her boxes. The wall-to-wall carpet was stained and threadbare. "And this is the bathroom."

I grimaced. The bathroom had a tub half the average size, but the condition of the tiles—most were broken with grout missing. And as we returned to the front room, more details jumped out at me: peeling wallpaper, a dark stain on one of the ceilings—which could mean a previous leak, or a current leak, which meant there was a possibility for mold . . .

This is unacceptable.

Above my thought, Elizabeth began to talk about her plans for renovating the house. Something about pulling up the carpet, sanding the floors herself, and changing out the stove, since she was in the market for a small commercial oven. Removing all the blinds since most were torn. And there was more, but her words had gotten to be too much. I blurted out, "That's a lot to sink for a rental. Are you sure that you want to live here?"

"What do you mean?" A crease formed in between her eyebrows.

"You're in a month-to-month lease. Meaning that just as you can back out of this deal anytime, so can the Thornes. You shouldn't have to put in so much work and then—"

A hand on my elbow halted my speech. "Why don't we . . . unload my truck."

This wasn't the time to unload his truck. If anything, this was the time to turn around and deposit her things back at Sampaguita. "Quinn—"

I was tugged away, out onto the front porch and then down the path. Though I was flummoxed, it did not escape my notice that the sounds under that canopy were magnified, and our footsteps echoed along with the chirping birds.

There was no way my child was going to stay in this place.

"You can't do that, Celine," Quinn said when we made it to the rear bumper of his truck. "You can't tell her where she can and cannot live."

"Were you present during that tour? Didn't you see what I saw?"

He lifted both palms as if that would settle me down. "I did see, but she's an adult who has chosen where she wants to live. Did you look at her face? She didn't appreciate what you said. And most importantly, she's hard pressed to live here, at least for now, because she doesn't have much of a choice."

He unlocked his truck's tailgate and brought a box flush to the edge while I paced. He was right. Elizabeth was in a bind because of me, so that meant that only one solution remained. "Then I'll back out on the sale."

"What the . . ." Quinn hiked his hands on his hips. "Um, no, you're not."

"Why not? I'll say that I changed my mind. I need to find a house, too, and it's my house until escrow is officially over. I'll lose a lot of money, but what's money without family?"

"Family? What are you talking about?"

"Libby. Our daughter." The three words flew out of my mouth like wedding doves when finally set free. And in that split second that Quinn's face flipped to confusion, I gasped and backtracked. "I mean, she feels like she could be my daughter."

"That's not what you said. And you called her Libby, not Elizabeth."

All of me scrambled to think of an explanation, so I tried a less far-fetched reason. "I . . . I guess in my mind, she is our daughter."

"Why do you feel like that?"

"Because in another life, I would have chosen you from the start, and we would have started a family, and one would have been Libby."

I braced myself to be ridiculed or interrogated, and maybe even left behind right there on the gravel driveway. Instead, Quinn came closer, and perched on his tailgate. After a pause, he said, "I often thought of what would have happened if we'd ended up together from the start. I imagined we had a family, with four kids."

I crossed my arms to hug myself, suddenly cold. Beyond that, it was justification that some things were beyond explanation. "Four, really?"

"Yep. Four wild girls. Wild as in independent, go-getters in their own way. Our house would have been loud; there wouldn't be a moment's peace."

My throat clogged with emotion. With this need to tell him he was right. If only I could show him. "Four would be exhausting."

"But you would have been a great mom."

I rooted my eyes to the ground. If he only knew—if he only knew how I'd tried but failed, and how I wanted to do better. That from today onward, he would get all of me. That Elizabeth, Sonya, and my girls would always know I cared about them. "You would have been a great dad."

"I would have been a helluva fun dad." The pride was evident in his voice, and it took me out of what could have been another guilt-ridden moment. Instead, a giggle burst out of me, along with a single tear. Because yes, I would miss my life in that other place, and maybe in jumping in with both feet here, I had to choose, but having a version of Libby around . . .

"Come here." His voice snapped me out of my thoughts. I stepped up to him so I stood in between his legs. He set his hands on my waist, grounding me to him and this earth. "I don't expect for you to open up to me fully about why you feel that way about Elizabeth, because I have a hunch that there's more to it than you're letting on. I hope that one day, you'll trust me enough to. But I know you well enough to know how you take care of people. You take care of them, care for them, and love them like family. And because of that I hear your worry about Elizabeth.

"But you simply cannot make decisions for other people. And if you care about her that much, you'll respect that she knows what she wants for herself. When a person feels judged, they're less likely to stick around."

He was right; I knew he was right. My experience had proved it. For Elizabeth and I to grow in our relationship, she had to trust me. To earn that trust meant I needed to trust her too.

"Okay," I finally said.

"Sure? You good?" He looked me in the eyes. "You're not going to run back in there and throw a lighter at the house, are you?"

"Ha! That's an idea. But no. You're right. I promise to be good."

He nodded, letting me go, and for a beat I mourned his touch. I took steps backward, and he stood, handing me a box. "Ready? The only muscles you should be moving are the ones below your neck. Got it, big spender? Damn, I can't believe you were all, *I don't care how much it costs me; I want my house back.*"

Though he'd said it lightheartedly, and I'd blown off the joke, none of it was funny to me. I would do anything necessary at this point to keep my family together. I just didn't know how to do that when it was spread so far apart.

Chapter Thirty-Three

"Wow, what a difference a day made," Elizabeth said. "I can't even believe how empty it looks."

"Three loads of packed boxes, countless bags of garbage, and an encounter with a mouse later, and you're almost on your way." I stood up from sweeping dirt into the dustpan and dumped it in yet another garbage bag, then plopped down on the couch. We were back at Sampaguita, in the little house, tidying up after moving most of Elizabeth's stuff into the cottage. "All you need is for your movers to come and grab all your furniture, and you'll be all set."

Today's adventure with Elizabeth had taken a full eight hours, and every muscle in my body ached. But I had to admit, the cottage had since improved when we'd brought her lamps in. A rug on the floor, and maybe some plants, would make it more homey.

"It's wild." She looked up at the ceiling. "How much a room changes once you put your things in it. I wonder what the new owners will do to this little house. Or, the big house even. Maybe I shouldn't think about it. It's making me a little sad."

"Same." My mind had continued to whir through the afternoon. I couldn't let go of the notion that I wasn't doing enough. When I'd arrived, closing on the house had been the goal. That goal had evolved to spending more time with Elizabeth, to getting to know her, to showing her what I couldn't show Libby.

Now, I wasn't sure what I wanted.

Elizabeth tilted her head toward me. "Are you going to miss this house?"

"Yes. Honestly, I'm having a little bit of seller's remorse. How about you? Are you excited to make that cottage yours?"

She smiled. "You know what? I think so. I'll always love this place, but what you said last night made me think. That all the good feelings from this house will make it to the other side. And today, after our visit there together . . . I have so many ideas that will make the house mine. And I'm so happy that Quinn's going to help me change my contract to a yearly one, and discuss some of my requests like a new stove." Her smile was sheepish. "You were right to say that maybe I shouldn't settle for a month to month."

"I've no doubt that you're going to wave your magic wand and it's all going to be beautiful."

"Though, be honest. You were a second away from telling me not to move in."

I shrugged, gritting my teeth. "Guilty, but can you blame me? At first glance, the house looked so rough. But I admit, as you started to clean up, and then you told me of all your plans, it sounded better and better."

Elizabeth had shown us colored sketches and a notebook filled with DIY projects. It had put me in my place—to assume that she hadn't had a vision. Another lesson learned.

My phone buzzed. It was a text from Nelson:

We're done for the day. Are you nearby so I can update?

"Day two of the estate sale is done." I slapped my hands on my thighs and hefted myself to my feet. "Nelson needs me next door, and honestly, I am ready to head to bed."

She raised a finger. "Hold for just a sec." And after truly what felt like a second, she returned with something held behind her back. "We didn't really get a chance to get to the nitty-gritty with our barter for the piano, so I wanted to start by giving you something. But before I do so, will you promise to . . . for lack of a better word . . . use it?"

The smile on Elizabeth's face was quite suspect. "This sounds sketchy."

"Just say yes."

"Fine, yes." Because I was tired, and also, saying yes to her would be my pleasure.

And from behind her, she presented *Little Women.*

I stammered a shaky response. "W-wow." My brain was at a loss for words. This was a generous gesture, and the fact that she was willing to gift me this book, her comfort book at that, made me want to whoop in celebration. This must've meant that she trusted me. That she cared.

But this book represented everything about the past. How I'd failed, how I'd escaped into work, the intervention, and my unwillingness to listen to my family. On the night of Libby's funeral, when I had thrown that book in the fire, I'd thought that had been my lowest point, but I realized now that that had simply been the beginning of the journey.

I didn't want to return to that. Nor did I want to remember it.

She shook the book out at me. "I'd like for you to have it."

"No." The answer came out quickly, but at the concern on her face, I backtracked. "It's your book."

"It's also your piano, and you gave it to me. How do you expect for me to accept a piano if you can't even accept my book?"

It was a logical statement, and this offering shouldn't be a big deal. More so, this obviously wasn't the same book I had thrown in the fire, right? Just like the piano, it was a version of it.

And, bottom line, I couldn't refuse Elizabeth. She would be insulted; this was a new chance for us, and I wasn't going to ruin it. So, though every muscle resisted, I reached out for the book.

Much like with everything that had been a version of something from the past, my nerve endings fired at the familiarity of the smooth leather against the skin, the weight of the book, and the divots in the cover. I could almost hear the rain slapping against the window from the funeral reception.

"Now, you promised you'd use it, which means you have to read it," Elizabeth said, seemingly satisfied, bouncing on the balls of her feet.

I flipped through the pages, finding highlighted passages, notes on the margins, underlined sentences. "You annotated it."

"Like I said, it's a favorite. In fact, I read a couple of scenes last night. There's this line Marmee says about seeing light behind the clouds. And it reminded me of you. Like you could have said it yourself, and maybe posted it on your socials as a quote. Anyway . . . thank you." Cheeks reddening, she threw her arms around my neck in a hug.

So shocked was I that my body froze, but slowly, my arms wrapped her torso. My body savored every second: the way she felt in my arms, her hair against my cheeks. I reined in the tears, though inside I was folded over, sobbing with gratitude. "You're welcome. I'll see you tomorrow?"

"Yep. I'll be ready to clean this place up to a shine."

Later that night when I lay down to bed, I set the book on the pillow next to me, still unopened. I wasn't yet ready to turn to the first page, but I fell into slumber for the first time without wishing to wake up somewhere else.

Chapter Thirty-Four

Nelson and his crew arrived the next day shortly after I'd had my first cup of coffee, and the sight of the line of folks ready for the estate sale was a jolt to the system like a starting gun of a race.

"This is it. Day three." Nelson entered the foyer with enthusiasm, raising his clipboard with a megawatt smile.

He spread out the paperwork on the dining room table, which hadn't yet found a buyer. It was a list of all the contents of the home; yellow highlights delineated the things sold. There were at least a dozen pages. For a home's memories to be boiled down to scribbles on pieces of paper was sobering, even if I hadn't been the actual person who'd owned these things.

"I know it's just stuff, but it's decades' worth of stuff. Gone," I said.

"It's overwhelming if you think about it that way. I look at things a little more different. These things had many years here, and now they will go to another family, where they will have a second life. Maybe a third. They'll make a difference in those families' lives. Imagine if we had that power, to keep starting over. The impact we could make."

"A lot, for sure," I agreed, because before this last week, I wouldn't have believed it could happen. But here I was, in this limbo in which I continued to suspend disbelief—there was no choice not to—because I was living a different version of my life.

I was left to my thoughts as Nelson's people began work, when a text chimed in from Elizabeth:

I'll be hanging out here for the day.

That didn't sound good. I trudged toward the little house and knocked on its door. Elizabeth unlocked the door and opened it several inches, squinting against the sunlight. Her hair was in a messy bun, loose and askew. Her eyes were bloodshot, nose red, as if she had a cold.

"Elizabeth. What happened?"

"My mother happened. But I don't want to talk about it."

Curiosity and secondhand guilt clamored in my chest. Was this how my Libby had looked when she and I had gotten into arguments? We'd had doozies of discussions, once over the fact that she'd refused to share the financials of how her business was doing when I'd offered my help to make it profitable. She'd accused me of not trusting her, and I'd simply wanted to be involved. We hadn't spoken for a month. At the time, I'd imagined her indignant, but what if she'd been upset?

How much time had we lost in anger?

"Okay. But I think I can help," I said, knowing exactly what would make her feel better. "Get some clothes on."

Confusion passed in her eyes. "Where are we going?"

"Questions, questions. Just know you're getting a good cup of coffee because of it. Give me your keys. I'll drive."

Her lips quirked up, and she snapped up her keys from her kitchen counter. She tossed them to me in a graceful arc. "All right. I'll be right back."

While I waited for Elizabeth to get dressed, my phone buzzed in my purse.

Sonya:

You should be getting a call from Trisha Blake

Sonya:

Your therapist

Sonya:

Please pick up her call, k?

                                                  Celine:

                                                     k

Sonya:

You have to make time for this

                                                 Celine:

                     Ok fine but also I did speak to Rex

Sonya:

And

                                                 Celine:

                                    We broke up.

The phone rang in my hand, though I declined it. I couldn't update Sonya at the moment—this time was for me and Elizabeth.

                                                 Celine:

                               Later? Busy right now.

Sonya:

I'll be waiting for your call!

Elizabeth returned a few minutes later, now in a pair of sweats, and we swiftly walked to where her car was parked.

"So where are we going?" she asked as she slid into the passenger seat.

"You'll see." I grinned while backing out of the space. There was another vehicle ready to take our spot, with the estate sale starting in ten minutes. "Hopefully it will give you a little boost."

Our destination was only two miles down the road, and in five minutes I turned into the parking lot. Elizabeth squealed with delight, and her features brightened. For how complicated this last week had been, my daughter's smile was my reward.

We jumped out of the car. The signage of the LITTLE CAT CAFÉ was neon green and hung from the large front window, showcasing shelves for cats to parade in front of human eyes. As we approached the front doors, pairs of cat eyes tracked our movements.

"How did you know I needed this right now?"

"Well, since your baking stuff is all packed up, I figured this was the next best thing."

The door chimed when we entered the café, and I melted at how quaint the setup was. Round tables with chairs were evenly spaced in the dining area. Artistic black-and-white photos of cats hung in frames. Against one wall was the coffee counter, where a massive espresso machine sat. Two baristas chatted while tending to an order. And down the hallway was a room of cat towers where cats played.

"What do you feel like having?" I asked, though Elizabeth was already lingering at the mouth of the hallway.

"Actually, do you mind if I go on ahead?" Her body tilted away as if she was magnetized.

It brought me to giggles. "Be my guest."

Elizabeth was gone before the end of my sentence, so I decided on an espresso drink and ordered it.

After I was handed my latte, the bells of the front door rang once more, and a familiar voice rose above the rest of the chatter. I halted with the steaming cup against my lips, lamenting that there wasn't a second and secret exit from this current situation. So I girded myself and turned, a smile plastered on my face.

"Hello, Anne." My voice was just shy of screeching; I winced at how the woman had always had that effect on me. At eighteen, when Quinn and I had been dating. In my twenties, when I had shown up at her doorstep to visit with our first child, then second, then third, and then fourth. In my thirties, when all I could do was keep my children alive and I'd barely had enough time to brush my teeth. In my forties, when I'd started my coaching business.

She'd always greeted me with the same confounded sour expression, like she'd been sorting through her judgment for the most perfect one to lob at me.

It's because she cares about you.

Quinn's words from the other day returned to me, and I reeled back my criticism. My efforts with Elizabeth had worked; perhaps a good honest chance would allow Anne and me to get along.

But I was met with a distinct frown. Of course I was.

"Celine. I'm surprised to see you here." Anne took a to-go cup from the barista with an arched eyebrow. She was with two other ladies about her age, and they were handed their coffees too. "David, did you make sure that this is with skim milk and not whole? I can tell the difference."

"Yes, ma'am. It's skim," the poor guy behind the counter said.

She grumbled, disbelieving, then turned her attention back to me, peering, head tilting down to get a look at me without the aid of her glasses. "I didn't know you liked cats."

"I'm here with Elizabeth, actually." At her perplexed expression, I explained further. "My neighbor?"

She pursed her lips as if suppressing a giggle. "I know who she is. Don't you mean your squatter?"

"The baker," I clarified.

She guffawed, brushing past me to a Siamese on a high perch whose tail was whipping in a figure eight. Her friends followed her, and they took turns petting the cat. To my surprise, the woman even bent (yes, she bent down) to run a hand down another cat's back, lips moving in sweet baby talk.

She had been this way with the girls too—disarmingly sticky sweet.

From the other room Elizabeth shot me a questioning look, probably wondering if I needed to be saved. I shrugged. "Well, Anne, it was great to see you—"

"Are you planning to adopt a cat?" And again, with the over-the-nose peering action.

"Oh, no . . ."

"Right. You're not staying." She grunted. "That's too bad. The cat café is getting so full. We're always looking for forever homes for them."

"We?"

"You didn't know? This is my establishment."

"You?"

"Yes. Why that expression?"

"Well, you . . ." My thoughts tumbled and stumbled through the years of sparring with this woman. But the bottom line was that not once in three decades had I seen a cat in or around Anne's home. She'd had zero pets in my other life.

She challenged me with a look. And though I'd gotten quite a bit more honest and assertive throughout the years, I was clearly still no match.

"I mean . . . ," I tried again. "The look was of surprise because I hadn't heard about it till now. Where have I been?"

She seemed to relax, sitting down in the nearest chair. "It's a passion project of mine. I can't very well have so many cats running around my house with all the events I plan. Besides having all the cats in one place for when I need them, it's a vehicle to get them adopted. I always want to be part of the solution."

Maybe this was a trick and I'd become gullible since arriving, but an appreciation rose above my suspicions. "That's . . . wonderful."

"Celine." Her tone iced over so it felt like a chill had swept through the café.

"Yes."

"You and Quinn." She paused. "I've largely kept out of your business, but I do feel like I have to intervene."

I held back a snort at this absolute lie. This woman had always been in my business. With the way she'd spoken to me at the social, and how she was speaking to me now, it was virtually impossible that she had been able to keep her opinions to herself. "Intervene with what?"

Anne rolled her eyes. "Isn't he coming over to help you again?"

"Yes."

"And once you turn over the house, what do you plan to do? My nephew isn't a perfect man. He surely will never be, but even imperfect people deserve consistency."

"Wow." Did she think I was corrupting her nephew? "Quinn is a grown human. He surely can make decisions about his own relationships."

She tsked. "He's so desperate to have you back in any way that he's willing to do anything, risk anything. You need to know that so you understand the repercussions if you leave once more."

Unease filled me as both versions of Quinn occupied my head. How good they were, how they were willing to wait for me. "I love him, Anne."

"And yet, somehow, you cannot get it together. Perhaps love isn't enough?" She inhaled deeply and took a sip of her coffee. Her face screwed into a frown. "This is definitely whole milk. Dammit. This is what I get hiring people out of the goodness of my heart."

"Is everything okay?" Elizabeth appeared by my side, holding a kitten. It was a tabby, multicolored red and brown, and it curled in the crook of her arm.

"Yep. All good." I scrambled for conversation, to recover from what had felt like a sucker punch. "But who is this?"

"This is Cinnamon. She came in today." Anne gently ran a thumb down Cinnamon's forehead, and the cat stretched, prompting the three of us to ooh and aah. "She was found near the dumpster behind the ice cream shop. But she's a dear, isn't she? She really has taken to you, Elizabeth."

"She came right up to me."

"Perhaps once you're settled, you can come back for her."

"Do you think anyone else will pick her up?"

"There's no telling."

"I guess I can keep visiting until then." She kissed the top of Cinnamon's head, and went back to the playroom.

"If only . . . ," I whispered while watching her play, with another idea brewing.

"She needs to adopt the cat herself," Anne crooned.

"How did you know what I was thinking?"

"It's written all over your face. You want to make up for the fact that you've asked her to move."

"It's more than that." I thought of her tears the other night and this morning, and the inevitability of change. A cat could ease this change, if perhaps she realized I was gone. I wanted to leave her something from me, a being from my own heart, who could take my place. My chest tightened at this sudden need to know that Elizabeth would be fine. Her house, Quinn, and Mr. Loren. The cat. "How can I make sure that Cinnamon stays?"

"You can adopt her, and we can hold her for a few days."

"Great. I'll need that option, just until she can get everything into her new place."

"Are you sure you want to do that? I often discourage adopting pets as gifts even to family members."

"You said you needed some of these babies adopted, and I'm adopting."

"What I need is for a future owner to adopt."

My barter with Elizabeth for the piano came to mind—how intent Elizabeth had been to pay for it, how she didn't want to receive anything for free. I heaved a breath to unwind my impulse to simply adopt the cat. "Ugh. You might be right. I need another option. Can someone call me if there's interest in Cinnamon?"

"I suppose we could arrange that, but ultimately, it's first come, first serve."

"Fine, okay." I spat out the concession. "What do I need to do?"

"I'll have David take your number and hope he's better at making a phone call than being a barista." Then, from her reliably cold demeanor came a smile.

I stepped back, startled and unnerved by this rare show of emotion. "What?"

"Just that you seem . . . different. By now you would have rolled your eyes at me at least twice and forced the adoption paperwork through."

A cackle rocketed through me. "I feel like a completely different woman, actually."

"Well, I like it. I know we haven't always seen eye to eye, but I only want the best for you, and sometimes the way I show it might not be the way you would."

Her tone was sincere, gentle, and yet so forthcoming that my face went warm. She did care, and perhaps she had cared in my real life. It was her approach that I'd shied away from, like two magnets pushing away from one another. In this instance, one of us had flipped just enough so we stuck.

If this happened more often, what more could I learn from and share with Anne? And with Elizabeth, while I was here?

From the other room, Elizabeth yelped, then skidded around the corner. "Eureka!"

I laughed at the sheer joy on her face. "What is it?"

"I had a breakthrough. With the jingle."

Chapter Thirty-Five

Quinn's truck was parked in my driveway when Elizabeth and I returned from the cat café, and my heart buzzed at the sight of it.

"I'll head to my place, where it's quiet." She brimmed with excitement. "I'll check in when I'm done."

"Sounds great to me. Good luck." I watched her skip down the path to the little house with more pep to her step than how we'd left this morning. "Yay, Cinnamon!" My voice echoed through the backyard.

"No, you. Yay, you! Thank you for taking me!" Elizabeth raised both hands with spirit-fingers gusto.

My heart grew twelve sizes too big for my chest. A squeal threatened to burst out of me. This was all I'd wanted—to be a part of her happiness. To be included in her life and, at the same time, for her to know that she was independent of me.

Thank goodness for Anne, who'd been so wise to remind me that shoving my opinions wasn't love.

I turned toward the house in time to see Quinn come out carrying a decorative mirror. He was trailing after a couple and settled the mirror against their truck.

He was wearing a cozy fleece zip-up, fuzzy and warm looking. His hair was a little more unruly, boyish, and adorable. We hadn't spoken since he'd dropped me off after moving Elizabeth in, but my body didn't miss a beat. Was I ogling my own husband? Yes.

Once you turn over the house, what do you plan to do?

Darn Anne—she was still invading my thoughts. Because I didn't know the answer to the question. It would all depend on when and where and how I was supposed to wake up. Until then I wanted to give this time my all.

Quinn caught me staring at him, and he lifted a hand in a hello. He started my way, sending me right back to teenagehood. As he lumbered over, he stuck his hands in his pockets like someone had given him the rules on how to approach a woman, complete with a smoldering, shy look.

"Hey. Where did you go this morning?" he asked when he was a foot away.

"I took Elizabeth to the cat café, to perk her up a little."

Concern flashed in his eyes. "Everything okay?"

"Now . . . yes." I couldn't help but beam because I'd had a hand in it, albeit a small one. But it was short lived. Quinn's expression had turned serious.

"Did I do something yesterday? Gah, I knew I was too pushy about her getting smoke alarms ASAP." He pressed his lips together briefly. "The last thing I want is to act like her father."

"We're old enough that we could be . . . ," I managed to say, to bypass the temptation to reminisce about our three other children. *Did you install those car seats correctly, Mae? You should really make a spreadsheet to keep track of your bills, MJ. No, a dog might not be a good idea since you're in college, Amelia!* "But no, I don't think you were too pushy."

"I'm going to keep an eye on Thorne. I don't trust him."

"*Now* who's overprotective?"

His face broke out into a smile. "I can't help it."

"No judgment from me. You're talking to the woman who almost canceled escrow."

Knocking took our attention, and we turned to the house. Behind the window, Nelson was holding up an appliance.

"What's that thing he's holding up?" Quinn asked, squinting.

"I think it's a hair crimper."

His eyebrow plunged.

"You know what a crimper is. Don't you remember when . . ." I started to recall the time he'd had to help crimp the girls' hair for Halloween, but stopped short. "It's like a curling iron but for eighties babies." In response to his continued flummoxed expression, I pulled him toward the house. "Never mind. I'll show you instead of telling you. We should head in anyway."

As we entered through the back door, Nelson said, "Are you good with me putting some of the small items as free? We're in the last few hours, and it would be good to start to let go of the little things."

My mood took a tumble to morose at the words *let go*, but I pushed it aside. This was about an estate sale, nothing more. "Yes, and feel free to do what you think will be good for the sale."

"Here's our Celine." A familiar voice rang out in the crowd, with a tone of combined relief and annoyance. I looked up as Sonya, MJ, Amelia, and Mae emerged from the bodies.

Then, Elizabeth came in through the back door.

Past and present collided into one moment, and my vision swam with faces and voices, and the room tilted with memories. It was straight out of my dream the other night, with the slideshow of pictures of my girls as they grew up over the years.

I reached out for a steadying body—because my knees had buckled—right into Quinn's arms. Worry darkened his expression, and he helped me out into the fresh air. The whole group followed us outside, which made for a commotion.

Nelson caught up to us, face pinched into a frown. He scanned everyone in the group. "The first day we had a rabid fan, and today a reunion and a potential ambulance ride."

"No ambulance ride needed." I raised my voice above everyone else's, and the chatter subsided. "Seeing all of you here was just a surprise, and it caught me off guard. I'm fine."

My body had righted itself with the cool breeze, and I belatedly hugged my team and made introductions.

Hands stuck out for handshakes, and small talk ensued, but I continued to stand there in wonder. That this group of people, my whole family, was together. All my girls—my not-so-little women—were standing next to one another after two years since losing Libby.

Not the same girls, Celine.

To my conscience, I sighed. These weren't my daughters here in this world. My real daughters and my real husband were still out there.

But in that other world, there was no Libby.

I blinked rapidly to clear my brain and vision, and to force myself into the moment. Because the thought of choosing or picking which was better or worse or more important threatened to twist and tear my heart.

I was in *this* world, in which everyone was present, and shouldn't connecting with them be my first priority? There were no guarantees in any life.

But how could these women not tell that they resembled me and Quinn?

I shut my eyes. My thoughts were in a spiral, around and around, in which all I was doing was trying to get to the bottom of this whole experience.

"What is it?" Sonya asked. "Are you really okay?"

"Yes, I'm fine. It must have just been a little hot with all those people in there."

"Sure. It was the air that was hot." Sonya's eyes cut over to Quinn, examining him, recalling our history. "You're not fooling me."

I chortled, and the tension in my chest eased. Bless my dearest Sonya, who knew exactly what to say. "Why didn't you tell me you were coming?"

"I didn't want to promise until I could deliver. I wasn't sure if I could get everyone together on the same flight. And anyway, I kind of liked that expression on your face."

"What expression?"

"That you were happy to see us. It was golden, unlike a few days ago, when you looked at us like we were aliens."

"Ha!" Inside, I meant it as less funny and more a matter of fact that, yes, I was in another world.

"Anyway, we saw the pictures." MJ frowned.

"Pictures?"

"Of the social," Sonya said.

Next to me, Quinn groaned. "Am I in them?"

MJ nodded. "But don't worry; the both of you looked good, in a fierce sort of way."

"Which of course led to some requests for events. For more socials, smaller book club opportunities, and lunch clubs." Mae's eyes brightened pridefully.

"And merch sales are up!" Amelia added.

"Wow, your business is really a machine," Elizabeth commented.

"It is," Amelia declared with a proud nose in the air. "Celine Lakad is a big deal."

The women continued to banter in their quintessential way, with zingers and one-liners, and all I could do was watch and listen and marvel. As it had been in my real world, Amelia complained, MJ was the devil's advocate, Mae focused the conversation, and Elizabeth mediated.

"I hate to break up this reunion, but we have an estate sale going on," Nelson interrupted. "These customers are tearing up the place, and I need helpers to keep things neat and to answer questions. Basically, if they have a question, send everyone to me. Any takers?"

Sonya raised her eyebrows.

Gently nudging her with an elbow, I said, "C'mon."

Sonya whined, "I didn't expect to actually work. Then again, if we don't give these ladies something to do, they're liable to get into a catfight." She clapped her hands to get everyone's attention. "All right, ladies, you heard the man. The faster we get everything done, the faster we can go back to planning our next event. Right, Celine?"

"Right." The agreement shot out of me per usual, but the idea of attending events, of going anywhere without all of us together, was something I didn't want to entertain. I yearned for more of this closeness, this loud banter, this disorganization. The feeling of being drowned out by noise because every child needed to have the last word.

Now that we were all together, I couldn't fathom being apart again.

Chapter Thirty-Six

The rest of the day flew by, and the house emptied, one item at a time, and by the end of the night, only a small fraction of the house's contents remained.

The day's progress had been helped by the limitless energy of my family. At every junction was Mae, MJ, Elizabeth, or Amelia. Or Quinn, or Sonya. Seeing their faces—and hearing snippets of conversation, of one speaking to a customer, of another counting out change, of them bickering endlessly—felt like I was being handed a gift, or being showered by confetti. It was all my wishes come true.

But seeing the house empty was a different story. Now with most of the furniture gone, I was seeing it as Sampaguita, and melancholy had settled around me.

Sampaguita was my home. Our home. And having these people who looked like my family in this home was doing another number on my psyche. What was it with this place—it wouldn't give me a moment's peace. Just when I'd found what I thought was an answer, or made a decision, something else came along to knock my current plane off its axis.

Though this home would belong to someone else, in my real life, I still had a chance with Sampaguita, with my family. But would I remember this? Would this end up being a fuzzy dream that would eventually trigger déjà vu but not much more?

Nelson's distinct footsteps drew me from my thoughts, and I turned to him. Once again, he was holding up his clipboard. "Ready for an update?"

"Ready as I'll ever be." My voice echoed and bounced off the blank walls and the rug-free wooden floors.

"You have one last bed upstairs, as requested, in one of the smaller rooms. I'll return in the morning to meet the truck to take the last of the house's contents to the donation center."

"Elizabeth's mover should pick up the piano tomorrow too."

"Then that's the last of it."

"You've been so great, Nelson." I shook his outstretched hand, and followed him as he walked to the front door. "Truly. Are you sure you don't want to join us for dinner? We had Chinese food delivered."

He stepped out onto the front porch. "No, I appreciate it, but I have dinner waiting for me at home. Enjoy your time together. You have a fun set of people in there."

"They're definitely that and more." Now outside, my body soaked up the last of the setting sun. Today had been a frenzy, in the thick of people and voices—the open, quiet space provided some freedom for my thoughts to stretch out.

I'd sorely needed it.

But the respite was also like the eerie still air before a storm. More change was on the horizon. Though I wasn't sure when it would happen, I would need to go back to my real life.

But what if, when I returned, it didn't feel this good, or feel this *right?*

But what was right? What exactly were we supposed to expect from life? I coached to help people envision their dreams, to create what was right for them. Was I supposed to yearn for an easy and inauthentic life, with people who weren't exactly my family and where Elizabeth was represented, or was my real life what I wanted, where imperfection and loss had seeped into every crevice, where Libby was dead and our family was struggling?

And who got to make that decision for us? Right now I had no say. Throughout this experience, my only option had been to trudge toward an end goal and hope it was the right destination.

I feel like a completely different woman, actually.

I remembered what I'd told Anne Frasier earlier today, and blinked away the tears that had formed under my lids.

Because while I hoped, I also tried to learn. I tried to listen.

I tried to reform connections. I tried to forgive myself.

I also tried to savor special moments.

That had to count for something, didn't it?

Voices to my right took my attention, and I squinted out toward the fence line. Amelia was on the inside of the fence, speaking to Theo Loren on the other side.

Theo, as in the grandson of Mr. Loren. Theo, my son-in-law in my real life. They must've just met.

A smile burst out of me, unrelenting and giddy. This life! It was something.

My other life was something too. It had been amazing too.

"Hey, there you are." MJ was at the front door, and was breathless. "We've got the food laid out . . . and who is that with Amelia?" She stepped out in front of me and yelled without shame, "Amelia! Dinner!"

My first inclination was to shush MJ, but I halted to bask in this normalcy, even if it wasn't normal, not in the slightest.

Amelia ran up to us with a sheepish look. "Sorry, I got caught up. He was at the sale earlier, and he came back. He asked for my number."

"Only you, Amelia." MJ rolled her eyes.

"What?" She guffawed. "You just never know when you'll meet someone. And he's so cute."

And because I knew what this thing *could* blossom into, I said, "He's a nice guy. I've known him a good part of his life. You should get to know him."

"*Not* while you're on the clock, though," MJ said pointedly, walking ahead.

Shoulder to shoulder with Amelia, I tilted my head to speak to her. I intended to give her relationship advice; Theo had harbored a little crush on MJ before marrying Amelia years later, and I'd wanted to talk to her about staying focused on her career until Theo was ready to commit. But in looking at Amelia, I was reminded that she was capable and independent and didn't need it. "Well, I think he's cute too."

Her eyes lit up like spotlights. "Isn't he? I felt a spark between us."

"It's a sign. And don't worry about MJ. Like me, she's always here for you."

"Aw, I appreciate that. I love working with you and with everyone. You've really been like a second family."

I love you too, my heart screamed back in return. "I . . . I love working with you too."

But the mood had gone serious, so I smiled to cut Amelia loose from it. "Anyway, listen to me. I guess I'm feeling a little nostalgic from the move. Let's eat before my sappiness takes over."

The kitchen brimmed with conversation when we entered, with Chinese food set up buffet-style on the kitchen countertop. Paper plates and plastic utensils were passed around, and my daughters were first to jump in line.

My daughters. All of them, every single one in their unique splendor, ate and bantered like they used to, when I had taken this proximity for granted. My past self had had no clue how good she'd had it to have all that noise, the mini squabbles, the messy table, and the exhausted after-dinner cleanup.

I shoveled food into my mouth, relishing the moment. Kung pao chicken had never tasted so good.

"You look happy right now." Sonya stood next to me.

"I am *so* happy, but also sad and worried."

"Oh?"

"This right now? All of you here, the great food, and sitting around this old kitchen. It's so familiar, you know? Safe. But then it will be time to go . . . back to work, that is." My eyes drifted down to the floor, to help focus my words. "I'll love being back at work, but I'll miss this." I cleared my throat. "But I know I can't have it both ways."

"Why can't you? We can build in these moments of rest. And who's to say that you can't visit Louisburg? Heck, Quinn and Elizabeth can visit you wherever you are."

I shrugged, wishing it were that easy. "I guess I'm just all in my head. I keep going round and round about how it will all work out once the house turns over."

In the beginning of this experience, I'd doubted my senses. Now it wasn't so much that—rather, I believed that no matter what path I'd gone on, loss would've happened anyway. In my real life, Libby—in this life, thirty years with Quinn, and being a mother.

Loss was and would be inevitable. I hated that fact, that I couldn't escape it, even into a new world.

"Stress can really do something to a body, Celine. And you being in your head alone—it's not how we work as humans. We were meant to interact. We're supposed to be here for one another." She raised her plate in emphasis. "And some will be more qualified than others to take on the listening. And anyway, you're no spring chicken. We can use a little more help physically, emotionally, mentally. It wasn't part of our conversations growing up, to ask for help. We were told to hold it in, to be strong, to achieve. But we don't have to do any of those things. We can just exist."

I looked at my friend. "You're one of the wisest people I know."

"Psh. If you end up using any of that, I want a cut of the profit."

Cackling, I bumped her with a hip. "Deal. And a reminder that if I'm no longer a spring chicken, you aren't either."

"And yet, who made it to menopause first." She twirled lo mein onto a fork. "But you're not off the hook. You still need to see Trisha

Blake—if not while we're here, then in person when we get back to work."

"Okay." I inhaled deeply.

After dinner, Sonya, Mae, MJ, and Amelia gathered their things to head to the B and B.

"Are you sure that you don't want me to grab you a room?" Sonya asked. "I was told they have quite a few available."

"No. It's my last night here, and I want to finish it out."

"I understand." She smiled. Then, to Quinn and Elizabeth, she said, "I'll see you all tomorrow. Bright and early at six a.m."

A groan sounded through the crowd.

"I'll be sure to bring over my coffee maker," Elizabeth said.

As we watched them go, Elizabeth sighed. "That was fun. They were so nice."

My heart ached that she hadn't had the benefit of over two decades with them. Of being best friends with siblings who'd loved her to her core. "They are. You're just like them, kind and generous, and that's why you get along."

Her cheeks turned a rosy shade of pink. "Thank you."

"You're welcome." I shook myself out of a somberness that had crept onto my skin. "So, what's on your docket tonight?"

"The pantry and fridge."

"What can I do to help?"

"Nothing. They're literally the last things, and both super easy. Quinn, can I hand you a couple of bags to haul to the dumpster?"

"Yes. Just load it on the back of my truck."

"Great! See you both in the morning."

Elizabeth left through the back door; Quinn and I watched in silence until it shut behind her. Then, we faced one another.

Was it possible to look at someone who you'd grown older with and still find something new about him? With Quinn, little details popped up, like the streak of gray hair in his right eyebrow. The tiny mole dotting the lower curve of his earlobe.

I hadn't noticed those things on my Quinn. My attention had veered so much after Libby's death; I'd lived in a fog in which I'd pushed everyone away.

No longer. Currently, this Quinn had my full attention.

"So . . ." He smiled crookedly. "Why don't I clean up the kitchen?"

"Good idea." I tore my eyes away from his face, heat climbing up my chest at how hard that had been to do. Loving Quinn had never been the problem, but admittedly those heart-stopping bursts of want had faded over time, and in our grief. But this experience had flipped the switch to my desire, and I wasn't sure how to act on it. It was as if we were back to dating. "I'll go check upstairs for garbage."

"Sounds good." He executed a half step backward and paused, then, as if deciding otherwise, walked away.

When he did so, the spell of the moment lifted.

Had I been a little younger, I would have probably taken the stairs up by three, with how my heart was galloping. This thing between Quinn and me felt so brand new and giddy, like the possibility to rewrite our relationship existed. But was that real, or would it transcend to my next life? And was I willing to fall into this hope of a new relationship knowing that it would change once I made it back home?

Out of breath, I entered the attic and turned on the lights.

Compared to how it had been just days ago, the space was cavernous. It was hard to imagine that soon, it would be claimed by another family.

There was indeed a bag of garbage sitting in the corner next to the open closet, and when I grabbed it, I noticed something on the topmost shelf.

The item was easy enough to reach; it was a wooden birdhouse that resembled the one Theo had made and used as a makeshift mailbox for secret messages with my girls when they were much younger. Made of pine, it was rudimentary, like it had been constructed in a woodshop class.

I opened the hinged cover; nothing was inside.

Backing up, I caught sight of something else on that shelf. On my tiptoes, I touched something solid. My fingers clawed for purchase until the shelf jostled.

Thank goodness for what was left of my reflexes because I was able to jump out of the way before the shelf tipped sideways and came off the wall. A box tumbled, its top flying off, contents spilling onto the floor.

Photographs.

I rushed at the box, sat on the floor, and fingered through the photos. My thumb left prints across the glossy paper.

All the photos were of me and Quinn.

Since arriving, I'd judged this world's Celine. For how nothing in this home was personalized, for how little she'd left of herself. But here it was, evidence of a life, of her love life with Quinn. And from the looks of it, she'd kept everything, down to old stamped and postmarked letters.

Here you are.

This was the unfiltered Celine. One photo was of me and Quinn holding hands and on roller skates, my hair teased and bangs sprayed stiff. Then another was of a coiled corded phone receiver against my ear, my eyeballs rolled up in impatience while Quinn pressed an exaggerated kiss on my cheek.

This Celine loved Quinn. Twice they had tried to get together but hadn't been able to make it work. Now I was here, years after the fact. For all intents and purposes, Quinn and I could take our relationship to the next level. We could try once more.

Was that destiny? Were we soul mates?

In this world, it would seem so. But it all came down to the question that ruled above others. What would happen when I left?

Footsteps bounded up the stairs and through the hallway, pulling my gaze and attention to the door.

"Celine?" Quinn emerged, eyes darting around the room. When they landed on me, his body seemed to deflate. "I heard that crash and came up. You know you can't just grab things off of high shelves. You can get hurt."

"Speak for yourself. I'm only fifty-three."

His expression softened. "Right, but . . . even so. I can help you, you know."

"I know."

I'd always understood Quinn would be there. We had thirty-three years' worth of a marriage to show that had carried the weight of loss, of struggles, of joy and tiny moments like these, in these photographs.

He approached me, squinting at what had fallen out of the boxes; then his eyebrows lifted. "Pictures."

"Lots of them." One jumped out at me, and I picked it up. It was of Quinn in his army uniform. He was even more lean with a baby face. I was standing next to him in a simple sheath dress.

"Wow." He opened a palm, and I set the picture in his hand. "This was . . . the early days."

"Super early. You swept me off my feet." And yet, after the words left my mouth, I realized my mistake. In this life, I hadn't chosen Quinn, which meant that shortly after this photo, we'd broken up the first time.

"I was crushed when you chose not to come with me."

Except, instead of the vitriol, his tone had a frankness about it.

"I was afraid," I said, in full truth, remembering back to my thought process. Loving Quinn had meant dealing with moving, with deployments. It had meant leaving home. "I knew that life with you would be unpredictable."

"And look at you now. You belong to the world. You've done so much. You stayed with Rex because of predictability, and yet that really wasn't what you wanted, was it?"

This was another reason why I had fallen for Quinn. It was his ability to fight with me. He could banter; he could discuss; he could challenge me. He never minced his words.

With Quinn, my self-confidence grew. His absence with the army and his coaching jobs had made me stronger, despite how painful it had been to do it all on my own.

"What did you think I wanted?" I dared him.

He bent down and helped gather the photos and stuck them back in the box. In this life, this Celine had tucked away these photos as part of her past and placed them out of sight, and yet, she never had gotten rid of them. It had been a testament to her deep connection to Quinn.

It was also proof that she hadn't been just about image.

That *I* wasn't just about image, and *I* had deep relationships despite all my faults.

"You wanted something enduring when life inevitably changed." Quinn finished cleaning up and stood, offering me a hand. I was hefted to my feet. "You know how I feel about you. But it's not about feelings. It's about choosing to be with that person. It's deciding that that person is who we want."

He cupped my cheek, and ran a rough thumb against it. His touch seared my skin, the heat reaching into my heart.

"What do you want?" I whispered.

"I don't know if you're ready for that answer. Because that would mean more. It would mean asking something from you that you might not be ready to give. And, I don't know if I can be rejected again."

"I won't reject you." I said it in full clarity. I'd married Quinn Frasier, for better or for worse. And while it had taken a whole new world for me to finally realize where my path had detoured, now that he was in front of me, I wouldn't let him go.

I reached out to him and got on my tiptoes. I kissed him on the lips, and it was almost too painful. I hadn't kissed my husband in months—not like this, desperate and sorrowful, where we wrapped our arms around each other under threat of separation. "I love you, Quinn, in all times."

A blip of confusion passed over his expression, but I didn't amend my words. I meant them with my entire self, through different threads of time, through worlds, through dreams, and even through states of being. It didn't matter how many versions of us existed or if we were the only ones of our kind. Or if this was simply a story playing out within my psyche. My love for him would always be true.

"I love you, Celine." Then, he led me to the bedroom on the second floor, to the last bed in the house, and we made love under the bright moonlight.

Chapter Thirty-Seven

I woke up to the sun streaming against my face, stopping short of opening my eyes all the way, allowing the sun's rays to cloud my vision. Heaving once, and then twice, I girded myself for the reveal of where I was, unsure what I wanted the answer to be. I'd dreamed of notes hanging from swaying tree branches, being sung by birds flying in formation or perched on fences, and whistled by passersby. "Petals Fluttering" had invaded every part of me like a song that had been played a million times on the radio.

A beat later, I realized why it had become an earworm.

Elizabeth was singing downstairs. "In a bit of a rush? On a deadline to crush? Lucky Four Laundry to the rescue. Not a moment to spare. In and out and with care. Lucky Four Laundry to the rescue."

Relief and happiness pulsed through me along with the thrum of disappointment.

I'd thought—because my night with Quinn had been perfect and, for the first time in so long, I had gone to bed with clarity and peace—that I would wake up back with my family.

But, the piano playing downstairs lifted my mood by the second. Elizabeth was still here. Quinn and I had spent a glorious and intimate night together. Though he'd set his alarm early—he still had to bring the garbage to the dump because he hadn't the night before—we would have the rest of this day.

Time was something that could not be controlled, but how I spent it could be.

The phone buzzed on my nightstand, as if hearing my thoughts.

Quinn:

Awake?

Celine:

I'm up now

Quinn:

I got back from the dump. Jumping in the shower and I'll see you

soon. It's been too long away from you

Celine:

I miss you too

What was better: Waking up to music being played by my daughter, or a sweet text from my handsome husband?

Both. Both at the same time.

After showering and dressing, I padded down the stairs to the scent of coffee.

"Good morning," I said. The house was bathed with light. Without all the furniture, the space felt so open and freeing.

"Morning." Elizabeth lifted both hands like a conductor of an orchestra.

"I heard the jingle."

She grimaced. "Was it okay? Is it too cheesy? Not that I can change it now. I sent it in yesterday but for some reason couldn't get it out of my head."

"I love it. I do."

She relaxed into the seat. "Thank you for helping me with it."

"It was truly my pleasure."

She stood and followed me into the kitchen, where I poured myself some coffee in a random leftover cup. In an automatic gesture, I opened the fridge, only to find it empty.

"Are you hungry like I am?" Elizabeth said from behind the door.

I shut the fridge. "I am. What do you have at your house?"

"Hmm. Basics, I guess?"

"The triad? Green onion, garlic, and ginger?"

"Yep."

"Rice?"

"Long grain?"

"Good enough. Eggs?"

"Of course."

From the leftover kitchen items, we took inventory: An old stockpot. Olive oil. A cracked ladle. Also good enough. "Perfect. How about we make lugaw?"

A grin blossomed on her face. "Rice porridge? Yes please."

"Why don't you grab the rest of the stuff, and I'll search for bowls and spoons."

Elizabeth was back minutes later with a bagful of the ingredients but a sour expression on her face. "I can't believe you did that," she said.

"Did what?" My eyes were on the ceiling, calculating how much food was needed to feed our brood. It had been a while since I'd cooked for all of us.

"You adopted a cat for me."

My gaze darted to her, and what met me was an incredulous expression. "It's not what you think."

She snorted a rebuttal. "David from the cat café told me that quote: 'Cinnamon is ready to go.'"

Dammit, David. I sighed. To be honest, the potential adoption had slipped my mind. "I left him *my* number."

"Well, he called me. What I don't understand is why you did that."

"You looked so happy with Cinnamon, and your new place takes pets."

"But that's not the point." She shook her head. "You should have asked me."

"I didn't think you'd be upset. This isn't a big deal."

"It *is* a big deal, to me. With you trying to give me the piano, your clear disappointment at my new place. And now Cinnamon. I appreciate all of it—the sentiment, the intention—but honestly, it's almost insulting. That you don't think I can make my own decisions. Seriously, you're just like my mother."

Since arriving in this world, I had been hit with a range of emotions, from disbelief, to confusion, to anger. But this was hurt. "That's not fair."

"No, but inside, you don't think I'm good enough, that I'm capable enough."

"That's not true. I don't know where this is coming from—"

"Really? Then why didn't you sell the piano to me outright? Why did you insist on coming with me to my place? And why didn't you encourage me to adopt the cat rather than doing it yourself?"

"But I didn't . . ." My chest began to fill with dread. The words she was saying were in the same tone my Libby had used with me so long ago, when I'd tried to do things for her. After all, what was the point of having the privilege of financial stability if I couldn't provide for my family? But she'd taken it as insult.

She'd wanted to do it all herself, and my own assumptions had kept me from accepting it.

"It's because you didn't think I could step up to the plate," Elizabeth continued.

My chest burst with regret. "No, it's because you're my daughter and I want to give you everything you want and need!"

Her face froze, eyes wide and mouth open.

"I . . . what I meant was . . ."

"I have no idea what's going on in your head, but . . . that's just . . . weird! You calling me Libby the first time we met, and now this. I can't with this . . ." She dropped the bag where she was standing and headed out the back door.

As her figure disappeared down the path to the secondary home, I broke out into a sob. This was what I'd avoided the whole time I had been here, yet here I was again. Back to square one. Square two years ago.

Chapter Thirty-Eight

No. I couldn't go back to two years ago, or even a week ago. Back then, second chances hadn't been a part of my belief system. Back then, regret had fueled my every decision. Back then, I hadn't been willing to step outside my comfort zone.

So I set out after my daughter.

My journey wasn't far, because she was coming back up the path. Her arms were raised, and she was shaking her head, face twisted into a frown. "I'm so sorry. I didn't mean it. I knew that you were taking a break from your tour, and to imply that you were weird and that you had something wrong with your head . . . it was wrong."

All of me melted into a puddle. Because here was Elizabeth, worried about *me*. Then again, this was Elizabeth, a woman who thought about others. A person who cared and empathized. "It's me who's sorry. The moment I thought adoption, I should have consulted you and spoken to you about it. The truth is, though, that I didn't adopt Cinnamon. I asked to be notified if someone was interested. And I guess someone is."

Her face crumpled. "Gah. Really? I didn't hear any of that. I just jumped to all kinds of conclusions. I'm sorry. I don't mean to do that—I don't mean to get angry and to push people away. It's just how I am sometimes . . ."

Grabbing onto her hands, I squeezed gently, and she silenced. "You can't be sorry about that. You're exactly the way you should be. You're right; I should have talked to you first. Even Anne Frasier said so." I swallowed the swell of emotion rising up my throat. "Elizabeth, I called you my daughter because in my mind, in my heart, you have become my daughter. No one here knows this, but I lost a daughter once before, and meeting you, here, gave me a second chance. But I went a little overboard; I wanted to give you everything."

Her eyes dropped for a beat. "To be honest, in the last few days, I have wished . . . I wished that you were my mother."

My eyes filled with tears. "Really?"

"Yes. I even dreamed about it. Those women on your team? I dreamed that they were my sisters and Quinn was my dad . . ." Her face streamed with tears, though she half laughed. "Imagine that? I dreamed it last night."

"Was it a good or a bad dream?"

"It was so good. To be part of a family, and a big one at that. In my dream, I belonged with all of you."

If only I could have told her, in a way that would have been believable, that she indeed had had us. And that we—me, Quinn, Mae, MJ, and Amelia—had been lucky to have her. That in her twenty-three years, she'd graced us with her goodness, and we were better for it. Because of her, whenever I heard a piano playing or a cat meowing, smelled bread cooking in the oven or jasmine in the air, she was the first person I thought of. And that her death didn't negate her life and the prints she'd left behind with all of us.

Coming in, I'd wondered if life would've been better without the pain of losing Libby, even if it had meant changing the course of my life. Now, I would endure all the pain of Libby's death once more in exchange for the time I had spent with her.

"I can be your family if you want," I offered.

"I'll be your daughter, if you want, also . . . because I'm going to miss you when you have to leave."

The word *when* almost brought me to my knees. Like she knew our time was coming to an end. I leaned in and wrapped my arms around her, shutting my eyes in hopes I would never forget this moment.

Seconds later, we stood back from one another. I wiped the tears from her cheeks, though she had a veil of a smile on her face.

She and I, we were good.

I gestured toward the house. "The rest of the crew should be here soon. Do you want to go back and help cook?"

She nodded. "I wouldn't miss it."

Chapter Thirty-Nine

Twenty minutes later, the lugaw was simmering, and my mouth was sore from laughing. Elizabeth had just recounted how she'd accidentally baked the dough that she'd placed in the oven to rise.

We were interrupted by the doorbell. "I'll get it," Elizabeth said, leaving the kitchen; shortly after, a myriad of familiar voices filled the home. I peeked out into the entryway, where Sonya, Mae, MJ, and Amelia sauntered in in athleisure wear. All, except for Sonya, halted at the piano, where Elizabeth had sat down to play a few notes.

The déjà vu that washed over me stole my breath away.

"You cooking is an odd thing." Sonya nudged me out of my thoughts. "Are you really making this all by yourself?"

I migrated to the stove. "What can I say? You're a friend to a very talented woman."

"I mean, I already knew that." She smiled. "So?"

I did a double take. "So, what?"

"Are you holding out on me? Tell me before I burst."

The back door slammed open, and Quinn stepped in. He was wearing a flannel over a hooded long-sleeve, exuding warmth and coziness, topped off with his unshaven face. Then, he greeted me with a smile so pure that for a beat, I let go of the knowledge that today could be my last day, the second-to-last day, or forever.

At the thought, I waited for the strike of pain, a push into my thought spiral, of which I'd had so many. But at the moment, with the piano playing and food simmering in the pot, I let the time and its hold on me go.

Time wouldn't ruin my enjoyment of my newfound giddiness.

Why seek the hurt and the pain when there was love standing in front of me, looking as sexy as ever?

"Morning." Without a glance at anyone else, he came for me with a kiss and a hand firmly on my hip.

Whistles came from the ladies; Elizabeth trilled two keys on the piano. It reminded me of silverware against wineglasses at a wedding.

Sonya gasped. "Oh, hello, Quinn."

Quinn straightened, cheeks pink. "Sonya."

"Celine, I take it back. You don't need to update me, because I completely understand now."

A discussion started in the living room, and Sonya, Quinn, and I peeked in.

My heart swelled at my view, and I committed it to memory.

"It's like they've known each other forever," Sonya said. "I bet these four are going to keep in touch. I also think that the team is going to be much closer because of this experience."

"I hope so."

Sonya's watch beeped, and she twisted her wrist to look at it. "Back to reality. The truck'll be here in a few minutes."

"I need about ten more minutes on the lugaw, but as soon as it's done, you all can eat whenever you're hungry."

"Sounds good." As Sonya tore off to speak to the team, Quinn laced his hand in mine and took me deeper into the kitchen. "Can we talk?"

"Sure." Breathless, I toddled after him.

He took both of my hands into his; his skin was warm. "I just wanted to make sure that you and I are okay."

My face flushed with memories from last night. Quinn had been so skilled, so strong, so generous. "I'm definitely okay."

His face broke out into a relieved smile. "Good, I wasn't sure."

"Not even with all the noise we made?"

"You were extra loud." His gaze dropped down to my hands. "Sex was never the problem between us. For us, it's the days after."

In this world, he and I hadn't gotten it right. We'd feared commitment. We hadn't been able to compromise. In both worlds, we had given each other ultimatums. But from now on I wouldn't let it get to that point where we had to wager our relationship over an unknown answer.

I gave him a reassuring smile. Because nothing could take away from this moment of having my most favorite people in this house. In hearing all their voices—because Elizabeth had warmed up, and the four were using their outdoor voices, with Sonya hovering above them like the second mother she was—I felt complete. And though I wasn't sure what was coming up next, and despite the grief and pain that would always be a part of my history, I was present. I was here.

With certainty, I said, "Everything is perfect right this very second."

Chapter Forty

Later on that morning in the living room filled with movers, an unexpected chill came over me, causing me to shiver. "Brrr. Did someone turn on the AC?"

"Nope. I'm properly glistening. Can I borrow you for a moment?" Sonya waved from beyond my line of focus, from the kitchen doorway. All around us were strangers, though this time, all were wearing the same branded T-shirt of the junk-removal company. One was collecting the last of the wall decor. Another disassembled the couch so it could be brought out of the house.

Elizabeth's movers were here too. That group was in the second house, except for two who were in the process of moving the piano.

I wove my way to Sonya, excusing myself as I accidentally brushed past a person carrying a chair to the truck.

"Hi, yes?"

Sonya swiped a hand over her damp forehead, but her smile was radiant—she was having fun. As I approached her, one of the movers ran a finger down the piano keys, from high to low notes, and my body shuddered at the sound.

"Are we leaving the butcher-block island for the next owner?" she asked.

It took me a few seconds to comprehend her question. Meanwhile, the mover ran a finger up the keyboard from low to high notes.

"Please don't do that," I snapped back, irritated. There was too much noise—I probably needed to hydrate, and eat. Only a couple of hours had passed since breakfast, but I was antsy. Like I'd received a haircut, and there was a stray hair down my back. "Sorry, that's not what I meant."

Sonya's expression froze. "So did . . . you want to keep it?"

"Yes, I do. Thank you."

"Are you feeling dizzy like before?" Sonya asked.

"No. Not dizzy, just tired. Hangry, maybe." I forced a smile. Except the room seemed to shift minutely, like a blip in a record.

As Sonya went into the kitchen, a strong hand landed on my shoulder, and I looked up, to Quinn's face. He and Elizabeth had come from dropping off the final boxes at the cottage. "Hey. You okay?"

"Totally. Totally fine." At his dubious expression, I continued, "Is everything at Elizabeth's cottage?"

"Yep." He peeked behind us. "Now it's just that piano."

The two movers were working together to tilt the piano onto a large dolly. Notes echoed with every move, sending a flush of goose bumps along my skin. I looked around for an open window, or someone blowing down my neck—anything to explain the growing sensation that something was happening. That change was afoot once more.

My breaths grew shallow, and along with each inhale came a thought.

I need to say goodbye.

I don't want to say goodbye.

I can't wait to go home.

I want to stay.

I belong there.

I belong here.

I need to tell them I love them.

I hadn't felt this unsteady since that first day my world changed. I tugged on Quinn's elbow and scrambled for an excuse to bring my family together. "Can you get everyone in the study, where it's a little quieter . . . um, for a picture."

"Sure." Worry clouded his expression. "I'll be right back."

As I meandered toward the study, I gathered my thoughts on what to say. My instincts could be wrong. Perhaps my blood sugar was low and I simply needed to eat. Or this was the last day I would see these people for who they were.

It was the last day I would see Elizabeth.

Nelson was first in the study. "Hands down, this was the most successful estate sale I've had."

"You made it happen, Nelson." I offered my hand, and shook his with as much affection as I could. "Thank you, for everything."

"My pleasure."

Mae and MJ burst into the room, laughing. "We literally just climbed one of the backyard trees!" Mae plucked a leaf from her hair. "I haven't done that since I was a kid."

"She barely got up on the first branch," MJ said.

"You're such a brat." Mae gently slapped her on the arm. "Anyway, just an FYI, Celine, about the schedule." And in a smooth change of subject, she brought up a document on her phone. "We have to get on the road soon."

"Right. Um, can we talk about this later? How about the both of you stay here, and we can get a picture?"

"What a great idea," MJ said. "For memories and posterity. And, Nelson, don't you sneak off. I want you in it too."

I strode away from the chatter, though I was met by crashing piano keys, followed by curses from one of the movers. An urgent need arose to get to Elizabeth.

Theo and Amelia were just walking into the living room. "It's time for photos," I said.

"I can take the photo. I'm not part of the family," Theo said.

"Yes, you are." Because he would be soon enough. "And I bet Mae and MJ have figured out how to get everyone in the shot."

Amelia, with a confounded jaw-on-the-floor expression, led him into the study.

Quinn met me at the back door. "Sonya's on her way here. What do you have up your sleeve?"

"I wanted to get everyone together, just to say thank you, you know? It's been a journey."

"You make it sound like it's ending."

"I mean, it sort of is?"

He frowned. "Then we choose another journey. Together."

"Oh, Quinn." I wrapped my arms around him once more, tears clogging my throat. Unbeknownst to him, what he'd said had blanketed me with hope. That come what may, whether it was us here or in my real world, we might find ourselves together, to traverse another thirty years.

"You're kind of worrying me right now."

I looked at him, at his unsmiling face. "Don't worry about me, or about us. I love you. And I'll be here. Okay?" I uncoiled my arms from him, refocusing. "Elizabeth. Where is she?"

"I sent her a text. She's at the house and is coming up soon."

"Thank you."

Sonya came up the walk, hanging up her phone as she neared. "Where are we taking the photo?"

"In the study." I gestured to the back door. Through the open windows, one could hear my family's raucous laughter.

She snickered. "I guess I should go in there and wrangle them."

Grabbing her wrist before she walked in, I pulled her into a hug. "Thank you."

To my surprise, she didn't stiffen up. "We're hashtag team Celine. No matter what. Of course we would be here. You know, I'm more than just fabulous; I'm a good friend too."

"Not just good. The best. I hope I haven't burdened you. I hope I've been just as good of a friend to you."

She tsked. "We've been friends for twenty years, and you are, admittedly, a pain in the butt. But you've done your share in bailing me out. I love you. Seriously, though . . . you can count on me through the good and the bad. You've been there for me." She pressed her lips into a sardonic smile. "I'd better go before it rains on my face. It'll smear my foundation. I don't know what it is about today, but it feels momentous."

"It is. I'm saying goodbye to this house." I kissed her on the cheek. "I love you too. I'm grabbing Elizabeth. And I'll be right back."

"All right." She opened the back door. "And oh, Robin's on her way here to collect the keys."

Then, that afternoon, I'll grab the keys from you, and that is that. You're scot-free.

Scot-free.

Shit.

With Robin's words in my head, I strode down the path with the little house in view, my steps quickening across the stone walkway. The yard appeared to be blue green this afternoon, vibrant against the sun. Birds encircled the nearest apple tree, chirping. The scent of jasmine was so overwhelming that a headache began at my temples.

Beyond was the faint grumble of an engine.

I turned toward the noise; it was Robin's car rolling up to the property.

Then came the sound of those crashing piano keys. It was constant this time, because the piano was being rolled onto the moving truck. With each jostle of the instrument, my body lurched away from the main house, toward the second house.

My only thought: I had to get to Elizabeth first before . . . before . . . I wasn't sure, so distracted and bothered by the piano keys. To my ears, the sound became incessant and demanding.

I'm almost there.

Elizabeth came out the front door.

"Elizabeth!" A yell exploded from my lips. "I'm coming!"

She squinted at me, then shook her head, eyes blinking as if to clear them. She frowned. "Mom?"

"It's me, Libby. It's me."

Chapter Forty-One

Like light, life was a cycle of crests and troughs. Like light, my surroundings wavered until they cut out, leaving me in darkness.

Until I heard my name.

"Mom?"

That was me. Mom. I was a mother to four children. Four darling girls who gave me joy. Four girls who had made me the woman I was today.

But which woman? In which time? In which world?

My body startled awake at that thought, lungs contracting, chest heaving. My eyes flew open, and I was stunned at the bright lights above, the cold compress on my head, and the faces looking down at me.

Mae, MJ, Amelia, Sonya, Quinn.

No Elizabeth.

No Libby.

Chapter Forty-Two

"The last thing I remember was me running toward Libby. Then, everything went dark. The whole experience was so detailed . . . but it was all a dream." I wrapped the fleece blanket around me tightly while sitting on the hotel couch, and swiped at my recent tears. Quinn and my girls surrounded me, with Quinn holding my hand.

Two years of tears were intent on releasing themselves, and there was no stopping them, as if the dream had unlocked the dam that had kept them all back. The dream had been so vivid, so rich and multi-dimensional. It had been exactly like my current surroundings, in full color and texture and surround sound.

"That's such a wild dream," Amelia said. "Were Theo and I in it?"

MJ, sitting on my bed, snorted. "Seriously?"

"What? I'm honestly curious."

The memory of that time warmed me a smidge. "You met Theo in this dream. Since I wasn't your mother, you didn't meet Theo until you and your sisters—though you weren't sisters but coworkers—came to help me get the house ready. But, you hit it off right away."

"And me?" Mae asked.

"You were married but with no kids, and, MJ, you weren't an author, though you wished you were one."

To Quinn, who had been quiet, I said, "You and I started out rough, but we found our way back together."

His face was twisted into worry. "This was my fault. We shouldn't have done the intervention, especially before the event. It was wrong of me."

"It was all of us, not just you, Dad." Amelia stood. "My God, Mom, when you went down . . ." She pressed her hand against her heart.

"I'm fine now, Amelia. I am."

I squeezed Quinn's hand. "You felt that you had to do the intervention and give me an ultimatum . . . you all did. But I know you did it because you love me. It was hard to hear what you all said. I've yet to fully process it all, and it may take a while. But I love you. All of you, too, girls, and nothing will change that. And I promise to continue to listen."

"You and I, we will work this out, Celine. I love you, and even though I'd given that ultimatum, I wouldn't have ever left . . ." Quinn choked on a sob. "Through thick and thin—"

I leaned in to hug Quinn until his tears abated.

"You know, Mom, I've read so many time-travel, *Sliding Doors*–like stories," MJ said. "Sometimes it does make me wonder if some of it is real. That there could be a glitch in time, that we could have another chance elsewhere."

"It felt like another chance."

Mae wandered over to the window. "Do you blame yourself for Libby passing, Mom?"

"I did." I looked down and allowed the fresh tears to flow. "I'd equated my missing her, my wishing that she were closer, to blame. I do know that I can do better by all of you. To tell you how I feel. To share how much I miss Libby, to listen to you when you all do. To remember her out loud, even when it hurts. So, I'm going to Sampaguita."

"You will?" Quinn asked.

I nodded. "Sampaguita was our home. Libby's home. And I'm not afraid."

"I can't get over how you keep saying her name, Mom." MJ knelt in front of me. "Did she look good to you? In your dream?"

"She was beautiful, and feisty, and independent, like the three of you."

"We get it from you." Amelia came closer, and took my hand in hers. "And we know you tried your best, that you do try your best, all the time. It was something I didn't get to say before."

I paused to think on it. On this idea of what best was, especially for this moment. "When Libby died, she took a part of me with her. And I tried to pretend that things were fine. I thought that was what you all needed from me. But the more I tried to deny what I was feeling, the more I lost my way. Lost in stuff that doesn't really matter, when in the end, I was losing touch with you all.

"I want you all to still have your mom. Mae, I want your children to have their lola. Quinn, I want you to have your wife, still. And I want to be here, for you, with you, and for me. I think that's what best will have to be for me, for now. To face things as they are, not for the next step."

Amelia wrapped her arms around my neck, and she was followed by MJ and Mae. Quinn wrapped his arms around all of us. I felt the strands of their hair against my cheeks and heard their voices in my ears. "This has been so hard," I croaked out. "I miss her. I miss her so much."

My husband and my girls—the first, second, and fourth—began to cry.

"It's been so hard that I couldn't even say it aloud. But I'm ready to talk about it."

A knock sounded on the door, followed by the beep of the card reader. It opened to Sonya, followed by a woman wearing a comfy cardigan and jeans. She had dark-brown skin, black hair swept up into a claw clip, and a kind, soft expression. Her eyes bounced around the room before landing on me with a gentle smile.

This was the second stranger of the afternoon—the first being the hotel doctor who'd checked in on my physical health, when I'd been cleared of any emergency conditions.

Sonya gestured to the woman. "This is Trisha Blake. She's a clinical psychologist who we spoke of earlier before . . ."

Straightening, I reached out a hand, noting the name. Trisha Blake was also the name of the psychologist in my dream who I was supposed to contact. How many Trisha Blakes were there in the mental health field in the Boston area?

As we shook hands, I pushed down that runaway thought.

"It's a pleasure to meet you, Celine. I'm on the board and a doctor with Phone Therapy, an online therapy platform."

"You're here because my team thought I should talk to you."

Her cheeks darkened. "Well, yes. But it's totally up to you." She took a card from her pocket. "Or, you can access Phone Therapy via phone or web."

"I don't need your card," I said.

"If I could convince you that—"

Behind Trisha, Sonya dropped her chin to her chest.

I interrupted. "I don't need your card because I'd like to talk to you right now."

"And if it's okay with Celine, I'm available for couples therapy," Quinn added.

"Family therapy," my daughters said in unison.

Sonya raised her hand. "Hey. You'd better not forget about me."

I laughed through my tears. "I'd never forget about you. Any of you." Or Libby, or Elizabeth, or my dream at that magical home when jasmine bloomed.

Chapter Forty-Three

Louisburg, Massachusetts
The Same Day

The déjà vu returned in full force while I was driving onto Main Street, though this time in the passenger seat of a rental car, with Quinn next to me.

"Exactly how I remember it," my husband said.

"It really is." The sun was just starting to dip below the trees, and trailing behind it were the orange and pink of a spring sky. Pedestrians meandered on the sidewalks, some holding paper bags of the day's groceries. The occasional runner sped by, called upon by parents walking with their children.

It had been two hours since my therapy appointment with Trisha Blake. It would be the first of a series planned—I found myself comfortable in her presence. Comfortable being vulnerable. Comfortable crying, even.

There had been no mincing words at this first appointment. My road to healing would be long, and it would involve not only moving forward, but also looking back. And maybe glancing sideways at a dream that promised to haunt me at every turn. It might also mean coming to terms with letting go of that dream, to embrace this real world.

I did know, however, that one of these steps was coming back to Louisburg.

Sampaguita, after all, was there.

"How are you?" Quinn asked.

"Hanging in there." I heaved a breath, then reached across the middle console. He took my hand, the moment right out of my dream with Quinn when we'd moved Elizabeth into the cottage. Inside, I felt myself lighten. "I'm not mad at you, Quinn."

He seemed to deflate, and he did a double take, relief playing across his features. "I'm mad at myself. And I will be for a while. I turned my back on you. The only thought I had when you went down was that I'd given you an ultimatum when I should have said that I would wait. That I would meet you where you are."

"I needed to meet you where you were too. Things needed to change. I needed to tell you how I feel."

"We will agree to disagree. Except for the fact that I love you, and it's you and me. You and me."

Sampaguita rose in my vision as we drove down the long road, and instead of pain, what I felt was warmth. Like the rise of ensaymada dough, like the slow boil of lugaw, and like the boisterous laughter around a piano. "You and me, and Sampaguita."

"And our children," Quinn said as he parked curbside. He turned to me, and he burst into tears. I leaned in and cried, unable to contain the relief and hope pouring through me. "We're going to work on it," he said.

"We will, and I will," I promised with every cell in my body.

When our crying ceased, Quinn wiped the tears off my cheeks. "Ready?"

Nodding, I exited the car. As I held my husband's hand, the walk up the driveway and the stone path swept me away with a surreal feeling of peace. The smell of jasmine filled my nostrils and made me smile.

We climbed the stairs and walked into the front door.

It was not the house in my dreams, nor was it the house that I had raised my girls in.

It was Libby's house. Furnished in her style: simple lines, bright colors, comfortable. Books piled on tables, music sheet paper strewed on the coffee table. Much of which I remembered from the funeral reception.

And the piano, sitting in front of the back windows, with the fall-board down.

I was truly at Sampaguita.

Chapter Forty-Four

Louisburg, Massachusetts
Six Months Later

My fingers lifted from the keyboard. The chord echoed until it faded away to the wall clock ticking overhead. I exhaled, energy drained out of me.

Clapping sounded from my iPad, which was perched on a holder. I turned to face it, to my music therapist, Lance Goo. "That was wonderful, Celine."

"I know I have a long way to go. At least half the piece left."

"But what you've done, and all the work you put in, has been tremendous. Don't discount that."

"Trying not to." Except, it was hard. Therapy was tough work, and especially music therapy, where each note was bittersweet. Listening to myself play the piano had been like coming to terms with each of my memories and facing them for what they were instead of as a means to assign fault or blame to myself. But it was something for me to touch these keys, to press down on them.

"That's it for us today. Same time next week?" Lance's smile was encouraging. He knew that depending on the day, I would need to take an extra breath or perhaps barely make it through the first bars of music, but he never did give up. He continued to be patient; he never pushed me past my speed.

"I'll be here," I said.

When the screen went blank, I texted Nelson, Sampaguita's contractor, to tell him the coast was clear. Seconds later, the tile cutter turned on.

Quinn and I had decided to move back to Sampaguita shortly after our visit. We couldn't walk away from its memories. But, the house had to undergo major construction to upgrade systems that were no longer up to code. Which proved to be serendipity, because the renovation kept me busy while I was on an open-ended sabbatical from work, for much-needed rest, conversation with my family, therapy, yoga, and prayers. So I could be free to miss Libby and to celebrate who was here.

Two factors could exist simultaneously: grief and joy all in one shot.

It was okay.

Even if it wasn't, that was okay too.

I lowered the fallboard of the piano, then picked up the book waiting for me. Part two of my therapy, and that was to fulfill my promise to Elizabeth—read *Little Women*. I'd purchased a new copy, a thick mass-market paperback, unpretentious and unintimidating.

Okay, so it wasn't part of my therapy, but admittedly, the book had called to me, slowly but surely. A page about every other day was my speed.

Slouching on the couch, I covered my legs with a blanket and opened the book to my bookmarked page.

A sentence in, scratching grabbed my attention.

I lowered the book, but with no further noise, I resumed reading.

The scratching noise continued.

I halted and stilled my breathing. Wayward critters weren't rare in our backyard. Nor were raccoons in our garbage, or the occasional snake slithering in the grass. Unlike our town house in Annapolis, which had windows that kept traffic noise outdoors, Sampaguita was drafty, and perhaps that scratching was simply a branch rubbing up against the siding.

And then . . . a meow.

The hairs on the back of my neck stood.

No way.

I went to the back door and looked out into the backyard, to . . . nothing. Nothing but a peaceful, serene view of trees.

Stepping back, I dropped my gaze.

To a cat sitting proudly on the back stoop. But it wasn't just a cat. It was a multicolored orange-and-brown tabby. My heart rocketed to my throat; my body leapt forward, and I opened the back door.

It sauntered in with a whip of its tail, then hopped onto the piano bench.

ACKNOWLEDGMENTS

If you could have read the very first draft of this book!

Just kidding—I would never have let you read it. Because the journey this manuscript took was much further than any other manuscript I've written thus far, even prepublication. The drafts were all-consuming, and each revision was actually a rewrite. But every pass was warranted, to unearth Celine from who I thought she was, to what you are reading today.

This book would not have happened without a slew of people by my side.

Rachel Brooks, my agent, who backed this book from conception, from the jump, from the spark years ago. Thank you for believing in *all* of my stories, and even in my story potential. Editor Lauren Plude who acquired *When Jasmine Blooms* when it was called *Just One Wish* in my head, and then took it through multiple stages of revisions, and titles too. Our long talks about Marmee, about Celine, blew the doors off my imagination. Bonus brilliant editor Tiffany Yates Martin who knew what questions to ask so I could dig deeper—I'm so grateful for you! Combined, Lauren and Tiffany about knocked me off my butt and at the same time lured me back into the chair. Mega thanks to Ruby B. and my dearest Robin O'Sullivan for the generous sensitivity reads. Deep gratitude to Jeanette Escudero and Elise Cooper for dipping into an early copy and giving me your feedback. Hugs to all of Lake Union!!!

Especially to Jen Bentham, Mindi M. (your copyediting prowess is fire!), Riam Griswold, and Gabriella Dumpit. And finally, Caroline Teagle Johnson for this novel's stunning cover.

My lovely friends (also confidants and colleagues): April, Annie, Rachel L., and Jeanette. Mia S., Pris, Tracey, Nina, and Michele. Tall Poppy Writers, #5amwritersclub. Melissa Panio-Peterson for snatching up all the things I drop. Kristin Dwyer, for being a great friend and a stalwart cheerleader and publicist whose level head I've come to rely on.

For my own four who inspire everything I write: Greggy, Cooper, Ella, and Anna. Greg, my husband of almost twenty-six years—one breath!

To readers, reviewers, librarians, and booksellers: you are my heroes! It is because of you that I am publishing my eleventh full-length novel. Thank you for trusting me once more. I hope Celine speaks to you!

And finally, to Louisa May Alcott, who wrote a book that I clung to, with characters I fell in love with. *Little Women* will always be my most favorite book.

BOOK CLUB QUESTIONS

1. How was Celine like Marmee of *Little Women*? What would a modern-day Marmee look like to you?
2. In the past, Celine came to a fork in the road, and she wondered, *what if?* Did you have your own fork in the road? How do you think your life would be different?
3. How was Celine different in her what-if world?
4. In the beginning, Celine coped by diving deeper into work. When does work become an escape?
5. What symbols in Celine's life represent her character arc?
6. Why does Celine feel such regret over Libby's death? How does this regret manifest in her other relationships, in her real and what-if life?
7. Why was it important for Celine to mend her relationship with Quinn?
8. What about Sampaguita plays a pivotal role in *When Jasmine Blooms*?
9. What do you think this what-if world was?
10. How do you see Celine a year from the end of the book? Five years?

ABOUT THE AUTHOR

Photo © 2020 Sarandipity Photography

Tif Marcelo is a veteran US Army nurse and holds a BS in nursing and a master's in public administration. She believes in and writes about the strength of families, the endurance of friendship, and heartfelt romances and is inspired daily by her own military hero husband and four children. She hosts the *Stories to Love* podcast, and she is also the author of contemporary fiction, contemporary romance, and young adult fiction. Her website, including a link to her newsletter, is at www.TifMarcelo.com.